"You need to tell the sheriff *everything* that happened…"

Tires squealed around the corner, and a dark sedan with tinted windows approached at a high speed. Noah quickly ushered Ruthie and the boys away from the road. The car's front tire came up on the sidewalk.

Ruthie screamed and shoved the boys farther from the car. Noah turned as it raced past.

Ruthie grabbed Noah's hand. "If you had not moved us away from the curb, I fear what would have happened." Tears filled her eyes.

He wrapped his arm around her shoulder and then pulled the boys into his embrace, as well. "The car's gone, and we're all okay."

"But—"

He nodded to her, knowing there was a reason the car had jumped the curb, and it wasn't because the driver was going too fast. He was sure the guy was the same man who had come after Ruthie.

One thing was cert Ruthie and the boys were n the man's crosshai

Debby Giusti is an award-winning Christian author who met and married her military husband at Fort Knox, Kentucky. Together they traveled the world, raised three wonderful children and have now settled in Atlanta, Georgia, where Debby spins tales of mystery and suspense that touch the heart and soul. Visit Debby online at debbygiusti.com, blog with her at seekerville.blogspot.com and craftieladiesofromance.blogspot.com, and email her at Debby@DebbyGiusti.com.

Dana R. Lynn grew up in Illinois. She met her husband at a wedding and told her parents she'd met the man she was going to marry. Nineteen months later, they were married. Today, they live in rural Pennsylvania with their three children and a variety of animals. In addition to writing, she works as a teacher for the deaf and hard of hearing and is active in her church.

USA TODAY Bestselling Author

DEBBY GIUSTI

Dangerous Amish Inheritance

&

DANA R. LYNN

Hidden in Amish Country

LOVE INSPIRED
INSPIRATIONAL ROMANCE

LOVE INSPIRED®

INSPIRATIONAL ROMANCE

Recycling programs
for this product may
not exist in your area.

ISBN-13: 978-1-335-94962-2

Dangerous Amish Inheritance and Hidden in Amish Country

Copyright © 2021 by Harlequin Books S.A.

Dangerous Amish Inheritance
First published in 2020. This edition published in 2021.
Copyright © 2020 by Deborah W. Giusti

Hidden in Amish Country
First published in 2019. This edition published in 2021.
Copyright © 2019 by Dana Roae

This edition published by arrangement with Harlequin Books S.A.

For questions and comments about the quality of this book,
please contact us at CustomerService@Harlequin.com.

Harlequin Enterprises ULC
22 Adelaide St. West, 40th Floor
Toronto, Ontario M5H 4E3, Canada
www.Harlequin.com

Printed in U.S.A.

CONTENTS

DANGEROUS AMISH INHERITANCE   7
Debby Giusti

HIDDEN IN AMISH COUNTRY   243
Dana R. Lynn

DANGEROUS
AMISH INHERITANCE

Debby Giusti

In memory of
Becky Martin
February 28, 1950–April 16, 2019

A beautiful sister in Christ!
I miss you, dear friend.

Deliver me out of the mire, and let me not sink:
let me be delivered from them that hate me,
and out of the deep waters.

Let not the waterflood overflow me,
neither let the deep swallow me up,
and let not the pit shut her mouth upon me.

Hear me, O Lord; for thy lovingkindness is good:
turn unto me according to the multitude
of thy tender mercies.

—Psalm 69:14–16

Chapter One

Ruthie Eicher awoke with a start. She blinked in the darkness, hearing the patter of March rain on the tin roof, and touched the opposite side of the double bed, where her husband had slept. Two months since the tragic accident and she was not yet used to his absence.

Finding the far side of the bed empty and the sheets cold, she dropped her feet to the floor, tied the flannel robe around her waist and hurried into the hallway. Sorrow twisted her heart as she peered into her father's room, unoccupied since the buggy crash that had killed her husband and claimed her *datt*'s life, as well. Had her mother been alive she would have said it was *Gott*'s will, although Ruthie placed the blame on her husband's failure to approach the intersection with caution. According to the sheriff's report, the *Englischer*'s car had the right of way, which her husband failed to acknowledge.

Ruthie hurried to the children's room. Even without lighting the oil lamp, she knew from the steady draw of their breaths that nine-year-old Simon and six-year-old Andrew were sound asleep.

Danki, Gott. She lifted up a prayer of thanks for her

two wonderful sons, one blond, one brunette, both so different yet so loved. After adjusting the coverings around the boys' shoulders, she peered from their window and gazed out at the farm that was falling into disrepair.

Movement near the outbuildings caught her eye. She held her breath and stared for a long moment, unsure of what she had seen.

Narrowing her gaze, she leaned forward, and her heart raced as a flame licked the air.

She shook Simon. "The woodpile. On fire. I need help."

He rubbed his eyes.

"Hurry, Simon."

Leaving him to crawl from bed, she raced downstairs, almost tripping, her heart pounding as she knew all too well how quickly the fire could spread. She ran through the kitchen, grabbed the back doorknob and groaned as her fingers struggled with the lock.

"No!" She moaned and coaxed her fumbling hands to work. The lock disengaged. She threw open the door and ran across the porch and down the steps.

Cold Georgia mountain air swirled around her, along with the acrid smell of smoke. Rain dampened her hair and robe. She raced to the pump, grabbed a nearby bucket and filled it, then scrambled to the woodpile and hurled the water onto the flames. The fire hissed as if taunting her efforts to quell the blaze. Returning to the pump, she filled another bucket, then another.

A noise sounded behind her. She glanced over her shoulder, expecting Simon. Instead she saw a large, darkly dressed figure. Something struck the side of her head. She gasped with pain, dropped the bucket and stumbled toward the house.

He grabbed her shoulder and threw her to the ground. She cried, struggled to her knees and started to crawl away. He kicked her side. She groaned and tried to stand. He tangled his fingers through her hair and pulled her to her feet.

She turned, her arms flailing, and made out only a shadowed form of a man. A lady's stocking distorted his face. A knit cap covered his hair. She dug her fingernails into his neck.

He twirled her around and yanked her arm up behind her back. Pain, like white lightning, exploded along her spine. She reared back to ease the pressure.

The man's lips touched her ear. "Didn't you read my notes? You don't belong here." His rancid breath soured the air. "Leave before something happens to you and your children."

Her heart stuttered.

He threw her to the wet ground and kicked her again. Air whizzed from her lungs. She gasped, unable to breathe.

The back door creaked open, and Simon stood in the doorway, eyes wide. *"Mamm?"*

"Stay...inside." Ruthie glanced at the now smoldering logs. She was relieved by the dying fire, and even more grateful that the man had disappeared.

Andrew pushed past his older brother and grabbed the rope to the dinner bell that hung on the back porch. His face twisted with determination as he tugged on the heavy hemp. The peel of the bell sounded in the night.

Simon ran to where she was lying and fell to his knees. "*Mamm*, do not die. Do not die like *Datt*."

She wanted to reassure both boys, but all she could think of was that no one would answer their call for help.

* * *

Noah Schlabach stepped from his father's house and inhaled the smoke that hung heavy in the air. The chilling clang of a dinner bell pierced the silence. At this time of night, it signaled danger and need. The closest neighboring farm on Amish Mountain belonged to Eli Plank. Ten years ago, the crusty old codger had a bad heart and a cranky disposition. Doubting Eli's condition had improved, Noah climbed behind the wheel of his Ford pickup, flicked on the lights and headed along the dirt road that led to the bridge, which he hoped was still standing. Rain had fallen steadily since he had returned to the area twenty-four hours ago and had swelled the narrow river. There was a safer bridge closer to town, but the detour would delay his response to the bell's clamant call.

He'd last crossed the river the night he had begged Eli's daughter, Ruthie, to run away with him. Leaving her ten years ago had been the hardest thing he'd ever done, next to burying his brother, Seth, and his family. Coming back to sell their father's house was closure to the past and all its pain. If only he could rid himself of the guilt so he could embrace life again. But then, he didn't deserve happiness. Nor did he expect to find it.

The wind howled, bending the pines and pushing against the truck with a powerful force. He gripped the steering wheel as he neared the rickety bridge. The guard railings bowed in the wind. A board broke loose, fell into the water and floated downstream toward the town of Willkommen.

Had he remained Amish, Noah would have offered a prayer for his own safe passage over the aged structure, but if God hadn't answered Noah's prayers for his brother, He wouldn't answer his prayer tonight. Better to remain silent than to face God's rejection again.

The moon broke through the clouds and reflected off the churning river below. Glancing higher up the mountain, he spied the cascading waterfall. The early spring rains had been merciless, which added to the surge of water flowing down the mountain.

He eased the truck across the bridge and accelerated on the other side. The Plank farmhouse sat at the upper tip of the valley, not more than fifty yards from the riverbank. Too close to the water, but then Mr. Plank had never made good decisions about the way he managed his farm, or how he parented Ruthie after her mother's death.

A small boy with blond hair, not more than five or six, stood on the porch, ringing the dinner bell. Noah braked to a stop and lunged from the truck. A fire smoldered in the woodpile. Smoke trailed upward from what appeared to be a contained burn.

Turning, his heart sped up.

An older boy was kneeling over a woman who was lying facedown in the red Georgia clay. Noah recognized the dark hair and frail form.

Ruthie!

"Mamm," the child whimpered as Noah neared. "Help her," the boy pleaded. "Help my *mamm.*"

Noah touched her slender neck, searched for a pulse and let out a relieved breath when he felt a faint but steady beat.

She moaned and tried to turn over. Her neck and spine seemed uninjured, yet her eyes remained closed. Feeling her arms, he checked for breaks, then did the same to her legs and feet before he gently lifted her into his arms.

"Let's take your *mamm* inside."

The older boy hurried to the porch, where his younger brother held on to the bell rope as if his hands were glued in place.

"It's okay," Noah assured the shivering younger child. "Come inside and get warm."

Following the boys into the house, he asked, "Where's your mother's bedroom?"

"On the second floor." The older boy locked the kitchen door behind them, then led the way up the stairs.

Peering around the starkly furnished Amish home, Noah expected to see Eli. "Is your grandfather asleep?" he asked.

"*Dawdy* died two months ago," the young one said.

"And your father?"

"He died in the same buggy accident."

Noah's gut tightened. "There are just you two boys?" They nodded.

"And *Mamm*," the younger one answered. His fingers latched onto his mother's arm, which was hanging limp. Tears welled in his eyes.

"She's going to be okay." Although Noah wanted to reassure the child, he wasn't sure of any such thing. Ruthie had been used as a punching bag. Internal injuries could be deceptive and hard to diagnose. She needed a doctor, but knowing the Amish way was to treat first and use medical care as a last option, he would assess her injuries before he talked about taking her to the hospital in Willkommen.

The boys led him into a small bedroom. The covers on the bed had been thrown back. Ruthie's slippers sat on the floor. Carefully, he removed her muddy robe and laid her on the bed.

"*Datt* said we deserved it whenever we were hurt," the little one whispered. "But *Mamm* did not deserve to be beaten. Ever."

Had she been beaten before? "Did either of you see the person who hurt your *mamm*?"

Both boys shook their heads.

Noah touched her cheek. "Ruthie?"

She moaned.

"Talk to her, boys."

"*Mamm*, look at me. It's Andrew." The youngest one leaned over his mother and kissed her cheek.

Noah's heart tightened.

The other boy, his face shadowed, touched her hair. "Open your eyes, *Mamm*. Simon wants to see your blue eyes."

Andrew started to cry.

Noah put his arm around the young child and drew him close. "Shhh," he soothed.

The older boy turned to the nightstand. He struck a match and lit the oil lamp.

With the sudden burst of light, Ruthie's eyes blinked open. She stared at Noah, her brow furrowed with puzzlement.

"Your boys are safe," he assured her.

"Andrew?" She tried to raise her head.

"Here I am, *Mamm*."

"And Simon?" Slowly, she turned to look at her oldest child.

Noah followed her gaze, seeing the boy more clearly in the lamplight. Tall and lean, he had a shock of brown hair about the same shade as Noah's. Dark eyes, a strong nose and square jaw. One eyebrow arched slightly higher than the other. His lips were full. He offered his mother a weak smile, revealing dimples on each cheek.

Noah's gut tightened. He raised his hand to his own face. The realization hit him hard as he stared at the boy who looked surprisingly like him.

"Why did you come back, Noah?" Ruthie asked, her tone bitter as she turned to stare at him. "You left once—why did you return to Amish Mountain?"

Before seeing Simon in the light, he would have told her he was here to sell his deceased father's house and farm. Now he realized something other than his father's passing had brought him back to the mountain. Was it Divine Providence? Whether God was involved, he would never know, but one thing was certain—Noah had been led back to Amish Mountain to find his son.

Chapter Two

Noah!

Ruthie pushed aside the dream that troubled her slumber and opened her eyes to the light streaming through her bedroom window. Her head pounded with confusion as she struggled to remember everything that had happened last night. Mentally, she flipped through a number of details until she stopped at the fire and the man who had attacked her.

His words made her stomach roil. *You don't belong here. Leave before something happens to you and your children.*

Remembering the two notes with similar warnings that had been shoved under her door, she grimaced. Who was the hateful man and why had he beaten her?

She rubbed her hand gingerly over her forehead, feeling the lump, and shivered. Her whole body ached. Ever so slowly, she crawled from bed and shuffled to the window. Peering down, she was overcome with relief when she saw Simon and Andrew in the chicken coop gathering eggs.

Glancing toward the barn, her heart lurched. She

grabbed the windowsill to steady her weak knees and stared at Noah Schlabach, carrying feed toward the barn. Evidently, her dream had been real.

Moving as quickly as her groaning body would allow, she washed her face and hands and slipped into her dress. After sweeping her tangled hair into a bun, she covered it with her *kapp*, wiped her muddied feet clean and donned her shoes. She hurried into the hallway and inhaled the aroma of fresh-brewed coffee. Surely her imagination was playing tricks on her. The coffee tin had been empty for two weeks.

She gripped the banister and descended the stairs, her aching muscles and strained back objecting to every step. The smell of fried bacon assailed her. Bacon was a luxury she had not tasted in months.

Entering the kitchen, she stopped short as the back door opened and Noah stepped inside. Tall, muscular, more mature and even more handsome.

She swallowed down the lump that filled her throat and stared at the man she had once loved. "I—I..." she stammered. "I thought seeing you last night had been a dream."

"How's your head?" he asked, his voice warm with concern.

Her head was throbbing with frustration, but she refused to let him know how much seeing him unsettled her. "I have a headache. Otherwise, I'm fine."

In spite of her tight muscles, she straightened her spine and narrowed her gaze. "Did I not ask you last night why you came back?"

His mouth twitched, revealing dimples that used to play with her heart. "You did ask me that question."

"I remember dreaming I saw you, then I woke to find

you hauling feed to my barn." She rubbed her forehead. "My mind is a bit fuzzy this morning, and I cannot recall your answer. Why did you return to Amish Mountain?"

"Someone wants to buy my father's property. I'm here to sign the papers. Although after what happened last night, I'm not sure why anyone would want to live on the mountain."

"Some of us do not have the luxury of moving," she said with a huff.

"Sorry. As you probably remember, I was never known for my diplomacy." He stepped toward the stove, poured two cups of coffee and handed one to her. "Who beat you up, Ruthie?"

"It was not a social visit," she said, still irritated by his earlier comment. "We did not exchange names."

"The fire was started with gasoline. If not for the rain…" He shrugged. Both of them knew what could have happened.

Had *Gott* intervened? If so, maybe He cared about her and her boys, after all.

Ruthie raised the cup with shaky hands, then sipped the coffee, appreciating the rich brew she had missed, and stared at her near-empty pantry. "Where did you find coffee beans?"

"At my dad's place."

"Along with bacon?" She glanced at the cast-iron skillet warming on the back of the stove.

He lifted his eyebrows, a ploy Simon used when he wanted to make a point. "You used to like bacon."

"That was ten years ago, Noah. A lot has changed since then."

"I remember you were the prettiest girl in the entire area."

She sealed her ears to his sweet talk. She had been fooled once but would not be fooled again.

"I wanted you to go with me that night, Ruthie."

"You were young, Noah, and tired of being Amish." She grimaced inwardly. Because of Noah, she had almost walked away from her faith. How different life would have been if she had left with him.

The sounds of the boys' voices filtered into the kitchen.

"You've raised two fine sons." The word *sons* hung in the air. "Why didn't you tell me you were pregnant?"

The hurt and rejection she had felt so long ago bubbled up anew. She squared her shoulders defiantly. "I did tell you as soon as I realized what was happening to my body. I wrote you immediately and then wrote again and again. Why did you never answer my letters?"

"What?"

"You heard me, Noah. I did not know your address so I took letters to your father and asked him to mail them to you. I expected a reply, even if you did not want to acknowledge our son."

His eyes widened. "I never got any letters."

"Perhaps you forgot."

"Having a son is not something a man would forget."

She glanced away, unwilling to argue. Noah had made his decision all those years ago. She could not change what had happened then, but she would protect her son now. Simon had lost one father. He did not need to know he had a biological father, as well. Especially one that would stay a few days and then move on with his life. A life without his newfound son.

Needing to hide her upset, she went to the cabinet

and pulled out four plates, then set the table and filled glasses with water for the boys.

"I brought milk." He pointed to the icebox. "And packed the box with more ice."

"Did you check my pantry last night as well as my icehouse before you headed home?"

"I spent the night on your porch to ensure the attacker did not return. Once the sun came up, I felt you and the boys would be safe while I made a quick trip home for a few supplies."

Although touched by his thoughtfulness, she needed to remain strong. "Thank you, Noah, but I did not ask for your help."

"I'm well aware of that, Ruthie. You always were a bit stubborn as well as independent."

His words stung. "Stubborn because I did not run away from my responsibility? My father needed me."

"Didn't your husband come first?"

She bristled. "What do you mean?"

"I read about your wedding in *The Budget* newspaper. Ben Eicher wasn't from around here. Why did you both stay on the mountain instead of returning to his home?"

A good question, and one she should have asked before they married. Although a woman in her fourth month of pregnancy needed a father for her unborn child and could not be particular.

Marrying Ben had been a mistake, she had learned quickly, but by then she had been baptized and had committed fully to living the Amish way. No matter how Ben treated her, Amish women did not leave their husbands. Even husbands caught in addiction.

"Ben knew my father needed help," she said in defense of a husband who did not deserve to be defended.

At first she had not known he was a gambler, although it did not take long for her to realize the little money they had disappeared whenever Ben went to town. Still, she did not want Noah to know the truth about her husband and their dysfunctional marriage.

"Your father had a brother," Noah stated.

"Yah." She nodded. "My uncle Henry owns a bit of land south of here, but he left the area years ago."

"Perhaps he didn't think your family farm was worth saving, Ruthie," he continued, no doubt unaware of her upset.

"Is that what you told your father when you and Seth ran away in the middle of the night?"

Noah's face tightened.

The pain of learning he had left without her washed over Ruthie again. She had been naive to think Noah would change his plans for her. All she had wanted was a few days until she mustered the courage to tell her father she was leaving. Why had Noah not understood her need to wait?

"You have not mentioned your brother." Regretting her sharp tongue, Ruthie steered the conversation away from the past. "Did he return to the mountain, too?"

"Seth died, Ruthie. It's been almost six months."

The two brothers had been inseparable. Ruthie's heart broke for Noah. She lowered her gaze. "Forgive me. I did not know."

The kitchen door opened, and the boys bounded inside. "We found eggs." Andrew held up his basket. "Lots of them."

Noah tousled Andrew's hair and smiled at Simon. "Enjoy breakfast, boys." He stepped toward the open door. "I've got a couple of jobs to do outside."

"But you need to eat." Though relieved that Noah was leaving, she also wanted him to stay.

"I'm not hungry." Cool air swirled into the kitchen. "After breakfast, boys, come outside and we'll finish the chores."

"Go home, Noah," Ruthie suggested. "Get some sleep. We can manage without you."

He stared at her for a long moment. "You're managing, Ruthie, that's true. But I'm here for a few days. Let me help."

"Then you will leave again?"

"At least this time, I'll know who I'm leaving behind."

"What did he mean?" Andrew asked after Noah had closed the door behind him.

She ignored her son's question. "Wash your hands, boys, and put the bread on the table. We will have bacon along with our eggs."

Simon neared the window and peered outside. "He went into *Datt*'s workshop."

A warning tugged at Ruthie's heart. "I thought you locked the door."

Simon shrugged. "Maybe I forgot. We never used to lock it."

But things had changed.

Before she could answer, Simon added, "That man last night could have been here before."

She stepped closer. "Why do you say that?"

"I saw a man near the river last week."

A nervous thread tangled along her spine. "You did not tell me."

"He asked where the fish were biting. I told him downstream a bit. Funny, though—he did not have a fishing pole."

"What did he look like?"

Simon shrugged. "He stood in the shadow of a tree and held his hand up so I could not see his face."

"Did he leave right away?" she asked, trying to keep her voice even.

"After he asked who was buried on the hill."

Ruthie's heart thumped a warning. "What did you tell him?"

"I told him about *Datt* and *Dawdy*."

"About the accident?"

He nodded.

She would not fault her son, but Simon had revealed that she and the boys lived alone. Was the man who seemed interested in fishing the same man who had attacked her last night?

The sound of someone chopping wood drew her to the window. Simon and Andrew followed. As the three of them peered outside, Noah raised an ax over his head and then, with a powerful downward movement, split a log in two.

Andrew stood on tiptoe, his eyes wide. "Noah brought Simon and me moon pies this morning before you were awake, *Mamm*."

Moon pies had been Noah's favorite as a kid, although his *datt* rarely allowed such a frivolous waste of money. In spite of being Amish, Reuben Schlabach preferred to spend his hard-earned cash on liquid libations. Her own father called Noah's dad a drunk. Ruthie had considered him an unhappy man who regretted the life he had made for himself.

"Even after eating moon pies, I know you are hungry." She shooed the boys toward the sink. "Wash your hands."

Simon reached for the bar of soap. "Did I meet Noah when I was a child?"

A child? She almost laughed. Nine years old, and Simon was trying to be a man. "Noah left the area ten years ago. I do not recall him returning to the mountain until now."

Both boys lathered their hands with soap and rinsed them with the well water.

Simon reached for the towel. "Noah looks like someone I know, but I cannot remember who."

Ruthie's stomach tightened. The boys enjoyed looking at their reflections in the clothing-store mirror the few times they had gone shopping in town. Simon might not realize the truth yet, but as much as he resembled Noah, he would learn who his real *datt* was before long.

Noah was leaving, but would he leave soon enough?

As frustrated as he felt, Noah could have chopped down an entire forest. Ruthie needed wood so she could cook and keep her house warm. She needed other things, too. Her pantry was almost bare. He had checked the icehouse and found only a few pounds of frozen meat.

Thankfully, he had purchased hamburger and steaks when he was in town, so he was able to leave her enough beef in the icehouse for a few meals. He would return to town for more supplies as soon as possible.

In spite of the cool morning, he worked up a sweat before putting down the ax when the boys hurried outside. Andrew wore a milk mustache and had to run back inside for his hat.

"My brother wants to split wood, Mr. Noah. *Mamm* says he is too young to use an ax."

"She doesn't want him to get hurt. He'll be old enough

soon." Noah's heart warmed as he glanced at his son, slender and gangly with big feet and hands. Given time, Simon might grow taller than Noah.

"Have you split wood before, Simon?"

The boy nodded. "Sometimes I help *Mamm*. The ax gives her blisters that hurt her hands, but she never complains."

Forever stoic, Ruthie had also never complained about her infirmed father or her need to care for him.

Noah handed Simon the ax. "You chop while I stack. We'll work together."

The boy's face brightened. *"Yah, gut."*

"Just remember to spread your feet apart as wide as your shoulders and keep your eyes on the wood you plan to split."

Simon gripped the ax, adjusted his stance and glanced at Noah for approval.

"Move your feet out a bit," he advised.

The boy responded.

He raised the ax and brought it down into the middle of the log, splitting the wood on the first swing.

"Good job."

Simon puffed out his chest with the praise.

Before he could grab a second piece of wood, the kitchen door opened and Ruthie stepped onto the porch.

"Simon," she called.

The boy looked up.

"Stack the wood. Then you and Andrew fill the mare's trough with feed. Make sure she has water."

With a sigh, he handed the ax to Noah.

As the boy started to gather the wood, Noah stepped toward the porch where Ruthie stood. "He did a good job."

"You should have asked me first, Noah."

"I chopped wood when I was Simon's age."

"*Yah*, you did a lot of things, but you are not my son."

Simon was *his* son, too, but he didn't deserve the title of Dad. Not now. Not ever. Not when he had turned his back on the boy. Although, in his own defense, he hadn't even known he had a son.

Ruthie must have seen the confusion in his gaze because she came down the steps and put her hand on his arm. "You do not need to fill a role you have never known."

"A boy needs a father."

"Simon will grow into a strong man even though Ben is gone."

Her words cut him like a knife.

"Come inside," she said. "I kept a plate of food warm."

He shook his head and pointed to a distant pasture. "Some of those fence posts look ready to topple. The boys can help me. You don't want to lose the few head of cattle you have."

"Ben planned to sell them at market, but he died, and I…"

She glanced at the grave site, her face tight with emotion. Noah saw the grief she still carried.

"Simon mentioned your father died, too."

Ruthie nodded.

"I'm sorry."

"*Danki*, Noah."

He turned his gaze back to the pasture. "You could slaughter one of your steers for meat," he suggested, hoping to turn the topic away from the deaths of her father and her husband. "Your ice is low. We might be able to have some delivered from town."

She shook her head. "Not this month."

Was money the issue?

He noted the way she steeled her jaw with determination, trying to hold on to her pride. Ruthie was doing her best to provide for her boys.

He glanced at the peeling paint on the house and outbuildings, and the dilapidated barn. No matter how hard she tried, it wasn't enough.

"I've decided to go to town tomorrow. Why don't you and the boys join me? You could tell the sheriff about your visitor last night and any details you might have remembered."

"Everything happened so quickly." She wrapped her arms around her slender waist.

"Is there something the man might want that is yours? Or could he be an acquaintance of your husband?"

"An *Englisch* lady's stocking covered his head so I could not see his face. Simon told me about a man at the riverbank last week who asked where to fish."

"A sportsman wanting a tip on where to toss his line?"

"Maybe, except he did not have a fishing pole, and he wanted to know who was buried on the hill."

Noah turned toward the graves. "Your husband is buried there?"

She nodded. "Along with my mother and father."

"You and the boys shouldn't be left alone, Ruthie. I'll bed down in the barn tonight."

"As ramshackle as it is, the barn might collapse on top of you."

He smiled. "Then I'll sleep on your porch again."

"You have already done enough, Noah. Besides, I would worry about you if you stayed outside in the cold.

Go home and rest. With the doors locked, the boys and I will be safe in the house."

"I heard the dinner bell last night. Ring it if you need me."

"Do not worry about us. We will be fine."

But he was worried. A man had attacked Ruthie once. Noah had to ensure he did not hurt her a second time.

Chapter Three

Noah kept thinking about Ruthie and her two sons when he returned home later that evening. After eating dinner, he brewed coffee and took a cup onto the porch, listening to the hoot of a night owl and the scamper of squirrels burrowing through the underbrush.

He also heard the flow of the river. Rain had fallen intermittently all afternoon and more was expected over the next few days. He and the boys had shored up the pasture fence in between the hardest downpours. Other repairs needed to be tackled in the morning.

Ruthie might think she could handle the farm, but it was too much for her. The boys were good workers and helped as best they could, but they couldn't fill the gap left by Ben Eicher's passing. Although from the level of disrepair Noah had noticed, Ruthie's husband had failed to keep up the farm. Years of neglect under her father's hand had been, no doubt, compounded by a lackadaisical husband.

Noah finished the coffee and returned the mug to the kitchen, then grabbed his keys, climbed into his truck and headed toward the bridge. Thankfully, the water level had lowered a bit with the ease in the rainfall. He checked the bridge's underpinnings, and decided to brace the support beams as best he could tomorrow.

Leaving his truck on the far bank, he walked across the bridge to get a better view of the Plank farm, now shadowed in darkness. An oil lamp glowed in a downstairs window of the farmhouse, inviting him forward. He hurried to the porch and tapped on the door.

"Ruthie, it's Noah."

She opened the door. "Is everything all right?"

Her hair hung loose around her shoulders. A small triangular scarf covered her head and was tied under her chin, in lieu of her prayer *kapp*.

"I decided to check your property but didn't want to scare you. Are the boys asleep?"

She nodded. "They were exhausted after working with you today."

"I appreciated their help."

"And the questions?" Her eyes almost twinkled in the lamplight. "The boys are much too inquisitive."

His heart warmed as he thought of their nonstop chatter this afternoon. "Curious minds are quick to learn. They both take after their mother in that regard."

She raised an eyebrow and smiled. "Are you saying I was talkative in my youth?"

He laughed. "I'm referring to intelligence, Ruthie. You're a smart woman."

"A smart woman should be able to manage this farm better than I am currently doing."

"Your husband and father haven't been gone long." He looked expectantly at her.

"Two months." She let out a shallow sigh. "In some

ways it seems like only yesterday, yet when I look around the farm, I feel it has been neglected for years."

"Any sign of the guy from last night?" he asked.

"Everything has been quiet."

"Good." He glanced over his shoulder at the rocky terrain. "I'll search around the outbuildings and ensure nothing is amiss in the barn."

She motioned toward the living area. "If you would like to come inside for a cup of coffee afterward—"

He held up his hand. "I'll take a rain check."

"Then good night, and thank you."

Standing on the porch as she closed the door, Noah felt a weight settle on his shoulders. Everything within him begged to accept her offer. He wanted to learn who Ruthie Eicher was. He had known Ruthie Plank, but ten years was a long time. He had changed. No doubt, she had, as well.

With a deep sigh, he left the porch and searched the barn. The wood shop and other outbuildings were locked. He glanced over the pastures and the hillside, then walked back across the bridge and climbed into his pickup. For a long moment, he stared at Ruthie's house.

His father, in one of his drunken stupors, had mocked Noah, calling him a protector who wanted to keep everyone safe. The irony cut Noah to the quick after what had happened to Seth, his wife, Jeanine, and their adorable daughter, Mary.

Seth had never been happier than when he and Noah had worked on the dam near Chattanooga. After carefully saving enough money, Seth and Jeanine had placed a down payment on their starter home and had invited Noah to dinner that first night in the new house to share in their joy. The pride Noah had felt in his little brother had made his heart nearly burst.

Two weeks later, the dam gave way, and a wall of water washed over the housing area as the family slept.

Noah had worked on the dam. He had gotten Seth a job there and had told him about the new houses being built and the low-interest loans for people employed by the construction company.

If Noah hadn't been so helpful, Seth and his family would still be alive.

He started the engine and turned the truck around. Noah had come home to sell his father's property. The real-estate agent had a buyer. Tomorrow in town, he would see if the papers had been drawn up. Noah needed to move on with his life. There was nothing except memories on Amish Mountain.

Then he thought of Ruthie and Simon and little Andrew. His heart softened, yet he needed to be realistic. Although he had left the Amish faith before baptism, Noah had lived life as an *Englischer* for the past ten years. Amish and *Englisch* didn't mix, at least not when romantic relationships were concerned. There could be no going back to what they'd had so long ago.

Plus, he didn't deserve happiness or love or a family, and had to make certain he didn't get involved. Bottom line—the sooner he left the mountain, the better.

Ruthie extinguished the oil lamp and moved to the window. In the moonlight, she watched Noah walk over the bridge, climb into his truck and sit there for a long moment. Was he thinking of her or their son?

She had said too much about their circumstances. She did not want Noah to know they were hanging on by a thread. A very thin thread. Surely he would wonder about the Amish community and why they were not reaching out to the widow Eicher.

Truth be told, she had rejected their help. The shame of Ben's gambling and subsequent shunning pained her to the core, even after all this time, and the memory of his outrage during Sunday service haunted her still. Ben had called the bishop and elders hypocrites and stormed out. Ruthie had gathered the boys and followed him, holding her head high. All the while, her face had burned with shame.

Her father had always said a wife's place was beside her husband. If Ben was shunned, then she felt shunned, as well. Even after his death, she had not been able to embrace the community or accept their outreach.

After his shunning, Ben had gone to town once a month to gamble, collect the mail at the post office and buy supplies with whatever money was left after his poker games. She and the boys had remained at home to handle the chores. All too often, she had prayed her husband would not return. *Gott* forgive her for such thoughts.

Ben always returned in a foul mood, as if he had been forced home to a wife he did not love and an elder son he knew was not his own. At times, she wondered why he had married her. Was it for her father's farm or had he believed love could grow between them? After Simon's birth, Ben claimed the baby was the problem, but she knew the problem was Ben, who usually thought only of himself.

Ruthie turned from the window, carried her cup to the sink, washed it and placed it in the cupboard, her thoughts moving back to Noah and the way he had brought joy to her life when they were young. They had played together as children, and with time that friendship had grown into something more. Ruthie had been too free with her love, which she regretted, yet she never regretted the wonderful child who had come from their youthful tryst.

Footsteps sounded on the porch. Her heart fluttered. Noah had come back to see her.

Not waiting for his knock, she threw open the door.

"Oh, Noah, I am glad—"

Her heart lurched. The man with the stocking over his head was not Noah. Before she could slam the door, he pushed his way into the house. She gasped.

"What are you waiting for?" He leaned into her face. "Time is running out."

She squared her shoulders and steadied her voice. "What are you talking about?"

"Move off the mountain. No one wants you here."

"That is not true."

His eyes widened. "Are you calling me a liar?"

"I am calling you a fool to think you can frighten me."

"I'll make life miserable for you and your children."

He raised his hand as if to strike her. She grabbed his arm, and his shirtsleeve raised, revealing tattoos that covered his skin.

His face contorted, and he pushed her away with such force that she tumbled to the floor, landing on her hip. Pain ricocheted up her spine.

She struggled to her feet, knowing she had to be strong to protect her boys.

"Get out of here." She pointed to the door. "Leave me alone."

"I told you what will happen if you don't get off Amish Mountain."

Seething with anger, he stepped closer. "Don't make a tragic mistake if you want your boys to live."

He shoved her hard against a table and ran outside.

Ruthie stumbled and fell to her knees, overcome with a mix of confusion and fear.

Once again, footsteps sounded on the porch.

Her heart pounded. He was coming back.

She grabbed the edge of the table and tried to stand. She had to keep him from harming Simon and Andrew.

His footfalls drew closer.

She screamed.

Arms surrounded her. "Ruthie!"

Gasping, she collapsed into Noah's arms.

"He—he came back. He said he would…kill my boys. Help me, Noah. Help me save my boys."

Chapter Four

Noah held Ruthie close until she calmed. Having her in his arms tugged on his heart. So many memories flooded over him and reminded him how dearly he had loved Ruthie once upon a time. Now someone was doing her harm.

"Why is this man coming after you?" he asked once she moved out of his embrace.

She shook her head and cast her eyes down. "It is difficult to discuss."

"You mentioned coffee earlier," he suggested, hoping to ease her tension. "A cup would be good for both of us."

"*Yah*, you are right. I brewed a pot early and kept it on the stove so it will still be hot." She led the way into the kitchen and poured the coffee. After opening a cabinet drawer, she lifted out a large manila envelope, carried it to the table along with the filled cups and sat across from Noah.

"I do not want you to think badly about my husband, but it is necessary to tell you some things so you understand what is happening." She stared at the envelope and then glanced up at Noah.

"Perhaps you have already heard talk in town?" she asked.

"I didn't talk to anyone about you, Ruthie. I thought your father was still alive and that you and your husband lived elsewhere."

"If you had asked, you would have heard that my husband liked to gamble."

Noah saw the pain on her face.

"What started as an occasional problem grew worse with time," she admitted.

Noah took her hand. "I'm sorry."

"The hardest part was his disregard for the boys, especially Simon. Not that Ben was a better father to Andrew."

"He knew you were pregnant when you married?"

She nodded and pulled back her hand. "I was truthful. He said it did not matter that I was in the family way, but it did matter. Evidently more than either of us realized."

Her words cut into Noah. The thought of Simon being raised by a man who didn't love him was almost too much to bear. Noah carried the guilt for the deaths of his brother's family. To learn that he was also responsible for a child who had been slighted by his stepfather weighed him down even more.

"What about the church district?" he asked. "Did the bishop not offer counsel?"

"Ben did not accept criticism or advice, even from the bishop. When Andrew was a baby, my husband caused a disruption during Sunday services while the bishop was speaking. Ben called him a hypocrite and said all the elders were ungodly men who preached lies."

"Oh, Ruthie, how that must have hurt you."

She wrung her hands. "Ben said he wanted nothing

more to do with the church. Because of his gambling and his disregard for the bishop's counsel, he was removed from the faith, just as he wanted."

"You mean *Bann* and *Meidung*?"

"*Yah*. He was excommunicated and shunned."

"But you weren't. Surely the bishop would not hold what your husband did against you."

"I was Ben's wife. If he was cut off from the community, I was, too."

"You could have asked for help."

She glanced at him, her eyes revealing the shame she must have felt for all these years.

"As you know, Noah, we live on the mountain, far from town. What do the *Englisch* say? Out of sight, out of mind."

He nodded. The townspeople had not made an effort to help Ruthie because of her husband.

"Although to be honest, a few people checked on me after the incident in church. Following Ben's death, they reached out to me again, but I was still too shamed by my husband's actions as well as his shunning and refused their help."

"How does all this have bearing on what's happening now?" he asked.

She glanced again at the envelope. "Ben would go to town once a month to get the mail and to gamble."

Her voice was little more than a whisper. "The last time he went to town, my father went with him. My *datt*'s health was bad. He had grown so frail. I asked Ben to take him to the medical clinic for an exam, which I am certain interfered with Ben's gambling. On the way home, he raced through an intersection and never saw the approaching car that had the right of way."

"They both died in the collision."

Ruthie nodded. "Comforting the boys was hard. They did not understand how *Gott* could take both their father and their grandfather. Some people said it was *Gott*'s will, but that is difficult for children to comprehend."

She paused for a moment and then added, "It was difficult for me to accept, as well."

"You've been through so much, Ruthie."

"It is life, *yah*? We are given both the good and the bad. How we act in those difficult situations can either build strength or tear us down. I am determined to remain strong."

"You have always been strong and faithful to the Lord. You're showing the boys how a *gut* person lives, and they learn well from your example."

"I fear they are now learning how a hateful man can ruin a family's peace and well-being." She withdrew a piece of paper from the envelope, unfolded it and placed it on the table.

Pointing to the paper, she said, "This is what I found under my door two weeks ago. It states that I need to leave the farm."

Noah read what appeared to be a hastily scribbled note written in green ink. "Do you recognize the handwriting or the color of the ink?"

She shook her head. "Several days ago another note was slipped under my door."

Withdrawing the second slip of paper from the envelope, she sighed. "This one is also written in green ink and says I would be sorry if I did not leave within forty-eight hours."

Noah looked at the date on the second letter. "And the fire occurred last night as the deadline lapsed?"

She nodded. "I did not realize he would be so hateful. I fear evil has taken over his heart."

Noah tried to think why this property would be so important.

Ruthie folded the papers and returned them to the envelope. "The man talks about hurting my children. That is what frightens me."

"We need to tell the sheriff."

"And what will he do? Willkommen is far from the mountain. My children and I live here alone. I have no phone to call for help."

"Cell reception is almost impossible on the mountain, Ruthie. I've had trouble trying to make calls since I returned home, but if you need to contact anyone, you can try my phone."

"I cannot rely on you, Noah. You are here now, but you will leave as soon as your father's land is sold. I do not blame you. As you said, why would anyone want to live on Amish Mountain? It is true, but it is the only thing I have to call my own, other than my wonderful sons. I want to pass this farm on to them. Without the land, how would I grow food or raise chickens and have eggs? There is so much work to do with a farm, but I want to raise my children on this mountain."

As much as Noah admired Ruthie's determination, he knew she would be an easy target for the man who had come after her. Noah needed to talk her out of staying, but since he hadn't been able to convince Ruthie to leave years ago, he doubted he could convince her to leave now.

Perhaps there had been more to her staying back then than just caring for her father. The Amish felt a kinship with the land. It provided their livelihood, their food, their ability to sustain life.

In his youth, Noah hadn't been aware of Ruthie's love of the land. Now that he had nothing of his own and no one to hold on to, he could understand her desire to remain on the farm that had belonged to her family for generations.

He thought of his own guilt in his brother's tragic death. Noah had no right to find comfort in his childhood home and surrounding property. He would sell it all and continue to wander from job to job, even if a portion of his heart remained on the mountain, as it had so long ago.

Ruthie could not sleep. Every time she closed her eyes, she envisioned the man with the distorted face and the tattooed arm. Discouraged and upset, she rose from bed and walked to the window. A light from Noah's house glowed in the darkness. Perhaps he, too, was trying to make sense of her tangled life.

She had not wanted to tell Noah about her husband. The mistake of marrying Ben had been her own to make. She did not need pity, or for Noah to feel responsible for the struggles she had endured. Life had to be accepted, no matter how difficult. Ben often told her if she was a better wife, he would have been a better husband. Not that she understood his logic. Whenever he spoke such nonsense, she would busy herself with cooking or cleaning and steel her heart to his criticism. Her father had never offered praise and his words had been caustic at times, but Ben's belligerence was different, and no matter how hard she tried to shrug off his comments, they troubled her spirit and sapped the joy from her life.

What hurt her even more is that she had tried to be a

dutiful wife, but Ben's verbal attacks on her worth as a person, as well as a wife, took a toll until her heart had hardened.

If she had her boys, she had everything she needed. Keeping the farm was for their future, so she could provide something other than the memory of their childhood with a father who did not know how to love.

She stared again at the light in the distance. Once upon a time, she had been in love. She loved her children, but she would never be able to love a man again. No matter how much she remembered the past and what Noah had meant to her then.

Ten years was a lifetime. She had changed, not necessarily for the better. She accepted her life as it was and did not need to run from the pain. Joy had been part of her distant past, before Noah left the mountain, but it would not be part of her future.

Chapter Five

Noah had breakfast ready by the time Ruthie came downstairs the next morning. He poured a cup of coffee and handed it to her when she stepped into the kitchen.

"Looks like you could use a little caffeine."

"I need more than caffeine." She accepted the cup with a weak smile and took a long sip.

"You'll find the spare key on the counter," he said. "Thanks for letting me keep it overnight."

"I gave it to you in case there was an emergency. I did not expect you to cook breakfast for us."

"It's the least I could do. Plus, I'm worried about you. It might be wise to have a doc check you over, Ruthie. I told you that I plan to go to town today to get some supplies to work on your barn. Come with me."

"No. I am stiff and sore, but nothing is broken and I will be good as new in a few days."

He could see the dark lines under her eyes and the way she held her side. Ruthie was tough. Always had been.

"And you do not need to fix my barn," she insisted.

"I've got the time and the wherewithal. Plus it gives me a chance to spend time with Simon and Andrew."

"I am sure you have other things to do."

"Not until my father's house is sold. I'll check with the real-estate agent today. I called his office when I first arrived in town. His receptionist said it would take a week to get everything ready. I might hurry them along if I stop in today."

"You would not want to stay on the mountain longer than necessary."

He heard the subtle hint of sarcasm in her voice and raised his brow.

She ignored his gaze and took another sip of coffee, then placed the cup on the table. "The boys will be downstairs soon. Thank you for preparing breakfast."

"Breakfast is easy. I'm sorry I couldn't stop the man from hurting you last night."

The boys scurried downstairs and bounded into the kitchen. Andrew's eyes widened. "What smells so *gut*?"

"Noah has fixed us breakfast." Ruthie's smile was warm. "Come sit at the table, and I will pour your milk."

"But the chores," Simon insisted.

"I've cared for the animals," Noah assured him. "We can work together on the other jobs after we eat. It won't take us long." He pointed to the table. "Sit next to your brother. We'll eat while the food is warm."

Simon slipped into his chair. "My stomach is ready to eat."

"Mine, too," Andrew said, holding out his glass for his mother to fill.

"Noah has brought us many good things to eat, as well as milk to drink. What do you boys say?"

"*Danki*, Noah," they chimed in unison.

"It is *gut* to enjoy a meal with my neighbors." He placed a large platter of sausages and scrambled eggs in the center of the table. A smaller plate was piled high with buttered toast.

"Bacon yesterday and sausage today. It is like Christmas." Andrew took a long chug from his glass, then wiped his mouth with the back of his hand.

"Use your napkin," Ruthie instructed. "And we will wait for Noah to join us before we give thanks."

Noah hadn't asked the Lord to bless his food since his mother had died. His father had rarely sat at the table to eat following her passing, and Noah and Seth had quickly forsaken many of the Amish ways, including prayer before meals.

Simon and Andrew waited expectantly for him to sit. Sliding into the seat opposite Ruthie, he smiled at the boys. "Shall we bow our heads in prayer?"

They dutifully followed his suggestion, their eyes closed and faces serene. His heart warmed at their innocence. He turned his gaze to Ruthie. She stared at him, one eyebrow arched ever so slightly, as if questioning what he was doing coming back into her life.

Noah glanced down, mentally trying to calm his rapid heartbeat. Unable to focus on prayer, he pulled in a breath and quieted his mind. He needed to ensure his heart didn't get carried away with thoughts of Ruthie.

Bless her, he silently intoned. *And her children*.

He raised his eyes to find the boys staring at him and winked at Simon. "Shall we eat?"

Handing the large platter to Ruthie, he said, "Serve the boys and yourself first."

She arranged the food on the three plates and then offered it once again to Noah. "Breakfast looks delicious."

"At times it's nice to have someone else do the cooking." He glanced at the boys. "Simon and Andrew, you need to learn to cook so you can fix breakfast for your *mamm*."

"We do the outside chores," Andrew said, reaching for his fork.

"And you're good workers. I could tell that yesterday."

Simon spread jam on a slice of toast. "Your eye, *Mamm*. It looks worse today."

She glanced at Noah. "A bruise comes a day or two after the injury. Do not worry about your *mamm*."

"I do not want to see you hurt."

She patted his hand. "You are a *gut* son."

Noah's stomach tightened. A *gut* son who needed a man's guidance. Andrew needed that, as well.

Ruthie didn't want the boys to know the stranger had returned last night. Noah had to make certain the man didn't have another opportunity to hurt her again. What type of an animal would attack a defenseless woman? His stomach soured as he thought of what could have happened.

The boys were enjoying the food with enthusiasm. Again he thought of the pain the attack could have caused to both Simon and Andrew.

Much as he wanted to go to town today, he wouldn't leave Ruthie and the boys alone. Not when the vile man was on the loose. If only Ruthie and the boys would go to town with him.

"Noah plans to go to town today," Ruthie said as if reading his thoughts. "Would you boys like to join him?"

"Oh, *yah*," both boys enthused.

"It has been so long since we have gone anywhere," Simon said, serious as always and sounding much older than his years.

"Today will be an adventure, *yah*?" Ruthie smiled.

"What about the chores?" Simon asked.

"We'll do them before we leave," Noah assured him.

Ruthie nodded. "Finish your food and the three of you can head outside, while I tidy the kitchen. Many hands make light work."

"This day could not be better." Andrew downed the rest of his milk and finished the last of the eggs on his plate. "A *gut* breakfast and a trip to town make me very happy."

"What if the man returns while we are gone?" Simon asked, his brow wrinkled with worry.

"We will lock the doors to the house and will not think about him anymore today."

"I think of him when I see the bruise on your face."

"Then I must heal quickly so looking at your *mamm* does not upset you."

"That is not what I mean."

She nodded. "I understand, Simon. None of us want to see the man again, but we cannot live life in fear. We have to trust *Gott* to keep us safe."

"He did not keep you safe night before last."

"No, but the fire in the woodpile did not spread and nothing of significance burned. *Gott* protected us in that way, even if he allowed the man to hurt me."

"Bad things sometimes happen," Noah said, hoping to deflect the boy's upset. "But as your mother said, it could have been so much worse."

Simon squared his shoulders. "I will not let him hurt her again."

Noah admired Simon's determination and desire to protect his mother. For all his good intentions, Simon wouldn't be a match for an adult who weighed more and was, no doubt, adept at bullying people, especially defenseless women and children.

"You'll let me know, Simon, if you see anything suspicious, *yah*? We'll work together as a team to keep your mother safe."

"Can I be on your team?" Andrew asked.

"Of course. We three men will protect your mother." He nodded to Ruthie. "Now let's take the dishes to the sink, then we'll get our chores done and be ready for our trip to town."

"Are we taking the buggy?" Simon asked.

"I am sure our mare, Buttercup, would enjoy the trip," Ruthie said. "We will go by buggy."

The boys cleared the table and then hurried outside.

"I hate leaving you to wash the dishes," Noah said.

"They will not take long. Do you want me to pack a lunch?"

"If the boys like pizza, we can eat in town."

"You are spoiling them, Noah. What will I do with them when you are gone?"

Although her tone was light, her gaze was serious.

"We won't think about that now. Today is for enjoyment, *yah*?"

"Of course, Noah. Today will be a nice change, but we will remember that your time here will be short-lived. Soon you will leave, and we will go back to life as it was."

Noah's life would never be the same. From now on when he thought of Ruthie, he would also think of the son he only recently learned he had and the boy's brother. Both Amish lads needed an Amish father, not an *Englischer* who had left the faith.

* * *

Ruthie tried to calm her excitement. Going to town had been a rarity when Ben was alive. Since his death, she had too much work to do on the farm to think about leaving for even a few hours.

The boys shared her enthusiasm. Both of them scrambled into the buggy, talking about what they would see and do in Willkommen.

Noah seemed as pleased as the boys, and said, "It will be a fun day," as he flicked the reins and guided the mare onto the mountain road.

The weather was perfect. Sunny and bright, which matched Ruthie's mood. She had worn her black bonnet and pulled it around her face in hopes of hiding the bruise around her eye. Her ribs ached but not bad enough to be broken, and that was something else for which to be grateful.

"I checked the barn again this morning to determine what's needed to shore it up," Noah told her.

"Did you see the wood piled behind Ben's woodshop?"

He nodded. "I did. From the looks of the lumber, your husband was preparing to do the job himself. I'll just need a few more items before I start work."

"We can help you," Simon said from the rear.

"I'm counting on that."

Ruthie was grateful for the way Noah included her sons in the project. Ben had preferred tackling a job alone rather than guiding young hands through a new task. He had always been less than patient with their sons and with her.

"Age has given you the gift of patience," she said to Noah. Then she thought of his impatience in leav-

ing Amish Mountain so many years ago. If only he had
waited for her.

She turned to glance at the lush mountain scenery,
not wanting him to see the confusion that she knew was
written on her face. Confusion and pain, even after all
these years, because he had left without her.

"I was impetuous in my youth, Ruthie, and for that
I'm sorry."

Did he even realize how deeply he had hurt her? She
could not think of it again lest the pain overtake her.

"Virtue does not come easily," she mused, hoping
to deflect her focus onto something else. "My mother
said it takes a lifetime. Unfortunately, she did not have
long enough."

"You were always a loving daughter."

The boys chatted in the rear. Ruthie was thankful they
had not heard what she and Noah had said. She never
should have opened up the wound from her past. Noah
would be leaving soon. She did not want to be left with
a broken heart again.

Bracing her shoulders, she steeled her resolve. Noah
was *Englisch*, she reminded herself, as if that wedge between them was not evident. He had rejected his faith
at the same time he had rejected her. There could be no
going back to what had been so long ago.

Chapter Six

Noah recognized Ruthie's upset in the way she braced her shoulders and held her neck at an angle. She turned away from him, just as she'd done the night he wanted her to leave with him. She had used her father as an excuse, and the pain of rejection he felt had been so intense and immediate that Noah had fled the mountain, leaving behind that which he loved most.

In hindsight, his pride and concern for his own well-being had taken precedence over Ruthie's need to care for her father. He had lived with that regret for the last ten years.

With the boys sitting in the buggy, Noah knew this wasn't the time to go into their past. Although he doubted there would ever be a good time. Ruthie had found a husband, a man she loved in spite of his many flaws, and he'd been taken from her and the boys. Noah would be a hypocrite to wade into the midst of her mourning and pretend he could offer her something more. After losing his brother and his brother's sweet wife and adorable daughter, Noah didn't deserve a second chance when Seth had no chance at all.

He flicked the reins, feeling the frustration at his own failings well up in him again. Life wasn't fair. His father used to say that often in the context that others had more land or money or happiness. His dad had tried to find all that he was looking for in a bottle. Noah had chosen to make his own happiness through hard work, but neither of them had succeeded.

"How long until we get to town?" Andrew asked from the rear.

Ruthie turned and smiled. "Are you impatient, my son?"

"*Yah, Mamm.* I have wanted to go to town for so long. Now that it is happening, I am too excited to sit still."

"You must copy Simon and the way he remains quiet."

"Simon is quiet because he is older."

Simon shoved his young brother playfully. "Years do not make the difference. I was born quiet and you were born to talk and wiggle. *Datt* said we were born different."

"Because you are tall and I am short?"

"You will grow, Andrew. *Mamm* said I am ready to grow out of my clothes."

"And your hat and shoes," the younger boy added. "You said they are both too small."

Noah turned to Ruthie. "Perhaps we should stop at the shoe store."

"Spring is almost upon us, and summer will follow soon thereafter. The boys go barefoot when the weather is warm."

Ruthie's pride was keeping her from buying shoes. Pride and a lack of resources.

He lowered his voice to keep the children from hearing. "I would like to buy shoes for Simon. Andrew, too."

She shook her head.

"Think about it."

Upon entering town, he pointed to the real-estate office. "I need to check on the papers for the sale of my property. Do you want to go into the dry-goods store next door?"

Again, he lowered his voice. "Get new straw hats for the boys. If they sell shoes, buy them, too."

"The shoes can wait, Noah, and their old hats are fine."

"*Mamm*, my hat hardly fits," Simon moaned. Evidently he had heard a portion of their conversation.

"Please, Ruthie." Noah leaned closer so the boys could not see the wad of bills he placed into her hand. "Let me do this."

She stared at him for a long moment and then glanced back at Simon. "Noah is right. You both are outgrowing not only your shoes, but also your hats. We will get hats today and shoes at the end of the summer."

"Then it's decided." Noah smiled. "I won't be long. If you need something new, Ruthie, I would be glad to buy all the purchases. You and your family were always there for me when times were tough."

And when his father was on one of his binges, but Noah wouldn't mention that in front of the boys.

"Thank you, Noah. I will pay you back for the hats."

"No need." Except for her pride.

He turned the buggy toward the rear of the store and tied the mare to the hitching post. The boys eagerly jumped down while he helped Ruthie out of the buggy.

"I am not used to such attention," she whispered once her feet touched the pavement.

She stood still for a long moment. He didn't want to move lest the moment passed and she stepped away.

"You deserve attention, Ruthie," he whispered.

"We are no longer young teens, Noah." She turned to gather her sons. "We will see you when you are finished with your real-estate business."

Noah glanced along the street to ensure no one suspect was hovering nearby. The man who had come after Ruthie at her house was a coward and would hide until darkness, or when she was alone, before he struck again.

Noah would make sure she and the boys weren't left unprotected while he stayed in the area. But as he walked into the real-estate office, he knew he couldn't protect them for long. As soon as the sale of his father's property was final, Noah would leave Amish Mountain.

"Is it Ruthie Eicher I see?" the female clerk asked when Ruthie stepped into the shop with the boys following close behind.

Ruthie's first inclination was to turn around and leave the store, but the boys were excited about their shopping adventure, and she would not let her own desire to stay away from people ruin the day for her sons.

She nodded and stepped closer, trying to identify the Amish woman, near her own age, who had greeted them.

"You do not recognize me?" the clerk asked. "I am Fannie Martin. We went to school together."

The name surprised her since the slender woman standing in front of her looked nothing like the plump Fannie she remembered from her youth. "You are Daniel's sister."

"Yah." The clerk nodded. "I was a year younger and always thought you were the prettiest girl in the school."

Ruthie's cheeks warmed. "You should not say such things, Fannie."

"Of course I should not say them, but still I do. Are these fine boys your sons?"

She nodded, her heart swelling with maternal pride that could not be helped. If pride could ever be positive, it would be a mother's love for her children.

"What can I help you find?" the clerk asked.

"The boys wanted to look at straw hats."

"A shipment came in last week. You will find them on the last aisle in the rear of the store."

The bell over the door rang as another customer stepped inside. Ruthie recognized Sarah Deitweiler, a middle-aged woman with a pinched nose and unsmiling eyes. Sarah had spread rumors around town about Ben's vice. Ruthie sighed at the memory of Sarah's less-than-loving comments. Ruthie's Aunt Mattie, her mother's sister, had tried to ease Ruthie's upset, yet even her aunt found Sarah to be a troublesome gossip.

Not wanting to give Mrs. Deitweiler more fuel for her wagging tongue, Ruthie steered the boys to the back of the shop.

Fannie greeted the newly arrived customer with much fanfare, as if to ensure Sarah Deitweiler's shopping experience would be positive. Word of mouth was the best way to market, the Amish knew, but one disgruntled customer could sour a business's reputation.

"Is that Ruthie Eicher?" the older woman said loud enough to be heard throughout the store.

"You know her?" the cheerful clerk asked.

"I don't associate with her type. In fact, I find it

strange that she would show her face in town after everything that happened with her husband."

"Mrs. Deitweiler, a wife is not responsible for her husband's actions," the clerk said in Ruthie's defense.

"You may think that, child, but as you age, you will learn the truth." The older woman harrumphed. "I will leave now to do my grocery shopping and come back to purchase my dry goods another day."

Ruthie glanced down at her sons. Simon's face fell and Andrew's brow furrowed. The boys had overheard the woman's comment just as Ruthie had. She hated seeing their embarrassment.

Did they realize what it meant to be shunned? She had never mentioned their father's tirade, when he had walked out of the Sunday service after calling the bishop and elders hypocrites. Simon had been old enough to remember the stares of those gathered to worship that day. Now he placed his hand in hers and squeezed as if offering support.

"What people say about us is not important, boys. What is important is what is in our hearts and that we live our lives as *Gott* would want. You do not need to hang your heads or be ashamed. You are fine boys, and I am proud of both of you."

"But the woman did not want to shop when you were in the store," Simon said, pointing out what they both knew to be true.

"We will not try to guess her reason for leaving. Instead, we will look at hats, which is the purpose for our visit."

Although Ruthie tried to make light of what had happened, the boys had been deflated and their exuberance faltered.

Simon picked out a hat, then peered at the price tag. "My old hat is *gut*, *Mamm*. It keeps the sun from my eyes. I do not need a newer hat that will do the same thing."

"But—" Andrew started to object as he reached for a hat in his size.

Simon took his hand. "Andrew, this is not what we need now. Come, we will go outside and wait for Noah while *Mamm* shops for herself."

Touched by Simon's maturity, and also saddened that he realized how far she had to stretch each dollar, she ushered them both toward the door. "I need nothing today," she told the boys. "We will all wait for Noah outside."

The clerk was busy unloading new merchandise and did not see them leave.

Once outside, they sat on a bench near the sidewalk and watched the cars and buggies pass. The sun had gone behind the clouds and the breeze was crisp. Their adventure was off to a less-than-encouraging start.

Seeing Noah exit the real-estate office and hurry toward them, she feared he would have news of the imminent sale of his property. If he announced he was leaving in the next day or two, she would return to the buggy and ask him to take them home.

Instead, Noah smiled as he neared. "Did you find hats?"

"We will wait for another day," Simon answered for both boys.

Noah glanced at her, as if questioning what happened.

"We were not in the mood to shop." She returned his money when the boys were not looking and hoped he would not press for more details.

She had thought the shame of the past would end with Ben's death, but shame lived on even now. She could bear being rejected, but she did not want that for her children.

Chapter Seven

Noah could sense Ruthie's tension, and he read pain in her eyes. Something had happened in the store that was more upsetting than the price of hats. He wondered if it had to do with small-town gossip.

The boys hung their heads as if finding great interest in the pavement. Simon's shoulders slumped and his mouth drooped. Andrew rested his elbow on the arm of the bench and held his head in his hand. The sadness that covered both boys' faces tugged at Noah's heart. He wanted to wrap them in his embrace and right whatever wrong had happened.

This morning, they had all been so excited about the trip to town. Noah thought the day would be fun and an opportunity to be together. Evidently he had been wrong.

Last night, Ruthie had shared about Ben's past. From his own youth, Noah knew how scathing gossip could be. Some people thrived on spreading hateful tales that harmed not only the people involved, but also innocent bystanders, such as the boys. Neither Andrew nor Simon were responsible for their father's actions, yet they, too, suffered. Life could be unfair. Noah knew that all too well.

"What about your land?" Ruthie asked as if trying to focus on something other than their distasteful experience in the shop.

"The real-estate agent is out of town today. His receptionist said the papers aren't ready. Prescott Construction is the name of the company wishing to buy the property. I thought I'd use the computer in the library to find information on the construction firm."

"The post office is across the street from the library. I would like to get my mail."

"We'll stop there as well as the library."

Simon's eyes widened. "Could you show us how to use a computer?"

"If your mother says it's all right."

Ruthie pursed her lips. "Technology is not something the Amish embrace."

"Please, *Mamm*." Simon grabbed her hand, his earlier upset seemingly forgotten.

Following his older brother's lead, Andrew tugged at her other arm. "The library has books, *Mamm*. You want us to read more."

She nodded. "Books are good. I am not sure about computers."

"You could go to the post office while the boys and I go to the library," Noah suggested. "It won't take long."

"Can you use your phone to search for the information?" she asked.

"I'll have more success using a computer. Plus, Simon and Andrew will enjoy seeing how they work."

Ruthie tilted her head as if mulling over her decision. "You will be careful?"

She was no doubt worried about the man on the mountain. "I'll be as cautious with them as you would be. You can trust me, Ruthie."

She stared at him for a long moment, and he wondered if she was weighing that very point. He had destroyed her trust ten years ago, so he understood her hesitation. The boys sat quietly, seemingly holding their breaths as they awaited her response.

Finally, she nodded. "The boys can stay with you while I get the mail."

Noah almost sighed with relief, but he didn't want the boys to realize what a huge concession their *mamm* had made. Ruthie had guarded her children for so long. He imagined she had placed herself between them and her husband, always the protective mother never wanting anything to hurt her boys.

He had asked Ruthie to trust him. Taking the boys to the library wouldn't seem like anything major to most people, but Noah was grateful that she had placed her sons in his care, even if just for a short time.

"Come on, guys, let's escort your mother to the post office, then we'll head to the library."

The boys skipped ahead as Noah and Ruthie followed behind at a more leisurely pace. Ruthie's shoulders were tense, and she flicked her gaze up and down the street.

She was worried about the man from the mountain. Perhaps she was also worried about whom she would see in town. From what she had told him last night, Ruthie and the boys had remained isolated on the farm and away from townspeople who had witnessed her husband's tirade at that Sunday service prior to his shunning. Undoubtedly, she still carried the scars from her humiliation.

In a way, Noah could relate. As a youth, he and Seth

had been ashamed of their father. They heard the whispers behind their backs and saw fingers point when they came to town. Noah had left home to rid himself of the shame. After all these years, he realized he had allowed it to take hold of him, and no matter how far he traveled, he couldn't remove himself from the memories and the pain until he embraced his past, accepted his father for who he was and then worked to forgive him for the dysfunction he had caused in Noah and Seth's lives.

Regrettably, as much as Noah wanted to forgive his dad, he couldn't. The pain was still too real. Then he realized the truth about Ruthie.

For so long, he had felt stung by her rejection, yet being with her again made him realize he was the one at fault. He had left Ruthie. She couldn't forgive him because the pain of being abandoned was still so real to her. Plus, Noah had not only abandoned her, but also their child. Some wrongs could never be righted. Ruthie could never forgive him just as he could never forgive his father or himself.

Chapter Eight

By the time they arrived at the post office, Ruthie was feeling less unsettled. The few people they passed on the street had smiled and nodded in greeting. Mrs. Deitweiler was nowhere to be seen, and there was no sign of any tall man wearing black and sporting tattoos on his arm. The boys had regained their youthful enthusiasm, and even the sun peered through the overcast sky. Her earlier concern eased, and she smiled as Noah and the boys left her at the post office and headed to the library across the street.

She waved a farewell, although Simon and Andrew were focused on Noah, probably talking about computers and questioning how they operated. At least Noah glanced back and waved. Ruthie appreciated the attention he gave to her sons, but she remained all too aware of the man who wanted to do them harm.

Stepping into the post office, she was relieved to find only two people ahead of her in line. She waited patiently and approached the postmaster's window after the other customers had been helped.

Mr. Hardy was a kindly man who had managed the

local post office for as long as she could remember. His smile was warm and welcoming. "Ruth Plank Eicher. It has been a long time. I wondered if you would be coming to town."

"It has taken me a while to get here."

"You've got a pile of mail that I've been saving. Did you bring a satchel?"

She glanced down at her small handbag. "I have only my purse."

"I'll get a big plastic bag from the back." He paused to stare into her eyes. "I'm sorry about the accident, Ruthie. You and the boys doing okay?"

"*Yah*, *danki*, Mr. Hardy. The farm is a challenge, but the boys are a big help."

"Your *datt* was a friend. I miss him. He was fortunate to have you as a daughter. You are a good woman."

Her cheeks burned. She nodded her thanks and waited quietly as he found a bag and filled it with her mail.

"Do you still want me to hold your mail here until you come to town again? Or we could set up delivery to your home."

"Can I let you know the next time I stop in?"

"Of course."

Ruthie's heart was heavy as she left the post office. Glancing into the bag, she wondered what all the official-looking envelopes meant. She had buried herself on the farm for the last two months and had allowed the bills to mount. Now she had more with which to deal. With so little ready cash, she had wanted to provide the daily needs for her children instead of paying off bills, many of which Ben had left unpaid.

Focused on her own financial situation, she failed to survey the surrounding area and suddenly heard footsteps sounding behind her. She stopped at the intersection and looked back. Her heart lurched at the sight of a tall man dressed in black. He stared at her through narrow eyes. The man on the mountain had covered his face with a stocking, so his features had been unrecognizable. Could this be the same man who had attacked her?

The light changed and she hurried across the street. She glanced back. The man started jogging toward her.

The library was just ahead, but she did not want the man anywhere near her boys. She spied a flower shop on the far side of the library and hoped she could find safety there. Surely the man would not do her harm when other people were around.

Increasing her pace, she hurried past the library and slipped into the shop.

The clerk looked up from arranging a bouquet of roses. "May I help you?"

"I—I just wanted to look at some of your potted plants."

Glancing out the window, Ruthie saw the man hurry past the storefront.

"Let me show you what I have," the clerk insisted. She motioned Ruthie to the rear of the store and pointed out a number of potted plants, each more beautiful than the last. The woman rambled on about how to care for the plants to keep them healthy and blooming.

Grateful though Ruthie was for having a place to hole up, she was eager to join Noah and her boys at the library and was relieved when a phone rang. The clerk excused herself and hurried to the far end of the counter to take the call.

Ruthie slipped outside and glanced along the sidewalk, seeing only a woman pushing a baby stroller.

Letting out a sigh of relief that the man was gone, she hurried to the library and walked across the large stone portico. As she opened the door and stepped inside, someone bumped into her.

She glanced up. Her heart raced. The man in black. He must have backtracked to the library when the clerk showed her the potted plants.

The man's face twisted in recognition. "I thought I had lost you."

Her boys. Had he done anything to Simon and Andrew?

"What are you doing here?" she demanded.

"You dropped this."

She looked down at the letter in his outstretched hand.

"You need to be careful." He pointed to the bag she held close to her chest. "You wouldn't want to lose any more of your mail."

She took the letter, and before she could react, he was gone. She watched him run across the street and disappear into a wooded area not far from the post office.

Glancing down at the envelope, her breath hitched. The letter bore a stamp and had been mailed to her rural address. The script was the same as the writing on the notes she had received at home that demanded she leave the area, and all three missives had been written in the same shade of green ink.

Was he merely returning a letter she had dropped? Or was the man today the same person who had attacked her on the mountain?

Noah glanced at his watch, concerned about what was taking Ruthie so long. He should have waited for her at the post office until she got her mail. If the boys hadn't been so excited about visiting the library, he might have been more cautious.

He was ready to head outside to check on Ruthie's whereabouts, when she raced into the computer area, eyes wide and face flushed.

From her expression, he knew something had happened, and it wasn't good. "Stay here, boys. I want to talk to your mother."

Noah hurried to her side. "Are you all right?"

"A man dressed in black came after me."

"The same man from the mountain?"

"I am not sure. He gave me this envelope. He said I had dropped it." She was talking fast, the words spilling one after another out of her mouth.

"Calm down, Ruthie, and tell me you are all right."

She pulled in a breath and nodded. "He did nothing to harm me except make my heart nearly stop beating." She explained about him following her across the street.

"I dashed into a flower shop until he passed by. Then when I entered the library, he was there. Somehow he had doubled back. Perhaps when I was with the clerk in the rear of the store."

She held up the envelope. "He said I had dropped this letter."

"Did you see tattoos on his arm?"

"He wore a long-sleeve shirt." She shook her head. "Perhaps I am being foolish, but I feared he would grab me."

"Do you want to read the letter now?"

"Not now. I do not want the boys to know."

Noah understood. Ruthie always put her boys first. He admired her for that.

"Come, the boys are excited about the computer. We

will focus on them now and deal with the man later. I called the sheriff's office. We can talk to one of the deputies this afternoon."

"I am not sure, Noah. What will the deputy say?"

"He'll say you need protection."

"My father never wanted to deal with the authorities. Neither did Ben."

"But you are wiser than your father and your husband. Besides—" he glanced at where the boys sat in front of the computer "—you need to think of Simon and Andrew."

She nodded. "You are right. My safety is not as important as theirs."

"All of you are important, Ruthie. The man needs to be stopped."

He needed to be stopped now, before she was hurt again or he injured the boys. If anything happened to any of them, Noah wouldn't be able to forgive himself. He had made so many mistakes in the past, he couldn't make any more now that Ruthie and Simon and Andrew had come into his life.

Chapter Nine

Ruthie pulled in a deep breath to calm her pounding heart and racing pulse. She did not want the boys to suspect that she was upset. Andrew was still young and overlooked subtle nuances, but Simon had always been more attuned to her feelings. He could sense her upset even when she tried to appear calm. At the moment, she felt totally out of control.

Her concern was for naught. Both boys were so engrossed with the computers that they failed to notice anything different about her demeanor, for which she was grateful.

"This is cool," Simon enthused.

She did not know where Simon had learned about something being cool, but his statement was followed by laughter from Andrew.

Worried they were making too much of a ruckus, she patted both boys' shoulders and then held her finger to her lips. "*Shhh*. You need to be quiet."

Glancing at the large monitor, she shook her head. The bishop would not approve, of this Ruthie was certain, but when she leaned closer, she saw Bible verses printed on the screen.

Noah pointed to the lines of text. "I told the boys how the Bible can be accessed on the computer. We were looking up some of their favorite verses of Scripture."

Bible verses were not what she had expected to find on the screen. Once again, Noah had surprised her.

"What's your favorite text?" she asked, trying to keep her voice light in spite of her still erratic heartbeat coupled with her surprise at the boys' search for Scripture.

"Matthew 6:14 to 15." He pointed to Simon. "Look it up and read the verses to your *mamm*."

"I need to remember what you told us." Simon carefully tapped the keyboard.

"Now hit Enter," Noah prompted.

A new verse appeared on the monitor. Simon leaned closer. "The passage says, *'For if ye forgive men their trespasses, your heavenly Father will also forgive you. But if ye forgive not men their trespasses, neither will your Father forgive your trespasses.'*"

Ruthie was amazed at how easily Simon had pulled up the passage. She glanced at the text. Forgiveness sounded easy and it was the Amish way, but sometimes the results of one's mistakes caused too much pain. The act could be forgiven, but life would be forever changed.

"What about the man who plans to buy your property?" she asked Noah. "Did you find him on the computer?"

"Not Prescott Construction. He must not advertise on the web."

Ruthie pointed to the nearby youth section. "Boys, find a book to check out while I talk to Noah." Both

Simon and Andrew hurried to the area designated for children.

"You are teaching the boys something they will never use," she said to Noah once they were alone.

"When they are older and want to get a job in town, Ruthie, they will need to use a computer. Many Amish craftsmen use computers to keep in touch with their customers and to order their supplies. As I understand the *Ordnung*, technology can't come into the home, but in an office or an outbuilding it's allowed for business purposes."

"Perhaps you are right, but for now, we are farmers who do not need technology."

"Let me do a little more searching while the boys find books to read, then we'll have lunch. I promised pizza if that's okay with you."

"Pizza would be a special treat."

Noah was exposing the boys to so many things. She would not let their minds be turned to the ways of the world, but for one day, allowing them to experience something new would be all right. At least, she hoped it would not cause them problems when they returned to the farm.

Ruthie's mind would be filled with other thoughts, as well. Would she be content to hole up on the mountain with no one around?

Prescott Construction. Would a construction company be her new neighbor after Noah left the mountain?

Perhaps by then, the bridge would have fallen into the water, isolating her even more. Her shoulders slumped with concern as she thought again of the man who wanted to do harm to her and her children.

She turned and stared at the other library patrons,

searching for the man who had retrieved the dropped envelope to make sure he had left the library and had not returned. After what had happened, she never wanted to see him again, and she never wanted her sons to worry about a man who might attack their mother or bring harm to either of them.

"It's time for lunch," Noah said once they left the library. "I mentioned pizza earlier. Does that still sound good?"

"We like pizza," Simon said, serious as always.

Andrew tugged on Noah's hand. "Can we have pepperoni?"

"Whatever you want." He looked at Ruthie. "And whatever your mother says you can have."

"Pepperoni and peppers." Simon grabbed his mother's arm. "Please, *Mamm*."

"Yes to both, if Noah agrees. Anything sounds delicious to me."

On the way to lunch, they stopped to watch a train chugging through town. The boys were wide-eyed with excitement as the train whistle blew and the engineer waved a greeting.

"Someday I want to ride in a train," Andrew enthused.

"Yah." Simon nodded in agreement. "And I want to take that trip with you."

They were still talking about trains when Noah ushered them into the pizza parlor. "Table for four," he told the hostess.

"Family of four," she said into a microphone.

Noah swallowed down a lump of regret. If only they were a family. He had lost that chance ten years ago, when he had left Ruthie and his Amish faith.

A waitress hurried to help them and ushered them to a table.

The boys played word games printed on paper place mats while Ruthie watched.

Noah touched her arm. "Pepperoni and peppers?"

"The boys will love that."

"How about a second pizza with mushrooms and onions?"

She lowered her gaze.

"Isn't that what you liked years ago?"

She nodded. "You remembered."

"Why wouldn't I? We were close, Ruthie."

"Best friends growing up."

He smiled. "Along the way the friendship ended and something more developed."

She glanced at the boys, who seemed oblivious to their conversation.

"We are just talking about friendship," Noah assured her. "There's nothing to be concerned about."

Glancing over her shoulder, she studied the various customers already enjoying lunch. "I keep thinking about the man who followed me today."

"Do you see him here or anyone else who looks threatening?"

Trying not to be obvious, she peered at the people sitting around them. "There are a few men who are the same height, but no one looks like the man who followed me today."

Noah glanced at the corner table, where two men shared a pizza. Both were big and beefy and wore long-sleeved black polos and khaki slacks. A logo was embossed over their shirt pockets, but Noah couldn't read the lettering.

He dipped his head toward the table. "Either of those guys look familiar?"

"One man seems in his fifties, the other is much younger. From their clothing, it appears they work together."

"Maybe Prescott Construction," Noah mused as if grasping for straws.

"I cannot read the logo on their shirts. You could ask them who they work for," Ruthie suggested.

He shook his head. "Not today. Besides, if they are with the construction company, I wouldn't want to do anything to sour the land deal."

"Of course not."

He heard sarcasm in her voice.

"Did you notice anyone with a tattoo?" he asked.

"Because of the cool temperature, everyone is wearing long sleeves."

"A description of the tattoo will help the sheriff find the attacker."

"I still do not want to discuss this with law enforcement."

"Law enforcement will find him," he assured Ruthie.

But would the sheriff's department find him before he came after Ruthie again?

Chapter Ten

"Thank you for bringing us to town and for all the ways you are making this day special for the boys," Ruthie said after the waitress had taken their order.

"The boys are special to me, Ruthie."

She glanced away, unwilling to meet his gaze.

He touched her arm again. "It's okay."

"You are selling your property."

He nodded. "I am."

The waitress filled water glasses for the adults and brought orange drinks for the boys. Two pizzas arrived soon thereafter. The boys ate until they were seemingly stuffed.

Ruthie laughed as she reached for her third slice. "This is more pizza than I've had in years," she confessed.

Noah smiled. "I'm glad. Pizza is always good. This seems especially so. We don't want any leftovers."

Simon and Andrew stepped up to the challenge and each boy ate two more slices. "I'm full," they both said in unison when they finished.

Noah glanced at the bag Ruthie had placed on the

floor next to her chair. "Looks like you have a lot of mail to read."

"I should have come to town earlier."

"Have you talked to the post office about delivering mail to your house?"

The boys were once again engrossed in their place mats and laughing among themselves. Ruthie lowered her voice so they wouldn't hear. "The postmaster mentioned home delivery. Ben had arranged for them to hold the mail for his monthly trip to town."

"While you stayed on the mountain?" Noah asked.

She nodded. "I needed to stay to care for my father."

The waitress brought the check. "I'll pay at the register." Noah slipped from the chair.

Ruthie instructed the boys to wash their hands and faces in the restroom. She glanced again at the two men eating in the corner, realizing there was nothing familiar about either man except that they were tall and muscular.

As she looked around the pizza parlor, she saw a number of other patrons with similar builds. She had to stop seeing the man from the mountain every time a tall, bulky guy appeared. Men dressed in dark clothing seemed even more suspect to her.

She looked at Noah as he stood in line to pay the cashier. He fit the mold, as well. Tall and well built, he was wearing a long-sleeve navy blue shirt with dark trousers, yet she knew Noah would not do her harm. At least not physical harm. If she did not guard her heart, she would be hurt in unseen ways when he left. She did not want to get involved with any man again, especially Noah.

As soon as the boys returned to the table, she gathered her mail and handbag and followed them to the front of the pizza parlor.

A big man dressed in black with dark eyes and a scowl walked inside just as the boys neared the door. Simon nearly collided with him. Not the man who had stopped her at the library, but someone who gave her pause.

The guy grabbed her son's shoulders. "Watch where you're going, little man. You don't want to get hurt."

Something in the man's annoyed tone made Ruthie's stomach tighten. Everything happened so fast. He was standing in front of Simon one second and hurrying into the main dining area the next.

Wishing she had gotten a better view of his face, she grabbed both boys' hands and pulled them into a sitting area away from the door.

Simon frowned as if to say he was too old to hold his mother's hand. *"Mamm,"* he moaned.

She ignored his annoyance. "We'll wait here patiently for Noah before we go outside."

"I did not mean to get in that man's way," Simon said.

"Did he hurt you?"

Simon shook his head. "No, but he looked familiar."

"Could he have been the man you saw at the river's edge? The man who wanted to know where to fish?"

"I am not sure." He turned and looked into the dining area. "Where did he go?"

Ruthie glanced over her shoulder and studied the people sitting at various tables, but she did not see the big man with the dark gaze.

"Perhaps he went to the restroom," she suggested.

Noah paid the bill and joined them at the door. "Everything okay?"

Ruthie glanced again into the dining area. She was not convinced the man was in the restroom. Had he gone out a back door? If so, why had he passed through the pizza parlor? Was he here to spy on them?

"Ruthie?" Noah raised an eyebrow. "Is everything okay?"

"Yah," she said, unwilling to tell Noah about her concerns. "Everything is fine."

"The sheriff's office is on the next block," Noah said once they were outside. "We'll go there next."

"Thank you for lunch," Ruthie said.

He smiled. "I'm glad you enjoyed it."

"The boys did, as well." She gently nudged them.

Taking the hint, they both said, "Thank you for the pizza."

"We'll do it again, *yah*?" He patted their shoulders.

"Yah!" Smiles covered both boys' faces.

They skipped ahead on the sidewalk, giving Noah an opportunity to talk to Ruthie.

"You need to tell the sheriff's deputy everything that happened."

Her face grew serious. "I am not sure this is a wise idea. What can he do?"

"He knows people in town, Ruthie. He hears things. There may be a stranger causing problems. The deputy can question him and learn the truth."

She nodded. "If you think it will end the attacks, then I will talk to the deputy, although I do not know if he will listen to an Amish widow who lives so far from Willkommen."

"Too many Amish are wary of law enforcement, but the sheriff's deputies are not to be feared."

"I will follow your advice, Noah."

"Good." He glanced at the boys as they approached

the upcoming intersection. "Turn left at the corner," he cautioned.

Ruthie hurried to catch up to them. She glanced over her shoulder a number of times until Noah looked back, as well.

"Something's bothering you," he said.

"I am thinking the boys are much too visible in case the attacker lives in town."

"I should have brought the buggy."

"The exercise is *gut*, but perhaps I am also worried about what to tell the deputy."

"Just tell him the truth."

"I would not lie." She squared her shoulders.

"I didn't say you would."

The boys glanced at each store-window display they passed, finding wonder in the items for sale. "It is so long since we have been to town," Andrew said. "There is so much to see."

Tires squealed around the corner and a dark sedan with tinted windows approached at a high speed. Noah quickly herded Ruthie and the boys away from the road. The car's front tire came up on the sidewalk.

Ruthie screamed and shoved the boys farther from the car. Noah turned as it raced past. He focused on the rear license plate, but mud was smeared on the plate and he was unable to read the numbers.

Ruthie grabbed Noah's hand. "If you had not moved us away from the curb, I fear what would have happened." Tears filled her eyes.

He wrapped his arm around her shoulder and then pulled the boys into his embrace, too. "The car's gone and we're all okay."

"But—"

He nodded to her, knowing there was a reason the car had jumped the curb, and it wasn't because the driver was going too fast. With the tinted windows, he couldn't see the driver's face, but he was sure the guy was the same man who had come after Ruthie. The attacker was in town at this moment. Noah didn't want to scare the boys more than they already were, which is what he tried to silently convey to Ruthie.

She wiped her eyes and nodded back to him as if understanding that she needed to be strong for the boys' benefit.

Noah glanced in the direction the car had gone. The guy who wanted Ruthie's property was becoming unhinged. One thing was certain—Ruthie and the boys were in his crosshairs.

Chapter Eleven

Coming to town had been a mistake. Ruthie knew it in the depths of her being. She clung to her boys. Her heart pounded almost as fast as the automobile had raced past them.

"*Mamm*, who was driving that car and why does he want to hurt us?"

Simon's question deserved an answer, but a lump filled her throat at the thought of what could have happened. Noah must have understood her upset. He patted Simon's shoulder.

"The man was driving too fast, Simon. Cars are dangerous, as we all know. We must be cautious, even on the sidewalk."

"I did not see the car until it had already passed," Andrew said. His little face was drawn and pale.

Noah nodded. "You boys responded immediately and stepped out of danger. That was very good."

Both boys seemed to take pride in their ability to react quickly. "That man should not be able to drive along the streets," Andrew said, staring in the direction the car had gone.

"If the sheriff had seen him," Simon said, "he would have gotten a ticket and his license would have been taken away." He looked up at Noah. "We need to tell the sheriff about what happened so he can arrest that man."

"We'll tell him, Simon. That's a good suggestion. The sheriff needs to know."

Ruthie's father had insisted the Amish take care of their own problems and not involve law enforcement. She had agreed to talk to someone at the sheriff's office, but she did not want to reveal family difficulties to a deputy she did not know. "I am not sure what we should do."

"Mamm!" Simon tugged on her arm. "You told me to be truthful when things happen even if I am at fault so I can learn from the mistakes. That man needs to learn from his mistakes."

She offered her son a weak smile. "How did you get so wise, Simon?"

He shrugged. "Perhaps it was the pizza."

In spite of the boy's serious expression, they all chuckled.

Ruthie turned to Noah. "Simon is right. We need to let law enforcement know about this driver and the harm he could cause."

The sheriff's office was located on the corner of the next block. She swallowed hard as Noah opened the door and motioned them inside. A bench sat on the right just inside the door.

"Boys, sit there while Noah and I talk to the clerk."

The man at the front desk beckoned them forward. Ruthie gave her name and address. "I need to report a number of things that have happened."

The clerk reached for a tablet and pen. "What type of things?"

"I received threatening notes that said I needed to leave the area or my children and I would be harmed. Then someone started a fire in my woodpile and attacked me when I raced outside to put out the fire. The man returned the next night. I believe the same person ran his car onto the curb not far from here and almost struck all of us."

The clerk wrote down the information she provided. "Could I speak to the sheriff?" she asked.

"He's out of town, but one of the deputies is available."

"That will be fine."

The clerk took the paper on which he had been writing and motioned them forward. "I'll take you to the deputy's office. There's a bench in the hallway where the boys can wait for you, if you like. You'll be able to see them."

She glanced at Noah, who nodded his approval.

"Mr. Schlabach will be with me. He is a neighbor and has witnessed everything I mentioned."

"That will be fine, ma'am. Step this way."

The clerk pointed to a bench for the boys and then ushered Ruthie and Noah into a small office directly across the hall. He gave the paper he carried to the man behind the desk. Ruthie looked back to ensure she could see the boys. They opened their library books and started to read.

The sheriff's deputy was middle-aged with a sagging jaw and warm gaze. He rose and stuck out his hand. "I'm Deputy Sam Warren."

Noah introduced himself and Ruthie.

"Please sit down, Mrs. Eicher and Mr. Schlabach. How can I help you folks?"

Ruthie went over everything she had told the clerk and

then explained about the man who had questioned Simon near the river. She also mentioned the man at the library.

"Let's start with the person at the river. Can your son give a description of the man?" the deputy asked.

"Simon said the man was shadowed by overhanging branches so he could not see his face."

"What about you, Mrs. Eicher?"

"He wore a woman's stocking over his face. A knit cap covered his hair. His eyes were dark, but that does not offer much help."

"Have you seen a doctor since the attack?"

She shook her head. "My bones did not break, so I will mend on my own."

"That's good to hear, ma'am. What about the boys?" He glanced into the hallway where the boys sat. "How are they doing?"

"They remain inquisitive about nature and the outdoors, but I am concerned for their safety."

"And, no doubt, your own safety, as well." He dropped his gaze to the paper the clerk had given him. "What about the car that ran onto the curb? Did either of you see the driver?"

Noah shook his head. "He drove a black sedan with tinted windows. I couldn't see the driver and tried to catch the license-plate number, but the plate was caked with mud and unreadable."

"Convenient for anyone who doesn't want to be identified," the deputy mused.

"We pushed the children out of the way," Ruthie explained. "If not—"

The thought of what could have happened returned to haunt her.

"Is there any other information you can provide about

the man who attacked you that would be beneficial?" Deputy Warren asked.

"Tattoos."

The deputy picked up his pen. "What type and where on his body?"

"I do not know the type of tattoos." She pointed to her left arm. "His shirtsleeve came up at one point, and I saw the marks covering his skin from his wrist up."

"All the way up his arm?" Warren asked.

"I saw only as far as the shirtsleeve was raised. About midway to his elbow, so I cannot say about the rest of his arm."

"What about the colors of the tattoo and the design? Did anything stand out?"

"I feared he would strike me. I saw only the marks and nothing that I recognized."

"Tattoos that cover the entire arm are called sleeves, Mrs. Eicher. Often the various details in the design have a common theme. Did you see anything you could identify? And did he have tattoos on his other arm?"

"As I said, I do not recall seeing anything except swirls of color on his left arm. Yellow, red, blue." She shrugged. "I saw nothing on his right arm."

"Anything else?"

"As I mentioned, he was tall and muscular." She glanced at Noah. "Somewhat like Mr. Schlabach."

The deputy stared at Noah for a long moment. "What were you doing at the time of the attacks, Mr. Schlabach?"

"I was at my house just across the river from Mrs. Eicher's home."

"Did you see the suspect either time?"

"I saw a man dressed in dark clothing running from her house last night."

"You saw him from your house all the way across the river?"

Noah shook his head. "I had checked Mrs. Eicher's property and then decided to return to talk to her."

"About what, Mr. Schlabach?"

"Why did I want to talk to her again?" Noah asked.

The deputy nodded.

"To tell her not to worry."

"Yet the man was accosting her at that very moment."

Ruthie's stomach rolled. The deputy was implying Noah was involved.

"The door to her house was shut," Noah said. "I didn't realize what was occurring inside until I saw the door open and the man run away."

"Did you follow him?"

"No, I..." Noah glanced at her. "I was concerned about Mrs. Eicher's well-being and entered the house to check on her."

"I see." The deputy wrote something on the paper.

Ruthie glanced at Noah. His gaze was dark. He seemed as surprised by the deputy's line of questioning as she was.

The deputy pursed his lips and turned back to Ruthie. "Did you have the feeling at any time either night that Mr. Schlabach could be the attacker?"

She laughed nervously. "No. No thought like that entered my mind. Noah is an old friend who has helped me since he returned to the mountain. The other man is hateful. His heart is hardened and he needs to be stopped."

"Amish Mountain is a distance from town, Mrs. Eicher. If you were *Englisch*, I would advise you to call me as soon as you see anything that seems questionable, but I presume you do not have a phone."

"That is correct."

"Do you have access to a phone?"

She thought of Noah's cell. "For the next few days. After that time, I will have no means to communicate with your office."

"Living high on the mountain could be difficult, especially if the man returns to do you harm."

"*Yah*, I am all too aware of what could happen. That is why I need you to protect me."

"I'll have a car patrol the mountain each night, but I can't do more than that."

"Do you know of new people in town who fit his description?" she asked.

"Ma'am, the description you provided could fit a lot of men in town. Tall, muscular. Since he wore a stocking over his head, would you be able to recognize him in a lineup?"

She shook her head. "I saw someone in the pizza parlor and wondered if he could be the man, but it is too hard to know."

"You mentioned a man at the library."

"I had dropped a letter and he returned it to me."

"Was he tall and muscular?" the deputy asked.

She nodded. "And dressed in dark clothing."

"Did he have tattoos?"

"It is a cool day. He was wearing a long-sleeve shirt. I collected my mail at the post office and hurried toward the library." She explained about hiding in the florist shop and then bumping into the man when she entered the library. "After he gave me the dropped envelope, he hurried outside, crossed the street and went into the woods."

The deputy nodded. "There's a vagrant who set up camp in that area. We'll bring him in for questioning."

"Thank you."

"Could I see the envelope he gave you?"

"Two notes have been stuck under my door. Both were written in green ink and the script was the same as on the mailed envelope the man gave me today."

As Ruthie dug into the plastic bag of mail, the deputy asked, "Has the man given you any indication of why he wants to do you harm, Mrs. Eicher?"

"He wants me to leave my property." She told him what had been written on the first two notes and then held up the envelope in question. "The man who lives in the woods handed this to me."

Tearing open the flap, she glanced at the deputy and then pulled out the folded paper.

"Might be a good idea if I handle this one, ma'am." The deputy drew a plastic bag from a lower desk drawer along with a pair of tweezers. Using the tweezers, he opened the letter and read it, then placed it in the plastic and sealed it shut. "He's giving you until the end of the week."

"Does he say what he will do then?" Noah asked.

"He'll make you regret staying on the land." The deputy scratched his jaw. "Sounds as if he wants your property. Any idea why he wants your land, Mrs. Eicher?"

She shrugged. "The setting is lovely with a river that runs between my property and Noah's. Perhaps he wants a mountain home."

"Mr. Schlabach, the man has not come after you?" the deputy asked.

"I have received no threats or attacks to my person. Although a real-estate agent contacted me some weeks ago about selling my property. Prescott Construction is interested in the land."

"So both of you own mountain land that two different people or groups want?"

They nodded.

"Do you know about the movie studio that's on the other side of the mountain?" the deputy asked.

"I've only recently returned to town," Noah said. "Why would there be a movie studio in such a remote spot?"

"Low taxes. Pristine scenery."

"Could the movie-industry people want to film on the land?" Noah asked.

"Or perhaps build mountain homes for their executives," the deputy added. "I'll talk to the Montcliff Studio folks. We had some problems with them early on. Things have changed for the better." He shrugged. "Still, I'll let you know if I find out anything."

He turned to Ruthie. "Mrs. Eicher, if you see someone who looks like the man, let me know. There are a lot of new folks in town these days. Seems Willkommen is growing faster than anyone expected. New housing areas attract city people looking for a country home."

"Do you mean city people from Willkommen?" she asked.

He shook his head. "No, ma'am, from farther south. I was referring to Atlanta."

"They are moving to this area of Georgia?"

"'Fraid so. Our peace and quiet might be a thing of the past."

"Hopefully they will not come to the mountain."

"Looks like someone is already there stirring up trouble. Lock your doors and keep an eye on the boys when they're outside."

"You are scaring me, Deputy."

"Ma'am, I'm just speaking the truth."

Upon leaving the sheriff's office, Noah turned to Ruthie. "You don't look satisfied."

"I had hoped the deputy would know names and already have possible suspects in mind."

"Investigations take time, Ruthie. The deputy is trying to be realistic."

"Maybe I ask too much."

"To raise your boys in safety is not asking too much. You've filed a report so now the sheriff's office can act if they find someone questionable."

"I hope they find the man and lock him up," Simon said, overhearing their conversation.

"We don't wish harm to come to the man," Noah told the boy. "But we need to ensure he doesn't hurt anyone else."

"Just so he does not hurt my boys," Ruthie said. She glanced over her shoulder and tugged on Noah's arm.

He followed her gaze and saw a tall man in dark clothing. As Noah watched, the man turned the corner and disappeared from sight.

Ruthie was imagining that any tall, muscular man she saw was out to hurt her and her sons.

"Take a deep breath and try to relax," Noah suggested. "The deputy will be on the lookout for the assailant. You must be careful but not unduly paranoid."

She didn't seem interested in his advice.

"I need to stop at the lumber store for some building

supplies," he explained. "Then we'll get ice cream before we leave town."

She studied the sky. "The clouds in the distance are as dark as my current mood. I am ready to head home, but I do not want to ruin the end of the day for the boys."

"The supply store won't take long. We'll be riding up the mountain within the hour."

She nodded as if satisfied with his answer.

"Climb in," Noah told the boys when they arrived back at the buggy.

He helped Ruthie to her seat and then scooted next to her. After a flick of the reins, Buttercup eased back onto the main street. The lumber store was on the south side of town. Ruthie kept her focus on the people and cars they passed, no doubt searching for her attacker.

Noah hated that Ruthie was living in fear, but her children were in danger, and she would do anything to keep them safe.

Once they arrived at the lumber store, Noah hopped to the ground and tethered Buttercup to the hitching rail. "I won't be long if you want to stay in the buggy."

"We'll go with you," Ruthie replied quickly.

"I know you're worried about the boys, but from your frown, I also wonder if you're upset with me, Ruthie. Did I do something wrong?"

She shook her head. "You have been wonderful, Noah. I will never be able to thank you."

"The smiles on the boys' faces are thanks enough, though I would feel better if you smiled, as well."

She nodded. "Ben always said I was much too serious."

"And determined. You set your mind to something and you keep at it until you succeed."

"Things came more easily to you, Noah. I had to work for any skill or knowledge in school."

"Yet you made everything look easy, Ruthie."

They hurried into the lumber store and Noah found what he needed. After checking out, he loaded the items into the rear of the buggy.

Andrew tugged on Noah's hand. "Are we going to get you-know-what?"

Noah winked at Ruthie and then glanced down at Andrew. "I don't know what you-know-what is."

The boy motioned for him to bend down. "Let me whisper in your ear."

Noah enjoyed the game and stooped down.

Andrew cupped his small hand around Noah's ear and whispered, "Ice cream."

Straightening, he smiled. "That's a great idea. Do you think your mother and Simon want some, as well?"

Andrew nodded. He grabbed Simon's hand and whispered in his ear.

Simon's eyes twinkled and he nodded to Noah. "*Yah*, please. That sounds very *gut*."

"Are you boys keeping secrets from your mother?" Ruthie rolled her eyes, acting playfully indignant.

Andrew covered his mouth with his hand and giggled. "Close your eyes and we will take you there."

The boys guided her along the street and into the ice-cream shop, where she pretended to be surprised. Simon nodded to Noah and then motioned to Andrew, who was enjoying himself. Noah patted the older boy's back, proud of him for joining in and not spoiling his younger brother's fun.

From what he'd seen so far, Simon had a good heart and a sincere concern for others. Pride swelled within

Noah, though he couldn't take credit for the boy. Ruthie had raised Simon. Her husband had, as well. Noah had done nothing for his child and couldn't even buy him a new hat and a better-fitting pair of shoes. At least he could buy him ice cream.

The boys ordered triple-scoop ice-cream cones with three different flavors and then tried to decide which they liked best.

"I like them all," Andrew said. He rapidly licked his cone as the ice cream melted.

Ruthie had one scoop of chocolate, and Noah splurged on two scoops of mint chocolate chip.

Once they finished the treat and wiped their hands and faces, they were ready to drive home. When they stepped outside, Noah eyed the dark clouds that hovered overhead and wished he had paid more attention to the weather instead of the fun he was having with Ruthie and her boys.

As he rounded the corner to the rear of the supply store, where he'd parked the buggy, Noah saw a man standing near the rig. A tall, muscular man wearing dark clothing.

The guy glanced at them, then turned and hurried down a back alley.

Ruthie was talking to the boys and hadn't noticed the man. Noah didn't want to worry her, but having someone snooping around the buggy was a concern. After the boys climbed in and he helped her to the seat, he checked his purchases from the lumber supply, relieved to find everything in place. Ruthie's mail looked undisturbed. He quickly inspected the wheels and the underside of the buggy. Nothing seemed amiss.

The stranger was probably walking through the parking area and had inadvertently passed close to Ruthie's buggy. Noah was making too much of something that was nothing more than happenstance. Plus, he didn't have time to track down the guy. From the dark clouds rolling overhead, they needed to start back to the mountain if they hoped to make it home before the rain.

Chapter Twelve

Halfway up the mountain, the rain started to fall, fat drops that pounded the top of the buggy. A stiff wind drove the rain at an angle, drenching Ruthie and Noah. The boys got wet as well, even though they were hunkered down in the rear seat.

"Simon, make sure the bag of mail stays dry," Ruthie called back to him.

"The bag is plastic, *Mamm*. The envelopes are dry."

She grabbed blankets and wrapped them over the boys and then around her legs and Noah's.

The temperature dropped at least ten degrees, and the gusting mountain air and driving rain made the ride even more uncomfortable.

The buggy started to shimmy. Noah pulled back on the reins to slow Buttercup's pace.

Ruthie glanced around the outside of the rig. "The back rear wheel is wobbling."

Noah steered the mare to a clearing on the far side of the road. Before he could pull her to a stop, the wheel flew off and rolled down the incline.

The buggy shifted. Ruthie screamed.

"Hold on, boys," Noah warned as the buggy tilted, throwing Ruthie to the ground. The boys fell against the side of the buggy, then tumbled out, landing near their mother.

She screamed and crawled to her children. "Simon, Andrew. Oh, *Gott*, help us."

Heart in his throat, Noah jumped to the ground and hurried to check on both boys. They were stunned but sat up without a problem.

Tears ran from Ruthie's eyes as she gathered the boys into her arms. "I feared you both were hurt."

"Are you all right?" Noah kneeled beside her, touching her arms and legs to ensure nothing was broken.

"I am not so fragile to break in a fall."

Ruthie was strong-willed and determined, but her husband and father had died in a buggy accident. Noah knew the fear she had to have felt seeing her boys tumble from the buggy. His own heart had nearly stopped, too.

He led Ruthie and the boys to shelter under a large oak tree and wrapped the damp blankets around them. The rain continued as Noah retrieved the wheel and worked to reattach it to the buggy.

Noah thought of the man who had been snooping around the buggy. Loosening a few bolts could cause the wheel to shimmy off-kilter with time, which is probably what happened. When Noah had checked the wheels, all the bolts were in place, but evidently not screwed in tight enough.

He dug through the supplies he had purchased at the lumber-supply store and found bolts that would fit the wheel. He also found a toolbox in the rear of the buggy.

"You need help?"

Turning, he saw Simon, who had left the cover of the trees.

Noah appreciated the offer. "If you hold the wheel, Simon, I can slip the bolts in place."

Working together, they reattached the wheel. The mare would have to go slow, but they would be able to get home.

He helped Ruthie and Andrew into the rear of the buggy, where they would be at least somewhat protected from the rain.

"I will sit next to you," Simon announced.

"You'll be more comfortable in the back with your mother and brother," Noah encouraged.

"*Yah*, but it is good to be here with you."

Noah's less-than-thorough inspection of the buggy in town had placed Ruthie and her boys in a dangerous situation, yet he heard no accusation in Simon's tone, nor did he see anything except admiration in the boy's gaze.

In spite of the mistakes his biological father continued to make, Simon would grow into a fine man. Of this, Noah was certain.

Ruthie was too shaken to think of anything except that her boys had not been hurt. When she had seen them lying on the ground, she had thought the worst and her heart had been ready to break. Only two months ago, Ben and her father had been killed, although Ben's failure to stop at an intersection had placed him at fault. Still, no matter who was at fault, her husband and *datt* were dead, and today's accident had made her fear her boys had been injured.

With a grateful heart, she offered a prayer of thanks that her sons had been spared. Sensing Noah's upset, she tried to control her own emotions. She knew he held himself responsible, but he had done nothing wrong. No one would suspect someone would tamper with their buggy wheel. But someone had.

Again, she thought of the man in the pizza parlor, as well as the man who had tracked her down in the library. Could either of them be the man who had attacked her twice on her farm?

Hoping to keep Andrew warm, she wrapped him in her arms and pulled him close. Simon had to be chilled, but he was trying to be so grown up. Ever since Ben had died, he had considered himself the man of the house. Simon had taken on that role without her prompting, and she admired his internal sense of purpose, although she did not want him burdened with responsibility at such a young age.

Both boys were enamored of Noah, and as much as she enjoyed seeing them happy, she feared their spirits would be dashed when he left in a few days. To protect the boys she should stop Noah from coming around, yet she knew without a shadow of a doubt that Noah would do anything to keep them safe. With the hateful man on the loose, she and her sons were in danger, but knowing Noah was never far away provided a sense of security that would surely end when he sold his father's land and moved away.

Drawing Andrew even closer, she glanced down at the bag of mail and worried about what to expect tonight as she sorted through the bills. She would wait until the boys were in bed before she opened the envelopes, but the thought of what she might find unsettled her.

Tired and wet when they got home, she heated water on the stove and poured it into the washtub. Both boys

bathed, enjoying the warm soak, then dressed in flannel pajamas.

After their filling lunch in town, Ruthie fixed peanut-
butter sandwiches and wedges of cheese and apple for
their evening meal.

Noah had parked the buggy in the barn, promising to
work on the wheel later, and had gone home to change
into dry clothes.

Her body ached, made worse by the cold. A hot bath
would help ease the soreness, but by the time she tucked
the boys in bed, the bath water had turned tepid, and she
was too tired to refill the tub.

She washed her hands and face and changed into dry
clothes. After throwing another log into the woodstove,
she pulled her bent hickory rocker closer to the warmth
and turned up the oil lamp.

Reaching into the plastic bag, she sorted through the
mail. The flyers and pamphlets could be tossed, but she
placed the important correspondence in a pile on the
side table.

Her heart sank as the pile grew. She threw away the
junk mail before she opened the bills, one after another.
Her stomach churned as she realized how much debt Ben
had accrued. He had cautioned her never to buy on credit,
yet he had done that very thing more than a few times.

The fact he had taken out credit cards troubled her.
She needed to talk to the bank manager the next time
she went to town to see how much money was left in
their small savings. She feared it was near rock-bottom,
which only compounded her misery.

Overwhelmed with concern about her financial situation, she sighed before she reached for the next letter in
her pile. The return address read Prescott Construction,

the same buyer who was interested in Noah's farm. She ripped open the envelope and noted the letter had been written six weeks earlier and had probably been waiting for her at the post office all this time. The company expressed interest in buying her land.

As much as she wanted to keep her property and turn it over to the boys someday, she needed to be practical. If her financial situation was as dire as she believed it to be, she had to make some tough decisions. Selling the farm would break her heart, but taxes would soon be due on the land, and she needed money to buy feed for the livestock and seed for the fall crops. Money she did not have.

Was the offer from Prescott Construction the answer to her financial problems? She did not want to leave the mountain, but she might not have a choice.

Another thought surfaced that gave her pause. Could the man who wanted to do her harm be involved with Prescott Construction?

Chapter Thirteen

Noah returned to Ruthie's barn later that night to fix the broken wheel and soon saw her leave the house and walk to the graveyard. Despite the sweater she wore, she rubbed her arms against the cool evening air and paused at each grave, head bowed and shoulders slumped. Noah sensed the heaviness that appeared to weigh upon her heart. More than anything, he wanted to comfort her and apologize for not being more proactive today. Had he done a better job checking the buggy wheel, he could have had it professionally repaired before they left town. The ride home would have been wet but uneventful. Instead it had almost been a disaster.

As he watched, Ruthie kneeled on the damp earth and tugged at the weeds growing between the graves, no doubt wanting to ensure Ben's final resting spot wouldn't be blighted, as his life had been. The sight of such a caring and considerate woman mourning her husband with servitude wrenched his gut and brought a bitter lump to fill his throat. Ben didn't deserve Ruthie's love. Nor did Noah, yet she was too young to be a widow with two sons to raise by herself.

Her husband had been shunned, and Ruthie suffered with the shame. She had not been ostracized from the community, yet she had rejected any offer of help from the bishop and his church. Noah hoped that would change over time.

Eventually some handsome farmer would come courting. At first, he would help her with her farm. They would get to know each other until a bond formed that might eventually lead to love.

Ruthie was too pretty and sweet and hardworking to be ignored by the single Amish men in the area.

They were probably giving her an opportunity to mourn before they came knocking at her door.

Noah fisted his hands, surprised by the frustration mounting within him. Not at Ruthie, but at the men who would be vying for her hand. None of them would be good enough for her, but perhaps they could offer her what she wanted—to live Amish on her land.

Noah thought back over his years in the *Englisch* world. He had hoped life would be different when he left the mountain, but he had all too quickly learned that the internal struggle eating at him in his youth—his sense of inadequacy and need to isolate himself from his drunken father—remained constant.

He had also learned that the *Englisch* world, like the Amish, required hard work and steadfastness. He had done well with his jobs, and seeing Seth find love and have a family had brought him joy. Then the dam had collapsed and everyone he loved had been swept away.

Except Ruthie. She was the last link he had to the past. When he thought back to his youth, he had wonderful memories of their time together.

He continued to watch her as she pulled weeds and

intermittently wiped at her eyes. Was she crying? Her tears broke his heart and confirmed she was not looking for anyone else to fill her husband's shoes. Even if Ben Eicher hadn't deserved her love and attention.

Glancing at the upstairs bedroom window, Noah wondered if Simon and Andrew were asleep. The boys were both so full of life and energy. The thought of them brought a smile to his lips and a joy to his heart that pushed past the pain of seeing Ruthie grieve for her deceased husband.

No matter how much Noah cared for the boys, he still needed to leave, so Ruthie could move on with her life. It wasn't what he wanted, but it needed to be done for her sake—for her future and that of the boys. Noah would only stand in the way of her happiness.

He turned back to the broken wheel, but his heart was heavy, and he decided to call it a day and return to his father's house. Things might seem better in the morning, although he doubted anything would be different. Ruthie would remain the dutiful wife grieving her husband's death, and Noah would be the man who had left her pregnant and alone. *Gott* help him for what he had done, even if he hadn't known about the baby growing within Ruthie's womb. Leaving her had been a huge mistake, and leaving his child compounded the guilt that welled up within him. Tonight, the pain of what he had lost was almost too much to bear. He needed to distance himself from Ruthie. She would continue to mourn her husband's passing while Noah mourned his youthful mistake that still ate at his heart.

After returning the tools to their rightful places, Noah peered from the barn to ensure Ruthie had gone inside. The now neatly weeded cemetery was empty except for the simple grave sites that marked the passing of her family.

Rain started to fall as he headed home. The river had continued to rise over the last few hours. If the water overflowed its banks, Ruthie's home could be flooded as had happened years ago when they were both children.

"She doesn't need any more problems, Lord."

Noah glanced back at her house, realizing that was the first time he had prayed aloud since the Chattanooga dam had broken.

Maybe he was starting to heal. Walking across the bridge, he shook his head at his moment of optimism. He would never heal, and that would be the burden he had to endure for the role he played in his brother's death.

Stopping on the far side of the bridge, he turned to stare at Ruthie's home, all the while ignoring the rain. As a kid, he'd enjoyed visiting his best friend, who eventually grew into the woman he loved. How had what started out so good turned so wrong? She had married someone else because Noah had thought of himself instead of what Ruthie needed.

Why hadn't he loved her enough to stay because he wanted her in his life? Some would argue that he was young and self-centered, both of which were true, yet he couldn't forgive himself for what he had done to Ruthie and, unknowingly, to Simon.

He turned back to his father's house and thought again of the lonely nights when his *datt* was drunk and ready to whip him for some imagined problem. Noah had never been good enough, but at least he had been the one his father punished instead of his younger brother. Seth had escaped their father's physical abuse, not that it made Noah feel any better right now.

Tonight, he felt once again like that boy going home to find his father either passed out in the house, or ready to take a strap to his backside.

Life back then had been tough, but that was the past and he needed to focus on the present. Being with Ruthie and the boys over the last few days had brought Noah joy, although he would leave soon. He didn't deserve happiness, and without Ruthie and the boys he would never be truly happy again.

Ruthie stood in the unlit downstairs of her house and stared out the window, watching Noah walk back across the bridge until he faded into the darkness.

Tired as she was, she hoped the night would be un-eventful. The day had been a seesaw of emotions that had sapped her energy. Tonight she wanted to sleep without dreams of a man with a stocking over his head. She wanted to feel safe and secure in her own home without fearing what was going to happen next.

The deputy said he would have someone patrol the mountain. Would he be true to his word and would she even notice when law enforcement drove by? It was doubtful their occasional presence would deter anyone who wanted to do her harm.

She headed to the bent hickory rocking chair by the stove. After lighting the oil lamp, she reread the letter from Prescott Construction. If only she knew what to do.

Earlier, she had walked to the cemetery, where her mother and infant sister were buried, to draw strength and, hopefully, get answers.

Having her mother die in childbirth had rocked her world as a young girl. Her father had gone to get the midwife and told Ruthie to take care of *Mamm* while he was gone. He had returned soon after her mother had taken her last breath. Brokenhearted, Ruthie held on to the last words her mother had whispered on her deathbed. "Take care of your father."

Ruthie had tried. That was why she had not run away with Noah that night, much as she had wanted to. She had planned to talk to her father and soften the blow of her leaving, and work out some arrangement for his care. All those plans were for naught because Noah had left without her, never realizing how he had broken her heart.

She laid the letter from the construction company on the kitchen table, turned off the lamp and slowly climbed the stairs to her bedroom. Once again, she pulled back the curtain and stared at the farmhouse on the opposite side of the river. A light glowed in a downstairs window.

She imagined Noah with a cup of coffee in hand, staring pensively back at her. How had their lives become so mixed up when they had been so much in love?

Some things were never meant to be, and perhaps she and Noah had never been meant for each other.

That realization made her heart ache as she crawled into bed and closed her eyes. All she could see was Noah's handsome face and his eyes twinkling with laughter as they used to do when they were both young and in love.

Chapter Fourteen

Noah couldn't sleep. He kept thinking of the buggy accident and what could have happened.

The rain increased through the night. Concerned about the rising river, he donned a water-repellant windbreaker, grabbed his Maglite and walked to the water's edge. The river churned as it flowed down the mountain, the current strong with whitecaps. If the river overflowed its banks, nothing would remain in its path.

He played the light over the bridge, checking the underpinnings, and realized he had not shored up the rotting wooden beams as he had planned to do. Tomorrow the bridge would be his first priority.

To ensure the muddy bank on Ruthie's side of the river was holding firm, Noah crossed the bridge. A noise sounded in the night. He flicked off the Maglite and made his way carefully along the river's edge. As he neared Ruthie's house and outbuildings, the sound came again, metal against metal.

Drawing closer, he saw movement.

Thunder rumbled overhead, then a bolt of lightning

crashed to the earth. For a split second, he saw a man running from the chicken coop.

Noah raced after him. Another bolt of lightning struck. A tree cracked and branches crashed to the ground.

The man disappeared into the woods behind Ruthie's house.

Thunder roared and lightning once again brightened the night sky.

Noah ran to the chicken coop. As he drew closer, he realized the sound he had heard was the wire fence being cut. Some of the chickens had already escaped through the gaping hole that would allow a fox or coyote to attack those that remained behind.

His heart skipped as he thought about what the man might do next, and what could befall Ruthie and her boys.

Ruthie woke when a giant bolt of lightning struck nearby. She sat up with a start, hearing the raging storm. Concerned by the howling wind and torrential rain, she slid from bed, peered through the window and saw Noah. Hurriedly, she slipped on her robe, glanced into the boys' room to ensure they were asleep and then raced downstairs. Like a strobe light, the sky flashed bright, then dark, then bright again.

She opened the door as another bolt of lightning lit the sky and glanced at the chicken coop. Her heart pounded. Even from this distance, she could see the cut fencing and the chickens scattered about the side yard. There was another burst of light and she gasped.

Spray-painted on the wall of the chicken coop were the words *Leave now*.

"Mamm?" She turned to find Simon on the stairs.

"Go back to bed. It is only a storm, Simon. We are not in danger."

Turning back, she watched Noah wrangle the chickens into the henhouse. He grabbed tools from the barn and quickly closed the gaping hole before he hurried to the porch.

"You saw the coop?" Noah asked as he shook water from his jacket.

She nodded, then glanced over her shoulder, relieved her son had complied with her request. "Simon has gone back upstairs, but I fear he may have seen it, as well. Who would do this?"

"I saw someone running, but I couldn't catch up to him."

Her shoulders slumped and she was overcome with discouragement. "Maybe I should sell the farm."

"What?"

"Come in. I will show you the letter I received from Prescott Construction. I wanted to pass the land on to the boys, but so many bills came in the mail we picked up today. I am tired of trying to make ends meet while fighting off the vile man who wants me gone."

"You don't have to make a decision tonight, Ruthie."

She appreciated the concern evident in Noah's voice, but she had her back to the wall, figuratively, and needed a way to support her boys.

"I should return to town and talk to the real-estate agent about Prescott Construction's interest in my land," she admitted.

"We'll go together. I have to take the buggy to the repair shop. What I did tonight was a quick fix, but I don't want you going up and down the mountain without an expert checking the wheel."

"Could we go tomorrow?"

He nodded. "But first thing in the morning, I need to work on the bridge. We'll leave after that."

"I do not want the boys to know about selling the farm. At least, not yet. Once I find out what arrangements the company is willing to make, then I will know whether this is something I should do."

She glanced out the window. "When the rain lets up, I have to remove the writing from the chicken house. The boys have gone through so much. They do not need to worry more about their mother."

"I'll take care of it, Ruthie. There's spray paint in my dad's garage. I'll cover the writing. It won't look attractive, but we can buy paint in town. I'll repaint the structure and repair the wire."

Confused as to what to do, she wrapped her arms around her waist and sighed. "I do not want to give in to this man. If he wants me to leave, perhaps I *should* stay."

"To prove to him that he can't run you off?"

"Exactly. If my well-being was all I had to worry about, I would sink in my heels and remain here, but I worry about the boys. I have been schooling them at home, yet the needs of the farm are great and there is little time for lessons. I see them falling behind with their studies. In town, they could go to school with the other children."

"You love the mountain, Ruthie."

She smiled weakly. "Whether you realize it or not, so did you, Noah, but you left. This has not been a problem, *yah*?"

"I wouldn't be truthful if I told you it was always easy."

"Have you thought of returning to the Amish life?"

"At times."

"Yet something holds you back?" she asked.

"I never felt that I fit in. Perhaps it was because of my *datt*. Drunks are not living life according to the *Ordnung*. The district looked askance at my father. They also looked askance at Seth and me."

"You did nothing wrong."

"Perhaps I was too thin-skinned. The *Englisch* world taught me to be more independent and not worry about what others thought."

She nodded. "I should learn the same from you."

"You're not comfortable in town?"

"Perhaps I am too thin-skinned, as you mentioned."

"You were always well liked. Although because of your husband, I'm sure these last few years have been difficult."

"Things change, as we both know." She sighed and then pointed to the kitchen. "Shall I fix tea, or would you prefer coffee? Plus, I have a feeling you did not eat after our trip to town. I have cheese and bread."

"I'm fine, and the chicken coop needs attention. The boys rise early. It's best if I paint over the message tonight."

"It is still raining."

"And it may continue all night. You might hear me outside. Don't be alarmed. Lock your door and stay inside. I'll see you in the morning."

He had to be tired. They had both had a long day. His clothes were wet, and the weather was growing even more severe.

"You have done so much for me, Noah. I do not know how to thank you."

"Letting me spend time with you and Simon and Andrew brings me joy, Ruthie. For this, I should thank you." He started for the door, then hesitated and glanced back. "I'm sorry how everything turned out. I was impetuous and bullheaded. I should have thought of your needs instead of only my own."

With a nod of farewell, he strode out of the house and hurried toward the bridge. She locked the door and climbed the stairs. From her bedroom window, she watched when he returned and spray-painted over the vile message.

Once the job was done, he glanced up, no doubt seeing her in the window. He raised his hand and then hurried back across the bridge.

Shortly thereafter, lights came on in his family home.

As a girl, she used to stare out her window and think of a time when Noah would court her and ask to marry her. In her mind, it would have been the normal progression after all the years they had grown up together.

She turned away from the window, remembering how many nights she had cried herself to sleep after Noah had left the mountain. Her heart had broken, and at the time, she had feared she would not have the wherewithal to continue on.

Then came the realization that new life grew within her. For all her heartache, Ruthie had vowed to move on with her life for the sake of her child. She did not have Noah with her, but she had his child, and she would do everything to ensure that child was loved and embraced totally.

Then Ben had entered her life. He had sweet-talked

her and put on his best behavior. Not long after their wedding, his true personality surfaced. By then, there was no going back, and once again, she had tried to make a life for herself and her baby. Not the life she had envisioned growing up with Noah, but a life that would provide a home for her son nonetheless.

Yet without a father's love, that home had never felt whole. With Noah back just for a few days, everything felt good and solid and filled with mutual support, though she needed to remember that Noah had left the faith and was no longer Amish, which meant there was no future for them together.

She feared getting hurt again when Noah left for a second time. Worse than her own pain was the fact that her boys would suffer, too.

Perhaps Noah should leave now before he became even more a part of their lives. But he had already worked his way into their hearts. She saw it in the boys' enthusiasm when they were with Noah, and she knew it when she was with him, as well. It was too late to put up her guard. Noah already had a place in her heart. Truth be told, he had always had one, even if they could never be together because of their differing faiths.

Another thought gripped her heart. When Noah left, she would be alone without anyone to help her protect her sons. The hateful man was determined to drive her off the mountain.

With Noah gone, she feared he would succeed.

Chapter Fifteen

Morning came early and brought clear skies, which was a welcome relief. Noah downed a cup of coffee, loaded his truck with lumber and headed to the bridge. Before long, he heard his name and glanced up to see Simon and Andrew running toward him. He laughed at their excitement.

"Did you tell your *mamm* you would be at the bridge?"

"She said to ask if you wanted our help. If so, we can stay. Otherwise she said we need to do our chores."

Ruthie stood on the porch of her house. He waved to let her know the boys had made it to the bridge and would be staying to help. The work went quickly. He enjoyed Andrew's chatter and Simon's tempered comments when his younger brother got too rambunctious.

Once the bridge was stabilized, Noah loaded his tools in the truck and told the guys to hop in the passenger side. He rewarded their hard work with moon pies that they gobbled down and then wiped their face and hands on his handkerchief before they drove to the barn and unloaded the rest of the wood there.

"Let's get the animals fed. Your *mamm* will call us soon for breakfast."

"She said we will not have eggs this morning," Andrew informed him. "*Mamm* thinks the storms and some kind of varmint upset the chickens."

Ruthie was right, but the varmint wasn't a fox or coyote. It was a two-legged kind.

"Maybe we can go to town and buy some more chicks that do not get spooked in the night," Simon suggested.

"Are we going back to town?" Andrew's eyes grew wide. "Twice in one week?"

Noah held up his hands. "You boys are getting ahead of me. I'm not sure when we'll go back to town, but no matter when we go, we need to ask your *mamm* about buying chicks before we jump to any conclusions."

"I hope she says we can go soon," Andrew said, "because I like eggs."

With three of them working, the chores didn't take long. Noah marveled at the boys' willingness to work and the weight they carried. Ben must have instilled a good work ethic in the boys. Or, more likely, it was due to Ruthie's mothering. Either way, Noah appreciated the fine young boys who were eager to pull more than their fair share of the load.

Ruthie called them for breakfast, so they washed at the pump and hurried inside.

Andrew inhaled the savory aroma when they entered the kitchen. "Are we having bacon for breakfast?"

Ruthie smiled. "Biscuits and sausage gravy."

"Yum! Next to eggs, that is my favorite."

Simon rolled his eyes and gave his younger brother a playful shove. "You like everything *Mamm* fixes."

"*Yah*, and I like what Noah fixes, too."

Ruthie gripped a large wooden spoon and pointed it at her sons. "Did I see you boys eating moon pies?" she asked, her eyes twinkling with amusement.

They stood still with hung heads and looked guilty.

Noah laughed. "That's my fault. I keep them in my truck. Simon and Andrew worked so hard on the bridge they needed nourishment."

She lowered the spoon and laughed as she hugged the boys. "Moon pies are not necessarily nutritious, but they are good."

"They're yummy, *Mamm*."

"You look like you want another one, Andrew," she said with a chuckle.

"I could eat five of them."

"Well, instead of moon pies, we will enjoy breakfast. Fill Simon's glass with milk, then open a new bottle to fill yours, Andrew."

She pointed to the cabinet. "Simon, get the plates and carry them to the table."

"What can I do?" Noah asked.

"Would you mind pouring coffee?"

"My pleasure."

Her cheeks pinked. The bruise on her face had faded, and she had a lightness in her step that he hadn't noticed yesterday.

Maybe it was because the rain had stopped and the sun was shining. Noah's mood was upbeat, as well.

"Why does the chicken coop have black paint on one side?" Simon asked, staring through the window.

"I had some paint at my house and wanted to see if your mother thought the coop would look better painted black."

The explanation seemed to satisfy the boy.

"I like red better," Andrew said.

"Then we can get red paint in town, along with some chickens."

"I am not sure we need more chickens." Ruthie raised an eyebrow.

"But we want eggs," Andrew reminded her.

"Yes, we do," Ruthie agreed with her son. "We can buy a dozen or two at the store."

"Are we going to town today?" Andrew asked after he had poured the milk.

"Noah and I need to run some errands. I thought you boys might want to visit with Aunt Mattie."

"It has been a long time since we saw her," Simon said as he arranged the plates on the table.

"Do I know Mattie?" Noah asked.

"My mother's baby sister. She moved to the area the year Simon was born."

"You and the boys don't see her often?" he asked.

"She was out of town when we buried Ben and my *datt*. A few weeks later, she left a card and brownies on the porch asking me when she could visit, but I was not ready for visitors."

Noah understood. After her husband's death, Ruthie was hesitant to allow people back into her life. Even a loving aunt.

"Aunt Mattie will not recognize you boys as tall as you've grown," she said, smiling at her sons.

"The last time we visited, she made chocolate-chip cookies and homemade ice cream," Simon informed Noah.

Andrew rubbed his stomach. "The cookies were good, but the ice cream was delicious."

"Mattie's house is not too far outside of town," Ruthie

said. "We can stop there first. As long as she agrees, you boys could help her with the chores while Noah and I run our errands."

"If you drive the buggy, Ruthie, the boys and I can follow you in the pickup. That way we can leave the rig overnight at the repair shop in town, if need be."

"They will enjoy riding with you, Noah."

Eager for another adventure, Simon and Andrew ate breakfast and finished the chores, then climbed in the pickup with Noah.

"I'm still concerned about the wheel," Noah told Ruthie, "so hold Buttercup to a slow trot. The boys and I will be right behind you."

He rolled down the windows and led them in singing church songs he remembered from his childhood as they followed the buggy down the mountain.

Mattie's house sat along a farm road about three miles from town. Ruthie pulled Buttercup to a stop in the driveway and seemed a bit nervous when she climbed down from the buggy and motioned the boys forward. Before they stepped onto the porch, the front door opened and a grey-haired Amish woman stepped outside, clapping her hands with joy.

"It has been too long." She opened her arms and hugged them all at once.

Andrew tried to wiggle out of her embrace. Simon glanced over his shoulder and rolled his eyes at Noah.

"Ruth Ann, you have been too long away from me," Mattie said. "It warms my heart to see you again and—" She stepped back to look at all of them. "And these boys have grown so big. You must come inside. I have cookies."

Andrew's eyes widened. "Aunt Mattie, the last time we were here you made ice cream."

"I remember, Andrew. Would you like to do that again? I'll need help turning the churn."

He held up his arm and showed his muscle. "I am strong."

"I know you are, and Simon is, as well. We can make lots of ice cream."

Ruthie touched her aunt's arm. "Mattie, this is Noah Schlabach. His family lived in the house across the river from us."

Mattie smiled. "I have heard about you, Noah. It is nice to meet you at last. You will come in for coffee and cake."

"And ice cream," Andrew added. "Right, Aunt Mattie?"

"Andrew," Ruthie chastised. "You are being much too insistent. Where are your manners?"

"I am sorry, *Mamm*. I must have left my manners at home."

"He is a wonderful boy." Aunt Mattie beamed. "Just as Simon is, and we will make ice cream in a bit."

"A cup of coffee and cake sound wonderful, Mattie, but we cannot stay long. We need to go to the real-estate office in town. Noah is selling his father's land."

"So many are selling their property."

"Amish farmers?" he asked.

"*Yah*, north of town a large development is being built. The bishop is not happy with the growth. He fears we will lose our peaceful way of life."

"In the past, there was nothing north of town," Ruthie said.

"So true, my dear, but things change. I wonder if they will start a new development on the mountain."

"Why do you say that?" Ruthie asked.

"You mentioned someone is buying Noah's property. It sounds as if homes will be built there, as well." She shook her head and tsked. "Too much growth too fast is never good."

Noah thought of his father's land and Ruthie's being divided into small lots dotted with homes that would mar the landscape. Did the man want Ruthie to flee from the mountain so he could have access to her land? How dark the man's heart must be if he would ruin a woman's life for his own personal gain.

A troubling thought caused Noah to flinch. Just like Ruthie's attacker, Noah had been thinking only of himself when he had left Ruthie ten years ago. Although she had continued on without him, Noah would never be able to forgive himself for causing her pain.

"Take your time in town and enjoy this beautiful day." Aunt Mattie stood on the porch with Andrew and Simon as Ruthie and Noah prepared to leave. "The boys and I will have ice cream waiting for you."

Ruthie regretted her own self-imposed estrangement from her aunt. After Ben had been shunned, she had become more reclusive and had only visited her aunt a few times in the last five years. Mattie had understood and had not barged in on Ruthie's privacy.

Today her greeting had been warm and sincere. Now that Ben was gone, Ruthie needed to visit more often. Being with her aunt would lift her own spirits and bring joy to the boys, as well.

Noah followed Ruthie to the buggy shop in town. Ivan Keim, a beefy Amish man with a ruddy complexion, owned the shop and agreed to check the wheel.

"I have three large jobs ahead of yours so I will not get to it for a day or two," he said. "You can board your horse at the stable in back. Unhitch your buggy and leave it here. My son will help you with your mare."

Once Buttercup was taken care of, Noah held the passenger door for Ruthie and helped her into his pickup truck.

"I have not ridden in such a vehicle before, Noah. This is an adventure, as the boys would say."

He laughed. "They wanted to sing songs on the way to Mattie's house. Did you hear us?"

"I heard nothing except the clip-clop of Buttercup's hooves on the pavement."

"Next time, we'll sing louder."

"A singing when we get home tonight might be fun."

He nodded. "I'm sure the boys will enjoy showing off their talent."

"But I do not want them to be prideful, Noah."

"I don't think you'll ever have that problem with Andrew or Simon. They are hard workers and considerate boys who will grow into fine men."

"Someday they will marry and give me grandchildren. This is my hope."

"Simon is not yet ten, Ruthie." His eyes twinkled playfully. "Aren't you moving a little fast?"

She laughed. "*Yah*, I want them to remain young, but I also think of children in the future who will carry on the family name."

"The Eicher name?" The buoyancy in Noah's tone faltered.

"At least their last name is not Plank," she countered.

"Meaning you married Ben so Simon would have a surname other than your own."

She could not bear to look at Noah. What he said was true, but she had been too caustic with her words. Had she wanted to cause him pain, the same way he had hurt her long ago? That was not what *Gott* would want her to do. She must ask forgiveness for her disregard of Noah's feelings. She must also wipe the hurt from her memory so it would not fester again.

"I would like to take back my words." She hung her head and was unsettled with remorse.

"I'm sure it was hard for you to be pregnant without a husband."

"I was not as concerned for myself as I was for my child, but that time has passed. I should not look back."

"I'm sorry, Ruthie."

"It is over. We will speak no more about what happened."

"It's not over if you're still hurt by what happened."

She turned to gaze into his eyes. "Some pain leaves quickly, like a stubbed toe or a hangnail. Other pain lasts a lifetime." She glanced out the window again. "I accept your apology. I hope you will accept mine. We do not need to mention this again."

He hesitated for a long moment, then said, "On a different note, I like your aunt."

Ruthie nodded as she adjusted her seat belt. "Mattie is a *gut* woman."

"She obviously enjoyed seeing you and the boys again."

Her sweet aunt did not harbor any ill will toward Ruthie, and she had never chastised her for marrying Ben. The problem was in Ruthie's mind, not Mattie's.

"Let's talk to Deputy Warren first and then we can

stop at the real-estate office," Noah suggested. "Hopefully Vince Ashcroft will be there today."

"I hope he will know if Prescott Construction is still interested in my land. As I told you, I have a stack of bills that must be paid."

"You could take out a loan and pay it back little by little."

"Which would only place me deeper in debt."

"You wanted to pass the farm on to the boys," he said, as if she did not remember her reason for holding on to the land.

"I still do, Noah, but I have to use my head as well as my heart. My heart tells me to remain on the farm. It has been my home for twenty-seven years, but my head reminds me that if I cannot pay my bills I could lose everything, including my farm."

"I can help you, Ruthie."

She held up her hand to stop him from saying anything more about her financial situation. Although she appreciated his offer, she would never be able to live with herself if she accepted his pity or his money.

"I am not sure what I will do with the land, but one thing is certain. I will not let that terrible man on the mountain take anything that belongs to me."

She pursed her lips before continuing. "Talking to the real-estate agent will provide information that might help me make a decision."

Noah sighed. "I hate to think of you leaving the mountain when the boys seem to love it there."

"You loved the mountain, Noah, yet you left."

"I thought we weren't going to talk about the past?" She nodded. "My mistake."

Shame on her for returning to the very subject she

had said was off-limits. What was wrong with her these days? When she was around Noah, her mind played tricks on her. At some moments, she saw herself as a young woman starting out in life with the man she loved.

Letting out a sigh, she shook her head. The thought was so unsettling, thinking of where they both were now. One *Englisch*. One Amish.

"Is something wrong?" he asked.

Glancing out the passenger window, she tried to act as if she was not concerned about anything, when in reality her heart was heavy. The man on the mountain was a constant worry and threat to her own well-being and her children's, but the bigger threat was Noah. The longer she was around him, the more comfortable she became. How could she separate herself from the memories of the past? Being with him brought everything to the forefront and made her realize what she had lost when Noah had walked away. She should have run after him, but she did not know where he had gone. If only he had come back.

But he did come back, a voice bubbled up within her.

The voice was right. Noah had come back, but he was ten years too late. Even more unsettling, he had left his Amish faith and had come back *Englisch*!

Perhaps she had been foolish ten years ago to believe they would have remained committed to the Amish way if they had left the mountain together. She liked to think her influence would have kept Noah Amish. Now she could do nothing to change his mind about the life he had chosen to live.

Amish and *Englisch* did not mix, as much as she wished it was not so.

Chapter Sixteen

As they drove through town, Ruthie studied the people, looking for tall, muscular men with tattoos on their left arms. She did not see many tattoos, but she did see a number of big, bulky guys who could easily be the man who had come after her on the mountain. If only she could remember something else about his clothing or appearance.

Noah pulled out his cell. "I'll call the sheriff's department to ensure Deputy Warren is in his office." He tapped in the number, asked to speak to the deputy and then paused.

"I'll check back later." He disconnected and glanced at her. "Deputy Warren is at city hall with the mayor. He should return in an hour or so. We can stop by then and tell him what happened last night."

Ruthie wanted to know if the deputy had made any arrests. She was being optimistic, but she wanted the attacker apprehended and locked behind bars.

Noah braked the truck to a stop at the red light. He pointed toward the appliance store on the corner, and

Ruthie followed his gaze. A large-screen television sat in one of the windows.

A commercial caught their attention. A big man dressed in a plaid suit stepped on-screen and gestured toward a billboard behind him. The sign read Your Home's a Castle with Castle Homes!

Noah groaned.

"What's wrong?" Ruthie asked.

"That's Floyd Castle. He used the same line in Tennessee."

"You know him?"

"Only by reputation. Seth bought one of his homes." Noah explained about the dam's collapse and Seth's death along with his family.

"Oh, Noah." She grabbed his arm. "I am sorry."

"It was my fault."

She shook her head. "How can you say such nonsense? You had nothing to do with the dam collapsing."

"I'm the one who told Seth about the development and the discount given to those who worked on the bridge."

"You did not know what would happen."

"I encouraged Seth to leave home even though our *datt* never laid a hand on him. Seth didn't get into trouble, but he came with me because we were a team, two kids always trying to outsmart their father."

"You were the older son, Noah. Your father was angry about life. He took that anger out on you."

"He was ashamed of himself, Ruthie. That shame ate at him and led him to drink. When he drank he saw himself as someone else, someone better or more successful. The sad thing is that down deep, I truly believe my father was a good man. If only he could have realized he had worth and that people would accept him for who he was."

"He changed when your mother died. My father did as well, when my own mother passed."

Noah nodded. She saw the regret in his eyes.

"The woman is the heart of the family," Noah said. "When the heart is gone, the body dies. My father didn't want to live without my mother, and he made it difficult for his children."

She could relate. "We had similar backgrounds. Perhaps that is why we became so close."

"It was more than our families." He turned to stare at her.

Ruthie's breath hitched. She glanced away, unwilling to lose herself to the memory of what they had had so long ago.

The light changed to green. Noah turned left and headed along the side street. There were railroad tracks ahead, and the lights were flashing.

"Looks like we'll be stopped by the train."

She smiled, glad to have something else to fill her thoughts. "The boys never tire of watching them pass."

The crossing guardrail on the opposite side of the street lowered, but the one on their side failed to engage.

"Something's wrong," Noah said as he pulled the pickup to a stop.

The roar of the approaching train filled the air, and the earth beneath them vibrated.

Seemingly concerned about the broken guardrail, Noah glanced in the rearview mirror and frowned. Ruthie looked back. A red truck pulled up right behind them. As the train neared, the truck inched closer.

"I'm not sure what that guy's doing," Noah said, his voice tight with worry.

The red truck tapped their rear bumper, pushing the pickup forward.

Ruthie gasped.

Just that fast, the truck tapped them again, sending them onto the tracks.

The train's deafening whistle blew. The engine loomed over them. Ruthie braced for impact and screamed.

Noah floored the accelerator and steered around the working guardrail to the other side of the tracks.

Time stopped for one long moment before Ruthie realized they had escaped without a collision.

Heart in her throat, she looked over her shoulder and watched the train race through the intersection. The truck that had rear-ended them turned around and dashed away.

"Oh, Noah, we were almost killed," Ruthie gasped. Tears filled her eyes and her hands trembled. "What happened?"

"We were shoved in front of the train by someone who wanted to do us harm."

"The man from the mountain." She dropped her head in her hands. "When will it end?"

Everything had escalated in that moment. Being pushed in front of an oncoming train ratcheted up the danger even more. Before this, the man on the mountain had wanted Ruthie to leave her land. Now he wanted her dead.

Noah steered his pickup to the side of the road and braked to a stop, then reached for Ruthie and pulled her into his arms. Her face was pale and she was shaking.

"It's okay, Ruthie. Neither of us was hurt."

"The train came so close. It was the man on the mountain. His attacks are getting deadly."

He held her until her trembling eased.

"Take a deep breath. The danger has passed."

"Yet the outcome could have been so different, Noah."

The man needed to be stopped, but they had to determine who he was first. Once they notified the sheriff's office, the deputies would be on the lookout for the red truck. Even with law enforcement's help, Noah still needed to be vigilant to ensure nothing else happened to Ruthie.

She pulled in a deep breath and eased out of his arms.

"Do you know anyone who drives a red truck?" he asked, relieved to see color return to her cheeks.

She shook her head. "The people I know drive buggies."

"I couldn't see the license plate. I'll call the deputy sheriff and tell him."

The deputy was still out of the office. Noah told the clerk about the driver of the truck obviously trying to do them harm. "Tell all your deputies to be on the lookout," Noah said. "This guy has got to be stopped. He's getting more aggressive and he means business."

"We'll find him, sir. You can be assured of that."

Noah wasn't so optimistic.

"You do not look satisfied with law enforcement," Ruthie said after he had disconnected.

"They don't seem to be as involved as I would like them to be."

"I am Amish, Noah, and I live on the mountain. As I mentioned to you before, out of sight, out of mind."

"Maybe, although I hate to think that would be the

case. We'll talk to Deputy Warren this afternoon when he returns to his office. Hopefully, he'll be more concerned about your situation."

"What about talking to the real-estate agent?"

"I'll call them now."

He tapped in the number and the receptionist answered on the third ring. "Ashcroft Real Estate, Tiffany speaking."

"This is Noah Schlabach. I stopped by yesterday in hopes of talking to Vince Ashcroft. Is he available today?"

"Mr. Ashcroft should be in his office after lunch."

"One o'clock?" Noah asked.

"Closer to one thirty."

"Are the papers ready for the sale of my land?"

"Could you refresh my memory, sir?"

Noah let out a frustrated sigh. After the train incident, he had run out of patience. "I have a home and acreage on Amish Mountain. Prescott Construction made an offer on my property."

"That's right. I remember. I'm sorry, but I don't have information about the offer, sir. You'll have to talk to Mr. Ashcroft."

"Do you have a point of contact for the construction company?"

"I didn't see a name on the initial correspondence."

"Schedule me for one thirty," Noah said.

"Could you repeat your name?"

"I could and I will." He glanced at Ruthie and shook his head. "Noah Schlabach. Shall I spell my last name?"

"No, sir. I've got you down for a one-thirty appointment with Mr. Ashcroft."

"Thank you, Tiffany."

He disconnected. "If Tiffany is any indication about how Ashcroft Real Estate operates, we might be dealing with the wrong real-estate agent."

"Hopefully, Mr. Ashcroft has information on Prescott Construction. Perhaps if I decide to sell my land and move to town, the boys and I would be safer."

Noah wouldn't dissuade Ruthie from doing what she thought was best for her family, but he wanted her attacker stopped. Now.

"I could apply for a job as the real-estate agent's receptionist," she added. Her lips tugged into a brief smile, which relieved him even more.

"Can you use a computer?" he gently teased.

She nudged his arm. "You know I cannot, which only proves your point about the boys yesterday. You might be right, Noah. Simon and Andrew will need to get jobs when they are older, especially if we live in town. Computer skills are necessary, even for the Amish."

"You can still follow the *Ordnung* within your home. No computers, no televisions, no technology in the house."

"'No fun,' the boys would say, once they are exposed to the ways of the world."

"You might underestimate them. I lived in the world for the last ten years, yet I still see the good in living Amish."

She tilted her head. "But I thought you were ready to leave the mountain?"

He was, yet when he was with Ruthie thoughts of settling down and embracing his Amish roots took hold of him like a dog tugging at his pant leg.

Looking away, he shook his head. "I'm not sure what I want."

"Sometimes it is hard to know. Have you asked *Gott*?"

"He and I have been somewhat estranged."

"Maybe it is time to get to know each other again."

"You might be right." He squeezed her hand. "Do you feel up to a visit to Mountain Bank? It's not far from here."

"I want to ask them about my account, so, yes, stopping there will be fine."

Noah drove the few blocks to the bank and pulled into the parking lot at the side of the large stone structure. "Let's talk to the bank manager. He might know something about Prescott Construction."

Before they reached the entrance, two men barged out of the bank. One was a portly man wearing a plaid suit. Noah recognized Floyd Castle and tapped Ruthie's arm to get her attention.

The other man was tall and muscular. He wore a long-sleeve black shirt and khaki pants. "We saw him at the pizza parlor," Ruthie said, her voice low. "He was sitting with another man in the rear of the restaurant."

Castle pulled at his collar. "Look, Burkholder, I don't care what kind of problems you're having. You sold me on the idea of a lake and said you could make it happen. Now you're making excuses."

"The deal's taking longer than I expected."

"That's your problem, not mine."

Both men hurried to a white sedan with dark windows. The man called Burkholder took the wheel, and the sedan pulled onto the main road, heading north.

"We need to find out who Burkholder is," Noah suggested. "Someone who works at the home-development site, for sure."

"Castle did not seem happy."

"Nor did Burkholder. Looks like there might be trouble with Castle Homes."

They hurried inside and asked to speak to the manager. The receptionist led them to a small office, where a bald man in his midforties stood to greet them. He stuck out his hand. "George Masters. How can I help you folks?"

Noah introduced himself and Ruthie, and explained that they lived on the mountain and were considering selling their properties. "Prescott Construction has made an offer on my land. Vince Ashcroft notified me of their interest. He's been out of town, but I'm hoping to meet with him later this afternoon. I'd like to know who I'm dealing with and thought you might have information about the construction company."

The manager tugged on his jaw as he thought for a moment. "That's not a local firm. Of course, we've got a lot of folks passing through town these days. Let me check my computer."

He tapped his keyboard and stared at his monitor. "They haven't done business with us or they would be in our system. But that name sounds familiar."

"I thought the same thing and did a computer search but came up with nothing."

"Wish I could help. I do know there's a lot of interest in new property these days. The mountain would seem like prime real estate, especially for someone, maybe from the movie studio, wanting to build a getaway retreat. I don't want to talk out of turn, but there are two real-estate companies in town. Willkommen Realty is an established firm. They're reputable and well thought of by the local townspeople and business owners."

"Are you saying there might be a problem with Ashcroft Real Estate?"

The manager shrugged. "I'm not saying anything except Vince came to town not long ago. I wouldn't want you to get involved with someone who was less than reputable."

Ruthie scooted closer in her seat. "Mr. Ashcroft is not reputable?"

Masters spread his hands. "I'm just telling you he's new and inexperienced."

"I appreciate your honesty," Noah said. "We saw a Castle Homes commercial on television. He must be building in the local area."

"North of town. Ashcroft Real Estate is handling the sales. Got himself on Mr. Castle's good side." Masters shook his head. "I'm not sure how, although it should be a gold mine for him if he plays his cards right."

Noah looked at Ruthie. She raised an eyebrow. "Mr. Ashcroft likes to gamble?" she asked.

The banker smiled. "He's gambling on Castle Homes drawing people from other parts of the state. I'm not as confident about the attraction."

"You don't think buyers will want to move to the North Georgia mountains?" Noah asked.

"Some folks will, but he's planning on three building phases of one hundred homes each. That's a lot of newcomers to town. The bank will enjoy opening new accounts, but I've got to tell you, this town will be hard-pressed to take care of that many folks, especially if they move in within a short period of time. A lot of the locals are worried. I tried to tell Castle to go slow, but he's got these grand ideas about making a fortune. He's dealing with another bank in town, though he stopped by to see if I could offer him a better loan, which I couldn't."

"He's been successful in other areas of the country," Noah said.

Masters nodded. "True, but his company was nearly wiped out with what happened in the Chattanooga area. Not sure if you read the papers, but a dam broke and his housing development was flooded. Folks died. Houses that hadn't sold were washed away. Castle had insurance but not enough to cover his losses."

"My brother and his family were in one of those homes, Mr. Masters."

"I'm mighty sorry. A tragedy, for sure."

"Why did Castle choose Willkommen for his next housing project?"

"Land was relatively inexpensive here compared to the big cities. The way I see it, he wants to turn his company around and thought this would be an easy sell. He rushed in without doing enough homework."

Noah was interested. "What do you mean?"

"His community is centered on a man-made lake. Somewhere he got the idea he could feed it with a natural spring, only there's no such thing in that area. He cut down the vegetation and ended up with a dust bowl that is less than inviting. Ask anyone in town. They'll tell you the same thing."

"We saw him outside your bank in a heated conversation with another man."

"Probably Brian Burkholder, his foreman. From what I gather, Burkholder claimed if they dug a lake, he could ensure it would fill by the grand opening next week. Even with this current rain, the lake is less than one-third filled. People don't want to see a mud hole when they are looking at possible home sites."

"Sales aren't going well?" Noah asked.

Masters shrugged. "He's tight-lipped about everything, but that's what I hear."

The bank manager drummed his fingers on his desk. "Anything else I can help you folks with today?"

"Could you check my bank account?" Ruthie asked. "My husband kept track of our finances. He died recently, and I want to ensure the balance in the checkbook is accurate. The only identification I brought is the bank statement. I hope that is sufficient." Ruthie handed him a statement that included her account number.

"That will be fine, Mrs. Eicher, and I'm sorry about your loss." He typed the account number she provided into his computer. "Ruth Ann Plank Eicher?"

"That is correct."

"I knew your dad. He often talked about his daughter who cared for him."

Ruthie's eyes widened. "Did he bank here?"

"No, ma'am. You might want to check North Georgia Bank."

He tapped the keyboard. The printer hummed. He pulled the paper from the machine and handed her the printout. She studied the information before folding the paper and tucking it in her purse.

Noah leaned forward. "Could you check to see if my father had an account?" He provided his father's name and his own driver's license for identification.

"Reuben was a customer." Masters typed something into the computer and nodded. "You're on his account." The banker handed Noah the printout.

"I'll leave the money in the bank for now, but after the land sells, I might decide to close the account."

"Whatever you decide works for us."

"Thanks for your help." Noah stood and shook the banker's hand.

"Good seeing you both."

Noah hurried Ruthie to his truck. "Let's see if Vince Ashcroft is in his office. I'm interested in what he has to say about our properties. Plus, I want to know why all of a sudden someone wants to buy land on Amish Mountain."

Noah felt like he was in the middle of a giant jigsaw puzzle. He had a number of pieces, but none of them fit together. One thing was certain, the land was secondary compared to Ruthie and her boys. His first priority was to keep them safe.

Chapter Seventeen

Noah parked in the rear of the real-estate office. He opened the passenger door and escorted Ruthie inside. The receptionist he had met yesterday smiled. "Mr. Schlabach, right?"

He nodded and introduced Ruthie. "Is Mr. Ashcroft available?"

"He just arrived. I'll tell him you're here." She slipped from behind her desk, hurried down the hall and entered an office, closing the door behind her.

Not more than thirty seconds later, she returned. "Mr. Ashcroft would be happy to see you now."

The real-estate agent stood as they entered his office. He extended his hand and offered them a wide smile and a limp handshake.

Vince Ashcroft was pushing fifty with a receding hairline and bushy eyebrows. A small tuft of facial hair protruded below his lower lip and looked like a smudge of dirt on his otherwise clean-shaven face.

"Sit down and we'll discuss the contract from Prescott Construction." He tapped on his keyboard and then studied his monitor. "You've got the Amish Mountain property on the north side of the river."

"That's correct." Noah nodded. "I'd like to know the construction company's offer and how soon we can close the deal."

"Didn't I mail that information to you?"

"I never received anything."

Again Ashcroft tapped his keyboard. His printer hummed into operation. He pulled a piece of paper from the machine. "Here's the offer they're making." He pointed to the amount with his pen.

"I don't know what property is going for around here," Noah admitted, "but that seems low."

Very low, plus Noah was less than satisfied with Ashcroft claiming he had sent papers Noah had never received.

"If you had land in town, I'd say you were right. But Amish Mountain is a different ballgame, so to speak. We don't have any comparable sales in that area. You could counter."

Noah sighed. "I had hoped everything could be wrapped up quickly."

"And it will be if you decide to accept their offer. As long as their funding comes through, we could have the sale completed by the end of the week."

"Let me think it over."

"Certainly, although they might find another property if you drag your feet too long."

Noah didn't want to be pushed into accepting a low bid. "Do you have any idea why they're interested in the land?"

"As I mentioned, Prescott Construction contacted me by email. You'll find their email and mailing addresses on the printout I gave you. We haven't discussed anything over the phone."

"Do you have their number and a point of contact?"

"Ah…" Ashcroft hesitated. "Let me check the computer." He studied the monitor and scrolled through a few pages. "Hmm? Strange. We don't have a point of contact or a phone number for them."

"That seems unusual."

"It's an out-of-state company…" The agent shrugged. "Some people like to keep their anonymity."

"And when they do," Noah said, feeling even more unsettled, "I always wonder why."

"I own the neighboring property," Ruthie interjected. "Prescott Construction contacted me by mail and expressed interest in my land, as well. Have they mentioned acquiring my farm?"

Ashcroft shrugged. "They haven't mentioned any other land, but I could email the company."

The agent glanced at Ruthie. "Do you want to sell?"

She held up her hand. "I am interested in finding out how much they are willing to spend. Depending on their offer, I would decide whether to sell or not."

"You farm the land?" Ashcroft asked.

"That is correct."

"With your husband?"

"My husband passed away two months ago."

"I'm sorry for your loss, but I can certainly understand your desire to move off the mountain."

"I do not want to move, Mr. Ashcroft, but I am making inquiries."

"I see. How many acres?"

"Fifty-five."

"Nice. I'm sure I can find a buyer for you." He made

a note on his tablet and then asked, "What about the mortgage?"

"It is through a local bank."

"Without any lends or other loans attached to the farm?"

"That is correct."

The agent nodded. "I'll email Prescott Construction and see what they say about your property."

"Thank you, Mr. Ashcroft."

"Of course." He glanced at his watch. "I hate to cut this short, but I have a meeting to attend. Is there anything else I can help you with?"

"How long before the papers would be ready to sign if I accept the offer on my land?" Noah asked.

"Two or three days, tops. Call my receptionist when you come to a decision."

"Cell service on the mountain is hit-or-miss. I'll stop by your office in the next few days."

"I'll see you then." Ashcroft rounded his desk, shook their hands and then opened his office door. "Good talking with you, folks. I'll be in touch."

As they stepped into the hallway, Noah spied a poster advertising Castle Homes' grand opening next week.

"This is a new development in town?" he asked the receptionist, hoping to get more information.

"Yes, sir. It's located about five miles north of Willkommen. Take Wagner Road and you'll see the signs for the office. There's a model home to tour if you're interested."

"Someone's out there now?"

She nodded. "The office is open until five thirty."

"Thanks, Tiffany."

"No problem. I almost forgot, I just received something from Prescott Construction. On the phone, you asked about a point of contact. Brian Burkholder's name is on the offer."

"He works for Mr. Castle?"

She shrugged. "I don't know about that, but I saw his name on the papers."

"You've been a great help, Tiffany."

She smiled. "Ashcroft Real Estate aims to please."

As they left the real-estate office, Noah leaned closer to Ruthie. "Did you get the idea Ashcroft wanted us out of his hair or was it my imagination?"

"After what the banker said, I wonder if he is a reputable agent, Noah. I would not want his inability to broker a deal to impact the sale of your father's land."

"I've got a strange feeling about Ashcroft, as well as Prescott Construction. I smell something fishy and we're quite a distance from the river."

They hurried toward his truck.

"Let's check out Castle Homes," Noah suggested. "I want to see what Floyd Castle is up to. He wheels and deals, and I don't like fast-talkers who always want to make a quick buck. Plus, I want to learn more about Brian Burkholder."

Noah checked his watch when they climbed into the truck. "Bottom line, I don't trust Castle. His foreman might also be questionable."

Before Noah turned the key in the ignition, a car raced out of the real-estate parking lot and turned north. A small sports car. Vince Ashcroft sat behind the wheel.

"Our real-estate agent seems to be in a hurry," Ruthie said.

Noah nodded.

Ashcroft had gotten flustered when Noah asked for

Prescott Construction's phone number. The real-estate agent was being less than forthright. He knew more than he wanted to let on and that worried Noah. What was Ashcroft hiding, and who really wanted to buy the mountain land?

"Can we stop at the sheriff's office before we visit Castle Homes?" Ruthie asked. "The deputy may have information about the red truck that pushed us onto the train tracks. Plus, I want to find out about the man who lives in the woods. The deputy said they would bring him in for questioning. I need to know what they learned."

Noah checked his watch. "Deputy Warren should be in his office, which isn't far from here."

After a series of turns, Noah parked on the street in front of the sheriff's office and ushered Ruthie inside.

The clerk smiled in recognition. "You folks here to talk to Deputy Warren? He's at his desk. Go on back."

The deputy was as welcoming as he had been the day prior. "How are the boys?" he asked.

"They're making ice cream with my aunt Mattie."

"Such fine lads." The deputy pursed his lips. "I understand you had another incident in town."

Noah explained about his pickup being shoved onto the tracks as the oncoming train neared.

"Did you see the driver?"

"Unfortunately the windows were tinted. I called your office after it happened and talked to the clerk," Noah said. "I doubt it was a coincidence since so many things have been occurring. Someone's trying to frighten Mrs. Eicher."

"And they are succeeding," she admitted.

"The dispatcher relayed the information about the

red truck to the deputies on patrol. No one has seen the truck, but we'll continue to be on the lookout."

"You'll let us know if you locate the truck and the driver?" Noah asked.

"Definitely. Have any other problems developed?"

"The man returned last night." Ruthie explained about the cut chicken coop and the threat spray-painted on the henhouse.

"One of our patrol cars was up there around nine p.m. before the storm hit. He didn't see anything amiss."

"What about the movie studio?" Noah asked.

"The head of the studio met with the mayor this morning. I spoke with the studio director following their meeting. He's working hard to ensure a good partnership with the townspeople and was concerned to hear about violence on the mountain. He'll have his security team on the lookout for anyone matching your description."

"Did you mention the tattoos on the man's arm?" Ruthie asked.

"I did. In the past, we didn't see many heavily tattooed folks in town, but that's changed over time, and even more so since the movie studio moved to the area. The head of the studio assured me his security folks will question anyone who seems suspect, and he'll call me if they uncover anything."

"Their cell coverage must be better than mine," Noah mused.

"They put up a tower to solve that problem. You're situated on the wrong side of the mountain."

"Evidently."

"What about the man who has been living in the woods?" Ruthie asked.

"The one who returned your dropped envelope?"

"*Yah*, did you get a chance to question him?"

"We searched the woods, but he had cleared out of his campsite and was gone. Those transient types don't hang around long, especially when they know they're not welcome."

"Maybe he headed back up Amish Mountain," she mused.

"Give us time, Mrs. Eicher. We'll find your attacker and take him into custody."

Noah explained about overhearing the argument between Castle and Burkholder. He also mentioned that the receptionist in the real-estate office claimed Burkholder was part of Prescott Construction.

"Well, isn't that interesting." The deputy pulled on his jaw. "Does Burkholder want your land for his own personal reasons, or is he acting as a front for Mr. Castle?"

"That's what I've been wondering," Noah admitted.

"Either way, you folks need to let us handle this from here on out. Don't mess where you're not wanted. You've already got one man coming after you, Mrs. Eicher. I wouldn't want anyone else to get upset with either of you. We'll do our job and let you know what we uncover."

Ruthie's spirits were low when they left the sheriff's office. She had hoped the man in the woods was the same man who had accosted her. She wanted him locked up and not able to hurt her or her boys. The deputy said to give law enforcement time, but Ruthie didn't have time if the man came after her again.

Chapter Eighteen

Noah and Ruthie left town and headed north on Wagner Road. The two-lane paved highway meandered through a forested area of tall pines and sturdy hardwoods. Rounding a bend, they came to the foot of a narrow valley that had been cleared of vegetation. Wind whipped down from the mountain, blowing dirt and debris.

"This looks like the middle of the desert instead of the Georgia mountains," Ruthie said as she eyed the naked land.

"They've removed the trees and destroyed the vegetation," Noah said. "Then they'll charge new home owners additional fees to landscape their property."

Signs pointed them to the home office. Noah pulled into the parking lot. "Let's see if we can find someone who can show us around."

No sooner had they climbed from the truck than a tall, lanky guy, in his late twenties with red hair, wearing a black polo and khaki slacks, hurried from the office to greet them. *Castle Homes* was embossed over the pocket on his shirt.

Ruthie eyed the logo as he neared. "Brian Burkholder

and the other man we saw at the pizza parlor wore the same shirts."

"I'm Dave Herschberger." He shook Noah's hand and nodded to Ruthie. "You folks looking to buy a home?"

"We stopped at the real-estate office in town," Noah explained, "and saw a poster for the development."

"Yes, sir. We'll have three hundred homes by the time all phases of the project are completed." He pointed to the office. "You'll find maps and brochures inside. Also, an artist's rendering of the entire area."

"How long before you're built out?" Noah asked.

"That depends on sales. The homes are moving fast so we anticipate twenty-four months to have the first phase completed."

"You bought Amish farms?" Ruthie asked.

"Some of the land belonged to the Amish. Other pieces of property belonged to regular folks." He nodded to Ruthie. "No offense, ma'am. I guess you call us fancy. Mr. Castle pays top dollar. His offers were too good to pass up."

"Seeing your last name, I wonder if you were raised Amish?" she asked.

"No, ma'am. Fact is my last name's Hersch. Mr. Castle likes us to use Amish names so we fit in with the local folks. I don't think it has much bearing on people from Atlanta coming to buy a new home, but from what I heard, it helped convince some of the Amish farmers to sell their land."

"Yet Mr. Castle did not change his name," Ruthie said.

"No, ma'am. But then everyone knows Mr. Castle."

"Did you work with Mr. Castle on his Tennessee housing development?" Noah asked.

"No, sir. I'm from Georgia and started working for him a month ago."

"By any chance, do you know anything about Prescott Construction?"

The guy shook his head. "Doesn't sound familiar. I could call our building foreman if you'd like. He might know of the company."

"Brian Burkholder?"

"That's right. Do you know him?"

"I've just heard the name." Although Noah would like information about why Burkholder and Prescott Construction wanted land on Amish Mountain.

Dave pointed to the office. "Let's go inside and get a cool drink while I show you the brochures."

Noah didn't want a cool drink, but he wanted to see Castle's concept for the development.

The air-conditioning was on in the trailer and the thermostat was set low. Ruthie rubbed her arms when she stepped inside.

A three-legged easel held a large poster board with a drawing of the final housing development. The town of Willkommen could be seen to the south of the site, with Amish Mountain in the distance to the west.

Noah stepped closer, noticing a large central area colored blue. "Is that a lake?"

"Yes, sir. That's one of the main drawing cards for our development. A two-hundred-acre man-made lake, perfect for fishing or boating. A beach will be on the eastern edge with picnic grounds. Plus, there's a playground, pool and tennis courts nearby."

"The developer thought of everything."

"'Your home is your castle—'" Dave began, reciting the builder's motto.

"'In a Castle home,'" Noah interrupted, finishing for him.

The guy smiled and handed both of them brochures. "There's a map of the home sites. Why don't you folks take a look around?"

"You mentioned calling your foreman about Prescott Construction."

"That's right." He tapped a number into his phone, waited for a moment and then shook his head. "He's not answering. I'll contact John Zimmerman. He's the assistant foreman."

This time the call connected. "John, I've got a couple interested customers here at the office who will be looking around the site. One of them wondered if you knew anything about Prescott Construction." The redhead nodded. "I see." He smiled at Noah. "I'll tell him." Another pause. "That's right."

Dave disconnected and stuck his phone in his pocket. "John knows of the company. Evidently someone took it over not too long ago. Prescott Construction is headquartered in Tennessee."

"Did the assistant foreman work on Mr. Castle's home development near Chattanooga?"

"No, sir. He came onboard when this project was in the early stages. I've heard him talk about the dam in Chattanooga a few times so he might have worked on the dam but not Castle's housing project."

Noah's neck tingled. "How was he involved?"

"Seems he mentioned the concrete supplier."

The concrete that had failed to hold. Whether it was poorly designed or poorly constructed would take a long time for the inspectors to determine. Until their investigation was final, Noah was suspicious of anyone tied to the dam.

He tried to place the assistant foreman. "What's Zimmerman look like?"

Dave shrugged. "About my height. Brown hair." He glanced at a poster on the wall. "There's a photo of both the foreman and the assistant foreman."

Noah and Ruthie moved closer. "He was the man we saw eating pizza with Brian Burkholder," she said to Noah.

He nodded. The two guys sitting in the corner.

Both men were tall with dark hair and dressed in the same Castle uniform that Dave wore. Standing in the foreground was Vince Ashcroft. The real-estate agent was shaking hands with Floyd Castle.

Noah leaned in closer and read the names identifying each person. Assistant foreman John Zimmerman and foreman Brian Burkholder.

Everyone used a German last name. Noah motioned Dave closer. "You're telling me the foreman's name is really Brian Burk."

The man smiled sheepishly, as if realizing he had said too much. "Ah, no, sir. The foreman's last name is really Burkholder."

"What about Zimmerman? Is his real name Zimmer?"

Dave laughed nervously. "Look, it may sound strange, but Mr. Castle knows the little things that make a difference when you're purchasing land. What can I say?"

He had already said too much. Bottom line—Castle couldn't be trusted. If his workers used false names to fit in with the local Amish, no telling what else he would do to see his development succeed. Although how this site north of town had anything to do with either Noah's land or Ruthie's property was the question Noah couldn't answer, yet everything pointed to a connection.

Noah put his hand on the small of Ruthie's back and guided her toward the door. "Why don't we look around outside?"

Dave hurried after them. "Wait, folks. I'll give you my card."

He grabbed a business card from a nearby desk and handed it to Noah. "We've got a home offer for you." Glancing at Ruthie, he added, "And you, too, ma'am.

"Stop back after you drive around," Dave continued. "We can go over some numbers. The model home's open next door. Be sure to check it out. You'll enjoy all the comforts of a Castle home."

Noah knew the comforts that could be washed away in a wall of water all too well.

Once Ruthie and Noah stepped outside, she said, "Dave seems a bit aggressive to me."

"He's repeating all of Mr. Castle's phrases. Castle's the one who seems to be moving fast and going in big for this area of North Georgia."

"I hate to think what will happen when all these people move to Willkommen. It makes me glad I live on the mountain."

"Let's drive around the site. Maybe we can get a different perspective on what's going on here."

The streets were marked, but only a few were paved. From the sizes of the lots, the houses would be close together with little green space.

Stopping at the top of a hill in the rear of the development, Noah pointed to Amish Mountain in the distance. "Notice anything up there?"

They both got out and walked to the edge of the road.

Ruthie held her hand over her eyes to shield the sun's glare. "Is that my house?"

"Between the trees. I can see the waterfall farther up the mountain and the river that forms at the bottom of the falls, and then runs down the mountain, passing between our farms."

She stared at the mountain and nodded. "Your house is barely visible to the right of the river. I never realized a natural valley leads down the mountain toward this area."

"Because the river turns at the junction of our properties and flows along the southern valley to the other side of town. That's where we always focus."

"Ever since seeing the rendering of the lake, I keep wondering where Castle plans to get the water." She turned to Noah, her face drawn. "Looks like they could get it from the river with just a little engineering. Lowering your side of the riverbank and damming up my side would redirect the water down the northern valley."

Noah nodded. "Then Castle has his lake."

"So how's Prescott Construction involved?"

"Brian Burkholder is the common thread that ties everything together." Noah hesitated for a moment and then added, "What if Prescott Construction or Brian Burkholder doesn't want Castle to succeed? Castle may not know who's behind Prescott Construction."

"Or, does Prescott Construction want our land so Burkholder can up the price and sell it to Mr. Castle for a profit?" Ruthie added.

"Maybe, especially if he and Castle have some negative history from their days in Tennessee."

"I do not like any of this, Noah."

They climbed back into his pickup and started down

the hill. As they rounded one of the sharp curves, a dump truck filled with gravel raced around the bend and headed straight toward them.

Ruthie screamed.

Noah turned the wheel. His pickup swerved out of the way just in time. Gravel flew from the top of the truck and pummeled his pickup, nicking his windshield.

"That was intentional," Noah said as he strained to catch sight of the driver.

Ruthie patted her chest as if to calm her heart. Her eyes were wide, her mouth drawn.

"Are you okay?" he asked, seeing her ashen face.

"I saw the man driving the truck." She grabbed his hand. "Oh, Noah, he had a stocking pulled over his face just like the man who attacked me on the mountain."

Ruthie's heart continued to pound at an erratic rate. The near miss had scared her. Seeing the man behind the wheel of the dump truck had scared her even more.

The man on the mountain who had attacked her wore a stocking pulled over his face. From the distorted features of the man driving the truck today, he had to have pulled a stocking over his face in the same way. She could not describe his features, yet everything within her had shuddered when she saw him. Her inner voice of warning screamed that the mountain attacker was after her again.

"A feeling came over me that it was the same man." She hugged her arms around her, hoping to ease the inner tension that wound her tight as a spring. "Then I realized he was wearing a stocking. It is more than a coincidence, Noah. He has to be the same man."

"We'll stop at the Castle Homes office. I want to let

them know what happened and see if we can discover who was driving that truck."

Dave was talking to another couple when they stepped into the office. A young female receptionist approached them and asked if she could help. Noah explained what had happened and that they needed to learn the name of the driver.

The other couple left the office with brochures and maps in hand and Dave stepped toward them. "Did I overhear that you folks had a problem?"

Noah repeated what he had told the receptionist. "Who was driving the truck? The guy needs to be reprimanded."

"Of course. I'm so sorry for what happened and relieved you weren't hurt."

"Gravel chipped my windshield, and we could have been severely injured."

"I'm sure Castle Homes will cover the damage as soon as we talk to the driver." He pulled out his phone. "I'll call the foreman. He'll locate the driver so we can get to the bottom of this situation."

He tapped in a number and raised the phone to his ear, nodding when the call was answered. He repeated the information.

"You're sure?" He frowned and then sighed. "I'll pass on the information."

Disconnecting, he turned to Ruthie and Noah. "The foreman says we don't have any dump trucks on the worksite today and no orders for gravel deliveries. He wondered if you confused the truck with another possible buyer who was touring the housing sites."

"Buyers don't usually drive dump trucks filled with gravel."

"You're right, sir. The foreman's down by the lake if you want to talk to him. I'm sorry I can't be of more help."

Ruthie and Noah left the office and climbed into the pickup. "I have caused too many problems," she said as she buckled her seat belt.

"You weren't the one driving the dump truck. We'll try to find that truck. The Castle foreman may think he didn't have a gravel delivery today, but we didn't imagine the truck and his aggressive driving."

They scoured the building site without success. "Let's head to the lake," Noah said finally. "I want to talk to the foreman personally."

But the only work crews they saw were carpenters stubbing a new home. Noah pulled to a stop near one of the workmen.

"I'm looking for the foreman. Have you seen Brian Burkholder?"

The guy shook his head. "Not today."

"Dave, at the office, said we'd find him here," Noah explained.

The workman glanced around the site as if searching for the foreman. "Sorry, sir. He must be working somewhere else."

"We might as well go," Ruthie advised. "We've driven around the entire area."

"Yet Dave talked to the foreman." Noah sighed. "Which only confirms my suspicions about this whole development and Castle Homes in particular. As I said before, something's fishy."

The workman tapped another man's shoulder and pointed to Noah's truck. The guy shook his head and approached.

Bending down, he peered at Noah through the passenger window Ruthie had lowered. "You folks are looking for the foreman?"

Noah nodded. "That's right."

"Drive down that road." The guy indicated a narrow lane on the far side of the lake. "He's got a trailer about half a mile from here. If he's not on-site, you can usually find him there."

"We appreciate your help."

Noah circled the lake and passed a house in the final stages of completion.

Ruthie tugged on his arm and pointed to the mountain. "The valley is even more visible from here."

He nodded. "You're right about shifting the direction of the river, especially at the source. Trying to divert the flow of water farther down the mountain from our properties would be more difficult."

"Castle is promising a lake and Prescott Construction is buying your land, and maybe mine, in hopes of selling Castle the water access he needs for a huge profit."

"Although," Noah said, "Castle could have made us an offer himself instead of going through Prescott Construction."

"*Yah*, but perhaps Burkholder did not tell his boss how he plans to get the water, especially if he hopes to make money from the deal."

"If Burkholder is going behind the boss's back, he might be getting anxious. Maybe he sent the notes and attacked you to ensure you would sell so the deal would go through in a timely manner."

"Yet he has not attacked you," she added.

"Because he's convinced I will sell, Ruthie. You received the offer from Prescott Construction when you stopped at the post office. How long ago had the letter been mailed?"

"Almost six weeks ago. Do you think Brian Burkholder feared I would not sell so he decided to scare me off the property?"

"Crazy as it sounds, I think that was his plan."

She hugged her arms. "We need to call Deputy Warren and tell him to question Burkholder. Then I want to get Simon and Andrew and return home, Noah."

"Let's locate the trailer before I call the deputy. After that we'll make a fast stop for paint so I can work on the chicken coop."

She nodded. "If we must, but I am worried. Not about the mountain property, but about the boys. With everything that has happened, I do not like having them out of my sight."

"Then we'll wait until another day to get the paint and go directly to your aunt's house."

"Ben said I was too protective, but I watched my mother's condition become life-threatening in a short time."

"I remember. Your father blamed you."

She nodded. "He waited too long to go for the midwife. Deep down, he probably knew he had made a mistake, but it was easier to say my inattentiveness had somehow caused her death."

Noah rubbed her hand. "I'm sure the boys are fine."

"I pray they are, but my anxiety will not ease until I see for myself."

"We'll drive just a bit farther before we turn around. I'd like to ensure that guy was telling the truth about the foreman's trailer."

As Noah steered the pickup away from the curb, Ruthie tugged on his arm. "Look at that house."

A team of men were painting the trim. "Notice the man carrying the bucket of paint?"

The guy was tall and muscular. He wore a short-sleeve shirt. His left arm was covered with tattoos.

"That is the man who returned the envelope to me at the library. The man who was living in the woods. He must have gotten a job with the painting company."

"Can you be certain it's the same man?" Noah asked.

"He looks like the same man, but—"

Ruthie flicked her gaze around the construction site searching for the missing gravel truck before she turned back to stare at him. He glanced at her, then nodded as if he recognized her.

Her stomach knotted. After seeing his face, she was sure he was the man at the library. Was he also the man on the mountain? Could he be the man who had driven the gravel truck or the red pickup?

Chapter Nineteen

After leaving the lake area, Noah drove along the dirt road that flanked the back of the cleared housing development. He pointed to a trailer in the distance that was parked in a small thicket of trees.

"Looks like Burkholder found a little shade for his trailer," he said to Ruthie.

"I do not want him to see us, Noah. We need to turn around and head back to town."

At that moment, a red truck sped around the trailer and headed toward them.

Ruthie screamed. Noah turned the wheel and drove off the road. The truck accelerated and raced past them.

A red truck with tinted windows.

"Oh, Noah," Ruthie gasped. "That was the third time today we have almost been in an accident."

"But nothing was accidental about any of those near collisions. Did you see the driver, Ruthie? I'm sure it was Brian Burkholder."

"I only saw a blur as the truck passed. The same truck that shoved us onto the train tracks."

"You're right about that." Noah pulled out his phone and tapped in a number. "I'm calling Deputy Warren."

The call went to voice mail. Noah explained what they had discovered. "We think Brian Burkholder just left the area in a red truck."

He disconnected and pocketed his phone. "Let's take a closer look before we turn around. Then I'll try to call Deputy Warren again."

He parked beside the trailer. "Wait in the pickup."

She shook her head. "I'm going with you."

Together they hurried to the side door. Noah knocked. When no one answered, he knocked again.

Leaning toward the window, he cupped his hands around his eyes to cut down on the glare and stared inside.

The interior of the trailer looked like a tornado had spun through the confined space. Papers were tossed helter-skelter. A coffee cup had been overturned on a table. Another cup was shattered.

Stretching to see more of the chaos, Noah groaned.

Ruthie tugged on his arm. "What is it?"

"Someone's on the floor. He isn't moving."

Noah rapped on the window. "Brian? Brian Burkholder?"

"Noah, this frightens me."

"Go back to my truck, Ruthie."

She glanced over her shoulder and then shook her head. "I am not going anywhere without you."

He pulled out a handkerchief, wrapped it around the doorknob and opened the door.

A cloying, acrid smell of blood wafted past him. "Stay outside, Ruthie."

He stepped into the confusion. "Brian?"

The man pictured in the Castle Homes poster—the same man they had seen at the pizza parlor—was lying in the middle of the trailer. His mouth gaped open.

Kneeling, Noah felt for a pulse. When he withdrew his hand, it was covered with blood.

Peering from the doorway, Ruthie gasped.

"Don't touch anything. I'll call Deputy Warren again."

"What do you think happened?"

"Someone got to him."

"The man driving the red truck?" Ruthie asked.

"I'm not sure." Noah glanced at the shelf behind the table. "Look at that framed photograph of a young man."

He leaned closer. "It says, 'Thanks for being such a great dad! Your son, Prescott.'"

Ruthie's eyes widened. "Brian Burkholder named the construction company after his son."

Noah wiped his hand on his handkerchief, then hit Redial on his phone.

The deputy answered.

Noah repeated the information he had left on voice mail and explained again that they were at Castle Homes and had gone searching for the foreman. He mentioned that the man who had returned Ruthie's letter in the library was painting homes in the area and also told him about the red truck that had raced past them.

"We found the foreman in his trailer," Noah said at last. "But he's dead."

"Can you identify the body, ma'am?" Deputy Warren stared at Ruthie. Noah stepped closer and put his arm around her shoulder.

"Is this the same man who attacked you at your home?" the deputy asked.

She glanced at the dead man and blinked back tears. "I do not know. He has the same build, but as I told you, the man who accosted me wore a stocking over his face."

"What about the tattoos on his arm?" The deputy had lifted his sleeve so she could see the markings.

"I do not know if they are what I saw on the man who attacked me. The colors look different. I cannot be sure."

"The red truck that raced past you looked like the vehicle that pushed you into the way of the oncoming train?"

She nodded. "*Yah*, this is so. We thought Brian Burkholder was driving the truck, but then we discovered his body in the trailer."

The crime-scene investigators were going through the trailer searching for evidence. The coroner had proclaimed Brian Burkholder dead and his body would soon be taken to the morgue so the pathologist could do an autopsy.

The foreman had been stabbed three times in the chest, which appeared to be the cause of death, although the pathologist would make the final determination.

"We've got some of our guys tracking down Vince Ashcroft, the real-estate agent." Deputy Warren glanced at Noah. "If the two of them worked together and if Mr. Burkholder tried to coerce either of you into turning over your property to him without telling his partner, Ashcroft could have gotten angry and decided to take matters into his own hands. We'll talk to Mr. Castle and see what kind of an agreement he had with Prescott Construction."

"Check out Chattanooga," Noah suggested. "I have a hunch Burkholder was involved in that dam collapse."

"Will do." The deputy's phone rang. He pulled it to his ear. "Deputy Warren."

Turning away from Noah and Ruthie, he conversed with the caller, then disconnected, pocketed his phone and stepped back to them. "The red pickup's been found. It belongs to the assistant foreman, John Zimmer. Evidently, he also goes by the name Zimmerman. He's definitely a person of interest. As soon as we can locate him, we'll haul him in for questioning."

"See if he has tattoos on his left arm," Ruthie said.

"Will do, ma'am."

The deputy glanced at the notes he had taken. "I've got everything I need from both of you. Where can I find you if I need any additional information?"

Ruthie looked at Noah. "I feel sure Aunt Mattie would let us stay with her."

He nodded. "That sounds like a good plan, at least until the deputy assures us the murderer is behind bars."

Ruthie provided her aunt's address.

Deputy Warren wrote the address on his tablet. "I'll have one of our guys follow you to your aunt's farm. Use caution until we make an arrest."

He turned to Noah. "How's cell coverage at the aunt's house?"

"Hopefully better than on the mountain. You've got my number?"

The deputy nodded. "I'll let you know as soon as we find the killer."

Noah shook the deputy's hand. "Thanks for your help."

Ruthie felt even more unsettled as they left the crime scene. A man had died, and another man was being hunted down. Was he the man who had come after her?

There were so many people of interest, as the deputy had mentioned. One of them wanted to do Ruthie and her children harm. Seeing how the killer had stabbed Brian Burkholder only compounded her worry. She had known the man who had attacked her was vile, but he had grown more brazen and his attacks more threatening. Now, without a shadow of a doubt, he not only wanted to do her harm, he also wanted to kill her.

Thinking of the danger she and her children were in made her tremble.

She glanced back and let out a sigh of relief when she saw the sheriff's deputy following them.

"How soon will it be over, Noah?" she asked.

"Hopefully before long, Ruthie, although we need to be careful until the perpetrator is apprehended."

"Poor Tiffany. She could be working for a killer."

"I regret taking you to his real-estate office. And to think we considered having him sell our land."

"The *Englisch* have strange ideas about the Amish. Some think we are ignorant of our rights and legal standing. He probably thought my farm would go into foreclosure if he forced me to leave."

Noah nodded. "Then he could buy your property at a cut-rate price."

"If not for you, Noah, I might have left permanently for fear of what he would do to Simon and Andrew."

Noah reached out and squeezed her hand. "I'm glad I could help."

"My mother always quoted the Scripture that says, 'With *Gott*, all things work together for good.'"

"Your mother was a wise woman. *Gott* prompted me to return to the mountain and take care of my father's property."

"At the perfect time." Ruthie glanced again at the sheriff's car behind them. Perhaps the worst had passed, especially if they could stay at Aunt Mattie's farm where Ashcroft or Zimmer or whoever killed the foreman and had attacked her would not find them. The killer would be arrested, she was certain, and all her fears would be put to rest.

"I'm eager to see the boys," she told Noah. "It seems like more than a few hours since we left them. So much has happened."

"Reconnecting with your aunt Mattie was a good thing, Ruthie."

"*Yah*, I see *Gott's* hand in this as if He is inviting me back to the Amish community."

"You would receive help and support."

"The boys would enjoy having friends and returning to the Amish school. I have tried to teach them, but they miss seeing other children."

"All that will change now."

Noah's words reassured her. The killer needed to be apprehended first, then she and her sons could return home.

Would Noah return to his father's home, as well? He had wanted to sell the farm, but the Prescott Construction deal was a thing of the past.

Perhaps now he would decide to stay and rejoin the Amish faith. The thought of having Noah as a neighbor warmed her heart for a moment until everything that had happened came back into focus. Once her attacker was arrested, she could relax. Until then, she needed to be cautious and careful. The vile man had come after her before. As long as he was free to roam the mountain, he would come after her again.

Chapter Twenty

Ruthie knew Noah was as upset as she was about finding the foreman murdered. A light rain shower fell as they left town and drove to Mattie's house. At the turn-off, Noah raised his hand in farewell to the sheriff's deputy who had followed them along the country road. The deputy honked, turned around in the drive and headed back to town.

Andrew was on the covered porch cranking the ice-cream churn when Noah parked in front of the quaint Amish farmhouse. Mattie rose from the porch rocking chair and hurried down the steps to greet them, ignoring the rain.

"Where's Simon?" Ruthie asked, a note of concern in her voice as she took her aunt's outstretched hand.

"Resting inside."

The two women dashed up the steps to the porch.

"His stomach hurts, and he looks pale," Mattie explained. "I am glad you returned early. When he was not interested in churning ice cream, I knew something was wrong."

Ruthie hugged Andrew and placed the palm of her hand on his forehead, relieved that he felt cool.

"Do you want ice cream, *Mamm*?" he asked. "It is almost ready."

"You are working hard, Andrew. Let me check on Simon first."

"He is sick."

Which is what Ruthie feared. She hurried inside and found Simon resting in the downstairs guest room. One glance at his flushed face and glassy eyes and she knew his upset stomach was caused by more than eating too much cake.

"What hurts?" she asked, running her hand over his hot cheeks.

"Everything."

"Are you nauseous?"

He nodded. "And my head is pounding."

She turned a worried gaze to Noah, who had followed her inside along with Mattie.

His expression confirmed he was equally concerned about Simon's condition. "Do you have a doctor who sees the boys in town?"

"Simon and Andrew are rarely sick, and I have not had the need." She looked again at her son's feverish gaze and weary eyes. "Until now."

"Doctors are always on duty at the emergency room." Mattie stepped closer. "Take Simon to the hospital in town. I have money in the bank in case you are worried about the cost. Andrew can stay here with me. We will eat ice cream, and he can help me bake cookies. I will fix enough dinner for all of you to enjoy, and you can spend the night if it is late when you return from town."

"I had hoped we could stay with you until a bad man

is apprehended." Ruthie explained some of what had happened, taking care not to say too much in front of Simon.

"You, Noah and the boys are always welcome here. My house is larger than I need. Having it filled with family will bring me joy."

"Thank you, Mattie." Ruthie hugged her aunt. "You are too kind to give us lodging. Knowing Andrew is with you when we take Simon to the hospital will calm my worry as well, at least for my one son. Plus, if Andrew stays with you, he will not be exposed to other people's germs."

She turned to Noah and grabbed his hand. "I have not asked if you mind driving us back to town."

"Mind? Of course not. Simon needs to see a doctor."

Working together, they eased Simon to his feet and slowly walked him outside. The rain had stopped, but the air was thick with humidity.

"I do not feel good," the boy moaned as Noah helped him into the truck. Ruthie slid in, wrapped her arm around him and positioned Simon's head on her shoulder. Heat radiated from his body, and she feared his temperature had risen even higher than when she first touched his forehead.

Noah climbed behind the wheel. The worry in his expression mirrored her own inner turmoil.

Ruthie had been so focused on the man who had come after them, and then on the idea of selling the land, that she had been less than attentive to Simon this morning. Could he have had the fever earlier without her realizing he was sick?

"Did you think Simon seemed ill this morning?" she asked Noah, hoping for confirmation that she had not neglected her son's care.

"He and Andrew were in great spirits when we drove down the hill," Noah replied. "The illness has come on quickly."

His response eased her concern that she had ignored some sign of his ill health this morning. "Simon never gets sick."

"The weather has been bad, especially with all the rain. I shouldn't have let the boys help me fix the bridge."

"That did not make him sick. This is something else, but I do not know what it could be."

"The doctor will be able to diagnose the problem."

Ruthie closed her eyes. Gott, *please let it be so.*

The emergency room was filled with sick people. Many were coughing and holding their heads. Some were wrapped in blankets, or leaned against loved ones for support.

Noah found three chairs in the corner. He and Simon remained there while Ruthie headed to the end of a long line of people waiting at the registration desk. After slowly making her way to the front, she accepted a stack of forms from the clerk and returned to where Noah and Simon sat to fill them out.

Simon started to shiver. Noah asked for a blanket and then held the forms while Ruthie tucked the covering around her son.

Glancing down at the top paper, Noah's gaze homed in on the block for father's name. Ruthie had written Benjamin Eicher.

A heavy weight settled over Noah's shoulders. Even though he hadn't known about Ruthie's pregnancy, Noah had given up his right to be called Simon's father when he left the mountain ten years ago. No matter how much it pained him now, he had to realize the truth. He was not part of Ruthie's family, no matter how much he wanted to be.

Simon's face was pale, and he continued to shiver even with the blanket. Ruthie pulled him closer and rubbed her hand over his forehead. Her face was tight with worry.

Noah patted her hand, hoping to offer support. She smiled weakly as if grateful for his presence.

"As I mentioned earlier, I have never had to use the emergency room before." She glanced at the crowd of sick patients waiting to be seen. "This is not how I expected it to be."

It was still daylight. Knowing how illness often struck in the middle of the night, Noah feared the crowded conditions could get much worse.

Within the hour, Simon was called into a triage room. The nurse listened to Ruthie's explanation of his symptoms before she took his vitals.

"His temperature is one hundred and three degrees," the nurse announced. "Blood pressure is normal, pulse is elevated. His oxygen level is ninety-eight."

"What does that mean?" Ruthie asked.

"It means he'll have to wait to see a doctor."

She handed Simon a pill and a glass of water. "This should bring down his fever. After he takes the medication, return to the waiting room and we'll call you shortly."

Shortly turned into two hours.

The nurse took Simon's temperature again. "It's one hundred two point eight degrees. The doctor will be in soon."

The physician was an older gentleman with tired eyes

and a sagging jaw. He examined Simon, then ordered blood work and rapid flu and strep tests.

"I'll be back with the lab results," he assured them as he left the room.

Simon fell asleep on the cot, and Ruthie and Noah sat nearby as they waited even longer for the results to come back from the lab.

"He's a good son," Ruthie whispered to Noah.

"You've done a great job raising him."

"He brings me so much joy. He looked like you even as a baby. Sometimes I marveled that people did not realize who his father really was."

"I'm sorry, Ruthie. I had no idea."

"We cannot undo the past."

The doctor returned with the lab results. "The cultures will take another twenty-four to forty-eight hours before we can identify the organism, but I can tell you for certain that your son has a serious infection. Do you have a well, Mrs. Eicher?"

"*Yah*, we do."

"Has the well water been tested recently?"

"I do not know that it has ever been checked."

"With all this rain, we're seeing an increase in contamination. Pasture runoff often causes problems. Get your water checked. I'll notify Public Health and ask them to send someone to your house."

"No one is there now."

"Not to worry—it'll take them a few days to get to you. Until then, I'd buy a kit at the hardware store so you can check for various contaminants. One will be for bacteria. It won't differentiate which organisms are causing problems, but it will let you know if bacteria has gotten into your water supply. Until you talk to the Public

Health folks, boil your water for at least a minute, then cool it in a sealed container before you use it."

"I have heard people mention having to shock their wells. Is this something I must do if I find contamination?" she asked.

"Public Health can help you with that. They'll provide guidelines on how much bleach to use." He made a note on a clipboard. "Let's keep Simon overnight so we can get his temperature down. I want to ensure he doesn't develop complications."

More time passed until they got a room and then admitted Simon. Once he was settled in his hospital bed, Ruthie put her head in her hands.

Noah rubbed her shoulder. "He's going to be okay."

"If what the doctor said is true, I allowed the boys to drink tainted water."

"Wait until the well is tested before you jump to conclusions, and remember that contamination happens. Most folks test their water twice a year."

She bit her lip. "Which proves that Simon's illness is my fault for not ensuring the water was safe."

"You heard the doctor. The increased rainfall could be the reason."

"What if the man tampered with the well? So much has happened. He told me he would hurt my children."

She shook her head and glanced away, as if not wanting Noah to see her upset.

"Right now, focus on Simon getting better," he encouraged. "I'll go to the cafeteria and bring back some food. You haven't eaten since breakfast."

"Food would be *gut*, and some water. Clean water that will not cause infection." She wrung her hands. "If the water is bad, then Andrew could get sick, as well."

"He was fine when we left him."

"*Yah*, and I pray he continues to be all right." She hesitated a moment and then added, "Two milk bottles were in a bucket of cool water overnight. Simon drank milk from an open bottle that was almost empty. Andrew's milk was poured from the new bottle. Suppose the man tampered with the open bottle of milk?"

"The lab tests will determine what caused Simon's illness. Tomorrow we can check on Andrew. Until then, we will stay with Simon and pray his condition improves."

Ruthie would pray for Simon's condition to improve and for Andrew to remain healthy. She would also pray for law enforcement to capture Brian Burkholder's killer and the man who wanted to do her and her boys harm.

How much longer would they have to live life looking over their shoulders? She wanted everything resolved as fast as possible. Bottom line, she wanted her family to be healthy and safe.

Chapter Twenty-One

Noah hurried to the cafeteria and returned with hamburgers and fries. Ruthie hardly touched the food, but she drank the bottle of water.

After he had eaten, Noah settled into an easy chair in the corner of the room. Ruthie rested in a recliner next to Simon's bed. She closed her eyes and was soon asleep.

Simon's breathing was even, but his coloring remained pale. Before coming back to the mountain, Noah hadn't known he had a son. Now he worried he might lose the boy he had grown to love in just a short time. Truth be told, he had loved him that first night when he had seen him in the light of the oil lamp. The similarity between them was so great there had been no question that Simon was his son.

If Noah had known Ruthie was pregnant ten years ago, he never would have left her. His father couldn't mail Ruthie's letter because Noah hadn't told him where he and Seth were living. He had communicated with his father much later, but by that time, Ruthie's letters would have been long forgotten.

Noah drew closer to the bed and touched his son's

cheek. "*Gott*, it has been a long time since I have talked to You. I've made a lot of mistakes. Not being here for my son is one of them. Get him through this illness, then help Ruthie find a good man to help her with the boys. She deserves a better life than she's had. Provide for her needs. I'll set up a fund for Simon and Andrew. Both boys are so special. If Seth hadn't died, I might be ready to open my heart again, but I seem to make a mess of everything You've given me that is good. Don't let me hurt Ruthie or Simon again. Please."

Noah stood at the side of the bed for a long time while Simon and Ruthie slept. Throughout the night he continued to pray for his son, and for Ruthie and Andrew, and asked the Lord to bring good from all the pain.

Ruthie woke with a start when the nurse entered the room early the next morning. She sat up, rubbed her eyes and glanced around, unable to find Noah.

"I'm sorry to disturb you," the nurse said with an apologetic smile. "Your husband went to get coffee and something to eat. He said to tell you he'd be back in a flash if you awoke."

"My husband?"

The nurse nodded. "Yes, ma'am. He's been awake all night and stopped by the nurses' desk a number of times asking about his son. We tried to reassure him, but he has been quite anxious."

Ruthie nodded. "We both have been concerned."

"Everything appears worse in the middle of the night." The nurse studied the monitor. "Simon's vitals look good. I'll get his temp in a minute. The phlebotomist will be in soon to draw his blood."

"More tests?"

"I'm afraid so. The doctor wants to ensure he's improving."

Ruthie stood and neared the bed. "Looks like he is a sleepyhead this morning."

"It's early. I'll come back in a bit for that temp. I hate to bother patients, especially when they're sleeping so soundly." She hung another antibiotic bag and left the room.

Ruthie raked her fingers through her hair and repositioned her *kapp*. She stepped into the bathroom, then splashed water on her face and rinsed her mouth.

After returning to Simon's bedside, she glanced out the window. A low cloud cover fell over the countryside. From the dark sky, more rain seemed likely. She was concerned about the rising water.

Once before, the river had flooded. Her mother had been alive, and they had moved the few furnishings they had upstairs. She had had the foresight to take bread and jam and some nonperishable food items to the second floor, along with jugs of water.

"*Gott* will provide" had been her mother's response as the water rose.

Ruthie had been little and remembered looking across the rain-swollen river to Noah's house. His home sat higher on the mountain and escaped the flood.

For two days, Ruthie and her family had holed up in the hot upstairs, and then the rain had stopped and the sun appeared.

"*Gott* has answered our prayers," her mother had said with her usual optimism.

Within twelve hours the water had left the house, although mud and debris remained on the first floor and had to be swept out and mopped clean. Noah and his family came to help, and by the second day, the floor-boards were damp but free from the mud. *Mamm* had aired out the house for days. The sun and a mountain breeze had been in their favor.

At that time, *Datt* had been a jovial man with a ready smile and hugs for his daughter. He had changed after her mother had died.

"Breakfast."

She turned at the sound of Noah's voice and smiled. His hair was somewhat disheveled and his eyes were tired, but he was as handsome as the young man who had stolen her heart years ago.

"Two coffees, plus platters of eggs and sausage. Also croissants and fresh fruit."

"Croissants?"

"Something different, *yah*?"

She nodded. "*Yah*. But the food smells delicious and I am hungry."

"How's our patient?"

"Sleeping soundly, which is probably good. The nurse did not want to wake him to take his temperature. She will return in a bit."

"So we can enjoy our meal without interruption from the medical staff."

"The phlebotomist is due shortly."

"What did the nurse say about Simon?"

"The results of the lab tests will provide more infor-mation."

Ruthie bowed her head. Noah was silent until she glanced up.

"Enjoy the food," he said.

"You always anticipate my needs, Noah."

"I was awake and hungry. I knew you would want to eat, as well. Don't give me more credit than I deserve."

"You deserve a lot of credit."

"I deserve a lot of blame, as well. I should have stayed, Ruthie."

"You needed to make your own way."

"At your expense. A good man would not leave someone he loved behind."

Her heart pounded with Noah's words. He had loved her. If only circumstances had been different.

A knock sounded at the door. "Morning. I'm Janice, from the lab."

"Simon is still sleeping."

"I've got a few more patients to draw on this floor. How 'bout I come back in a few minutes? You can enjoy your breakfast a little longer."

"That is very thoughtful. Thank you."

Ruthie ate in silence, unwilling to meet Noah's gaze. She needed to keep her focus on the present and take each moment as it came.

Noah is leaving, her voice of reason continued to warn her.

Plus, he was *Englisch*.

She steeled her spine and reached for the coffee. She would not let her heart be broken again. Once was one time too many. If it happened a second time, she might not survive.

Chapter Twenty-Two

Noah was anxious to hear what the doctor had to say, but it was late morning before the physician made his rounds.

"How are you feeling?" the doctor asked after he had poked and prodded Simon's stomach, listened to his heart, and checked his pupils.

"I am hungry," the boy announced. His face was pale and he still had a fever.

The doctor glanced at the breakfast tray. "You didn't eat breakfast."

"I would like real food like my *mamm* cooks," Simon explained, "instead of watery cream of wheat and dry toast."

The doctor nodded. "I'll have dietary change you to a nonrestrictive diet. Lunch should be more appetizing."

"Gut," Simon said with a weak smile.

"How does your head feel?"

"Like it is stuffed with cotton. My stomach is better, but it rumbles."

"You were a sick young man when you came in." The doctor glanced at Simon's file. "Your condition has improved, but only slightly, which concerns me. We need to be sure the antibiotic is working."

"When can he go home?" Ruthie asked.

"Not this soon. We'll see how he does tonight. Tomorrow might be a different story."

After the doctor left, Simon turned to his mother. "Why do I have to stay here?"

"Because you are sick."

"What about Andrew?"

"He is at Aunt Mattie's house, though I am concerned he might be sick, as well."

"I could check on him," Noah suggested.

"I would rather see for myself that he is all right."

Noah's phone rang. He stepped into the hallway and nodded when he heard Deputy Warren's voice.

"I wanted to give you an update," the deputy said. "We questioned Vince Ashcroft, the real-estate agent. He was in on the land-acquisition deal with Burkholder and Zimmer. Evidently the assistant foreman had come up with the initial concept of redirecting the mountain water, but Burkholder claimed it was his own idea when he talked to Mr. Castle. Zimmer became belligerent and the two argued."

"So you think Zimmer killed the foreman?"

"He's more than a person of interest at this point. Our guys went over his red truck from top to bottom. Guess what they found under the driver's seat?"

"A knife."

"You got that right. No prints but he probably wiped it clean. There was blood on the blade and we're having Forensics check to see if it matches the foreman's blood."

"As you might recall, a black sedan tried to run into

Ruthie and her children when we were in town. Does Zimmer own a second vehicle?"

"No, but the guys at the construction site usually leave their keys in their cars. Easy enough to borrow someone else's set of wheels."

"And what about tattoos?"

"Tell Mrs. Eicher that John Zimmer has tattoos on both arms."

"I'll tell her. Is he in custody?"

"We've spotted him outside of town. I'll let you know when we make the arrest."

After disconnecting, Noah stepped back into the hospital room. Simon was asleep, and Noah kept his voice lowered as he shared the information with Ruthie.

"Are you saying the assistant foreman decided to use force to get me off my land so he could buy the property without going through Prescott Construction?" Ruthie rubbed her hands together.

Noah nodded. "That seems to be right. Evidently he didn't trust Brian Burkholder."

"Greed is an ugly vice," she said.

"And it caused one man to lose his life. Law enforcement is closing in on Zimmer. They've spotted him outside of town."

"I will be glad when he is apprehended."

Noah glanced at the clock on the wall. "Ivan Keim should have checked the buggy by now. I'll walk to the repair shop and drive the buggy back here to the hospital. That way, as soon as Deputy Warren informs us that Zimmer is in custody, you can take the rig to Mattie's house to check on Andrew while I stay with Simon."

Ruthie smiled with relief. "That would be perfect, Noah."

* * *

Ruthie hated to see Noah leave the hospital. She had appreciated his support and had been touched by his concern for her son. Their son, she corrected herself.

Simon's eyes fluttered open when the nurse came in to check on his IV bag. "Your husband went home?" she asked Ruthie.

"He is running an errand in town."

"Simon takes after his dad."

The boy glared at Ruthie and nodded his head toward the nurse when her back was turned, as if to say she was totally confused.

"You should have corrected her, *Mamm,*" Simon said once the nurse had left the room.

Ruthie shrugged, trying to act nonchalant about the woman's comment. "There is no reason to correct her, Simon. She thinks what she thinks."

"Still, she should be told that Noah is not my *datt.*"

"Yet, he is a *gut* man."

"*Yah,* I would be happy to be his son, but it is not so."

Ruthie's stomach was in turmoil. How long would it take before Simon realized the truth?

Knowing he might ask more questions, she remained on edge until he eventually fell asleep.

Her back and hips ached after sitting so long. Needing to stretch her legs, she rose quietly, headed into the hall and then walked at a fast clip to the far end of the hospital wing. Turning, she headed down another hallway and then another, enjoying the chance to get at least a little exercise. Before long she found herself in an older section of the hospital that appeared to be in a remodeling phase.

Realizing she had walked too far, she turned and

started to retrace her steps. A noise sounded behind her. She glanced over her shoulder but saw no one. Concerned that she was alone in a secluded area, Ruthie hurried along the hallway and glanced at the overhead signage, needing to determine the way that led back to Simon's wing.

Footsteps sounded behind her. Her heart rate, already elevated from the brisk walk, increased even more.

"Still trying to get away from me?" A man's voice, coarse and belligerent, echoed in the empty hallway.

Glancing over her shoulder, she gasped, seeing his contorted face wedged within a woman's stocking.

"You tried to run from me, Ruthie. Now that I found you, I won't let you get away from me again."

He tried to grab her arm. She saw scratch marks on his hands.

"No!" She shoved past him and ran down the corridor.

He chased after her. His footfalls caused her heart to beat nearly out of her chest.

She was lost in a maze of hospital hallways that all looked alike. As she ran, she tried to read the direction signs.

He was close behind her. Too close.

Her feet slipped on the waxed floor. She screamed, caught herself and raced on again.

Where was the door that led into the main section of the hospital? She had to get away from him and make sure Simon was all right.

Security! She needed hospital security.

"Help!" she cried.

He chuckled—it was a menacing sound that made her pulse race even faster. Fear jammed her throat and twisted along her spine.

Her stomach tightened.

The door dividing the old section of the hospital from the new appeared ahead. She ran full steam against the swinging doors and nearly knocked over an elderly gentleman when she burst into the newer wing.

"Watch where you're going," the man growled.

"I am sorry, sir."

She skirted him and kept running.

Simon.

Everything inside her was screaming for her son. Was he okay or had the hateful man attacked Simon before he had come after her?

Ruthie moaned, unwilling to think about what could have happened.

She turned into Simon's hallway and stopped short outside his room. Pulling in a quick breath, she pushed on the door and stepped into his room, still struggling to regulate her breathing.

Simon's eyes widened. "*Mamm*, what is wrong?"

"Nothing is wrong." She patted her chest in hopes of calming her pulse and her racing heartbeat. "How are you feeling?"

Ruthie glanced over her shoulder. Where was the hateful man? Had he left her, or was he outside the room waiting for her even now?

"You look like you have been running, *Mamm*."

She rubbed her fingers over her son's flushed cheek. "A fast walk for exercise."

"You never could tell a lie."

"What do you mean?"

"I mean you were running. Was someone coming after you?" He glanced at the door, worried.

"You are making more of this than you should. I hurried when I realized how long I had been gone. Did you sleep the whole time?"

"I woke up once and saw a man standing next to my bed."

Fear gripped her heart. "What happened then?"

"He turned around and left the room, and I fell back to sleep. The next time I woke up, he was gone."

Ruthie trembled and her stomach roiled. Was it the same man who had chased after her?

Would he ever leave her and her boys alone?

Chapter Twenty-Three

Ivan Keim greeted Noah with a warm smile as he entered the buggy shop.

"Your buggy is ready." The shop owner wiped his hands on a towel. "You did a *gut* job reattaching the wheel to the axle. You have worked on buggies before this?"

"My father's buggy had problems over the years. I was his mechanic, but not by choice."

"It is a way to learn. If you need a job, I could use help."

Noah appreciated the offer. "I'm here to sell my father's land, then I'll be moving on."

"This area is a *gut* place to settle down, marry and raise a family."

"I grew up here and am well aware of the benefits."

"You were Amish, *yah*?"

"I was. Perhaps you knew my *datt*. Reuben Schlabach?"

Ivan rubbed his jaw. "Reuben lived on the mountain."

"You knew him?"

"I knew your mother. She was a wonderful woman. Your father was not the same after she died."

"By chance, do you know of Prescott Construction? They are interested in buying my father's land."

Ivan shrugged. "So much building. We will lose our peace, *yah*, when so many move into the new homes north of town."

"Castle Homes?"

The buggy maker nodded. "He buys farms from the Amish and then destroys the land. It is a shame."

"You've heard he plans to have a lake there."

Pursing his lips, Ivan shook his head. "I do not think his lake will find water."

Noah agreed. He paid Ivan and hitched the mare to the buggy. Leaving the shop, Noah checked the surrounding area. At the next intersection, he spied a tall man in dark clothing hurrying along the sidewalk. If only Ruthie had been able to positively identify the man who had attacked her.

On a hunch, he stopped by the sheriff's office. Deputy Warren was there. "Have you apprehended Zimmer?"

"Not yet, but we're closing in on him."

Noah told him about the man he had seen on the street.

"We'll check it out," Warren said. "And I'll let you know when we have Zimmer in custody."

Noah left, discouraged that the assistant foreman was still at large as he headed back to the hospital. Exiting the elevator on Simon's floor, his heart lurched when he saw hospital security outside the boy's room. He hurried forward to determine the problem.

Ruthie's face was flushed and her eyes wide as she

rushed to meet him in the hallway. Quickly, she explained what had happened.

"Did anyone call the sheriff's office?" he asked.

The hospital-security folks shook their heads.

The man who seemed to be in charge stepped closer. "Our guards are searching for the man throughout the hospital, sir, but I haven't notified the sheriff yet."

Noah pulled out his phone. "I'll call his office. I stopped in a few minutes ago and talked to the deputy we saw yesterday, Ruthie. He needs to know Zimmer might be in the area."

"I saw scratches on his arms today," Ruthie said. "I fought back both times he attacked me on the mountain. I am not sure if I scratched him or if they are from someone else."

"Scratches on both hands?" he asked.

She nodded. "*Yah*, both hands."

"I'll pass that information on to Deputy Warren."

Noah hit the prompt and connected with the sheriff's department. The deputy came on the line and Noah shared what Ruthie had said about the scratches.

"Security is searching the hospital," Noah explained. "Timing would have been right for the guy who attacked Ruthie to have been the man I saw on the street."

"One of our deputies spotted someone who matches your description in the downtown area. We're closing in."

Noah and Ruthie left hospital security in the hallway and returned to Simon's room. His eyes were closed and he moaned in his sleep.

"How is he?" Noah asked, stepping to the boy's bedside.

"I am not sure. They thought he was improving, then he had a setback."

"Another fever?"

She nodded. "The nurse took his temperature before calling security about the man who came after me. The doctor is concerned Simon's medication might not be working. He said the organism could be resistant. If Simon doesn't show more signs of improvement soon—"

The worry on her face told Noah what he needed to know.

Simon moaned again, then his eyes blinked open.

Noah stepped closer to the bed. "Hey, champ. How are you feeling?"

"Gut." Simon smiled weakly.

Noah squeezed his hand. "Your mom and I are right here with you. You're going to be okay. Get some rest now so the medicine can do its job."

Simon nodded, then closed his eyes and drifted back to sleep.

Ruthie moved to the bedside. "I have never seen him so sick."

"The medicine will work, Ruthie."

"Was it the well water? If so, I fear Andrew could be sick as well, yet I do not want to leave Simon when his fever is still high."

"Do you know anyone who lives near Mattie who has a phone?" Noah asked.

She shook her head. "You are also worried."

"I'm more worried about the man who wants to do you harm."

Ruthie's face was pale. "Too much is happening, Noah. You and I made mistakes in our youth, but I know God provides his mercy. Scripture says, *For where two or three are gathered together in my name, there am I in the midst of them.* We are Simon's parents. My mother always prayed for me and said *Gott* listens when parents pray for their children."

She held out her hand. "Let us put aside our differences and the pain from the past and pray together for the health of this son of ours."

Noah had been the one to make the mistake of leaving Ruthie. She had always done what was right. She loved her son. Noah did, too.

He took her hand and closed his eyes.

Please, Lord, he prayed silently. *Help Simon. Help our son.*

Ruthie's voice faltered as she started to pray aloud. "*Gott*, You know we love Simon. He is a wonderful boy with a huge heart. Noah and I have made mistakes, but we love this child, and we ask for his healing. We also ask that Andrew does not get sick. Stop the man who wants to do us harm and let us both know what to do about our land."

Her eyes fluttered open and Noah's heart nearly burst with love for her.

He stepped closer. "Ruthie, I—"

"Oh, Noah." She stepped into his embrace. All he could think of was her sweetness and how he had always loved her.

He pulled her closer and lowered his lips—

His phone rang.

She stepped away. Confusion lined her face.

"I'm sorry." He raised the phone. "Noah Schlabach."

"We got him." The deputy's voice sounded in Noah's ear. "We've apprehended the guy in black. He's got scratches on his hands. Said he was playing with a stray cat. He's coming in for questioning. I'm hoping we'll get a confession. Stop by my office later and I'll fill you in on more details."

"Thanks. I will."

Noah disconnected and turned back to Ruthie. "They're hauling someone into the sheriff's office. Deputy Warren will interrogate him. They're hoping for a confession."

A tap sounded at the door and the nurse hurried into the room. "Sorry to bother you folks. The doctor wants Simon's temperature checked again."

She nudged the boy. He blinked his eyes open before she placed the thermometer in his mouth. Once the device buzzed, the nurse smiled at Ruthie. "His temp is down a bit, which is encouraging."

"*Gott* is good," Ruthie said. Tears filled her eyes and she took Simon's hand and smiled.

A lunch tray arrived, and Simon sat up and ate slowly. Relief washed over Ruthie's face and joy returned to her gaze.

"The buggy's outside," Noah informed her. "Why don't you ride to Mattie's house and check on Andrew. You'll feel better once you know he's okay."

"You are right, Noah."

"While you're gone, I'll call Willkommen Realty about listing my property with them."

She frowned. "You still plan to sell your land?"

"I do. What about you, Ruthie? Have you decided about your land?"

"My family is buried on the mountain, Noah. My mother and father and baby sister."

And Ruthie's husband, whom she didn't mention. Noah had made a mistake so long ago to leave Ruthie. Another man had taken his place.

Ruthie kissed Simon's cheek. "I will be back as soon as I check on your brother."

"*Mamm*, I want to go home."

"*Yah*, you and I will go home soon."

The boy looked at Noah. "What about you?" he asked. "Will you go home with us, Noah?"

Noah's heart broke seeing Simon's confusion.

"I'll take you and your mother home."

"And then what, Noah?" Ruthie asked.

She looked at him like she had the night he had left her ten years ago.

Noah had made so many mistakes, starting with abandoning Ruthie. He had also lost his brother and his brother's family and didn't deserve to find love or to have a family. No matter how deeply he cared for Ruthie, he could not stay on Amish Mountain. She needed to go on with her life. A life without him.

Ruthie squeezed Simon's hand, then left the room, without saying anything more to Noah.

He didn't blame her. He had left her once. He would leave her again, but she would be better off without him. He knew that to be true, even though his heart would break this time just as it had done before.

Chapter Twenty-Four

Tears burned Ruthie's eyes as she left the hospital and hurried to where Noah had hitched the buggy. She rubbed Buttercup's mane. "How are you, girl? Ready to take me to Aunt Mattie's house so we can check on Andrew?"

The horse nuzzled Ruthie's hand as if expecting a treat. "Perhaps Aunt Mattie will have a carrot or an apple for you."

She climbed into the buggy, upset with herself, and flicked the reins. All along she had been concerned about growing attached to Noah. Although she had tried with all her might to keep up her guard, once again she had been pulled in by his charm. Her heart did not have a chance.

Noah had done chores and fixed meals and made her boys take pride in who they were and the jobs they did around the farm. He had taught them to fix fences and how to shore up the barn, and they had helped to check the bridge to ensure it was stable.

Plus, he had given them positive affirmation, and showered them with attention. Both boys had yearned for signs of love from Ben, but he was never one to show his feelings. Ruthie was sure her husband had loved Andrew. She feared he had always harbored resentment toward Simon. Not that she had kept anything from Ben before they were married. She had told him about Noah and their youthful mistake. But Simon was not a mistake. He had been wanted and loved from the moment she realized she was in the family way.

Before their marriage Ben had been accepting. After the ceremony his true feelings had surfaced.

She wiped the tears from her eyes. Ben was gone. Now she had to take care of her sons. *Please, Gott, let Simon continue to get better and keep Andrew from getting sick.*

Before she and the boys returned to the mountain, she needed to get a kit to test her well water. How terrible if contamination had caused Simon's infection.

Dark clouds rolled overhead and the musky scent of rain hung in the air. The wind picked up, and she tightened her grip on the reins. She should have been more aware of the dark clouds in the distance before she started on her journey. Hopefully, she would not be stuck at Mattie's house when she needed to return to the hospital to ensure Simon was improving.

If Andrew was sick, she would take him with her and have him checked by a doctor, as well.

Noah would be there, but soon after that he would sign papers to sell his land through the other real-estate firm in town.

How would she explain his leaving to her boys? They were still struggling with Ben's passing and her father's death, and had all too readily accepted Noah into their lives. Now he would be gone.

"Life is not fair," Ruthie said to herself. She heard disappointment in her own voice, tempered with a bit of anger.

After Ben's death, she had hoped life would get easier, but that was not the case. New problems had arisen one after another, starting with the man who had come after her.

Raindrops fell, gentle ones at first, then bigger drops that slapped against her skin and dampened her dress and bonnet.

She pulled the blanket around her legs to keep them dry and narrowed her gaze to better see into the distance.

A car raced by and threw water against the buggy.

"Ach!" she groaned, wiping her face and hands on the blanket.

She glanced back, no longer able to see the town in the heavy downpour, and then turned onto the side road that led to Mattie's farm.

The sky grew even darker, and the temperature dropped. Ruthie shivered and stared into the pouring rain to keep the mare on the road and headed in the right direction.

The roar of an automobile sounded behind her. She glanced back and spotted headlights. The car was traveling much too fast. She pulled the mare to the side of the road and waited for it to pass, expecting the vehicle's wheels to splash water that would drench her and the inside of the buggy.

Instead of zooming around her buggy, the auto braked to a stop. Ruthie's heart lurched. She glanced back but was unable to see the driver through the car's tinted windshield. A dark sedan, like the car that had driven onto the curb and almost struck her children.

She flicked the reins. The mare started to trot.

The car accelerated.

Ruthie flicked the reins again. Buttercup increased her speed.

The car swerved around the buggy and braked to a stop.

She drew back on the reins. The mare stopped short and balked.

"Easy, girl."

Ruthie's chest constricted. The driver's door opened and a man stepped out. He was tall and muscular and dressed in black with a woman's stocking over his head.

She leaped from the buggy and started to run.

He ran after her.

She raced toward the woods that edged the roadway, then slipped in the rain-drenched soil but continued on.

"No!" she moaned. When she glanced back, her heart jammed her throat. He was right behind her.

She entered the woods, jumped over a fallen log and kept running.

His heavy footfalls sounded behind her.

Her side ached. Branches scratched her arms and snagged at her dress. A root caught her foot. She flailed her arms to keep from falling.

He grabbed her shoulder. She tumbled to the ground.

He kicked her ribs. The air whizzed from her lungs. She tried to crawl away. Her bonnet and *kapp* flew off. He grabbed her bun and yanked on her hair. She screamed in pain.

"Why were you running away from me?" he demanded.

"Who are you and what do you want?"

"I want your land."

"Are you with Prescott Construction?"

"They wanted to buy the land that belongs to me." He jammed a thumb against his chest.

"What?"

His sleeves were raised, exposing a tattoo that covered his skin and scratches around his wrists on both arms.

"I told you to leave," he said. "Your father wanted the farm to stay in the family. He thought you would run off with that boyfriend of yours."

"My father is dead," she said, confused by the man's ramblings.

"He wrote his will ten years ago, thinking you would abandon him. Our parents divided the land between your father and me when all of it should have gone to me. I'm the youngest. That's the Amish way. But they didn't trust me to farm all the land so they gave me a smaller, rocky portion and gave your father the land along the river."

He ripped off the stocking.

She startled, recognizing her father's brother. "Uncle Henry? *Datt* said you two had reconciled."

He laughed. "I begged forgiveness for my transgressions and for leaving the faith. I told your father we needed to be family again and that I would care for the land after you left if anything happened to him."

"I do not understand what you are saying."

"Your father said you were in love with Reuben Schlabach's son. He thought you would leave the farm and the Amish way of life so he had a will drawn up. You were to inherit the farm upon his death, but if you left the property, the land would automatically go to me."

"My *datt* thought I would abandon him?"

"Because you loved the Schlabach boy."

"But I did not leave with Noah."

"Yet the will remains. That's why I wanted you to leave. With you gone, the land would pass to me. I agreed to sell it to Prescott Construction, but today, I learned the foreman planned to double-cross me. He said he could buy the land on his own and didn't need me. Now he's out of the picture."

"You killed Brian Burkholder."

Her uncle sneered. "I made it look like Zimmer, the assistant foreman, killed him."

"I do not believe what you are saying," she countered, hoping her prideful uncle would reveal more information.

"The foreman and assistant foreman had argued recently," he told her.

Ruthie's ploy had worked, as he continued to talk.

"I borrowed Zimmer's red truck to make it seem like he was coming after you," he said.

Ruthie egged him on. "So you planted the murder weapon in his pickup?"

Henry nodded. "My plan worked. Law enforcement arrested him. He'll stand trial and go to jail, while I sell your land directly to Mr. Castle for far more than the foreman planned to give me."

"You do not care about the farm staying in the family. You only care about yourself."

"I gave you an opportunity to leave the mountain, but you were too stubborn. Now you'll have an accident on your farm that will take your life. The river is rising. How tragic if you die in the flood."

"No!"

"Get up. We're going back to my car."

"I am not going anywhere."

"You will unless you want me to harm Andrew."

Her blood froze. "Do not hurt my child."

He jerked on her arm. She stumbled to her feet.

"If you do what I say, the boy won't be harmed."

He tugged her arm behind her back. She gasped. The pain seared along her spine.

"You do not know where to find Andrew," she insisted.

"Don't be a fool. You can't hide anything from me, including your son. I've got him, and you won't be able to find him. Unless you cooperate."

Her heart nearly broke. "I will do whatever you say, but do not hurt Andrew."

He shoved her through the underbrush to where his car was parked and grabbed rope from the backseat. Working quickly, he tied her hands and feet and shoved her into the trunk.

"No, please. I will not cause a problem. Do not leave me in here."

"Just for a short while."

He slammed the trunk closed.

Her heart pounded nearly out of her chest.

She heard the creaking of the buggy. Was he hiding the rig in the wooded area? Few people traveled the road to Mattie's house. If the buggy was out of sight, no one would know she had been captured.

Noah was at the hospital waiting for her return. Mattie was at her house. How long would it be until someone realized she had disappeared?

Heart in her throat, Ruthie felt the engine start and the car begin to move.

If only Noah would come to find her, yet with the buggy out of view, he would never know what happened.

She raised her legs and kicked, trying to force open

the trunk, but it held and she remained locked in darkness. Tears burned her eyes and her heart broke thinking she might never see her boys and Noah again.

Simon slept fitfully. Each time he woke, he asked for his *mamm*.

Noah glanced at his watch. Ruthie hadn't been gone long, but he was concerned. Soon after she left, the sky had turned dark and a terrible storm had unleashed its fury.

He should have insisted on driving to Mattie's farm while Ruthie stayed with Simon. Although as upset as she had been about Andrew, she probably wouldn't have agreed.

Noah had thought getting away from the hospital for a short time would be good for her. Now he envisioned her soaking wet and struggling to keep the buggy on the road.

Once she arrived at her aunt's house and found Andrew doing well, he hoped she would remain there until the storm passed.

Noah checked the weather app on his phone. Rain was expected to continue well into the night.

Simon woke again. "Where's *Mamm*?"

"She went to Aunt Mattie's house to check on Andrew. She will return soon."

Simon glanced at the window and saw the downpour. "I worry she will have trouble in this storm."

Noah was worried, too.

Please, Gott, he prayed. *Protect Ruthie and keep her safe.*

Chapter Twenty-Five

The car stopped. Ruthie pulled up her legs, ready to strike. When the trunk opened, she kicked her uncle in the chest. He yanked her up and shoved her out of the car. A sharp piece of metal dug into her arm. She gasped and tried to butt him with her head.

"You never give up, do you? But you can't outsmart me."

"Where is Andrew?"

"I won't tell you."

"You are hateful."

He laughed. "You should have cooperated and left the mountain so I wouldn't have to use force."

"Why does Mr. Castle want the land?"

"Your farm and the Schlabach property sit at the source of the river. Redirecting the water at your end will send the river down a northern valley."

"So Castle Homes can have water to fill the lake, but what happens if the river cannot be diverted?"

"I can make it happen once the land is mine, but time is running out. Castle needs the lake filled by next week. I agreed to provide the water. If you hadn't delayed, I would already have the detour completed and the money in my bank account."

"You are hurting the farmers south of town who rely on the river."

"That's not my problem." He untied her legs but kept hold of her arm and shoved her forward. "Now get going into your house."

Ruthie stared at the churning river that had started to overflow its banks.

She thought back to her youth when the river had flooded and water had come into the house. She feared it would happen again. If only she could overpower the man and escape his grasp.

Where was Andrew? She would do nothing to bring harm to either of her sons. She would rather die herself than have anything happen to her boys.

Noah became increasingly concerned about Ruthie as the storm continued to pummel the area. Lightning cut through the sky and thunder roared.

He took Simon's hand. "How are you feeling?"

"Better. My head and stomach no longer hurt."

"Can you stay alone here at the hospital for a while? I need to drive to Aunt Mattie's house. Your mother went there to check on Andrew. She probably hasn't returned due to the storm. I'll bring her back in my truck."

"I will be fine. Do not worry about me."

"You're a good boy, Simon. Your mother's proud of you and so am I."

He smiled and Noah noticed a brightness in his eyes, which was encouraging.

"I'll come back as soon as I can."

"Be careful, Noah. This storm is bad."

He stopped at the desk to inform the nurse he was leaving.

"I'll keep checking on Simon," she assured him. "I have ice cream that I'm sure he would like for a snack."

Noah thanked the nurse, then hurried outside and ran to his truck. His clothes were drenched by the time he slipped behind the wheel. He shoved the key in the ignition and pulled out of the parking lot as the rain intensified. The day turned dark as night and thunder rumbled overhead.

His cell rang. He hit speed dial and turned the phone to speaker. Deputy Warren's voice.

"We hauled in that guy who lived in the woods and returned Mrs. Eicher's letter the day you visited the library."

"I told you Ruthie and I saw him yesterday at the Castle Home site. He's working for one of the painters."

"And claims he's renting a room and plans to make a better life for himself."

"You don't believe him?" Noah asked.

"I wasn't satisfied with some of Zimmer's responses. He's still being detained, but I'm not certain we've got the right guy."

"You think the man in the woods could be the killer?"

"I'm not sure, that's why I wanted to talk to him. He saw you and Mrs. Eicher heading to the foreman's trailer yesterday. He also saw the red truck racing along the lake road soon after you and Mrs. Eicher passed by."

"Did he identify Zimmer as the driver?"

"That's the thing. He's seen the assistant foreman on the building site, but Zimmer wasn't driving the truck. Another man was. An older guy. Early fifties, who sometimes hauls gravel for Castle."

"Are you saying Zimmer isn't the killer?"

"I'm saying there could be someone else we need to find. Be careful."

Noah disconnected and prayed again—the prayer he had continued to say since he had left the hospital.

"Protect Ruthie, Lord, and keep her safe."

Noah was worried. He had to find Ruthie. He had to find her now.

Chapter Twenty-Six

Ruthie struggled against the ropes around her hands and waist that held her bound to a kitchen chair. Her uncle had gone back to his car. The storm had grown worse, and she knew the water had to be rising higher. Her only hope was to free herself and escape while he was outside.

Using all her energy, she scooted the chair back toward the cabinet where she kept her cooking utensils. If only she could open the drawer, grab one of the knives and cut the ropes.

Between the booms of thunder, she listened for footsteps on the porch, then shoved the chair back again and again. Her legs ached with the effort. She glanced over her shoulder. A little farther and she would be near enough to try to open the drawer. If only she could.

Again, she inched the chair back, seeing the scratches it made on the floor. Nothing mattered except getting free. As unstable as her uncle acted, she knew he would never let her go.

She scooted back again. The chair was close. She raised her arms, tied behind her, and grasped the knob on the drawer, then tried to pull it open. She groaned. The chair was too close.

She inched the chair away from the counter, then raised her hands again. This time the drawer opened.

Pulling in a lungful of air, she stretched her arms even higher to grab one of the knives. Her fingers latched onto a handle. She lifted it out only to have it drop to the floor.

Discouraged, she glanced down. A spoon. Not what she needed.

She tried again, and a wave of euphoria swept over her as her fingers touched the sharp blade of a knife. She almost cried with relief when she pulled it free.

Working quickly, she turned the knife in her hands and rubbed the blade against the rope with a back-and-forth motion.

The blade nicked her finger. She gasped and repositioned it. The rope was thick and the knife dull, but she continued trying.

Outside, the storm bellowed. Lightning illuminated the darkness.

Footsteps sounded on the porch.

Frantically, she hacked at the rope.

The door opened. Her uncle stepped inside, carrying a briefcase, and glanced at her. His faced twisted. "What are you doing?"

"Nothing." She tucked the knife against her arm.

He grabbed the chair and turned her around.

"Aren't you clever?" He jerked the knife from her hand. The blade scraped her wrist.

"Where is Andrew?" she demanded.

"If you obey me, he won't be hurt."

"Is he here at the farm? The river is rising. Do you have him in one of the outbuildings?"

He opened his briefcase and removed a stack of papers. "I'm going to untie your hands, but if you try anything, I won't let Andrew go."

"Please," she said, "he is a little boy. Do not hurt him."

Henry pulled the kitchen table closer to Ruthie and untied her hands. She rubbed her wrists, feeling the circulation return.

He shoved a pen into her right hand and pointed to a line on the first paper.

"Sign your name here. The land goes to me because of your father's will. He placed the will in a safe deposit box at one of the banks. In case he was lying, I'll still have these signed forms deeding the farm to me."

"I do not know if my hand will work."

"Don't play games with me."

She took the pen and signed her name.

He turned to another page. "Sign here."

He pointed to another page, and another.

She dutifully signed on each line.

"Now let me know where you have taken Andrew. If anything has happened to him—"

She could not finish her sentence. The thought of her son being hurt cut into her heart.

Her uncle retied her hands behind her back and returned the signed papers to his briefcase.

"You're a fool, Ruthie, just like Ben said."

"You knew my husband?"

"What a waste of a man. He wasn't even a good poker player. He regretted marrying you, but he needed someplace to live. His family had kicked him out. You were an easy mark for him."

She did not care what he said about Ben and the way he had felt about her. There had been no love between them, though she had tried to be a dutiful wife. Somehow she had thought he had loved her in the beginning, though everything had changed too quickly.

"Tell me about Andrew," she pleaded.

The guy laughed. "Again, you're such a fool and so very gullible. I don't have Andrew. I tried to grab Simon in the hospital, but the nurses were always around so I followed you when you left town."

Relief swept over her and tears burned her eyes. Andrew must still be with Aunt Mattie, safe and protected.

"You tricked me," she said, "into signing the papers."

"I have your signature and that's all I need. Everyone will be upset about your passing."

"What?"

He glanced out the window. "The river is rising. The weather forecast is for continual rain for the next twelve hours. The water will enter the house soon."

Terror filled her, but she would not let him fool her again. She thought back to the flood when she was a girl. The water had come to the top of the kitchen counter. She glanced at that counter now, knowing her head would remain above water. Someone would eventually come to look for her. How long she could survive, she did not know, but she would not drown.

She wanted to rail against the man, yet she needed to placate him and play into his pity.

"Let me go. I will not say anything about you. I will not tell anyone that you forced me to sign the papers."

"Once again you are proving your foolishness. You would get that boyfriend of yours and run straight to the sheriff."

"I would not. I will talk Noah into signing over his property to you."

"That would be an added plus, but I realized I don't need his land. By shoring up the river on your side, the water will naturally form its own channel down the northern valley. I have gravel ready and sand to dam up the southern shore."

"The river is racing too quickly. You will never succeed, not when the water is this high."

"I worked on a dam in Chattanooga and know how to make it work."

She glanced at the cabinet. As soon as her uncle left, she would scoot the chair back again and get another knife from the drawer. This time she would be successful and cut through the rope.

"What are you thinking?" He stepped closer and saw the drawer. He pulled it open, then dumped the knives onto the counter and pushed them back toward the wall, too far for her to reach with her hands tied behind her back.

"And just in case you could get to the knives, I'll make sure you don't last long enough to try to free yourself."

Fear raced along her spine.

He grabbed the back of the chair and flipped it on its side.

Her head hit the floor, and she cried out in pain.

"I'll come back to remove the ropes after you're dead so no one will suspect foul play."

"Someone will see the marks on my wrists. They will know my death was not accidental. They will find you, Henry, and try you for murder."

He grabbed the briefcase and turned to gaze at her. "Your body will be bloated by the time they discover you, Ruthie. No one will look for marks on your wrists. Besides, I'm already a murderer."

"Please," she said.

He laughed, then hurried outside, slamming the door behind him.

Thunder rumbled overhead and another downpour of rain rattled against the tin roof.

Ruthie did not have long before the water would enter the house. She could raise her head a few inches off the floor, but once the water rose that high, she would not survive.

At least Andrew and Simon were safe. She loved them dearly. And Noah? She loved him, as well.

Noah turned off the mountain road and headed to Mattie's house. His heart was in his throat knowing something was wrong. Ruthie wouldn't have stayed away from the hospital this long no matter how bad the storm was.

The rain was blinding. Lightning zigzagged across the sky as if the storm was waging war against the earth.

He kept his eyes peeled as he drove, looking for signs that the buggy might have gone off the road. He crossed over a culvert that was swollen with rainwater.

His gut tightened—he feared Ruthie could have been caught in the rapid current.

The drive along the back road seemed to take forever. Every time he increased his speed, the vehicle would hydroplane. The pickup skidded twice. He eased up on the accelerator until he couldn't stand it any longer and then increased his speed again. He needed to find Ruthie as soon as possible and ensure she was all right.

He came around the final curve in the road and saw her aunt's house in the distance. After turning into the drive, he slammed on the brakes, leaped out of the truck and raced to the porch.

Aunt Mattie's eyes were wide when she opened the door. "Has something happened to Simon?"

Noah shook his head. "He's improving. I need to talk to Ruthie."

"Ruthie is not here. I thought she was at the hospital with you."

Noah's chest compressed and he exhaled a lungful of air. "She didn't stop here to check on Andrew?"

The boy ran to the door. "Noah, where's *Mamm*? And how is Simon?"

"Your brother is better." He didn't want to worry Andrew, but he needed to speak truthfully to Mattie.

She understood his hesitation. "Andrew, go get the cake I cut today. Noah can take it to the hospital for your brother and mother."

Once the boy raced into the kitchen, Mattie grabbed Noah's hand. "How long ago did Ruthie leave the hospital?"

"Long enough for her to have gotten here, had cake and returned." He raked his hand through his hair and turned to glance at the dark sky and torrential rain. "Where is she, Mattie?"

"I do not know."

Noah couldn't wait any longer. He raced to his truck and guided it back onto the road. Glancing in his rearview mirror, he saw Andrew on the porch holding a tin that, no doubt, held the cake. Much as he hated to disappoint the young boy, Noah had no time to waste. Ruthie was in danger. Had the man found her, and if so, where would he take her? Law enforcement was looking for him in town. The only place left was the mountain.

He reached for his cell and called the sheriff's department. The phone went to voice mail. With the bad weather, there was no telling where the deputies were needed. He envisioned accidents on the main road, perhaps flooding in the southern valley, downed power lines and people caught in the storm.

"This is Noah Schlabach. Ruthie Eicher is missing. I fear the man who attacked her has kidnapped her. I don't have any information, but do whatever you can to find her. I'm heading up the mountain to her property if the river hasn't already overflowed its banks. I'll try to keep you posted, but cell reception isn't good and the storm doesn't help."

He disconnected and threw the phone onto the console.

Needing an update on the rising river, he flipped on the radio. Static buzzed, followed by the announcer's voice.

"The main mountain road is flooded. Take the northern route if you're heading up Amish Mountain."

Noah's heart sank. The detour would take more time. Time he didn't have. Yet his instincts screamed that he had to get to Ruthie's farm.

He angled across one of the side roads and crossed the lower bridge to the northern shore that would lead to his father's property. He hoped the bridge connecting his farm to Ruthie's would still be standing.

Water covered the road, but he continued to drive at a rapid speed. Noah didn't care what happened to him, but he had to find Ruthie. Her life was in danger—he knew that for sure.

He had to find her before the terrible man who had

attacked her turned on her again. This time the man on the mountain wouldn't be satisfied with striking Ruthie and kicking her. This time he would kill her.

Chapter Twenty-Seven

Ruthie glanced at the woodstove and spotted the poker. Would the metal tip be sharp enough to cut through the rope?

She jerked back on the chair and inched her way toward the stove. Her cheek rubbed against the floor. She fisted her hands to counter the pain and kept moving the chair little by little. Her progress was slow, but anything was better than doing nothing. If there was hope, she would continue to fight for her life.

Water flowed under the front door and fanned out on the hardwood floors. A braided rug soaked up some of the moisture. A second surge of water flowed in, circled the rug and headed toward where she was lying. She pushed herself back again and again, nearing the stove as the water inched toward her. Another wave of water traveled across the main room and splashed against her arm.

Her heart nearly stopped.

She pushed again, then reached for the poker. It slipped from her hands and dropped to the floor behind her, knocking against her head.

As much as she wanted to cry, she would not sacrifice her precious energy when she was fighting for her life.

Again, she scooted the chair and repositioned her hands closer to the metal rod.

Another surge of water flowed around her ear.

She stretched her arms behind her and flailed her fingers, searching for the poker.

Her hands touched something hard and circular. She grabbed the metal rod, overcome with relief. Slowly she inched her fingers along the poker until she felt the blunt tip.

Blunt?

She shoved the rod against the rope, holding her bound hands, but without a sharp end, her efforts were for naught.

She closed her eyes. *Please,* Gott, *save me.*

When she opened her eyes, another wave of water streamed across the floor and splashed against her cheek. In a short time, the water would rise higher and cover her nose and her mouth.

Ruthie could not think of that now. She had to get free. But how?

Amish Mountain was barely visible with the low cloud cover and blinding rain. Noah gripped the wheel with white knuckles and forced his truck up the hill. The rain-soaked earth couldn't absorb any more moisture, so water covered the road.

Mudslides could be a problem. *Please,* Gott, *don't let that happen. I have enough worries trying to find Ruthie.*

The storm raged outside the truck and sounded like a monster attacking the earth.

Lightning brightened the sky, creating an eerie hue that flashed on and off.

The engine sputtered going around a curve. He eased his foot off the gas pedal. "Come on. Don't give out on me now."

Nearing the final turn, he held his breath and rounded the bend. His father's farmhouse and the bridge were still standing. In spite of the raging river, both structures remained intact. He spied a car parked on the distant shore.

"Stay with me, Lord," he prayed as he coaxed his truck over the rickety bridge that swayed in the storm. Water washed over the underpinnings and sloshed against the wheels of his pickup.

"Don't let the engine stall," he said aloud.

Once across the river, he parked on higher ground, then leaped from his truck. Thunder crashed overhead and rain pummeled him. For half a heartbeat, the storm ebbed before the next clap of thunder rumbled across the sky. In that momentary lull, Noah heard another sound— the sound of a loud engine.

He followed the noise around the back of the barn and down to the river. The rapid current was flowing at breakneck speed and the water had flooded over the riverbank.

The rain eased for a moment, and he saw a bulldozer pushing soil and debris into the water, forming a man-made dam. A dump truck sat parked nearby. Gravel sprayed across the side of the riverbed.

A guy dressed in black operated the bulldozer. The angry current tried to tear apart his work, but he backed up again and shoved an even larger mix of gravel and soil into the river.

Surely the man wasn't in his right mind to be operating heavy equipment at the edge of a flooding river, and no telling how he had gotten the bulldozer and dump truck up the mountain. Noah glanced around to ensure he didn't have an accomplice or two hiding in the bushes.

From what Noah could tell, the man was working alone, and he was making progress. Water spilled over the opposite bank of the river and washed down the mountain, along the northern valley Noah and Ruthie had seen when they'd toured Castle Homes.

Ruthie had been right. The guy wanted her land so he could detour the water and form a new river that would feed into Castle's lake.

Noah raced forward. The man backed up the bull-dozer, nearly running over Noah.

He grabbed the man's arm and yanked him from the seat. The guy swung his fist and hit Noah in the chin.

Ignoring the pain, he grabbed the man's arm again.

"Where is she?" Noah screamed above the roar of the storm. "What did you do with Ruthie?"

"Get outta my way. This is my land now."

Noah jabbed his fists into the guy's stomach. The man doubled over, coughing and gasping for air.

"Where is she?" Noah grabbed his shoulders and held him up. "Where's Ruthie?"

"I told you this land is mine. You're trespassing."

The guy struggled to free himself. Noah wrapped his hands around his chest and half dragged, half pushed him toward the barn. Using electrical tape from the tool rack, he bound his hands and feet, then dragged him to his pickup and hoisted him into the bed of the truck.

The guy groaned.

Noah grabbed his shirt and leaned into his face. "You've got one more chance. Where is she?"

The guy nervously flicked his gaze toward the Plank house.

"She's in there?" Noah shoved him aside and raced to the house. The river had already flooded over the porch.

"Ruthie?" Noah pushed open the door. All he could see was the rising water.

He called her name again. Movement by the wood-stove alerted him. An overturned chair.

His pulse raced. Ruthie was tied to the chair, with her nose and mouth underwater. At that instant, she raised up her head and grabbed a breath.

Heart in his throat, he ran to her, lifted her out of the water and righted the chair that still held her bound.

"Oh, Ruthie!" He found a knife on the nearby counter and cut through the ropes. All the while, she gasped for air, then coughed and sputtered.

"I tied up the guy who attacked you, but I didn't think I would find you in time." He looked into her eyes. "Talk to me. Are you okay?"

She rubbed her hands together and then patted her chest and coughed.

More water swept into the house.

"We need to get out of here now." Noah lifted her into his arms and carried her across the room, through the water and out the door. The rain pelted them, but he had Ruthie and he wouldn't let her go.

Chapter Twenty-Eight

Ruthie collapsed onto the seat of Noah's pickup. She was shaken to the core and kept thinking of what could have happened if Noah had not saved her. Overcome with emotion, she dropped her head in her hands and started to cry.

He climbed behind the wheel and pulled her into his arms. She nestled closer as the tears fell.

"Shhh," he soothed, rubbing her back and giving her time to regain her composure.

Warmed by his embrace and drawing strength from him, she eventually wiped her hands over her face. "You saved me, Noah. I am so grateful, but I am also wet and dirty."

He smiled. "You're beautiful and you're alive, but we need to get out of here before the water rises any higher."

He started the engine and turned onto the road heading up the mountain. "There's a narrow roadway that weaves around the back of Amish Mountain. It will take us longer to get to town, but it's far from the river. I'm driving directly to the hospital so the doctors can examine you. No telling what you were exposed to in the water."

"I need to see the boys."

"Andrew is fine. He's with Mattie. Simon's fever is down and he was feeling better when I left the hospital."

"The man who tried to kill me was my uncle Henry. He said he had Andrew and would harm him if I did not turn over my land to him. I signed the papers he provided in order to save my son."

"Both boys are being cared for, and we'll determine if the papers you signed are legal later." He wrapped a blanket over her, and she pulled it close.

"You saved me in the nick of time, Noah. I could not have lasted a second longer. The water kept rising, and..." She paused for a long moment. "I...I did not think I would survive."

"And I didn't think I would ever find you."

"My uncle stopped me on the way to my aunt's house and forced me into the trunk of his car. He hid the buggy in the woods. I am sure Buttercup is frightened to death by now."

"We'll get her. I looked for you when I drove to Mattie's farm, fearing I would find the buggy crashed on the side of the road."

"Which was almost the case. Where is Henry now?"

"In the back of my truck."

"What?" Glancing through the rear window, she saw her uncle and sighed, overcome with regret that her own kin had tried to kill her.

"Henry needed to get rid of me so he could have the farm." She explained about her father's will that supposedly gave her uncle rights to the land if she ever left the property. "The foreman planned to buy the property from him, then changed his mind. Uncle Henry killed him and tried to kill me."

Noah rubbed her shoulder. "It's over, Ruthie."

"*Yah*, but I will feel better once I know the boys are all right."

"We'll get to the hospital as soon as possible."

"Did you talk to the real-estate agent about your land?" she asked.

He nodded.

Ruthie's heart sunk. Why had she thought Noah might change his mind?

The flashing lights of the deputy sheriff's squad car appeared on the road ahead. Noah pulled up beside the car and rolled down his window, obviously happy to see Deputy Warren.

"I got your voice mail, Noah. Looks like you didn't need me."

Noah explained what had happened and then pointed his thumb to the rear of the truck. "I've got the man who attacked Ruthie tied up in the rear. Arrest him, Deputy, for the murder of Brian Burkholder, as well as the attempted murder of Ruthie Eicher."

The deputy looked at Ruthie. "Did he hurt you, ma'am?"

"He tied me up and left me in my flooded home to drown, but Noah saved me."

The deputy stepped from his car and slapped Noah's shoulder. "You're a good man, Noah Schlabach. We could use you around this neck of the woods if you decide to stay."

Noah squeezed Ruthie's hand before he stepped to the pavement and followed the deputy to the rear of his pickup. Ruthie slipped from the pickup and watched as he lowered the back of the truck bed. Noah grabbed the tape binding her uncle's legs, pulled him to the edge and then eased him to his feet.

"I'm innocent," Henry railed. "Noah Schlabach trespassed on my property," her uncle said to the deputy. "I've got the deed in my briefcase."

"And where's your briefcase?" the deputy asked.

"Probably floating down the river," Noah said as he herded the guy toward the rear door of the squad car that Deputy Warren held open.

"We'll take you downtown and have a long talk. You can tell me about beating up a defenseless woman and leaving her to die in a flood."

Once Henry was secured in the rear of the squad car, the deputy addressed Ruthie. "Ma'am, I'll connect with you later and take your statement. Don't worry about this guy. He's staying behind bars."

Noah shook the deputy's hand and then helped Ruthie back into the pickup.

The deputy raced down the mountain, siren screaming and lights flashing as Noah climbed behind the wheel.

"We'll take it a bit slower," he said with a smile.

"Just so we get to the hospital so I can see Simon."

"We're heading there now."

People stared at Ruthie's wet and muddy clothing when she got to the hospital, but she did not care. All she wanted was to see Simon and ensure her son was all right.

When she stepped into his room, her heart nearly burst with relief. Not only was Simon sitting up in bed looking bright-eyed and energetic, but Andrew and Aunt Mattie were also there. The boys were playing checkers while Mattie sat knitting in a nearby chair.

Andrew spied her first. *"Mamm,"* he shouted. Hopping off the bed, he raced with open arms to hug her.

"Oh, Andrew, it is so good to see you."

She gave him a hug and, still holding his hand, hurried to the bed and hugged Simon with her other arm. "You are cool. Your fever is gone."

"And I feel strong, *Mamm*. The nurse said I can go home tomorrow."

Home? She worried where that would be with the flooded house on Amish Mountain.

"We were worried about you," Mattie said as she placed her knitting on a bedside table and hurried to embrace Ruthie.

"I am a mess."

"You look wonderful. One of the Amish farmers who lives near me spotted your buggy and mare. Both are safe in my barn. After that, Andrew and I called the Amish taxi and rode here in his car. We were worried. Simon and Andrew suggested we pray together, which is what we did. The boys knew that *Gott* would answer their prayers."

Ruthie smiled with maternal pride and gratitude for her two sons. *"Gott* did answer your prayers, boys. He brought Noah, who saved me from that hateful man. The sheriff has him locked up now, so we no longer have to worry."

"What about the farm, *Mamm*?" Simon asked. "Are we staying or leaving?"

"We are staying, Simon. Although we will have to work hard to clean the house after the flooding."

Simon looked at Noah, his gaze intense. "What about you? Are you staying or leaving?"

Ruthie was not ready for the boys to learn that Noah

was leaving. She needed to prepare them a bit before she gave them the news. They would be so disappointed, and she did not want this moment of reunion to be ruined with more upset.

"Perhaps Noah will tell us at a later time."

"No, Ruthie, I can tell you now."

"I do not think that is wise. Simon is just starting to improve, and we are all tired and have been through so much."

"Which is the perfect time to tell you that I'm staying."

"What?"

"Yay!" the boys cheered in unison. Andrew grabbed Noah around the waist and Simon slipped from bed and hugged him, as well.

"Simon, get back in bed," Ruthie insisted.

She felt light-headed and unsure she had heard Noah correctly. "You are not selling your land?"

"That's correct. I'm staying on Amish Mountain. It's my home. I have wonderful neighbors and an Amish community that I never should have left."

"But—"

"I made a mistake years ago, Ruthie. I left you and I left my heart with you. I've tried to make a life for myself, but I was going through the motions when all along I wanted to be back here with you."

He glanced at the boys. "And with Simon and Andrew, these wonderful young men who have also stolen my heart."

Ruthie was confused and unable to share in the boys' excitement. Had Noah been away from the Amish faith so long he did not realize that which would continue to separate them?

"Is there a problem, Ruthie?" he asked, no doubt seeing her concern.

Why did he not realize they could never be together when…?

"You—you are *Englisch*, Noah," she blurted out.

He smiled. "Not for long. I plan to talk to the bishop as soon as possible."

Had she heard him correctly? "Are you sure this is what you want to do?"

"I've never been surer about anything. As long as you don't mind me staying. I know you're still grieving and—"

She gripped his arm and stepped closer. "I grieved for you when you left. We must have exchanged hearts because you took mine with you."

"You're sure?"

"Cross my heart." She laughed as tears of joy flowed down her cheeks.

"I never thought you would want me back, Ruthie, so I never came home."

"We both made mistakes, but that is in the past, and what is important is the present." She looked at the boys. "And the future."

"A future together, Ruthie."

She nodded and rested her head on Noah's shoulder as they both smiled at Simon and Andrew. "Yes, dear Noah, a future where we are all together."

The nurse knocked and entered the room. "Looks like everyone's been out in the storm."

Ruthie explained to the nurse some of what happened.

"The doctor is at the nurses' station. Let's have him check you over. He might want to run some tests."

Before Ruthie left the room, Mattie had Noah call

the Amish taxi for her. "Andrew and I will go home and prepare the house. I want all of you to stay with me until the flooding ends and your homes are ready to be lived in again."

"That is so generous," Ruthie said.

"We are family, Ruth Ann. Family takes care of its own. We have been separated too long. We will not let that happen again."

Ruthie hugged her aunt.

"I will ask the taxi driver to return to the hospital with clean clothes for you to wear," Mattie said. "We are about the same size. I even have a new *kapp* that should fit you. I am certain the nurse will let you shower here. I doubt she wants the river mud in her hospital room."

"Thank you, Mattie. We will see you tomorrow."

After Mattie and Andrew left, Ruthie headed for the nurses' station. The doctor prescribed an antibiotic due to the water she had swallowed. "If you start feeling sick, I'll want to see you again."

"What about our well situation?"

"I doubt your well water was the problem, Mrs. Eicher, since your younger son didn't get sick, but you'll need to have it tested after this flooding."

Ruthie told him about the two milk jugs and her concern that Henry had contaminated one of the jugs.

The doctor rubbed his jaw and nodded. "That would certainly explain why only one of your sons became ill. If not for the flood, we could culture the jugs, although I'm sure they're long gone by now. I'm just glad you brought Simon to the ER in time. We'll keep him on oral meds for the next ten days. If he shows any signs of reoccurring infection, you'll need to bring him back."

"Thank you for taking care of my son."

"He's a good boy. I hope we'll see more of you and your family in town."

"*Yah*, we will come often, I am certain."

Later, once she had showered and changed into the clothing Mattie sent, Ruthie started to relax. The deputy stopped by and had her write up what had happened and then sign her statement.

"Don't worry," Deputy Warren assured her. "Henry Plank won't get out on bail. He'll stay behind bars, and I feel sure the jury, when he goes to trial, won't have any problem with their verdict. You'll have to testify, ma'am, but he confessed to killing Brian Burkholder and attacking you. He also said he had tainted some milk left outside at your house."

The deputy glanced at Simon. "That might be what caused your boy to get sick."

Ruthie was relieved that the well water had not been the problem and thankful for the doctor and medical staff at the hospital.

"Mr. Plank said you had signed papers he had downloaded off his computer that deeded the land to him. We talked to one of the county lawyers who assured us the forms you signed, if they ever turn up after that flood, would not be legally binding."

"I am relieved," Ruthie said, "and I appreciate you checking with a lawyer."

"Happy to help, ma'am."

The deputy glanced out the window. "I doubt you folks have heard what happened. That dam the guy managed to put in place detoured a good bit of water into that northern valley, which means the south side of town suffered no flooding."

"So his plan had positive results."

"The townspeople who didn't get their shops flooded feel that way, although the construction in the Castle Homes area has a problem."

"What happened?" Noah asked.

"Water washed out some of their new construction. A number of folks who planned to purchase homes have changed their minds. The Atlanta paper published an online story about the foreman's death and people are calling to say they're not interested in buying a Castle home."

The deputy held up his hand. "There's more. The bank said if Castle can't make this month's mortgage payment, his land will go to foreclosure."

"Castle will lose everything?" Ruthie asked.

"Yes, ma'am. He's talking about a development in Mississippi that he plans to tackle next."

"He's always trying to make it rich," Noah said.

The deputy nodded in agreement. "Money and power are important to Mr. Castle. That is a shame. He needs to learn the importance of truth and service to others."

Deputy Warren paused for a moment and then added, "There's an interesting side story that the Atlanta reporter uncovered. Brian Burkholder's son, Prescott, lived in Mr. Castle's Chattanooga development that flooded. Seems Prescott saved a lot of folks' lives that night, including children who couldn't swim and wouldn't have survived without him. He went back to get a young family with a little girl named Mary, but he didn't make it. They all perished, but the young man was a hero for sure. That's why Burkholder named the company after his son. He planned to use any profits he earned from Castle to help the survivors of that flood."

"By any chance, do you know the name of the family Prescott tried to save?" Noah asked.

"Seth was the man's first name." The deputy rubbed his jaw. "Give me a minute and I'll remember the last name."

Ruthie looked at Noah's expectant gaze and reached for his hand.

The deputy nodded. "Seth Schlabach." His eyes widened as he glanced at Noah. "Any relation?"

Stepping closer, Ruthie wrapped her arm around Noah's waist. She could sense the lump in his throat when he spoke.

"Seth Schlabach was my brother."

The deputy patted Noah's shoulder. "I'm sorry for your loss."

"It helps to know that someone tried to save them."

"Just like you saved me," Ruthie said.

Deputy Warren stood quietly for a long moment and she knew he had been touched, as well.

Finally, he said, "I talked to some of the local townspeople, Mrs. Eicher. They want to help clean up your property."

"I—I never thought they cared, although the bishop and some of the women stopped by the farm a few times, usually when Ben was in town gambling. I refused to see them. It was my hurt pride after the church had shunned my husband. I understood why it happened, but my heart remained closed to their outreach even after Ben died."

The deputy nodded. "Folks feel real bad about you having to manage the farm by yourself. I talked to the bishop. He plans to visit you soon. The district will pay for Simon's hospital bills."

Tears burned Ruthie's eyes.

"The bishop said he hopes you'll come back to Sunday services."

She smiled and looked at Simon. "That would be *gut*."

"I need to talk to him, as well," Noah said.

"You all are staying in town for the next few days?"

"My aunt Mattie has room for us. You can find us there."

The deputy smiled. "I'll let the bishop know."

Noah and Ruthie walked the deputy to the elevator and said goodbye to him there.

A small waiting room was across the hall. Noah took Ruthie's hand and guided her into the room, then pulled the door closed behind them.

"I wanted to talk to you in private, Ruthie."

"What is it?" she asked, suddenly worried. "Have you changed your mind about staying?"

"No. I'm here for good. But I wanted to ask you something and perhaps it's too soon with Ben gone such a short time."

"What is it, Noah?" She was even more concerned.

"Ruthie, I've loved you forever. I told you that earlier, and it's true. You've always had my heart. Coming back, I realized how foolish I had been, how stupid. I had everything, and I left it here so that I could make my own way because of my father and my lack of understanding. I wasn't man enough to forgive him, so I caused you and Simon so much pain."

"It is over, Noah."

"No, Ruthie. I don't want it to be over. I want it to be the beginning of us together. You and the boys and me. I'm not doing this very well because I'm not sure what you will say and that has me tongue-tied."

He hesitated and then took her hands and stared into

her eyes. "Ruthie, will you forgive me and let me make it up to you? I want to marry you when you have time to sort through everything that has happened. I love both your boys as my own and promise to be the best father I can be to Simon and Andrew. Will you give me a second chance?"

He hesitated for a moment and then added, "Will you marry me?"

"Oh, Noah, you do not need a second chance. You have always had my heart. I have never stopped loving you. Yes, I will marry you. Nothing would make me happier and I know the boys will be overjoyed, too."

"We don't have to rush into anything. I'll need to be baptized first."

"We have waited so long. Your baptism cannot come soon enough."

He pulled her close and lowered his lips to hers, and everything she had ever wanted in life came to fruition in that one kiss. The promise of a future together, of more children, of a new home on the mountain and a wonderful life with Noah as her husband.

"I have never loved anyone else," she whispered as he kissed her again and again.

Eventually, she pulled back and giggled like a schoolgirl. "Simon will wonder what happened to us."

"He'll know something's going on by the way you're blushing."

"And you." She laughed. "You have the biggest smile I have ever seen."

"That's because you've made me the happiest man in the world."

Arm in arm, they walked back to Simon's room, to see their son. Tomorrow at Mattie's house they would tell both boys about Noah's desire to return to the Amish faith and their upcoming marriage. When the boys were older, they would tell them who Simon's father really was. Ruthie felt certain the information would be well received.

As they stepped into Simon's room, Ruthie glanced out the window. The rain had stopped and the sun was shining. In the distant sky, she saw the most beautiful rainbow as a sign from *Gott* that the storm had ended and the future would be bright and filled with love.

Epilogue

"Hurry, boys," Noah called to Simon and Andrew. They both ran from the house wearing their new straw hats and athletic shoes. Andrew stopped on the porch to tie his laces, then hopped down the stairs and raced to the buggy.

"I can run so fast now." His smile was wide and his eyes bright.

"Race you to Aunt Mattie's mailbox and back," Simon challenged.

Noah laughed as he watched the boys run. Andrew won but only because Simon slowed so his younger brother could pass by him.

Returning to the buggy, Simon winked at Noah, who winked back.

"Andrew's growing so fast," Noah said to Simon. "Soon he will be as tall as you."

Andrew stood on tiptoe and came up to Simon's chin.

"Yah." Simon joined in the fun. "He is tall like a weed."

"I am tall like a sweetgum tree," the younger boy countered.

"Then you produce spiky seed pods that cause pain when I step on them," Simon added.

Andrew shook his head. "Not with our new shoes. We do not have to worry where we step now."

"As long as you remember to wear your rubber boots when there is mud," Noah cautioned.

"Like after the flood?"

"Yah." Noah nodded. "You were *gut* workers as we swept the mud from the old house."

"Mamm said it still smells."

"That's why we're building the new house."

"Where we will live after your wedding."

"Yah, Andrew." Noah patted the boy's shoulder. "That's right. A new home for our new family."

Simon rubbed Buttercup's mane. "Andrew and I were talking about the wedding when we went to bed last night."

"Oh?" Noah would have enjoyed hearing that conversation.

Andrew stepped closer. "We are both glad you are going to be our new *datt.*"

Noah's heart warmed. "Thank you, boys. I'm glad, as well."

"But," Simon added, "it does not seem that you are a new *datt.*"

"Meaning what?" Noah asked, confused by the boy's comment.

"Meaning it seems that you are our *datt.* Not a new one, but the one who we have waited for all our lives."

Noah wanted to say something about Ben being a *gut datt,* but he was overcome with gratitude and did not want to change anything about the moment as he gazed at his son.

"You have always been in my heart, Simon." He glanced at Andrew. "And you, as well, Andrew. So thank you for allowing me to have a place in your family. Thank you for allowing me to be your *datt*."

He opened his arms and the boys stepped into his embrace. Noah's heart soared with joy for these two sons of his. He had asked *Gott* to forgive him for leaving Ruthie so long ago. She had endured so much. The boys had, too. Now they were together as a family, which was more than Noah deserved and more than he had ever expected, but then Ruthie had assured him that *Gott* was a generous provider.

Ruthie stepped from the kitchen, carrying a basket filled with their picnic lunch. Simon ran to help her and placed the basket carefully in the rear of the buggy.

"Climb in, boys." Noah motioned them into the buggy. "Let's go to our new house and enjoy the lunch your *mamm* prepared for us."

Aunt Mattie came onto the porch and waved. "Remember the bishop is coming for dinner this evening."

"We'll be home in plenty of time," Noah promised as he flicked the reins and encouraged Buttercup up Amish Mountain.

The sun was bright and the air smelled sweetly of honeysuckle.

"It will be *gut* to move back to the mountain after the house is finished," Simon said.

Noah reached for Ruthie's hand. "Remember, Simon, home is anywhere as long as we're together."

Ruthie's eyes beamed and her skin glowed. The lines of worry and concern that had weighed her down were gone, replaced with an infectious joy that he remembered from their youth.

The boys sang as they rode up the mountain, their voices harmonizing. Ruthie and Noah joined in, and between the songs, they laughed and joked.

Turning onto the farm, they passed the old house and headed to the new one, positioned higher on the rise and away from the river. Even if it flooded again, the water wouldn't come into their new home.

The boys hopped down and raced along the meadow, chasing butterflies and enjoying the fresh air and the open spaces.

Noah pulled Ruthie close and pointed to the valley. "Castle Homes is gone and the area will soon bear new growth as the trees return."

"It is like a distant memory that I do not want to recall." She squeezed his hand. "All I want to think about is our wedding and our future together."

"The boys told me they're glad I will be their new *datt*, then added that it seemed they had been waiting for me all along. I should have corrected them, but my heart was overflowing with love for both of them and I didn't want to spoil the moment."

"I told you, Noah, you have always been in my heart. They knew you because I carried you within me. My love for you never ended, and even the years when we were apart, you were with me."

"You led me back to the mountain, Ruthie, and back to the Amish faith. I thank *Gott* for that."

"You returned when I needed you most. You saved us from my uncle. I might have left my land, and look what I would have lost."

They stared at the valley that stretched below and the gentle river that flowed between their properties.

"The new bridge looks sturdy," Ruthie said. "You did a *gut* job rebuilding it."

"The underpinnings survived the flood, and the bridge stayed intact long enough for me to save you. My father built that bridge soon after he and my mother married. I have been remembering those happy times when Seth and I were children."

"You have forgiven your *datt*?"

"*Yah*, and that forgiveness has healed the wound within me that festered for so long."

Ruthie smiled. "I found my father's will along with a note he wrote to me explaining that he knew you and I were meant to be together, but he also knew the farm needed to stay within the family. Henry had convinced my father that he wanted to reconcile and be part of the family again so my *datt* arranged for the farm to go to him if I moved away from the mountain."

"Your *datt* loved you, Ruthie."

She nodded. "In his own way, he did love me."

"Now, with my father's land and your father's land joined together, we will have a flourishing farm."

"You will teach the boys to be *gut* farmers."

Noah wrapped his arm more tightly around her waist. "There will be much to do, but they are hard workers, like their mother."

She smiled and scooted closer.

"I am glad the new house will be ready before the wedding," he said. "Your aunt Mattie told me the boys can stay with her for a few days following the service so we can enjoy our new home together."

"What do you plan to do when we're alone?" Ruthie asked.

"Tell you how much I love you and have always loved

you. I want to share every moment of every day with you, Ruthie. Together we'll farm the land and help our boys grow into wonderful men."

"And other children?" she asked, her eyes twinkling.

"That's something I'm planning for. Little girls who look like you and boys who look like Simon. We can add on to the house, if need be. I also want to renovate my father's home. It's rundown and needs work, but someday Simon might want to live there."

Ruthie nodded. "With his wife and children."

"Our grandchildren." Noah smiled. "We have a wonderful life ahead of us."

She snuggled deeper into his embrace. "The future sounds better than I ever could have imagined, Noah."

"I love you, Ruthie. I've always loved you. Thank you for forgiving me and inviting me back into your life."

She shook her head. "Noah, I told you. You have always been with me. I never said goodbye, because deep down in my heart I knew you would come back to me."

She raised her lips to his. "And you did."

* * * * *

HIDDEN IN AMISH COUNTRY

Dana R. Lynn

To my husband, Brad. Even after so many years, you are still my best friend and the love of my life.

Fear thou not; for I am with thee:
be not dismayed; for I am thy God:
I will strengthen thee; yea, I will help thee;
yea, I will uphold thee with the right hand
of my righteousness.
—*Isaiah* 41:10

Chapter One

Someone was watching her.

Sadie Standings whipped her head around so fast that her light brown hair swung across her face, blocking her vision. Shoving her fingers through her hair to push it out of the way, she searched the area behind her. The parking lot at the local shopping mall was busy, filled with people who had stopped on their way home from work, but none of the other shoppers appeared to be looking in her direction. Seeing no one suspicious, she scrunched her eyes into a squint, desperately trying to catch sight of whoever was watching her. Still, she saw nothing.

She should have been comforted.

She wasn't. Unease still pricked at her.

Despite all evidence to the contrary, she knew that she was under surveillance. In fact, she had known since the day before when she had spotted the man with the cold blue eyes watching her as she left the post office. He was so familiar. When she had seen him, she had a flash of what she thought may have been a memory, but it had made no sense. In her mind, she could hear a cold voice calling to her, shouting, but couldn't make out the words. Was it a threat? A warning? Although she couldn't understand the words, the tone was harsh.

Although it seemed improbable, she knew that she had seen him somewhere before and instinctively cringed. A chill had run through her when his posture stiffened at her reaction. Had she offended him? She didn't think so. Since then, she'd had the sensation of hard eyes boring into her. It was like walking around with a target on her back, like the one her brother used when sighting in his rifle before hunting season.

The spot between her shoulder blades tingled again, like a spider skittering across her skin. He was there. Somewhere he was out there, watching her. Briefly, the idea of going to the police crossed her mind, but she quickly vetoed it. What would she tell them? That she believed someone she'd bumped into was following her, but she hadn't actually *seen* him following her? Oh, and she thought she might have met him before, but had no real recollection of doing so. Yeah, right. They'd think she was crazy or making the story up.

Thankfully, she was in a parking lot full of other shoppers, so there was little chance that anyone would come after her. Still, she didn't like the feeling of being out in the open. Hoisting her purse higher on her shoulder, she held the bag close to her body and pushed herself to move faster. The October wind bit into her skin as she practically ran the last few feet to her car. Her eyes teared at the cold. She didn't care what the people around her thought. Every instinct inside her was screaming at her to flee.

She held out the key fob and pressed the unlock button several times as she approached her vehicle. The lights flashed in two short bursts. Opening the driver's side door, she threw herself inside. Her elbow slammed into the steering wheel in her haste. She ignored the sharp pain that shot down her arm. She pushed the key into the ignition with fingers that shook. The first time she tried to turn the key, it was stuck and wouldn't move. Not now. She'd had trouble with the ignition jamming before. Thoughts of being stranded here while someone with malicious intent drew closer crowded into her mind. Clenching her teeth, she held her breath and turned the steering wheel to the left. When it clicked, she tried to turn the key again.

Relief flooded through her as the engine roared to life. The sooner she arrived home and was locked inside her house, the better she'd feel. She was concerned that someone might try to break into her house, but she shoved that fear aside. She had good locks, and she didn't live alone in the house her family had owned for the past fifteen years. Her brother would be home shortly.

Pulling out of the parking lot, she sighed, allowing the tension that had built up inside her to drain away. She had half-expected someone to follow her, but no one did. Maybe she was being paranoid.

Suddenly her confidence that she had recognized the man dwindled. He probably just had one of those faces that looked vaguely like someone she had known. Even with the doubt, she couldn't completely shake the sensation that she had escaped from some nebulous danger.

She was being ridiculous.

She neared the intersection. Wow. She needed to pay attention to where she was going. She hadn't realized that she had driven so far already. She tapped the brake to slow as she neared the stop sign.

Her car didn't slow. Her insides quivered.

She pushed harder on the brake. In horror, she glanced down to see that her foot was all the way to the floor-board.

Her brakes weren't working.

The car stopped to the left started into the inter-section. She was going to wreck! Slamming the heel of her hand against the horn, she let out three sharp blasts. The driver jerked to a halt, yelling angrily as Sadie vroomed past.

She held the steering wheel in a white-knuckled grip and leaned forward, her eyes frantically searching the passing roads.

In less than a mile, she'd be at another busy inter-section. How far could she travel before she collided with someone? Making a split decision, she wrenched the wheel to the side and peeled off onto a dirt road. The road was at a slight incline. Her stomach began to set-tle as the vehicle started to slow as it continued uphill.

The relief vanished when she realized that on the other side of the incline was a steep drop. Her mouth was dry. The moment she crested that hill, her car would begin to accelerate again.

Frantically, she stomped on the brake, hoping against all logic that the brake would suddenly begin to work again.

It didn't. As she neared the top, she knew with utter clarity that if she didn't figure out a way to stop the car, she was going to crash and possibly kill herself and any-one in her path.

"*Dat*, they're going to crash!"

Ben Mast heard his son's shout a mere moment be-fore he heard the roar of a vehicle approaching way too fast. Throwing his hammer down on his work bench, he rushed out of the brown log-sided structure and raced down the gravel driveway to his seven-year-old son Nathaniel's side.

The red compact car swerved wildly down the hill, tires spinning on the slick surface.

Ben grabbed Nathaniel and dragged him back from the road, despite the boy's protests. If the driver left the road, he didn't want his son to become a victim of some *Englischer's* recklessness. His lips tightened in anger. Didn't these people care that others might be out on these roads? He knew for a fact there was a sign posted saying that children lived on this street.

The car zoomed past, the high-pitched whine of the engine searing the silent afternoon. He caught a glimpse of the driver's face and saw sheer panic. Why didn't she try to slow down?

A familiar clopping noise gained his attention. He whipped his head around, mouth so dry he couldn't have swallowed if he'd wanted to. A horse was coming up the hill. It was pulling a buggy with an Amish couple and several children. The man pulled on the reins, but the car was still coming. Where could the family go? Ben felt the inevitability of the collision clenching his stomach painfully.

"*Gott*, help them!" he shouted out.

The car swerved to the side, careening off the side of the road and plowing into an ancient maple tree with a horrendous crash. The tree shuddered, and the hood of the small car crunched in like it was made of cardboard. Steam burst from the engine, with a long, loud hiss.

There was no movement inside the car. Fearing the worst, Ben turned urgently to his son. "Go to Caleb and Lovina's," he said, pointing to the house across the street. "Caleb has a phone in his business office. Ask him to call for help."

Most of the houses on the road belonged to Amish families. Although there were a few *Englischer* homes, as well. Lovina and Caleb were their closest neighbors.

Nathaniel's head bobbed in a hurried nod, then he shot off across the street. Ben waited until he saw his son was with Lovina before he dashed down the street to the car. He knew that Caleb was probably already calling but giving Nathaniel a purpose would keep him out of harm's way. Ben reached the car and saw that the front windows had shattered upon impact. Glass crunched under his feet as he approached the driver's door.

"Miss?" The woman inside the car was hunched over the steering wheel, but he could see part of her face through the curtain of light brown hair. Blood was running down her cheek. Taking care not to cut his arm, he reached in through the broken window and placed his fingers on the side of her neck, feeling for a pulse. He found one. It was strong and steady. Ben sighed and closed his eyes, murmuring a soft prayer of thanksgiving.

The driver of the buggy stepped down to see if he could help. Ben heard the cries of children in the buggy. Looking up, he also saw that the woman sitting in the front looked very pregnant and quite ill.

"*Nee, denke.* Why don't you take your family home? My son went to Caleb's to call the ambulance."

The man nodded. "Once I get my wife and children home, I will come back to see if you need me."

Ben agreed, but his attention was back on the vehicle. He looked at the front of the car and frowned. There was so much damage. He didn't see how she could have escaped injury; possibly she had internal bleeding. She'd have to go to the hospital. He flinched. He had lost his wife to a cancer that no one had been aware of until it was too late. Their unborn daughter had also perished. The hospital where they had died would forever be stamped in his memory. He never wanted to step inside one of those places again.

He looked again at the woman. It would be easier to decide what to do if the door weren't in the way. If it even opened. He looked doubtfully at how the frame had been bent on impact. He had to try it, though. To his surprise, he was able to wrench the door open. It swung wide and hung at an odd angle, but he was already focused on the occupant of the car. She was so still. He wished he could see her legs better. He wondered if he should try and pull her from the vehicle but decided against it. He didn't want to risk hurting her any more than she already was.

"Is she alive?" Caleb's deep voice startled him. He'd been so wrapped up in his inspection that he hadn't heard his neighbor approaching.

"*Jah*. I can't tell how bad she's hurt, but she's alive."

Caleb wrinkled up his nose. "What's that smell?"

Ben froze. The distinct sharp odor of gasoline rose to his nostrils. Bending down, he saw the gas was dripping from her car. She must have punctured the line during the crash. He reversed his earlier decision. She might have internal injuries, but if the car exploded, she'd be dead.

"Let's move her from the car," Ben said.

The other man grunted in response. Between the two of them, they slowly maneuvered the woman from the vehicle. Ben surveyed her for any other signs of damage as he helped Caleb carry her across the street to his porch. There was blood on her left arm, but other than that and the cut on her cheek, she appeared to be whole.

He looked around. Some of the neighbors had emerged from their houses to see what was happening. "Stay back," he yelled a warning. "There might be a gas leak."

Some of them stayed where they were, although several went back into their homes, shooing their children ahead of them.

Sirens sounded in the distance. As they zoomed closer, Nathaniel ran up to him and stared down at the woman.

"Is she going to die, *Dat*?" The little boy's voice trembled. It broke his heart to hear it. He wanted to say no, but he would never lie to his child. Nathaniel had already learned the hard truth of human frailty. Although Ben and his son did not speak of his wife's illness, he knew that Nathaniel had not forgotten the agony of watching his mother waste away and die. How could he forget it?

"I don't know, Nathaniel. It's in *Gott's* hands. We have called the ambulance, that's all we can do."

The ambulance arrived. Ben waved at them to pull up the driveway. A police car pulled up behind the accident, red and blue lights flashing. The paramedics jumped down from their vehicle and rushed to the young woman lying on the porch. With calm efficiency, they started checking her vital signs.

"You shouldn't move someone from a vehicle if you don't know the extent of their injuries," one of the paramedics informed Caleb and Ben.

Caleb grunted, unimpressed. Ben felt it was up to him to give an explanation.

"*Jah*, I know that. We smelled gasoline and feared it was too dangerous to leave her in the car."

He watched as they lifted the still-unconscious woman onto a stretcher. Something about her pale face surrounded by wavy light-brown hair tugged at him. Almost like a memory, but hazy. Hopefully they would find some identification in the car and be able to notify her next of kin. His mind again traveled to the hospital where he had spent the last day of his Lydia's life. It had seemed to him such a place should have been filled with warmth to comfort patients but was instead filled with *Englisch* technology. The idea of the stranger waking up alone in such a place bothered him, although he told himself that it wasn't his concern.

He had done his part. He had made sure the emergency personnel were called. She was being well cared for. If she had family, they would soon be with her.

It didn't help. What if she didn't have family?

He couldn't get the horrified expression on her face as she barreled down the hill out of his mind. Had she run into the tree on purpose to avoid the buggy?

The police were finishing up their inspection of the car. The tow truck arrived and hooked it up.

"Not that she'll be able to do anything with this," the driver remarked, chomping on a piece of gum. "I'm guessing the insurance adjuster will say it's a total loss."

"Why'd she crash? Did you see what happened?" an officer asked Ben.

He shook his head. "I saw her coming down the hill. It looked like she couldn't stop, but that's all I know."

The officers finished up, and within twenty minutes the street was quiet again.

But Ben remained unsettled. Something about the situation continued to eat at him.

"*Dat*. I found this." Nathaniel held up something for his father to inspect. It was a cell phone. Ben's brow furrowed. It had probably slipped from the woman's pocket when he and Caleb had carried her to the porch. The Amish didn't use cell phones, not even in their businesses. Their bishop allowed them to have a landline phone in their businesses if it was necessary, but cell phones were considered excessive. But from his interactions with them he knew that the *Englisch* relied heavily on their devices.

It gave him an excuse to check up on her, just to make sure she was all right. The thought made him pause. It wasn't like him to be so concerned about what was happening in the *Englisch* world. He had a few *Englisch* friends he'd made through his work as a carpenter, but he avoided any deep attachments. He had learned his lesson the hard way. He couldn't rely on others to protect his family. And technology couldn't always help. He had lost his wife and their unborn daughter when Lydia had been struck with cancer, and no amount of *Englisch* technology or medicine had been able to save them. All he had left was his son and he was determined to be careful.

He would check on her, he decided, then he would leave. His conscience would be eased, and he would never have to see the woman again.

His mind flashed back to the memory of the driver's panicked face before she had hit the tree. She had obviously been aware of the danger. He couldn't recall any of the telltale clues that she was trying to stop.

His eyes flashed to the tree in question. The bark had been scraped off in several places. He could see bits and pieces of it littering the ground. Although the mangled car was gone, he doubted he'd forget the image anytime soon.

Why hadn't she stopped?

Chapter Two

"Sadie? Sadie, can you hear me?" a strange voice pleaded, over and over again.

Why wouldn't he just be quiet? Her head was pounding with every word he uttered. Irritated, she dragged her eyelids open to confront the man who kept talking to her when she just wanted to rest. Two blurry figures stood beside her bed. That didn't seem right. She blinked, and they wobbled before coalescing into one man. His messy brown hair and dark brown eyes gave her the impression of an excited puppy. He was obviously happy to see her.

But who was he?

Panic stirred inside her at the sudden realization that she had no memory of the man standing before her, a ridiculous grin stretched wide upon his face. He, however, obviously knew her.

"Who—who are you?" she gasped out, feeling like the panic was a steel band around her chest, making it difficult to take in a full breath of air.

His grin faltered and those brown eyes sharpened.

"Are you messing with me, Sadie?"

Sadie. The shock went through her. Her name was Sadie. The sound of the name was unfamiliar.

"My name is Sadie?"

The man's formerly grinning mouth was now a grim frown. His brow was furrowed. Concern emanated from him.

"Your name is Sadie Ann Standings," he began slowly, as if her ability to process information had disappeared along with her memory. She fought the urge to sigh in impatience. "My name is Kurt. Kurt Standings. I'm your brother."

She'd forgotten her own brother?

"You're my brother?" she blurted. She didn't doubt him, but it was so much to take in at once.

He shrugged. "Stepbrother, but our parents have been married since we were both eight years old. When they married, my dad adopted you, gave you our last name. That was sixteen years ago."

Which meant she was twenty-four. Why couldn't she remember any of this? He reached out a hand to touch her shoulder. She jerked it away from him, then winced at the hurt on his face. Still, she was relieved when he didn't try to touch her again. The thought of a stranger touching her so familiarly was disconcerting.

"Here," he said, pulling his wallet from his back pocket and drawing out a picture. A young woman with light brown hair and a younger version of the man standing before her stood behind an older couple sitting on a couch, smiling at the camera. She glanced at it and then back at him, awaiting the explanation. He jabbed a finger at the young woman. "That's you. This is your mom and my dad."

She looked closer and saw a clear resemblance between the two women.

"Where are our parents?" Shouldn't they have come the moment they heard she was in the hospital?

His face grew sober. "I'm sorry, Sadie. Dad and your mom, Hannah, were killed in a fire two years ago."

The loss swamped her, even though the people he talked about were strangers.

"What was your father's name?" she asked softly.

"Our father, Sadie. Your biological father was long gone. Our dad's name was Tim."

"Hannah and Tim," she whispered to herself, wishing she could remember.

"Look, we need to get the doctor in here." Kurt took the control near her bed and pressed the button.

Within minutes, a doctor and a nurse were in the room. The female doctor flashed a light in her eyes and asked her endless questions, most of which Sadie was unable to answer. She didn't recall her family, where she went to school, anything about her job. She couldn't even tell them what she had been doing when her car had crashed.

"You swerved to avoid colliding with an Amish buggy and hit a tree instead." The doctor lifted her eyes from her laptop and slid her glasses up to rest on the top of her head. "The car was totaled, or so I hear. You're very fortunate that no one else was hurt."

Sadie detected a faint note of censure in the doctor's voice but wasn't sure why.

"I guess." If only she could remember!

The doctor nodded. "You must have been going very fast to have hit the tree so hard."

"What about my memories? Will they come back?"

This total blankness was intolerable. She couldn't imagine dealing with it for the rest of her life. A movement caught her attention. Kurt was frowning, his face disturbed. When he noticed her watching him, he smiled, but she could still see the strain in it.

The doctor's expression softened. "There's no way to know that. You may regain some memories, or you may regain all of them. In some instances, the amnesia is permanent. Your brother and your friends will undoubtedly be willing to help you fill in the missing memories."

"Of course, we will, sis. Don't you worry about it."

Which was silly. Obviously, she would worry about it. It was somewhat unsettling to have someone of whom she had no recollection talking to her with such familiarity. She wondered vaguely if they had been close siblings.

As the doctor was leaving, another stranger entered the room. Sadie felt her eyes widen. This stranger was taller than Kurt, and his dress was very simple. Blue button-down shirt, dark trousers, sturdy brown boots. His hair was dark, and so were his eyes. The lower part of his face was covered with a beard. No mustache, though. She blinked at the sight of an Amish man standing in her hospital room. The beard signified that he was married, or at least she thought it did. Huh. It struck her as odd that she could remember how the Amish dressed, but that she couldn't recall her own name.

"Ben!" Kurt strode to the door, astonishment stamped on his face. "What are you doing here?"

"Kurt. You know her?" He jerked the hand holding his hat toward where Sadie lay watching from the hospital bed. She could see the surprise in the rigidness of his posture.

"Know her? She's my sister." Kurt's voice retained its puzzlement.

Ben, whoever he was, hadn't said what he was doing there yet. Sadie listened avidly. Maybe he would have some details about what had happened to her. It was a rather desperate hope.

"Ah." Ben shifted. His eyes sought out Sadie. He blinked when he saw her watching him. A slow smile, that reminded her of a sunrise, took over his face. She'd been so focused on the beard that she hadn't noticed how gentle the deep brown eyes surrounded by several feathery laugh lines were. "It's *gut* to see you awake. You crashed in front of my house. My neighbor and I pulled you from the car. I found this after you were gone."

He pulled out a smartphone in a bright pink case and set it on the table beside her. It didn't look familiar, but then, nothing really did.

"Thank you for bringing it. And thanks also for helping me," she told him. "Do I know you?"

His thick eyebrows climbed up his forehead. "We've never met before."

She liked the way he talked, slow and soft.

Kurt stepped in before the silence could become uncomfortable. "She's got amnesia or something. Can't remember a thing. Her doctor popped in and said she may or may not remember everything."

That was a lot of information to be giving a stranger. Ben might know Kurt, but he had no true connection with her. She frowned at her brother, trying to let him know to stop telling his friend about her.

A knock sounded on the door. She sighed, wishing to be alone with her thoughts to sort out what she had learned. Kurt opened it. From her position on the bed she could make out a dark blue uniform and a gold badge. Finally. The police had arrived. Maybe she could get some answers. Kurt swung the door wider. "Hey, Keith. Do you have some news about my sister's accident?"

"Yes, as a matter of fact, I do." The officer entered the room.

Sadie sat up straighter. Kurt knew the officer, and the man hadn't said anything when he'd named her as his sister. Which meant she was, indeed, Kurt's stepsister. She noticed Kurt straightening his posture out of the corner of her eye as the officer approached her. She felt bad. To her, Kurt was someone she didn't know, but to him, she was his sister. If only she could remember!

"Keith? What caused my sister's accident?" Kurt's question brought her back to the present.

"There was a small jagged hole in the brake line. You most likely tore the line by going over rocks or rough terrain too fast. The line could have been slowly dripping for weeks without your being aware. You might have noticed your brakes feeling mushy. Too many people wait too long before getting their brakes fixed."

Kurt thanked the officer for his help. Sadie frowned. She had thought he would want to know what caused the accident, but she couldn't help noticing that his expression was even grimmer than before. His friend, Ben, seemed to notice something was wrong, as well.

"Kurt, are you well?"

Ben's voice was smooth and deep, unhurried with a slight accent. Not too noticeable, just somehow rounder than the speech she'd heard from others since she awoke.

Her brother glanced at her in a considering way. Then he apparently decided she needed to know what was going on.

"Sadie, you couldn't have had a leak for a long time." He drew in a deep breath. "You had the entire brake system, including the lines, replaced last week."

She shivered, though his meaning wasn't processing. "What are you trying to tell me?"

"This wasn't an accident."

"What do mean, it wasn't an accident?" Her voice came out strained, like she had to squeeze each and every painful word out.

Kurt—she couldn't think of him as her brother—gave her a look that was overflowing with sympathy. She was grateful he didn't attempt to touch her again.

"Someone tried to hurt you. Someone deliberately made it so that your car would run out of brake fluid while you were driving."

She shuddered. The fear and panic she had felt since awaking with no memory threatened to pull her under. Already she could feel the blackness dragging her down. She fought her way through it. The doctor had said that her memories might return.

The other man, Ben, shifted beside the bed. "If you feel your sister was in danger, shouldn't you have told the police officer who just left? You knew him."

That, she thought, was a valid question. Narrowing her eyes, she switched her eyes back to her stepbrother. He sighed, then he grabbed the chair and motioned for his friend to sit. While Ben cautiously settled himself, his eyes wary, Kurt strode to the other side of the room and pulled a second chair to the side of the bed. Sadie had the uncomfortable feeling that she was about to be interrogated.

"Okay, look, Sadie, I know you don't remember me, but I need you trust me. Okay?"

She nodded. "I believe that you are who you say. I'm sorry. I just don't remember anything!"

He sighed. "I know. I know. Look, the truth of the matter is that I think you are in danger, but I have no proof." He rubbed the back of his neck. "It's possible that it might be my fault. I think you might be in trouble because of my job."

Startled, Sadie forced herself to sit up straighter. She noticed that Ben sat forward, his gaze sharpening as he stared at her brother. The intensity of his glance made her momentarily lose focus on the conversation. When her brother began to speak again, she mentally shook herself and returned her attention to Kurt.

"Explain, please. How is it your fault that I may be in danger?" She stressed the word *may*, as she was still hoping it was all a bad nightmare and she would soon wake up with her memories intact.

"I can't get used to you not knowing things."

He wasn't the only one. Irritation stirred that he would find her amnesia an inconvenience. How did he think she felt?

"Kurt," Ben interrupted him, his deep voice rich with reprimand.

"Yeah, yeah, I know. That sounded really selfish. Sorry. I don't mean to be insensitive." He shoved a hand through his dark hair. "I'm a reporter. Nothing big. Smaller stories, mainly section B. I've slowly been getting more important stuff, though. Recently my boss put me on a new story. I can't tell you much about it, confidentiality and all, but I think I might have found something serious. Unfortunately, it's nothing I can take to the police. I have no actual evidence. Right now, I just have suspicions."

"One of your suspicions is that someone knows you're looking?" Ben asked.

"Yeah."

Sadie glanced from one man to the other. "I still don't understand how that affects me."

Kurt sighed. "It affects you because I think someone is telling me that you'll get hurt if I don't stop digging." Frustration rang in his voice. "I'm so close to finding something, so close, and I'm going to have to stop."

"Are you sure you can't go to the cops? That Keith seemed to like you well enough. Maybe he'd be able to find the information you are seeking."

Kurt snorted. "The moment it's learned I went to the police, any chance I have of uncovering the facts are gone. My boss will never trust me with another major project again."

It wasn't her fault. She knew it wasn't her fault. But she couldn't stop the trickle of doubt and guilt that wound its way through her. A new fear surfaced.

"Will they still come after me, do you think?"

He didn't answer her, which was an answer in itself.

"Kurt, you have to protect your sister." Ben shoved his chair back. The sound of the four legs scraping the floor made her cringe. Ben stood and paced away from the bed. "Your family must be a priority."

She appreciated him stepping in to speak up for her, virtual stranger that she was.

"I know I have to protect her," Kurt snapped. "I just don't know how to do that. Even if I stop digging, they're still there and will most likely come after me and probably her. I have to get more information so I can go to the police. Once they are involved, I'm sure we can find more protection."

Ben didn't let up. "And until then? How do you intend to make sure she is safe before then?" The Amish man slowed his pacing and took a deep breath. She could tell he was struggling to remain calm, although she had no idea why he was so invested in what happened to her. Was it just because he was friends with Kurt?

"You don't need to worry," Kurt said, lifting his chin and crossing his arms. "I'll figure something out."

Sadie's jaw dropped open. She couldn't hide her surprise. Maybe she felt this way because she couldn't remember her brother, but she was not impressed with him right now. Shouldn't he be more concerned about her? And about his own safety? Although, she had to admit, she had no idea what he had gotten himself into. That was a definite negative about having amnesia.

She flicked a glance toward Ben. He obviously wasn't any happier with Kurt than she was. Even through the beard she could tell that his jaw was clenched. His brows were lowered, and his dark eyes were flashing. "I stood beside my seven-year-old son and watched your sister's car slam into a tree. I will never forget the sound it made. When I got to the car, I thought she was dead. It was horrifying. There was gasoline on the ground. My neighbor and I pulled her from the car, wondering if the car would explode at any moment. I came here this afternoon because neither my son nor I could stop wondering if the woman we had tried to save would survive."

Silence followed his words.

She was touched by the care he had shown her.

"Your son, is he all right?"

Ben's glance settled on her. The kindness in those deep, sad eyes struck her. "Yes, Nathaniel is *gut*. He is very worried about you."

Kurt sat forward and placed his elbows on his knees. "I'm worried, too. Don't think I'm not. I just don't know what to do. I can't even think of many friends you could stay with. It would be one thing if you could remember, but you'd be so vulnerable without your memory. Unless…"

Suddenly he sat forward. Excitement lit up his face. "I know exactly what I can do and where you can go."

"Where?" Sadie shivered with apprehension. She might not remember Kurt, but at least she was certain of who he was. The idea of staying with someone she didn't know made her uneasy.

Her stepbrother gave her his wide cheerful grin. "It's perfect. No one would think to look for you there, and I could continue digging until I find what I need."

"Where?" she asked again, growing more tense by the second.

"You can stay with Ben. No one would look for you in Amish country."

Ben gaped at his friend, certain he had missed something. Kurt was desperate; he could comprehend the feeling, even empathize with it. In addition to that, he and Kurt had known each other for several years. Ben was a carpenter by trade, and they had met several years back when Kurt was writing a story on local businesses. He had included a section on businesses within the Amish community and had come out to interview Ben. They had formed a connection. When Lydia became ill the following year, Kurt had gone out of his way to assist and to be a support to his friend. He was the one and only *Englischer* that Ben considered more than a mere acquaintance. In fact, when Ben had decided to move away from the district where he and Lydia had both grown up, Kurt had helped him locate a new home.

Even so, the idea of the attractive young *Englisch* woman staying in his home was ridiculous. A widower did not ask a single woman to stay with him unchaperoned. It just wasn't done. He knew it would not be appropriate, and the gossip that would surely sprout from such an event could be devastating. Not to mention the trouble he would get in with the bishop.

Nee. He wanted to help. Truly he did. But not this way.

He tried to convince himself that he was making the right decision, but he couldn't keep the worry about what would happen to her once she left the hospital out of his mind. And almost as important, what he'd tell Nathaniel. His son had been almost in tears when Ben left to come to the hospital, afraid that the woman was dead.

With a start, he realized he was actually considering taking this woman into his home. He needed to put a stop to this foolishness.

"I am a widower," he told his friend sternly. "I cannot have a single woman living in my home, even temporarily, without a chaperone. You know this. That's not our way."

"I'm sure I'll be fine," a soft voice said. He turned his head and looked straight into eyes the color of warm caramel. Eyes that intrigued him, although he couldn't say why. "Please, don't worry about me."

He would worry, though. He knew he would. He just couldn't think of anything else to do. As he gazed into those eyes, he was reminded of someone, but the memory skirted just outside of his reach. This woman was familiar, somehow, but he knew that he had never met her. He shrugged the feeling away.

Kurt shifted in his chair, dragging Ben's attention away from the lovely *Englisch* woman with a bandage on her temple. He knew he was doing the right thing, but his conscience wasn't easy about it.

"I don't want to get you in trouble with your church. You know I don't. But isn't there a relative who could stay with you for a short time? Someone who could provide you with the chaperone you need? It will be for a short time. A week. Maybe two."

Before he could reply, Sadie turned her attention to Kurt with a puzzled frown on her face. "Don't I have a job? How is it that I can get away with just vanishing?"

Ben blinked. That was a very good question.

"You work as a high school counselor. There's no way you could go back to your job in the condition you're in. I have already contacted them and told them you've been in an accident. Obviously, they know nothing about the amnesia yet, but once they know, they'll agree. You have some sick time saved up, although only about three weeks. If it takes longer than that, you'll have to take unpaid leave."

Ben let their conversation wash over him without really hearing it. Every instinct he had was screaming at him that if he left her in the hospital, Sadie would still be in danger. The image of her pale and lifeless-appearing body trapped in her vehicle filled his mind. *Englischers* could be a very reckless and violent people. He still remembered the father of a childhood friend being murdered years ago by an *Englischer*. The killer, a local teenager, was still in prison.

He shook his head. He couldn't hold the actions of one man against all *Englischers*. Kurt, despite his lack of common sense at times, had proven himself to be a good and loyal friend. Ben knew that their family had suffered tragedies.

He couldn't get involved, though.

He opened his mouth to tell his friend how sorry he was that he couldn't help. Instead, he found himself saying, "Let me think about this and see if there's a way I can make it work."

Relief filled Kurt's eyes and a wide grin broke over his face. What had he done? He glanced again at Sadie. Unlike her brother, she was frowning. He could see the slight furrow in her brow.

"Ben, I appreciate your willingness to consider helping me out. I know that you are friends." She waved a hand between two men. "I don't mean any offense, but I don't know you. I don't even know Kurt, not at the moment, but he is my stepbrother. But we haven't met before today."

Kurt stepped closer to the bed. "I would never let you stay with anyone who wasn't trustworthy. Ben is as fine a man as they come. I promise."

The exasperated glance she threw at her brother had Ben biting the inside of his lips to keep from smiling. She may have been injured, but she had fierceness inside her. He was glad to see that.

"How do I know that I can trust your word?" she asked. Kurt looked a little hurt at that, but it was a fair question. She shook her head and then winced. "It's just that if I am in danger, and right now we can't really prove that I am, I hate the thought that I would somehow be bringing that danger into his home. He has a little boy he has to look after."

His heart warmed that she was thinking about his son. He needed to get back home. He had left Nathaniel with Caleb and Lovina. If he didn't go soon, he'd be getting home after it started to get dark. He hadn't gotten a driver since he hadn't planned on being gone that long.

"I need to head for home. I just came to assure myself and Nathaniel that you were well."

She was, for now.

Ben slapped his hat back on his head as he exited the building and strode briskly to where he had left his buggy. It had grown colder while he'd been inside. The chill bit at him. He ignored it. It would grow much colder. Dealing with harsh weather was just a part of his life. He had lived his entire life in this part of Ohio. He expected he'd probably die here, as well. Although, he was over an hour from where he'd grown up. He refused to allow guilt to take root. He'd moved out of the heart of Amish country in Homes County to get away from the memories of his dead wife. And to escape the expectations of his family.

Would Sadie's brother talk her into staying with him? he wondered as he pulled away from the town. He didn't know if Kurt's worries were founded or not. However, he had never known Kurt to be fanciful. Kurt might sometimes act without thinking, but he did seem to be very observant, which was probably why he had been entrusted with what appeared to be a dangerous assignment at his job.

Ben mulled over the facts as he knew them throughout the rest of the evening. He found himself distracted, thinking about the young woman he'd rescued that afternoon. With no memories, how would she know who to trust? Anyone could pose as a friend. Her brother wouldn't be able to be with her at all times. Just how serious was this story Kurt was following? If what Kurt said was true, and Ben had no reason to believe it wasn't, he was entangled too deeply to get out of it now.

It was very unsettling to not know what they were going to do. Part of him hoped that they would decide not to bring Sadie out to his home. Then he could just wash his hands of the whole situation.

He didn't know if he would be able to rest easy, not knowing if she was safe. Somehow, when he had pulled her out of that car, he had become invested in making sure she survived. It didn't make any sense, nor was it wise to become so deeply enmeshed in her life. He couldn't help himself, though. Seeing her unconscious, knowing she might not be safe, sat heavily on his mind even as he went to bed that evening.

Tomorrow, he thought, could bring more complications into his life than he wanted. Or than he was prepared for.

Chapter Three

Where was Kurt?

Sadie glanced at the clock on the wall for what must have been the twentieth time. He had promised to be at the hospital to pick her up by ten in the morning. It was now almost noon. She didn't know if she should be annoyed or worried, although in her present condition she was leaning more toward worried. Was such extreme tardiness something she should have expected from Kurt? She had no way of knowing, but that wasn't the impression she had gotten from him the day before.

She could try calling him again. The cell phone that his friend Ben had brought in was still lying where he'd left it. She had found Kurt's name and picture in her contacts. So she really did know him, even though she still couldn't recall a thing about him. She'd given herself a headache the night before, trying to remember anything about her life. It was all still blank.

Five more minutes passed. This was getting ridiculous.

A nurse walked in the room. "Honey, is your ride coming for you? Do you need us to call someone?"

Great, now the hospital was trying to kick her out. She pasted on what she hoped was a pleasant smile that disguised just how frayed her nerves truly were. "I'm sure he'll be here soon. I'll give him another call."

"That's a good idea. Let me know if you need any help."

The nurse gave her a comforting smile and retreated out of the room. Sadie snatched the phone from the table and tapped the phone icon next to her brother's name again.

This time, the call was picked up. She barely let him answer before she was talking. "Kurt? Where are you? They need this room for another patient. Are you coming to pick me up?"

"Ah, yes, Sadie. I'll be there soon."

The phone disconnected. She stared at the device in her hand, frowning. The voice was a bit muffled, but it hadn't sounded like Kurt's. There had been a lot of commotion in the background, though, so maybe she was wrong.

She stilled. In her mind, she replayed the commotion. Had someone been shouting *run*?

She glanced again at the phone, shivering as a chill settled into her body that had nothing to do with the cold. Whoever he was running from, they had Kurt. She had no way to prove it. It could have been another friend who had answered his phone, but she knew it was not.

What she did know was that someone was coming for her.

Galvanized into action, she jumped off the bed and grabbed her coat. Kurt had been very sweet the night before, leaving during dinner to bring her a change of clothes. Nothing fancy, just a simple pair of blue jeans and a T-shirt and a pink-and-purple flannel shirt. When she saw the clothes, though, she thought they must have been favorites, judging by the amount of wear in the knees and elbows. Which showed how well he knew his sister. What if she never got the chance to get to know him?

Stop it! This kind of thinking would get her nowhere. She could go to the police. She considered that option; surely it made the most sense. Except Kurt had been so adamant that he couldn't that she hesitated. She had no way of knowing if she'd put him in more danger by alerting the police. She didn't want to do that.

Nor could she go home. The ambulance driver had brought in her purse. She had her driver's license, so she knew where she lived. She also had an idea that if she went there, someone would be waiting for her. Panic started to churn inside her. Then she remembered. The early morning nurse had brought her a newspaper. There was a write-up of the accident in it. She snatched the paper. It gave the address where the crash had taken place. Ben had said that it happened right in front of his house.

She would go there. He wasn't really expecting her, even though they'd tossed the idea around of her staying with him. Last night she had not wanted to impose on him, a stranger. This morning, he was the only one she felt she could trust.

She made her decision. Grabbing up the newspaper and her purse, she left the room. The nurse at the station was talking with a doctor as Sadie strode by. She averted her face. Neither of them called out to her but continued what appeared to be an intense discussion about another patient. She rode the elevator down to the lobby, feeling

the walls closing around her the entire time. She tensed
as the door slid open with a soft whoosh, but no one was
on the other side.

Relieved, she pulled the hood of her coat up, both to
protect herself from the chilly air and to shield her face.
She walked past the reception desk and out into the cold.

Now what? There was no one meeting her, and she
had no car.

A car with a taxi sign pulled up in front of the hospital, and an older woman got out. She paid the driver and
started to head toward the hospital.

Sadie looked around. No other taxis were in sight.
This might be her only chance. She quickened her step,
trying to hurry without drawing attention to herself.
Please, don't leave.

The driver saw her and he smiled. She could almost
see him mentally adding on another customer. "You need
a ride, miss?"

She nodded. "Can you take me here?" She pointed at
the address listed in the paper.

"Absolutely! That's about a twenty minute drive. That
all right?"

"Fine." She hurriedly climbed into the vehicle. The
driver, a young man in his twenties, pulled away from
the curb and slid smoothly into the light traffic. She
glanced back at where she'd just left.

A man was jogging from the parking lot toward the
hospital. Pulling her hood so it hid the right side of her
face, she looked away. Something about the man struck
her as familiar. Half a memory of an angry face formed,
then it faded. She had seen him before. And he scared
her.

She had been right to leave the hospital. Whoever had

answered her brother's phone probably had him, and they were apparently coming to get her, too.

She bit down on the panic that was screaming to get out. Ben was the only one she could go to. Maybe he'd know what to do.

Her phone vibrated. Hands shaking, she looked at the text.

I got away. Hide. Don't text back. Danger. No police.

Kurt had gotten away. The very fact that he told her not to text back reassured her that it really was Kurt and not someone trying to get to her.

When the driver pulled up at the large two-story farmhouse, she distractedly paid him. There was something very solid and comforting about the look of the house. And, she realized, something familiar. Not specifically about this house, but about the feel of the place.

This was not her first visit to an Amish home, she decided. For a moment, she tried to grasp at the memory, but gave up as it continued to evade her.

A young boy watched her approach from the wraparound porch. He looked about seven. Ben's son was seven. She thought back briefly, trying to recall his name.

"Are you Nathaniel?" she asked gently.

He nodded, his eyes wide.

"Could you ask your father if he has a moment to talk? My name is Sadie."

The boy whirled around and dashed into the house, calling for his father. Sadie climbed the steps. The sudden adrenaline rush she had experienced as she escaped the hospital had gone, leaving her exhausted. Her bones felt like they had turned into half-cooked spaghetti. She just wanted to slump down against the wall and take a nap.

Footsteps pounded toward the door. She straightened her spine, embarrassed at her weakened state.

The man from the hospital appeared, his dark eyes astonished as he held open the door for her. His gaze swept the driveway behind her. Searching for Kurt, she realized. He wouldn't have expected her to show up alone.

When those eyes returned to her, she responded to the question in their depths.

"I need your help."

Ben stared at the woman in shock. He hadn't really thought that she would show up here, much less on her own. The silence between them stretched tensely before he realized that her face under the bandage on her temple was pale and drawn. There was an air of sorrow that hovered around her.

He was being rude. "Sadie. Come in. My son and I were getting ready to eat lunch. Please join us."

He could see the dismay that crossed her face and hurried to make her feel at ease. "It's no imposition. I made plenty."

He led the way into the kitchen. The little boy who'd greeted her sat at the table, his eyes excited. "Is it her, *Dat*? Is it the lady from the car?"

Ben chuckled. His son had run into the house telling him that the lady from the accident was at the door. Ben hadn't mentioned the idea that she might come and stay with them. The more he had thought about the idea, the more ludicrous it had seemed. He was a widower living with a young boy. Having a young woman in the house at night was not appropriate, and he didn't know who he could have stay with them. It would have been different had they been near his own family, but he and Nathaniel had moved to this district three years ago after Lydia was gone. They had friends, but no real family close by. He had done that on purpose, to escape from the expectations that he remarry and give Nathaniel a mother.

He had never expected to have her show up on his doorstep alone.

That alerted him that something had gone wrong. His stomach tightened. Kurt had been working on a sensitive project. A potentially dangerous one. Despite Ben's desire to keep his distance from the pretty *Englisch* woman, he needed to discover what had happened to Kurt.

The small group settled down to eat. Ben and Nathaniel both bowed their heads to pray silently, the way they always did before meals. When he opened his eyes, he saw that Sadie was staring at her plate uncomfortably. It had never occurred to him that she might not be a praying person. Kurt was, he knew, so Ben had assumed that his sister was, as well. Or had she forgotten?

That was an unsettling thought, that one might forget *Gott*. Even during the darkest times of his life, he never doubted that *Gott* was there. Truthfully, he had often wondered how he would have survived without his faith. Shame filled him when he realized that just a few minutes ago he had looked at this woman who was obviously in need and had basically been trying to decide how to best get rid of her because her presence in his life was not convenient. That was not who he was. That was not what he wanted to teach Nathaniel.

Questions burned inside of him. Questions that would have to wait until his son was no longer in the room.

"Sadie," he began the moment they finished eating and Nathaniel had skipped off. "Where is your stepbrother? I know we had talked about you coming out here, but I had gotten the impression that you didn't want to do that. Am I mistaken?"

The eyes that rose to meet his were wide with anxiety. "He never came to pick me up this morning. When I called his phone, someone else answered it. I could hear my brother yelling in the background for me to run. I think whoever he was investigating had found him." She reached into her back pocket and pulled out her phone.

"What—"

"Hang on," she shushed him. "I want to show you this text I received. I believe it's from my brother."

He read the text. No wonder she was terrified. Instinctively, he tilted his head and listened tensely. When he heard the sound of his son practicing his spelling words, he relaxed.

"Have any of your memories returned?" Anything she remembered could possibly help them right now. She shook her head, destroying that hope.

They both started when someone pounded on the front door. No one he knew would pound the door that way. And, he thought to himself, he didn't know anyone who would use the front door. Most people came around to the side.

He moved quickly across the house. He could see a young blond man standing outside. The man wasn't looking into the house; instead, he was glancing wildly around him as if searching for someone. Even standing as he was, inside, Ben could see that the man was bouncing on the balls of his feet, almost as if he was ready to be off in an instant.

"That's the taxi driver who brought me here," Sadie whispered at Ben's back. "He wasn't as jittery when I saw him before. Something must've happened."

Ben waved her back, motioning for her to stay out of sight. She gave him a disgruntled look but complied. Only when he was sure that she was not visible from outside did he open the door. No doubt she was still listening. He schooled his face into a bland expression. At least, he hoped he did.

"May I help you?"

"Where is she? That lady I dropped off here a while ago? She still here?"

The questions shot out of the young man so fast that they blended into each other. Ben couldn't very well say that he didn't know who the man was talking about. The man had probably seen her talking to Nathaniel before he left. He hesitated to give any clue about Sadie's whereabouts, however. His instincts said that the driver was honestly concerned about her, but his instincts had been off before.

"Why do you want to know?"

The driver glanced around hurriedly again. "Look, I think she's in trouble."

So did Ben. If this young man had wanted to harm Sadie, he'd had plenty of opportunity when she was in his car. Making a decision, he motioned for the young man to enter the house. He shut the door and turned back to find that Sadie had stepped from her hiding place.

Upon seeing her, the young driver exclaimed in relief.

"Man, I'm glad to see you!"

Ben saw her brow crease in consternation. She frowned and caught Ben's eye for a moment before she looked back at the driver.

"I'm sorry. I don't understand."

Visibly trying to collect himself, the driver shoved both his hands through his hair. "I went back to the hospital. The woman I dropped off earlier had booked me to come back and pick her up at a certain time. When she got into the car, she was very excited. She was telling me all about how a man had come in searching for a young woman who had been in a car accident. He claimed to be a detective."

"He was no detective!" Sadie burst out.

Ben wanted to ask her how she knew that, considering she had no memory. He didn't, though, for the basic reason that he agreed with her. If Kurt was right, the man searching for her was not out to help her. He hated to think that anyone from the local police force could possibly be involved, but that would explain why Kurt was so hesitant to go to the police.

"I don't know who he was," the driver responded. "All I know is that my customer pointed out the man who was looking for you as we pulled away. He sure didn't look like any policeman I ever saw. He looked mean. When he reached into his jacket to get his phone out, I saw a gun. I don't know if you've ever had the feeling that someone was up to no good, but that was exactly the feeling I got."

Sadie had gone pale.

"Sadie, no one knows you're here."

"So will you help me?" Her voice was nearly steady, with the barest hint of a tremble. She'd leave if he said he didn't want the risk. He couldn't turn his back on her, though. It wasn't the way he'd been raised. One didn't ignore those in need just because it was inconvenient.

"*Jah*, I will help."

The smile that lit her face was dazzling, radiant with relief.

It shook him how much he liked being the cause of that smile.

"Look," the driver said, reaching into his back pocket and pulling out a card. His features weren't as strained as they had been moments ago when he arrived, but he still had an air of concern about him. "I think you're as safe here as anywhere. And the dude's probably right. I mean, I doubt anyone knows that you're here. But I want you to have my card, just in case you find that you don't feel safe. I would be happy to take you to the police, or if you think of somewhere else you think you should go. Just call me. Just tell me to pick you up at— what's your name?"

He directed this last toward Ben.

"Ben Mast." He was slightly amused at the earnestness in the young man's expression. And oddly touched. He was surprised to find an *Englisch* youth with such compassion.

The young man nodded. "Right. Tell me you're at Ben's. I'll know."

Sadie looked at the card, then back up at the young man. "Thank you, Braden. I appreciate your help today. I will hold on to this. If I need help, I'll call."

Braden took his leave. Within moments, Ben was left standing in his kitchen with his son and the woman who had literally crashed into their lives, and now threatened their peaceful existence with her mere presence in their home.

Gott, *please don't let me regret this decision.*

He wondered if the prayer was too late.

Chapter Four

❧

Once the decision to allow Sadie to stay was made, there was no going back. But Ben could not allow an unmarried woman to remain in his house with only himself. Even if she remained hidden and no one else in the town was aware that there was an *Englisch* woman in his house, Nathaniel would know. Ben would not scandalize his young son by teaching him that it was okay to ignore the rules when they were not convenient.

And at the moment, the rules were the epitome of inconvenient. Still, rules were there for a reason. They helped to keep one out of temptation and close to *Gott*.

"You look very serious, Ben."

He hadn't realized that she had been observing him while he pondered the unique dilemma he found himself in.

He smiled at her, trying to ease the concern in her eyes. "*Jah*, I am trying to solve a problem."

"May I help?"

He could feel his smile wanting to change into a sarcastic smirk and kept his face still with effort. What would she say if he told her that she was the problem he was trying to solve? No doubt she would not be amused. *Nee*, he wouldn't be cruel. It was plain that she was feeling guilty about the situation she had put his family in. Not that he was blaming her. No one would choose to have someone chasing them. And she had to be going out of her mind worrying about her brother, the one solid connection she had at the moment.

"Listen, I need to go and talk with a neighbor. Could you stay here with Nathaniel for a few minutes? I will be back soon."

She nodded. "Of course. Whatever you need."

Ben passed her and headed out the door. Without thinking about it, he placed a comforting arm on her shoulder as he passed. He should have left without touching her. A jolt of electricity shocked him. She jumped, obviously having felt the same thing. Not *gut*.

Averting his gaze, he pretended that he hadn't felt the spark that shimmered between them, although he was fairly sure that his ears were turning red. Ben jammed his hat on his head and strode out, never looking back. He did not want to see the look on her face right now.

Jogging across the street to Caleb's house, he rapped sharply on the wooden door frame. Then he grimaced. It was not polite to pound on someone's door, but he was so rattled he was hardly thinking.

He could hear footsteps approaching, then the entrance was opened. Lovina looked surprised to see him.

"Ben? Is Nathaniel *gut*?"

"Jah." He nodded at the kind-hearted woman. Lovina was only a year or two older than his own twenty-six years, but she seemed older. He could hear the chorus of young voices inside her house. She and Caleb had four *kinner*. She also had a widowed aunt living with

her. "I was wondering if I might speak with you and Caleb. And Ruth."

Her eyes widened at the mention of her aunt. He didn't know Ruth that well, so it probably appeared to be a strange request. To his relief, she didn't argue or ask questions. "*Jah*, please come in."

He stepped inside as she left the room to gather her husband and her aunt. When the three returned, Ben cleared his throat. He had not planned what he would say, and the words seemed to stick in his throat. Finally, he drew in a deep breath and plunged into the story.

"Caleb, you remember that *Englisch* woman who crashed into the tree." It wasn't a question, for he didn't believe either of them would ever forget it. He would probably hear the sound of her car crunching against the tree in his nightmares.

"*Jah*, I remember well."

"Her name is Sadie. She is the sister of a friend I had met through my work. She has lost her memory, and her brother is not at home right now. I have been asked to look after her, at least, until he returns." He decided not to mention the true nature of Kurt's disappearance. "I told her I'd help, but—"

"Ack," Ruth broke in. "It is not proper for you to have a woman in your home without a chaperone."

Relieved that she understood the situation, Ben sighed. "*Jah*, but I believe I should help."

Ruth turned to her niece. "Lovina, I will be moving in to the Mast *haus* for a few days." She raised an eyebrow at Ben. He felt like a schoolchild being scolded. "You have a place for me to sleep?"

"*Jah*, I have a spare room for you." He'd have slept

in the barn, if necessary. Thankfully, that would not be needed.

"*Gut*. I will come over soon. You should not be in the *haus* alone with her."

"*Denke*, Ruth. I was in a bind."

The stern lines of her face softened. "*Gott* wants us to be charitable, Ben. He also wants us to guard ourselves."

He understood the warning and flushed.

Thanking his neighbors again, he left and rushed back to the house. The moment he entered, he saw that Sadie had cleaned up the lunch dishes and had started to sweep the kitchen. He appreciated it.

"*Denke* for cleaning up, Sadie." He glanced around the room. "Where did Nathaniel go?"

"He asked if he could go to his room for some quiet time. I told him that was fine. I figured you wouldn't want him to leave the house while you were gone. Not with all that's happened."

"You were right."

She narrowed her gaze slightly. "So? Have you solved your problem?"

He nodded. "I believe that I have."

She pulled the broom close to herself, holding on to it with both hands, and waited. She was a good listener, he decided, at least, when she wasn't feeling terrified.

"My neighbor's widowed aunt is coming to stay with us," he announced. "That way, both our reputations are protected."

Her eyes widened. He could see the alarm in the stiffness of her posture. Raising his hands, he made a calming gesture. "I was vague in the details, but we can't stay here together like this. It wouldn't be proper."

Tilting her head, she frowned at him. "We weren't doing anything wrong."

"Maybe not," he acknowledged, "but it is the Plain way. Ruth will be here soon."

She opened her mouth, no doubt to ask another question, but the question was never voiced. Knuckles knocking against the screen door ended the conversation.

"Ben! I'm here!" Ruth's voice boomed through the door. Ben glanced at his companion, choking back a laugh at the amused expression on her face.

"Door's open, Ruth," he responded. The older woman entered the house, her sharp eyes zeroing in on the two people standing next to each other in the kitchen. It wasn't hard to read the reprimand in her stare. Ben found himself backing away from Sadie without even thinking about it. Then he flushed. They hadn't been standing that close, and Sadie was still holding onto the broom.

"You're Sadie, ain't so?" the older woman demanded, inspecting the *Englisch* woman.

"That's right." Sadie inspected her right back, the corner of her mouth lifting slightly. Apparently, she wasn't offended by Ruth's gruff ways.

"I'm sorry that you were in an accident," Ruth murmured, her eyes touching on the bandage adorning Sadie's temple. "Are you in any pain?"

"Not much. My head did ache yesterday, but today it feels a lot better."

Ben was relieved to know that her condition was improving. Ruth quickly got herself settled into one of the spare rooms on the second floor. He showed Sadie to the room across from that. Ben discreetly moved some of his own belongings from his bedroom to the bedroom on the first floor near the kitchen. It wouldn't do to have his room so close to their guest. Ruth gave him an approving nod as she observed his actions. It was all as it should be.

Nathaniel, of course, was thrilled to have so many people in their house. It was quite the adventure for him. Ruth was known for her skill at baking, and before they sat down for dinner the house was already filled with the aromas of cookies and a fresh pot of hearty stew. Sadie had pitched in and assisted her, and he noted that she was familiar with baking and cooking. It was interesting how the memory worked, that she could still manage to perform tasks that she had forgotten she had ever learned, but she couldn't recall basic information about herself.

The remainder of the day and evening went past in a blur. That night, as he lay in bed, Ben considered all the events of the day. Who was after her? Just as important as that question, what had happened to Kurt? Ben fell into a restless doze after eleven. The following morning he awoke to the crowing of the rooster, feeling as if he had not slept more than a few minutes. All he wanted to do was turn over and sleep for another hour.

With a sigh, he threw back his covers. Lack of rest was irrelevant. Chores still needed to be done. The animals needed to be fed and he had a job to do. Customers who depended on him. Crushing the wish to stay in bed longer, he rose and dressed quickly in the dark, then headed out to begin the day's work. By the time he returned from the barn, the rest of the household was awake, breakfast was on the table and strong black coffee was on the cookstove.

The next two days passed without incident. Sadie didn't say anything, but he knew that she never relaxed her guard. She peered out the window multiple times a day. He also noted that whenever she went outside, her eyes were constantly moving.

"Sadie," he said gently on the third day, "I will not let you come to harm." He immediately felt like a hypocrite. How could he promise such a thing? He hadn't even been aware enough to see that his Lydia had been terminally ill, yet here he was telling this strange woman that he would save her from an unknown danger.

Nee, not him. "*Gott* knows what the danger is. He can protect you."

She rolled her eyes but didn't respond for a moment. Then she sighed. "If only I knew that Kurt was okay."

He found her concern for her brother touching, and interesting, considering he was a virtual stranger to her. "Have you remembered anything, say?"

She shook her head with a grimace. "Not a thing. Although some things seem so familiar to me."

"*Jah?* Give me an example."

They were in his workshop. She moved over to stand near where he was sanding the top of a large square table. He made the mistake of looking up at her once. The way her brown hair was warmed by the sun streaming in the window made his heartbeat bump. Flushing, he forced his eyes back down to his work and kept them there.

"An example," she mused, reminding him of their conversation. "Well, for one thing, I love to bake with Ruth. And it's not like I'm learning. When we made dinner last night, I found myself handing her ingredients before she asked for them. I *knew* what the next steps were."

He frowned, recalling the meal the night before. It was a recipe that Ruth and Sadie had put together without any written instructions. It was also, he remembered, a traditional Amish recipe. Yet she had assisted as if she had been making it her whole life.

"I wonder where you learned to make the dumplings. It's not a recipe most *Englischers* would know."

"I have no idea."

Ben continued to consider the information long after she returned to the house. He imagined that Nathaniel had probably met her at the door. Several times in the past few days, he had stopped just to listen to the sound of Nathaniel's laughter. His son sure did enjoy having the attention of a woman. They both did. *Best not get too comfortable*, he warned himself. As soon as the danger was past, she'd be gone, back to where she belonged.

For she would return. There was nothing Nathaniel, or he, could do to change that fact. She was an *Englischer*, just like her brother. And as much as he liked and respected both of them, there was no place for a woman like her in his Amish world.

What was taking Nathaniel so long?

Sadie paced the length of the front room, keeping away from the large window, though her eyes continually strayed to it, straining to see outside.

Nathaniel had run upstairs to gather his spelling homework. He had come in after school yesterday waving his new words at her. His teacher gave them new vocabulary every Monday. This morning Sadie had promised that she would help him practice it after he finished his chores. The moment they were done, he had bounded up the stairs, yelling that he was ready to practice.

She grinned at the memory. She knew that she should not allow Nathaniel to worm his way into her heart. It wasn't fair to any of them. She was only there for a short time. Until Kurt was found and had enough evidence to go to the police.

And then she would leave.

She caught her breath at the ache the thought caused. Of leaving adorable Nathaniel, who held her heart in his small hand. Also, she realized, she was sad at the knowledge that she would be saying farewell to Ben, no doubt forever. The man could drive her nuts with his calm logic and his unflappable demeanor. Except she had caught him watching her a time or two. Could he sense the attraction between them? She smiled. Then she shook her head, hard.

She was a fool. Why on earth would she want any attraction, any sense of true emotion, to develop between her and the brave and faithful Amish father? A future between them was impossible.

She paced again, stopping at the bottom of the stairs. Finally, Nathaniel ran down. His spelling words were not in his hands.

"I thought we were going to study," she chided gently.

The smile slid from her face as she took in the paleness of his face, the wideness of his brown eyes, as he stared up at her.

"Nathaniel! What's wrong? What happened?" She was vaguely aware that Ruth's singing in the kitchen paused. She didn't want the woman to know what was happening. She motioned for Nathaniel to join her on the other side of the room and indicated that he should keep his voice down.

Her heart thudded in her chest as fear spiked in her soul.

"I was looking out the window with these," he whispered, holding out a pair of binoculars. For the briefest second, she was distracted by the fact that he would use binoculars. "I saw a man with a gun. He looked mad. Sadie, I got scared."

The breath in her lungs seemed to grow heavy. Her head felt light. Could she have been found? She forced herself to be calm so that she would not make the child even more afraid than he was. Pressing her hand to her stomach to ease the twisting sensation inside, she focused on him.

"It's October. Maybe he was a hunter. Isn't it small game season right now?" She seemed to possess some basic knowledge of the sport and its timelines. She didn't think she was a hunter, but maybe Kurt was.

Nathaniel wasn't impressed. He gave her a look that would have amused her at any other time. At the moment, however, all she could think about was the cloud of danger she had brought to this peaceful household.

"Ain't no hunting rifle he was carrying. Hunters use rifles. This was one of those small guns, the size you might see an *Englisch* police officer carrying around. It didn't look like a police officer, though."

A chill settled over her. Somehow, she didn't think it was a cop, either.

"Nathaniel, what did he look like?"

"What did who look like?" Ben asked behind them. She had not heard him come home. Spinning, she came face-to-face with the man who was starting to take up way too much space in her thoughts. At his shoulder, Ruth was peeking into the room, her mouth pursed and her arms crossed. The option of keeping her out of what was really happened had just vanished.

"Dat!" Nathaniel dashed around Sadie and threw

himself at his father's legs, the binoculars held tight in his fist. "I saw a bad man with my 'noculars. Maybe the man who wants to hurt Sadie."

The adults were silent. Sadie saw the same shock that was ricocheting through her stamped on Ben's face. They had thought they'd kept the truth from Nathaniel. Obviously he had been paying closer attention than they knew.

"A man is trying to hurt Sadie?" Ruth surged into the room, hands on her hips. "Ben Mast, what is your son talking about? I thought this girl was in an accident and lost her memory."

Oh, this had the potential to be bad. Sadie clenched her fists at her sides. Ben, fortunately, seemed to take the question in stride, although his jaw did tighten slightly.

"*Jah*, Sadie was in an accident, Ruth. Her memory is gone, hopefully only for a short time. All that is true. Also, her brother is a friend of mine who asked me if I could help out since he didn't want her to be home alone." His gaze flickered in Sadie's direction before returning to Ruth's stony countenance. "What I didn't tell you is that someone may or may not be trying to hurt her to get to her brother. We cannot confirm that."

"Ben." Sadie began to pace, unable to stand still, to keep the fear from becoming a solid mass in her gut. "I should never have come here. I will call Braden—"

"*Nee!*" The objection shot out of Ben so fast, so sharply, she stilled. Her eyes were wide as she turned to stare at her host. His jaw was set and his brow was lowered over fierce brown eyes that glared at her. "You are my guest. You are also the sister of a friend who asked for my assistance. The friend who stood by me when I buried my wife and Nathaniel's *mamm*."

She'd had no idea that he and Kurt were so close.

Ruth had opened her mouth, but at his words, her disapproving expression melted like chocolate left in the sun, and her eyes misted. "*Jah*, he sounds like a *wonderbar gut* friend, Ben."

Ben turned to the older woman. "One of the best friends a man could ask for. I would like to continue to assist him. He would never ask it of me if it was not important. And I cannot turn my back on someone in need, Ruth."

She nodded, understanding deep in her eyes.

Well, that was fine and good for them, but had they forgotten the little boy?

"Ben, I understand what you're saying, but Nathaniel."

His eyes met her, silencing her protest. The connection she had started to feel for this man bubbled up and filled the space between them. "*Jah*, Nathaniel needs to be protected, too."

He turned to face his son. Nathaniel stood straight, his young body tense. He should have still been afraid, but Sadie could detect the excitement vibrating off him. Now that his father was in the room, the boy no longer feared what was coming, but seemed to sense an adventure was about to commence. What was it about boys?

"How?" She voiced the question that had been bothering her. "How will we protect Nathaniel?"

He turned from her to watch out the window. "Nathaniel, can you describe the man you saw?"

He ignored her question. She held her silence for a moment, because she had learned that Ben was a deliberate man. He wasn't ignoring her to be rude. Chances were that Nathaniel's answers would be factored into his response.

Nathaniel shrugged, but his face was avid. "He was an *Englischer, Dat.*"

The sigh that left Ben made her want to smile, but she didn't. "I know that. What else did you notice? Hair color? Clothing?"

Nathaniel thought a moment. When he finally answered, Sadie paid close attention, the fist around her gut clenching tighter with each word. Blond hair cut close, angry face, a scar on his neck, she knew that Nathaniel had been right; the man was not a police officer. She knew because this was the same man she had seen at the hospital. And somewhere tucked in the memories she was trying so hard to access, she believed she would find more about him. He was so familiar.

"That's the man I saw the day I left the hospital. The man that answered Kurt's phone." She needed to tell them everything. "I don't remember the details, but I think I know him from somewhere. And everything in me tells me that he means me harm and will not hesitate to harm those around me."

Ben nodded, his face giving nothing away.

Ruth spoke up. "Plain folk don't get involved with the problems of the *Englisch* world, but you have given your word to help, Ben. I don't like this mess Sadie is in. *Gott* is strong." She nodded to herself. "*Gott* can help you with this."

Sadie appreciated the woman's confidence, but she wasn't sure that she agreed. Somehow she didn't feel like she was one who relied on God for much. She would never tell Ruth that, though she suspected that Ben had guessed her faith wasn't very strong.

"Sadie, I think it's time you contacted the police and told them that Kurt is missing."

"He didn't want them involved."

"*Jah*, but that was when he couldn't prove your life was in danger. I think it's clear now that both of you are in danger. If this is true, they may be able to find him."

It made sense. She left the others and went to her room to contact the police on her cell phone. When they insisted on coming to the farm to talk to her, she didn't feel she had a choice.

An hour later, a police cruiser arrived. A single officer emerged from the vehicle. His dark hair was nearly black. She guessed him to be in his late twenties. He knocked on the door. Ben answered, and although it had been his idea to contact the police, she could sense the reticence in his manner. She rolled her eyes.

"Ma'am." The officer greeted her. "I'm Sergeant Ryder Howard with the Waylan Grove Police Department. I was the officer you spoke with earlier. I went by your house. You live with your brother, correct?"

She hesitated. "I don't know what I can tell you, sergeant. I was in a car accident a few days ago and have lost my memory. Kurt asked me to come here because he and Ben are friends, and he believed his latest assignment may have put me at risk." Briefly she outlined having seen the man at the hospital and Nathaniel's seeing him in the area.

Concern shadowed the officer's eyes, even as his face remained neutral.

"Oh. Well, that's too bad. I can tell you that nothing looked out of place. There was no sign of forced entry. No sign of upheaval. What was odd was that the front door was unlocked. When I contacted the paper, his editor said that Kurt was on assignment. He didn't feel there was anything odd about him being out of touch."

Sadie's shoulders slumped. Dejection welled up inside her. Was there nothing they could do?

"Miss Standings?"

"Yes, sergeant?"

"The fact that your brother was concerned and from what you have told me about the man you and the youngster have seen leads me to say, err on the side of caution. Come to the station, look through the profiles. If the man you saw is in them, it might help us. Either way, I would say you might want to find a different hiding place. We could probably locate one for you."

She blinked.

The police wanted her to go into hiding. She had hoped that her brother was being overprotective. But he hadn't been. Danger was, indeed, stalking her.

Chapter Five

Sadie sat beside Sergeant Howard in the cruiser, wishing that she had taken Ben up his offer to accompany her to the police station. He had done so much for her, though, and she knew that being in such a place would be uncomfortable for him. So she had told him that she would be fine.

As she had gotten into the car, he had watched her. She couldn't help but wonder if he was secretly glad to be rid of her, even if it was only for a few hours. She didn't think so. While he had accepted her decision, she sensed he was frustrated with it. Unhappy, even.

It made no sense, so she tucked it away and strove to focus on the task at hand.

Which was difficult, considering she couldn't help watching out for the man she'd seen at the hospital. A soft snort escaped her. Surely she didn't expect him to jump out at her, or to chase after a police car?

But she couldn't stop herself from scanning the roads around them and peering in the side mirror every minute or so to see if she could spot a man with close-cropped blond hair following them.

"We'll be there in under five," Sergeant Howard commented beside her. Apparently, she was transmitting her trepidation. For the fiftieth time since she'd entered the car, Sadie wished for the sturdy, reassuring presence of Ben beside her.

Stop it! It would be stupid to grow dependent on an Amish man.

She forced herself to put Ben out of her mind. When they pulled into the police station, she sucked in a deep breath and pasted a small smile on her face, attempting to project a calm and confidence that she definitely was not feeling.

Sergeant Howard led her into a room where he told her to take her time. For the next hour, she sat in front of a computer screen and poured over images.

And, suddenly, there he was. The man she had seen, his face angry and hard as his cold eyes stared out from the screen. She shivered. Deep in the recesses of her mind, she could hear a voice snarl. An image formed of this man standing over a body, a gun in his hand.

She squeezed her eyes tight to get the image to come into focus, but it was gone.

"This is the man," she said in a strangled rasp.

Sergeant Howard sat beside her. "Are you sure?"

She nodded. Now that she had seen the picture, she knew that she had seen him before. If only her memories would return.

"Mason Green. Hmm. He has a record for assault with a deadly weapon."

Sadie could well believe that. "I think he killed someone."

The police officer beside her sat up straight. "Why do you say that?"

It was too late to call back the words. The memory she had was so faint, she hesitated to tell him. But she knew she had to. Even if she was in error. "I could be wrong. My memory is weak, and I only get snatches at times. I have an image in my mind, and it looks as though he is standing over a body. I can't give you any more than that."

Still, he tried to pull more information from her until he was sure that she had given him all that she knew.

"It may not be a full memory, and it might not be accurate," he mused. "But I won't discount it, either. The fact that you may have seen him in your past and that he now seems to be following you is concerning."

She couldn't deny that. She was feeling a bit concerned herself.

The drive back to the Mast farm seemed to take much longer than the drive to the station. When they arrived, she drummed her fingers against the edge of the seat until the car was in Park. Then she was out of the car like a shot and up the stairs. By the time she arrived at the door, Ben was there holding it open for her.

His deep brown eyes searched her face, his frown growing fiercer, obviously not liking whatever he saw. "You found something."

"More than that. Ben, I think I remembered something."

At that statement, his brows rose.

She entered the house, aware of Ben and the officer behind her. Before beginning, she glanced cautiously around the room. This was not a conversation she wanted seven-year-old ears to hear. Ben seemed to understand.

"Ruth wanted to visit with Caleb and Lovina while

you were gone. I sent Nathaniel with her. He was happy to get the opportunity to play with the other *kinner*."

It struck her suddenly that it may have been odd that she never needed an interpretation of any of the German terms that peppered the speech of her new Amish friends. Maybe she had other Amish friends she couldn't remember. Or maybe she worked with Amish people at one point in her life.

Not wanting to be distracted, she pushed the observation aside as unimportant and quickly related to Ben what she had learned at the station.

"This man has been in jail before?" he asked.

She was glad he was speaking. When she had finished telling him about the man she'd identified and her recovered partial memory, he had stood silent for a long moment, digesting the information. Too long. She had been close to asking if he was all right when he finally spoke.

She looked to Sergeant Howard for the answer to his question.

"Yes, Mason Green has been in and out of jail several times. Minor things, mostly. But the last time, he had assaulted someone and put them in the hospital. He was sent to jail but has been out for a year now. If he's out and about with a gun, though, he's in violation of his parole. That means he'll go in again when we catch him."

"If you catch him." Ben sighed and scraped his hands over his face.

Sadie ached at the trouble she was bringing to his door.

The officer didn't deny it, either, which was disturbing.

"Sadie." Ben broke into her thoughts. When she looked at him, his eyes appeared to be shuttered. She couldn't help but regret that he was withdrawing from her. Whatever connection there was between them, he plainly wished to break it.

"Yes?"

"This man you think he killed, are you sure you do not know who it is?"

Frustrated, she stalked away a few feet. "Don't you think I would tell you? Honestly, Ben, I've been racking my brains trying to figure it out. I just can't get a good sense of what's going on. It's driving me crazy, not being able to answer the simplest questions. And then there's all the things I seem to know but have no idea why I know them."

He nodded.

She waited. The seconds ticked by. Restless energy squirmed relentlessly up and down her arms and legs as she waited.

A loud whistle broke through the tension that had invaded the room. She jumped.

"Sorry. It's a call from my department." Sergeant Howard touched the radio attached to his shoulder and tilted his head, listening to the dispatcher's voice that exploded into the room in a static-infused burst.

"Gunshots have been reported..." The report continued. One person had been confirmed injured. The gunman had escaped. He was described as a white male, late twenties, one hundred and eighty pounds. Blond hair. A scar on his neck. As the dispatcher continued, Sadie felt her ears buzz, and she shook her head to stop the dizziness that attacked her. Mason Green had shot someone. She didn't know the area that well, but she was willing to guess that the shots fired had been close by.

As the message continued, she watched as the color leeched from Ben's face.

Sergeant Howard barked a question into the radio. When the dispatcher responded, he flipped the talk switch on the radio. "I'm a mile from the location. On my way."

He turned back to the two people watching him. "Green was apparently hiding in a barn, maybe to sleep, maybe for other purposes. When the property owner entered his barn and surprised him, it appears Green assaulted him. That's all I know at present."

"He didn't even know the man he shot." Ben's voice was flat. That did not bode well.

"I believe this was a case of the victim being in the wrong place at the wrong time. I don't need to tell you guys that he's dangerous. If you see him, do not approach. Call me. Sadie, you have the number to the police station. Use it. I have to go."

They both turned to watch him leave.

"Ben—" she began.

He didn't allow her to finish.

"That's less than a mile from here, Sadie." He stalked to the window and peered out, as if he would see Mason Green watching the house. "I need to go find my son. Then we need to decide our next move."

She watched him leave to retrieve Nathaniel, her heart breaking that she had brought disaster to their door. That even now, some stranger might be dead or dying because she had interrupted the peaceful existence of these people and forced herself upon them.

A sob burst from her mouth. She turned her gaze upward, appealing to the God that Ruth and Ben had such trust in. "God, why is this happening?"

She didn't expect an answer.

Hollowness swallowed her from the inside out. Mason Green was after her. He might have already killed Kurt. And it appeared he had no compunction about killing the innocent in his quest to find her.

Who would be next?

Ben didn't tell Lovina why Nathaniel needed to come home immediately.

"Ack, Ben. I'm sorry. Ruth needed to go visit her sister, who fell this morning. She should be back in the next thirty minutes or so."

When she fretted that Ruth wasn't home yet, he was actually relieved. He had some hard decisions to make.

"You can let her know that we don't need her to supervise anymore."

"Oh. *Gut.*" Lovina blinked at him, startled. He let her think what she wanted. He needed to get his son home now and deal with the situation.

Nathaniel came when he was called. He started to pout at leaving his friends, but something in his father's eyes must have convinced that now was not a good time to test his parent's patience.

Ben bade Lovina goodbye, then headed for home, his stride long and impatient.

"Dat." Nathaniel tugged at his sleeve.

Beneath the youthful warble of his seven-year-old's voice, Ben grimaced when he detected the trace of fear. That man was prowling around his community, looking for Sadie. The fact that she couldn't remember why he would be after her didn't change the fact that her presence was what had lured him here. What if Mason

Green wasn't alone? How many men were, in fact, after the pretty brunette?

He knew the man who had been shot. Listening to the dispatcher so calmly talk about someone he did business with being hurt, and possibly dying, caused a storm of emotions to fight for dominance in his soul. Hot anger began to kindle inside his gut. His son should be out playing with other boys his age. Instead, he was being put into danger by some strange *Englisch* woman just because her brother had a slight connection to him.

Immediately, shame washed over him. Had he forgotten every lesson his own *mamm* and *dat* had tried to instill in him? Not to mention the basic virtues of charity and hospitality. Not long ago, he had watched Sadie's car slam into a tree, and he had doubted she'd survive. Now he was begrudging her assistance when he knew her life was in danger.

Asking *Gott* for forgiveness, he entered the house and found Sadie pacing within. For some reason, the sight drove some of his anger away. It seemed that she was always pacing. Sadie Standings was not a very patient person.

"Dat?"

Shaking himself from the darkness of his thoughts, he smiled at Nathaniel. *"Jah*, Nathaniel?"

"I'm scared."

Sadie shifted, drawing Ben's attention back to her pale face. She caught his eyes.

"I shouldn't have come. I'm sorry, Ben. I wasn't thinking. I just got so anxious with Kurt not coming to get me and that man showing up. I never meant to put your family at risk." She tightened her jaw, visibly gathering up her courage. A spark of admiration for her flickered to life before he squashed it. "I still have my cell phone. I can call Braden. He left me his card, remember? I'm sure he would be willing to come and drive me somewhere else. Somewhere safe. Or maybe I can call Sergeant Howard back. He did say they sometimes put people in places to keep them safe."

Ben frowned. Where could she go to be safe? She had no memory. And what if the men had been able to track her because of the taxi driver? Right now, they hadn't found her. Yet. Although the men were close. Could Braden get here before these men found her? And as for going with the police, that might be her best option, but he didn't like the idea of leaving her with them. Even though he was the one who had insisted she go, now he wondered if it had made trouble for Kurt.

Was he even considering abandoning her and breaking his word?

Apparently, he was.

"Wait." He hadn't planned to speak, but the word popped out of his mouth. Sadie cast a guarded glance his way. He couldn't, wouldn't turn his back on someone in need. Lydia would have been ashamed of him if she had been alive here today. The thought of his wife sent another pain through his soul. Lydia wasn't here, though. If he had paid attention when she'd gotten sick, maybe they would have diagnosed her sooner and she would have been healed. She and their daughter might be alive today. But he hadn't, because his priorities had been skewed. He had been so busy with his work and other responsibilities, that he had failed to notice that his wife was ill.

Well, he was going to make sure his priorities were right this time, if only so that his son could see their faith in action. Squaring his shoulders, Ben took a single step toward Sadie. The movement had her turning her caramel-brown eyes his way. The sensation of familiarity that he'd experienced in the hospital struck him again. Briefly, it distracted him. He couldn't allow himself to be pulled away from his goal. He would get his son and Sadie to safety. But the moment he achieved that, she was no longer his responsibility.

"Sadie, your brother is a friend of mine. I will help you."

Hope stirred in her disturbing glance. Hopefully he wasn't making a mistake.

"Are you sure, Ben? You'll still help me?" she whispered, her voice soft, as if he'd change his mind if she spoke with her normal volume. Their eyes met, and he felt as if he were snared in a honey-brown net.

Nee, he wasn't sure at all. But he was too involved to back out now. "*Jah*, I will help. But we can't stay here."

"Where are we going, *Dat*?" Nathaniel piped up, interrupting the tension slowly building between the adults.

Ben pivoted to face his child and squatted to put himself closer to eye level with the boy. It would not be long before Nathaniel stood tall enough that Ben wouldn't need to do this.

"I think we should head out to see *Grossmamma* and *Grossdawdi*. That would be fun, *jah*?"

The boy's eyes widened. "True? Will I see my cousins?"

Ben's heart squeezed at the innocent question. The devastation of losing his wife and their unborn daughter had nearly killed him. He wasn't certain that it wouldn't have if he had not had Nathaniel to remind him daily that he had a reason to live. For that, he praised *Gott* every day. The community he'd grown up in, however, had ceased to be a refuge for him. Everywhere he went, the places and the people were only reminders of his loss. And when his parents began to pressure him to remarry, to give Nathaniel a new *mamm*, his very spirit had rebelled. He'd uprooted his son and moved to outside of Holmes County with a shocking rapidity. His family had been stunned.

It had never occurred to him that he was being selfish, that his son may have needed more family than his father around him.

The emotion, the guilt, clogged his throat. "*Jah*, Nathaniel. I am sure that your cousins will be there. *Grossmamma* wrote and said that your *mamm's* cousin Isaac has returned to the Plain way. He has a new wife, he does."

Ben had always liked Isaac. They'd gotten into some mischief together as boys. It had saddened him when Isaac's brother died and Isaac abandoned the Plain life.

Ben grimaced. He hadn't abandoned the faith, but he had left his family when tragedy struck. He and Isaac were alike in more ways than he cared to admit.

"Won't your family object to your bringing a stranger, and a non-Amish woman, into their home?"

Standing, Ben turned to where Sadie was standing. He took a few steps toward her. The urge to put his hand on her shoulder and offer her comfort startled him, causing him to halt abruptly.

"My *mamm* would never turn anyone away, not when a body is in danger. *Nee*, they won't mind. They will be happy to have the opportunity to spend time with Nathaniel, too. It has been a while."

Nee, mamm would be happy enough to see them. *Dat*

would, too, although Ben knew that his parents would both be concerned that he had nearly been alone with an *Englisch* woman.

"We'd best get moving. It's a long trip to my parents' home in a buggy. I don't know that I want to take the risk of calling the taxi driver. One less person who knows where we are, the safer we will be."

At least, that was what he was hoping.

In less than an hour they were tucked into the buggy. Ben sat up front, driving the horse. Sadie sat directly behind him with Nathaniel chattering away next to her. She answered his myriad questions with patience. Every time she spoke, Ben listened to her voice, the smooth-as-honey tones. He couldn't help himself. He was aware of her presence behind him to an alarming degree. Several times, he imagined that he could almost sense her eyes resting on him, even while she carried on a soft conversation with his son.

Flicking his wrists to snap the reins gently, Ben urged the horse to a trot once they reached the main road. The familiar rocking motion was soothing, even with the occasional jarring as the wheels hit a rock or a pothole. Relief filled him. He needed all his focus to be on the road, which meant he had to force his attention to stay off the woman he was helping. Traffic was heavier on the two-lane highway. The day was cool, with the scent of rain in the air. It would be hitting soon. Already the visibility was down. It was almost like riding inside of a cloud, the mist and fog were so heavy. His cheeks and beard grew damp as the first cold drops fell.

He sent a concerned glance at the sky. This was not ideal weather to travel in by buggy. If he'd had his druthers, he would have hired a driver. He wasn't worried for himself, although he could already tell that he was going to be chilled clean through before they stopped. Nathaniel, however, was still so young.

"Nathaniel." He heard Sadie's warm voice drifting from the confines of the buggy. "Let's get you wrapped up under this blanket. We wouldn't want you to get sick."

Amazingly, the boy didn't argue at being treated like the child that he was.

Lightning sizzled ahead of them. Ben blinked at the brightness. That had been close. Thunder boomed three seconds later.

The storm was coming quick. He had no sooner thought it than the sky opened and the rain slashed down in sheets. Within seconds, he was drenched. Worse, he felt prickles of ice hit the bare skin on his face that was unprotected by the beard.

"I'm going to try and find a place we can wait out this storm," he yelled back to Sadie. "It's freezing rain. It won't be safe for us to continue on, especially not with the plows coming out."

Sadie leaned forward. He looked her way briefly. Her brows lowered, creating furrows in her otherwise smooth forehead. "Where?"

Ben's eyes swept the horizon. It was difficult to see far, but what he could see showed open highway.

Where was a very good question.

Chapter Six

The longer he waited, the harder it became to see. As it was, it was like trying to see through a downpour of Ruth's famous split pea soup, the rain was so heavy. Heavy black clouds hovered over them like an ominous warning.

Thankfully, Sadie had made sure that Nathaniel was kept warm and dry inside the buggy. Which was more than could be said of Ben, but he wasn't about to complain. *Nee*, instead, he would thank *Gott* for keeping his son safe. And for keeping Sadie alive and well.

He heard her soft laugh echoing inside the buggy. He could imagine her face and the glow in her eyes without turning around. He frowned, the faint image in his mind, just out of reach, teased him. What was it about her that was so familiar?

His reverie was broken by a sharp crack. The horse shied, neighing frantically. Ben pulled gently on the reins, attempting to soothe the nervous beast. He scanned the area for a fallen branch or a limb hanging from a tree—something capable of making the loud sound. Nothing appeared out of the ordinary.

The loud crack happened again. This time, the horse reared up, nearly unseating Ben. A covey of birds in a nearby tree took flight, squawking and flapping madly. Ben didn't bother looking around to see where the sound had come from this time. This time, he recognized that sound. It was a gunshot.

The question was, where was the shooter?

Another shot rang out. Ben yelled as agony seared across his arm. All thought of searching for a safe refuge for the night vanished. His most pressing need was just to survive and to protect the two people in the buggy who were calling out an alarm.

"Hold on!" he shouted to them. "We are being shot at. I can't see a car. He must be on foot."

Gripping the reins firmly in his hands, Ben flicked his wrists, giving the command for the horse to gallop. It wasn't a command one usually made in weather like this. It wasn't safe to travel in a buggy at this high velocity. But he didn't have any choice. Somewhere nearby a man with a gun was using them for target practice. He didn't intend to stand still and let them be caught.

The frightened mare bolted forward, dragging the buggy with her. As her head turned slightly to the right, Ben had a brief glance of the wildness and fear within the mare's eye. He hoped he'd be able to stop her once they were safe from gunfire. He would not allow himself to imagine that they would not get out of danger.

Nathaniel screamed once behind him, then his voice dwindled to a whimper. Ben winced as his son's quiet sobs reached his ears. Nathaniel was not a crier. It tore him to pieces to hear Nathaniel weeping now. Unfortunately, there was nothing Ben could do about it.

Vaguely he was aware of Sadie trying to keep the child calm.

All of Ben's attention had to be on the horse and the road in front of them. The mare was zigzagging on the road at a full gallop. Once or twice the buggy tilted alarmingly. Ben gripped the reins tighter. The edge of the leather strap dug into his palm.

A new sound caught his attention. A low rumble, which quickly built to a harsh roar. Glancing behind, he saw a motorcycle coming up fast on their left side. The rider was hunkered down on the seat, his blond hair plastered to his head by the rain streaming down the side of his face.

Mason Green.

The fact that Green was on a motorcycle gave Ben and those he was trying to protect one advantage. Mason needed both hands to steer, which meant he had the gun tucked away somewhere. Hopefully, the man wouldn't figure out how to shoot and drive at the same time. They would be in real trouble then.

He must not have been a hunter, Ben thought fleetingly. If he had been, he wouldn't have had so much trouble hitting his target. Shaking his head to clear the rain from his eyes, he strained to see where he might possibly go to try and lose the motorcycle bearing down on them.

A horn honked in the distance ahead. A large delivery van was heading their way. Ben felt a spark of hope. The road was too narrow to accommodate all of them. The motorcycle would have to back off. There was no way the biker could come up beside them with the van blocking the other lane. There was no shoulder on the right side of the road, so there was very little chance the bike would be able to approach them from that side, either.

As the van got closer, the horse skirted to the edge of the road. One wheel of the buggy slipped over the edge and Ben could feel it sway. Ben leaned to the left, trying to balance it. It was no use. With a shudder, the vehicle hitched. Behind him, Sadie gasped and Nathaniel was sobbing. A splintering noise on his right told him some of the spokes on the wheel snapped. The buggy heaved to the side, throwing Ben clear.

He hit the ground with a thud, mud splattering his face and drenching his clothes. All of this was minor compared to the agony that shot up his arm as he landed on the gunshot wound. Ignoring the pain, he jumped to his feet.

"Dat! Dat!"

Ben turned and his eyes met the horror-stricken gaze of Sadie. She was struggling to escape from the wrecked vehicle. To his relief, both she and his son appeared to be uninjured, although Nathaniel was crying.

He couldn't let Sadie get out of the buggy. They were stopped, and a killer was right behind them.

"Nee, stay there," he called out, his eyes searching the area desperately to see where the biker was. To his surprise, the man who had just tried to kill them was not coming any closer.

The delivery van was beside them. As soon as it passed, they would be in trouble. He opened his mouth to tell Sadie they were going to try and run down the embankment and escape.

The van didn't pass them. Instead, it pulled to a stop beside them and the driver stepped down and ran over to them.

Mason Green made a U-turn in the middle of the road

and roared off in the opposite direction. They were safe for the moment.

How had he known that they were in the buggy?

A chill settled in his heart as he realized that Mason must have located his house and seen them leave. There was no other explanation. He had tracked them like a dog tracking a coon. As soon as he had determined they were away from anyone who could rescue them, he'd attacked.

"Sir, are you hurt? Can I help you folks?"

"Yes!" Sadie cried out from the confines of the buggy. "Stay here, Nathaniel."

Ben turned to watch her scramble out, her blue denim jeans incongruous with the Amish vehicle. His mind was going foggy with the pain from the combination of his wound and the jar of the fall. Otherwise, he might have been tempted to laugh at the sight. She was so small and slender—she couldn't have been more than five foot three or four—it seemed impossible that she would be able to bear up under the weight of everything she'd been through the past few days. But she had. Her expression was fierce and determined, her lips pressed together in a straight line. She was not beaten down. His heart was glad.

She strode to where the driver was standing over Ben. "My friend was injured, obviously. He may need an ambulance."

"I will not go to the hospital." Ben was adamant. The hospital could do nothing for him. He glanced down at his arm. It was bleeding, but not badly. His jacket had protected it, for the most part. All he required was a bandage.

Sadie gasped. She was staring at his sleeve in horror. Before she could say anything, he swayed on his feet.

The delivery van driver grabbed his good arm, lending his assistance.

"*Denke*."

"Sure. Listen, I don't want to tell y'all what to do, but it sure does appear you should listen to the lady here. I can call 911 or I can drive you myself."

Ben shook his head. "*Nee*. I don't need an ambulance."

"Ben—"

"How's Nathaniel?" He cut her off, distracting her. "Are you *gut*, son?"

"*Jah, Dat*. I'm fine. That man was scary!"

That he was.

The driver was obviously conflicted. "Look, I can't just leave you sitting here in the middle of the road. Your go-cart or whatever you call it—" he gestured at the busted buggy "—is out of commission. And you all won't fit on the back of the mare."

"It's a buggy," Sadie replied.

"We don't ride horses," Ben said at the same time. Both facts were ridiculous and irrelevant at the moment. "Sadie, if you have your phone, you can call Sergeant Howard."

She shook her head. "I have it, but it's not charged at the moment." That made sense. There was no electricity at his house. "Even if it was charged, we need to get you and Nathaniel out of the cold as soon as humanly possible."

She was right. He wasn't as concerned about himself as he was about his son. And about her. She was a target out here. If the driver left, Mason Green might attack again. They had no way of knowing how far away he had gone.

"Could you give us a ride, maybe?" he asked the driver.

Relieved, the man nodded his head. "Absolutely. Where to? Want me to drive you home?"

Ben exchanged a glance with Sadie. They couldn't return to his house. Not now that they had proof that Mason Green had found Sadie and would kill her if he could.

"*Nee*. Not my *haus*. I'd appreciate it if you could drive us to the police station."

They received their share of odd looks as they traipsed into the station, that was for sure. To be fair, they probably didn't see very many bleeding Amish carpenters at the Waylan Grove police station. Nor did they normally see such men accompanied by young women in worn-out jeans and sneakers.

Sergeant Ryder Howard wasn't there when they arrived, but the chief of police, a lovely African-American woman with sharp eyes and short spikey hair in a stylish cut called him when Sadie introduced herself.

"He'll be here in fifteen minutes," the woman assured them. "I'm Chief Sheila Carson. We didn't get the opportunity to meet the other day when you were here. I have to let you know, your willingness to identify Mason Green might help us actually get him on charges that might lock him up for good."

"I hope so," Sadie said, her voice grim. She shuddered as she recalled the moment when Ben had toppled from the buggy. She'd thought for a moment that he'd been dead. "He came after us today and he shot my friend."

With an exclamation, Chief Carson turned to Ben, scouring him with a keen glance.

"Where were you hit?" she bit out.

"In the arm. I'm fine," he insisted.

"He refuses to go to the hospital," Sadie told the chief, frustrated at the stubbornness of the man. Didn't he realize that the injury could become infected? "If you have a first aid kit, I could look at my friend's arm while we wait for Sergeant Howard."

Within five minutes, Sadie and the Mast men were in the conference room, a first aid kit on the table. One of the officers had loaned her a charger, and her cell phone was plugged in. The chief had sent another one of the officers to the cafeteria to bring them something to eat while they waited. She wasn't that hungry, most likely due to nerves. But neither Ben nor his son seemed to have any trouble eating. Both of them had lowered their heads to pray silently, then they had silently scarfed down grilled cheese sandwiches, dipping them in bowls of steaming tomato soup. Nathaniel had wrinkled his nose at the first bite, and she had held in her laugh with difficulty. Ben had smirked, even as he took another mouthful.

"He's used to eating soup that was homemade," he explained. Ah. No doubt the soup was from a can, Sadie thought to herself.

"Okay, let me see your arm." She made her tone as no-nonsense as possible. He grumbled as he removed his coat, but she refused to give in. The least she could do was tend to his injury. He set his coat on a chair and rolled up his sleeve. Both items were torn where the bullet had hit.

The wound was just above the elbow. Had it been in a place where he'd have had to remove his shirt, she knew he never would have agreed to allow her to care for him. She could tell the situation made him uncomfortable, so she promised to hurry as she pulled on gloves and opened the kit.

When she saw where the bullet had grazed him, she sighed quietly. It was not nearly as bad as she had feared. Still, she was gentle as she cleaned the wound. It might have done better with a stitch or two, but she knew that wasn't going to happen. She applied a sterile dressing and taped it down.

"Keep this clean," she ordered him.

"*Jah*, I know what to do."

Did he really just roll his eyes at her?

With a small huff to disguise her grin, she gathered up the supplies, planning to remove her gloves and seal the bloody cloth inside them before discarding them. As her eyes moved to the blood on the white square of fabric, the room faded. Suddenly she heard voices as if from far away. A woman crying, loud harsh sobs, as if her world had shattered and she was left devastated. A man lay on the floor at Sadie's feet. It was the same man she had seen before, when she'd had a flashback of Mason Green. Now, though, she could clearly see the man. He was definitely dead, a gunshot wound gaping in his chest. His eyes, light brown in color, were open and staring.

He was Amish. She saw the hat lying beside him on the ground. The beard of a married man. No mustache. And again the woman crying.

"Sadie? Sadie!"

With a start, she came back to the present. Ben was standing in front of her, a concerned frown on his face. His left hand was raised, almost as if he wanted to touch her, to offer comfort, but wasn't sure if it was appropriate or if she'd accept comfort from him.

Nathaniel looked a little upset. She sent him a wobbly smile, desperate to hold the storm of emotions tamped down. For several seconds she battled. Then she made a mistake and looked back at Ben. He appeared to decide to risk her wrath and settled a warm hand on her shoulder.

"I'm here, Sadie. Did you remember something?"

It was more than she could take.

The tears she had dammed up burst forth in a torrent that shook her entire body. She couldn't breathe, she was sobbing so hard. She tried to stem the emotions, to get herself back under control. She placed both hands over her face, as if she could hide from him. She completely lost the battle when strong arms came around her, holding her close. Ben placed one hand on the back of her head and gently guided her face to his shoulder. She wept, and he accepted her tears, her pain, without a word.

"Am I interrupting something?"

Mortified, Sadie broke free of Ben's embrace. The shock of hearing Sergeant Howard's startled voice had the effect of drying up her tears instantly. Turning away, she rubbed her sleeve across her face, trying to scrub off the wet tracks on her cheeks. Not that he didn't already know she was upset.

A small hand crept into hers. Nathaniel. That sweet child. Without thinking, she stooped and kissed his forehead, letting him know she was fine.

"*Nee*, you're not interrupting." Ben responded to the officer's question, sounding remarkably calm and unperturbed. How she envied that! "I believe Sadie has remembered something. *Jah*, Sadie?"

Sergeant Howard's blue eyes flashed to her, alert. "Is that true? You've remembered something? Is it connected to what you remembered before?"

She didn't want to discuss it. However, knowing it might be important, she nodded reluctantly. "I'm pretty sure it is, yeah."

Biting her lip, she reached for the water she'd earlier ignored, more to give herself time to think than because she actually wanted it. The moment she took a swallow, though, she realized how dry her mouth and throat were. She gulped down half of the cold water.

When she set the glass down, Ben was still watching her, a slight smile tugging at his lips. She had chugged that pretty fast.

"Are you ready to tell us?"

"Sorry," she said, grimacing at the question. "I didn't realize how thirsty I was. I will tell you, but…" She cast a significant glance at Nathaniel.

"Ah, yes. One moment." The sergeant stepped out the door for a moment.

"Sadie, are you well?"

"Yes, I'm fine, Ben. If it will help them catch this guy, I will gladly tell them."

Sergeant Howard returned with a female in uniform and approached Nathaniel. "Hey, buddy, I want you to go with Officer Jill for a moment."

The woman held out a hand and smiled. Nathaniel gave his father a wild gaze but settled when his dad smiled calmly and told him to go.

The moment the two left, all attention returned to Sadie. She cleared her throat.

"Okay, then. Anyway, I don't know if your chief had mentioned it to you, but Mason Green chased us today and he shot Ben." She gestured toward the Amish man. Sergeant Howard nodded. Yes, he knew. That made it a bit easier. "So I asked her if I could clean the wound. When I was finished, I was picking up the cloths with his blood on it, you know? But suddenly, I wasn't here. I had a memory of a woman crying, and I saw a man lying on the ground, dead."

As she tended to do when she grew anxious, she paced a couple of steps away before turning back to them. "I'm sure it was the same man I saw before, only this time I saw his face. I didn't see Mason Green, but I saw the man he'd been standing over."

Feeling as if she had run out of air, she sucked in a deep breath before she finished describing the rest of the flashback, which was what she was positive it was. "The dead man? I don't know who he was, but he was an Amish man." She saw Ben straighten out of the corner of her eye, but kept her glance on the police officer.

"Amish?" He flicked a quick glance at Ben. "Are you sure?"

"Yeah. He had the beard, no mustache and a hat like Ben's. He also had brown eyes." This was part that really sounded crazy. "I think he had my eyes."

Chapter Seven

"What do you mean, he had your eyes?" The question erupted from Ben. When she winced, he realized he'd practically shouted at her. "Sorry. I didn't mean to yell. I am surprised."

Actually, he was shocked to his core. The implications of this memory, if it were true and if he were correct, could be devastating.

"I don't know, Ben. I really don't. I might be wrong. I probably am. But what if I'm not?"

Indeed.

He wished he could ask Kurt. Kurt had mentioned his sister many times. He adored his little sister. But never once had he hinted that the woman he considered his sibling might have Amish relatives somewhere. So where did that leave them?

"Hold on, Sadie. Are you saying you're Amish?" Sergeant Howard tilted his head and considered her.

"I have no idea. All I know is that my mother and Kurt's father got married sixteen years ago. My stepbrother is missing. And Mason Green, the man who I think I might have remembered standing over the body of an Amish man I may be related to has shot my friend, and would probably have killed me and Ben and Nathaniel if he'd not been scared away by the delivery van driver."

Silence filled the conference room after her words.

"You have to go into hiding until this is over."

The sergeant's words dropped like pebbles into the tense silence. Ben watched her face pale. Just twenty minutes earlier, she'd been sobbing in his arms, her heart breaking. He couldn't bear to see her hurting. An urge to protect her rushed upon him. If the police moved her, what if she was still in danger?

"Let me take her to my community, where I grew up." The words fell from his lips before he'd thought them through. "That's where we were headed when he attacked us."

"I would think that he would find you."

"How?" Ben challenged. "He has no idea where I grew up. It's several hours from here, in a different district. And Plain folk are not likely to spill another's secrets to an *Englischer*. Not that many know my family. I moved here three years ago, and Nathaniel and I have mostly kept to ourselves. I think Mason Green followed a taxi driver who drove Sadie to my house to the area. If we travel in another vehicle, the chances of him finding us again are slim."

The man did not look convinced. A knock on the door halted the conversation. Jill, the officer who had taken Nathaniel, opened the door and let the little boy back into the room. Nathaniel went over to sit by a window, clearly worn out.

"Hey, Ryder. Sorry to disturb you. We have a call. All available personnel."

"We do? I didn't hear a call come through." Sergeant Howard thumbed his radio. Nothing happened. "Huh. My radio appears to be broken. Okay, look, Ben, Sadie. You guys wait here. We will figure this out, but first I need to go and see if I'm needed on this call. Don't go anywhere."

He followed Jill out the door. When the door shut, they listened to his hard shoes clomp away.

"I can't stay here."

Ben glanced to see that Sadie had moved to his side. His nose caught a faint whiff of her clean scent before he put a couple of inches between them. Unable to help himself, he put a hand on her arm.

"You want to leave?"

She searched his face, her gaze pleading. "I have to, Ben. I think that my memories are starting to come back to me. And I am desperate to keep trying to find Kurt. If they hide me away somewhere, my hands are tied. Plus, I'd be alone. Alone and helpless, with no way to find the truth. I don't like that."

He wouldn't, either.

"*Gut*. We will wait until the police have left, then we will keep moving toward where my family is."

Astonishment lit her face. "You still want to go with me? What if I bring danger to your family?"

"Sadie, I was honest when I said I think my old district is the safest place for you. We must trust in *Gott*. He will protect us."

She breathed out a half laugh, half sigh. "I don't even know if I am a person of faith. It feels strange, though, hearing people talking about trusting God. I mean, how can you when so much bad happens?"

"*Jah*, I felt that way when my wife died," he murmured, keeping his voice pitched low so that Nathaniel wouldn't hear him. "For a time, I thought *Gott* had abandoned us. Abandoned me when He took my beautiful bride and my baby girl."

"How did you ever trust Him again?"

"I don't know how I would have gotten through that dark time without *Gott* in my life. He helped me see that bad things are not His plan, but that He does have a plan. I trust Him to know what is best for me."

She didn't look convinced. Given what had happened to her in the recent past, he couldn't say that he blamed her. How did you explain trusting *Gott* when your life was in chaos?

"If we are going to go, we need to go now." He picked up his coat and put it on again, careful not to irritate his wound. "Nathaniel, *cumme*. We must go."

"Goin' to *Grossmamma's haus, Dat*?"

He felt a twinge of guilt at the boy's tired voice. "*Jah*. We are going to *Grossmamma's haus*."

"How will we travel?" Sadie murmured, donning her own coat. She walked over to the far wall and unplugged her phone. "It's fully charged."

That gave him an idea.

"Do you still have Braden's number? Maybe he can recommend a driver we can trust."

In reply, she pushed a button on her phone and it sprang to life. "I saved his number in my contacts."

He waited while she called the driver. Impatience danced up and down his spine. He held himself still with an effort, refusing to fidget as if he were a *kind*.

"Hey Braden, it's me. Sadie. Listen we need a ride… Well, we're worried that the man after me might know your car, he came after me." Ben could hear the exclamation coming through the phone. He smiled briefly. "Oh, really? That sounds great. Thanks. Here."

To his surprise, she handed him the phone. "He said his own car broke down and is in the shop. He has a rental now that he normally wouldn't be caught in. He'll give us a ride in that without charge. No one should recognize it, but I don't know where to tell him to meet us."

Ben took the phone gingerly, more uncomfortable than he'd been in a long time, but this was an emergency. His bishop did allow them to use cell phones if it was really necessary. In the fewest words possible, he gave the driver directions to an intersection several blocks away. He didn't want the police seeing them getting into a car in front of the station. Or anyone else.

He handed the phone back to Sadie. "*Cumme*. We must go."

It was a true testament to how serious his tone was that the exhausted Nathaniel didn't even make a token protest as they left the station and walked the several blocks to meet up with Braden, even though it was still raining. They didn't recognize the car, of course. It was only when he pulled directly in front of them and rolled the window down that they knew him.

The moment they heard his doors unlock, the three runaways jumped in, scurrying across the back seat, Nathaniel in the middle. Braden put the car in Drive and started forward. Ben laid his head against the back of the seat for a second, allowing some of the tension that had gripped him to flow out.

"Where to, man?" Braden looked at them through the rearview mirror.

Ben gave him the address and the young man plugged it into his GPS.

As the miles ticked away, he couldn't quite shake the worry that Mason Green was still out there. Nor could he forget the flashbacks that Sadie was experiencing.

What if the amnesia she was afflicted with hid a dark secret? One that could hurt her as much as Mason Green?

How was he to protect her and his family from a danger that she couldn't remember?

The windshield wipers were set on high, swishing back and forth at full speed to keep up with the onslaught of rain streaming down the windshield. It was coming down so hard now that it wasn't even possible to distinguish drops. Rather, it was a constant sheet of water. When they had first gotten on the interstate highway, the traffic was flowing nicely at around sixty miles an hour. They certainly weren't going sixty now. She leaned forward so that she could peer over and see the speedometer. Just over forty. Great. Well, the one positive was that nearly everyone else had slowed down, too.

Sighing, she settled back against the seat. Ben reached across Nathaniel and tapped her shoulder to get her attention. "Relax. We're on our way to a new place in a car the man after you has not seen before."

He removed his arm and she immediately felt the loss. Which was just silly. She did not need to develop a crush on a man so out of her reach. Even if he was kind and brave.

And thoughts about him would not be a good idea either. She tossed him a smile to let him know she had heard him, then turned her head to watch the rain sliding down the window.

Nathaniel slumped against her right arm, his even breathing deepening to soft little snorting snores. It was adorable. She smiled down at the child snuggled up to her so trustingly. Ben shifted in his seat near the window. When she lifted her gaze, her heart melted at the tender expression on his face as he watched his son sleep. A rather robust snore escaped from Nathaniel. All three of the adults in the car chuckled softly. She was still laughing when her gaze rose and snared Ben's.

All laughter fled. The electricity that had been simmering between them for days flared to life. He had the deepest eyes she had ever seen. The rain pounding on the car, the radio quietly playing in the front of the vehicle, all of it faded until she was aware of nothing except the strong man sitting so close to her, with only a sleeping child separating them.

"Guys, we have a problem." Braden's voice was like being doused with icy water. Both Ben and Sadie jumped, their faces flushing. The sudden movement woke up Nathaniel. The child sat up straight with a cry.

"*Dat!* What's happening?" The fear in his young voice shredded her heart to pieces. No child should have to be afraid. Without thinking about it, she looped her arm around his slender shoulders and hauled him closer to her.

"*Alles ist gut*, Nathaniel," she murmured, the words for *all is well* flowing off her tongue like smooth cream. The moment the words left her mouth, she stiffened, her eyes opening wide. How had she known that phrase? Was it something she'd heard from Ben or Ruth? And why had it felt so natural to say it? Even if she had heard it, it shouldn't have been her instinctive way to comfort him.

"Sadie—" Ben begin, his face covered in confusion. The car slid slightly before Braden corrected it.

"What's the issue?" she asked the driver, keeping her

tone calm. She shared a glance with Ben. That conversation would have to wait.

Now that she was paying attention, she realized that they had slowed down. A lot. The rain hitting the windshield had altered. She could hear some of the drops *plink* as they made contact with the glass. Plink was not a word that should be associated with rain.

"Is that ice?" Ben asked, leaning forward slightly.

"Sure is. The road is getting slippy." She might have found the local word for *slippery* quaint and amusing if the situation hadn't been so treacherous. Knots were beginning to form between her shoulders as the tension inside her ratcheted up a notch. "I might need to take the back roads. The traffic won't be as heavy there."

"If that's what you think is best," Ben responded. She could see the crease that formed on his brow. He might have sounded calm, but he was worried; she could see the concern hovering in the deep shadows of his eyes.

God, if You're there, please help us. Protect Ben and Nathaniel and let us get to his home.

The prayer sprang from the depths of her soul. She had no idea if she was normally a praying person or not, but right at this moment, she knew that no one but the Almighty could get them out of the current mess they were in.

A semi truck zoomed past them, its speed creating a vortex that sucked them toward the fast lane. Sadie tightened her grip on Nathaniel and squeezed her eyes shut. Then they shot open again when Ben's hand closed over hers. He pulled it back when she looked at him. She knew he had been silently offering her encouragement, but it felt like more.

"Idiot driver. Does he think it's summertime?" Braden muttered darkly.

Once the car was no longer being pulled to the side, he sighed. A few minutes later, he moved up behind a slower-moving car. He switched lanes, passing a large sedan inching along. Sadie looked over. The woman at the wheel was staring ahead, her hands clenched on the wheel in concentration. This weather was an accident waiting to happen.

No sooner had the thought crossed her mind, then Braden exclaimed, his foot hitting the brake. She could feel the shudder as the antilock brakes kicked on and the vehicle began to skid. Outside the car, the air screeched with the horrendous clatter of metal crunching against metal. The semi that had passed them so blithely earlier had jackknifed and was completely blocking the road. Several cars had collided in their attempt to avoid the rig. Drivers were climbing out of the vehicles. She couldn't hear them, but it was obvious by their agitated movements that some of them were shouting. Fists were shaken in the air.

The violence of it disturbed her.

Even more disturbing, though, was the knowledge that they were not going to be able to follow through with their plans of traveling to the next exit and getting off the interstate. Which meant they wouldn't be able to use the back roads to get the remainder of the distance to Ben's family's home.

They were stuck, here in the middle of nowhere, on an icy interstate filled with other irate travelers. And the weather appeared to be growing worse. The icy downpour had become more snow than rain in the past few minutes while they'd been sitting still.

What if Mason Green was in one of the vehicles that was halting behind them? Granted, he didn't know what car Braden was driving. But they lost the advantage while they were sitting in an unmoving vehicle. All he had to do was get out of his vehicle and walk along the center of the road between the two eastbound lanes to see if he could find them inside the car. If he found them here, how would they protect themselves?

He really wasn't after Ben, Nathaniel or Braden. She knew that if he found them, she'd leave with Green to protect the others. Although she didn't think they would just let her go.

And that would put them in even more danger. She had no doubt Green would willingly shoot her companions to get to her.

The image of him standing over the body of another man intruded once again. Her stomach curdled. She swallowed hard and tried to breathe in through her nose to control the roiling of her gut. Fear prickled her skin, like tiny insects crawling over her.

"We can't just sit here!" she burst out.

"I'm really sorry," Braden said, lifting his hands in a helpless gesture. His face was frustrated. "There's nothing more I can do right now. Hopefully they'll be able to get some tow trucks and a crew out to move the semi and get us moving again. Until then, I'm going to have to sit right here. I don't like it, either."

"That doesn't mean we have to stay here," Ben said, his voice slow and considering. He was obviously working on an idea even as he spoke.

Sadie switched her eyes to the Amish man sitting so close to her. "What do you mean? What else can we do?"

He glanced quickly at his son before meeting her eyes.

"We're not that far from my old District. It's cold out, but we're dressed warm. We could probably walk the rest of the distance."

She pondered his words, mentally balancing the pros and cons. It might be their best option. Still, she hesitated to agree.

"Would that be too much for—" She really didn't want to say Nathaniel's name out loud, knowing that any sign that she felt he was weak would infuriate the seven-year-old. But her concern was real. It would be a lot to ask of the child. It was wet and slippery out, and judging by the way the trees on the side of the road were swaying, the wind was fierce.

Ben frowned, his own gaze troubled. "*Nee*, I think not. It will be hard. I do not know what else to do."

Biting her lip, she thought about it. "Ben, you and Nathaniel could go. He won't be after you if I'm not with—"

"*Nee*." He glared at her. "We all go, or we all stay. *Wir bleiben zusammen*."

The last was said deliberately. Nathaniel nodded with his father. "*Jah*."

Her breath shuddered out of her. Maybe she was wrong, but she was pretty sure she knew what he had said. *We stay together*.

His satisfied expression told her she was right. Why had she known that? Had she taken German in high school? Somehow, she doubted it. This felt more natural than a memory from a class years ago.

"Are you guys sure about this?" Braden asked.

"*Jah. Denke* for your help. We will walk from here."

The young man hit the door locks and his passengers all climbed out of the vehicle. They walked as quickly as they could over the slippery surface of the black top

covered with a thin layer of black ice. Ben assisted them
over the guard rail and the silent trio began to make the
slow trek down the shallow embankment.

The trees seemed so far away. Until they made it, they
would be out in the open. She was aware of Ben moving
to walk behind them. Not because he was slower, she realized, but because he was sheltering them with his body.
Anyone coming after them would have to get past him.

Their pace was slower than she would have liked but
it couldn't be helped. They were walking in thick mud,
which sucked her boots in and made them feel like they
had lead weights in the bottoms. Then there was Nathaniel. He wasn't a complainer, which she truly appreciated,
but he was only seven. His legs couldn't match the long
strides she would have used without him.

She flicked an angst-ridden gaze back toward the interstate they'd abandoned. The cars were backed up for
as far as they could see. Was Mason Green among them?
She couldn't shake the feeling that they had targets on
their backs. Anyone looking their way would see them.

After what felt like forever, they reached the tree line.

As they ducked behind the large pines and slipped into
the shadows, she looked back one final time, feeling as
if she were under a microscope. Had they been noticed?

Heart pounding, she plunged into the cover of the
trees.

Chapter Eight

They hadn't gone far before Sadie became aware of an echo behind them. She paused, pulling Ben and Nathaniel to a stop again. She held her breath, hoping to be proven wrong. There it was… Footsteps. Then suddenly the noise stopped.

They were being followed.

Sadie and Ben looked around. When they glanced back at each other, they both shook their heads. They couldn't see anything. Ben pointed down. She nodded. She knew his thought matched her own. Whoever was following them was using their footprints as a guide.

Grabbing Nathaniel's hands, Ben whispered to his son to stay quiet and follow. He led them off the path. They went down, down, down an incline. The rocks were slippery and they had to watch their step, but there would be no prints. That was an advantage. Her left foot skidded a bit on the slick surface. Any advantage they had would be lost if she fell down the incline and made a racket that would draw the killer to their position.

Ben seemed to know where he was going, she noted with relief. He'd grown up in this area, she reminded herself. It made sense that he would know his way around. He wore an air of confidence that gave her some hope that they could survive their current situation.

"*Cumme*, Nathaniel. Let me help you down."

Nathaniel sucked in his lower lip. The poor thing looked scared to death, but he obeyed his parent without question. Ben jumped down one particularly steep part, then reached up his arms for his son. Effortlessly, he swung the boy down by his side. Sadie was impressed with the unconscious show of his physical strength.

Her admiration changed to alarm when the man turned back to her. She gulped. There was not much she could do. She had to get down there, and they didn't have the luxury of time to let her try and make her own slow way down.

She allowed herself to lean into Ben's arms, setting her hands on his shoulders to keep her balance. When he pulled her down and swung her to his side, a strange breathlessness stole over her.

It may have been her imagination, but she thought that he held on to her a second or two longer than necessary. Then again, he might have been trying to ascertain if she was steady enough to stand on her own.

When he let go, she felt a pang of regret, but quickly shoved it aside. They didn't have time for her to be non-sensical.

Ben led his son and Sadie along a rocky path that wound through patches of mud-covered areas where the trees were less dense and erosion had worn away the rocks. They communicated mostly with gestures, as any sound could lead the villain hunting them down straight to them.

Suddenly, Ben stopped. Excitement filled him as he turned in a circle, looking around.

"Sadie," he whispered softly. "There's a cave near here. Its entrance is partially hidden by trees and shrubs. If we can get there, we can get out of the rain."

He cast a glance meaningfully behind them. She nodded to show she comprehended the secret message. If they hid in the cave, it might throw whoever was following them off the track long enough for them to escape.

"It's worth a shot," she whispered back.

"We're going to go to a cave?" Nathaniel didn't sound excited. She looked at Ben and could see the compassion there. Ben knew his son did not like the dark. A dark cave would not be his son's choice for an adventure.

"*Jah*. Sadie and I will be with you. Maybe we can dry off some, ain't so?"

The sigh that came out of the child lifted his shoulders in an exaggerated motion. Sadie saw Ben bite back a smile. The little boy was so endearing, Sadie covered her mouth with her hand so he wouldn't think she was laughing at him.

"Guess so, *Dat*."

Her heart melted at the brave acceptance. Putting her arm around his shoulders, she gave Nathaniel a gentle squeeze. "I don't like caves, either, but your father is right that it would be good to get out of the rain."

She was afraid to say more. Even though they were whispering and couldn't hear any steps behind them, it didn't mean that they were out of danger. Or out of earshot.

Keeping a firm hand in Nathaniel's, she followed Ben until they came to the mouth of the cave. He was right. The entrance was partially hidden. She might have missed it altogether had he not been there with her.

Hopefully, the person following them, whether it was Mason Green or someone else, wasn't familiar with the surroundings. If he wasn't, they might be able to hide out and escape.

Unfortunately, inside a cave hewn out of stone on a cold October day wasn't a warm place to be. With their clothes damp from the weather, it wasn't long before teeth started chattering.

Shivering, she moved beside Nathaniel and pulled him into her arms, trying to warm the little boy. She was shocked when Ben stepped to his other side and pulled both of them into his arms. She knew it was just from necessity. There was nothing romantic in the embrace. It was purely for the sake of survival.

Telling herself that, however, did nothing to stop the red tide of hot color that she could feel flooding her neck and up into her face. Her heartbeat kicked up. She was amazed that neither Nathaniel nor Ben seemed to be aware of how affected she was by the group embrace.

A scratching outside the cave got their attention.

Trepidation stole over her. The muscles in her shoulders and neck bunched. Something—or someone—was outside the cave. Whoever it was didn't seem to be trying to enter. She told herself it was probably an animal of some sort scavenging for the winter.

She didn't believe it. Whatever was out there was larger than a squirrel.

The hair stood up on the back of her neck. For no animal would have made that noise. It was a footstep, made by human feet.

Ben gestured for them to stay down. He went to peek out.

A second later, he rushed back inside. Unceremoniously, he lifted his son into his arms.

"Move," he hissed urgently.

She moved. They ran deeper inside the cave.

"We can't get out without being shot," he explained as they hurried. "It's Green. It looks like he's trying to blow up something at the entrance."

Horror shot through her. "We'll be trapped here."

No sooner had the words left her mouth than an explosion rocked the cave, showering rocks and debris in every direction.

The cave entrance disappeared in a hail of rocks, stones and debris. The blast knocked all of them to the ground. The cave had been shadowy and dim before. Now it was pitch black. Fear rose up inside Ben. Neither Nathaniel nor Sadie was making any sound. Frantically he sat up.

"Sadie? Nathaniel? Please answer." He held his breath as he crawled over the floor, searching for the others.

His fingers came in contact with Sadie's. He gripped her hand, and the backs of his eyes grew hot when she grabbed onto him. Nathaniel called out his name weakly. As quickly as he could, he followed his son's voice until he found him. The child was terrified, but Ben couldn't feel any wounds on him. He needed to know for sure.

"Are you hurt?" Ben asked them.

"I'm fine, but I can't see anything. What about you guys?" Sadie responded.

"I'm not hurt. Nathaniel?"

The dust settled around them. Nathaniel coughed a

couple of times. He didn't appear to be experiencing difficulty breathing, however, and Ben murmured a prayer of thanksgiving. A hand reached out in the dark and touched his arm. Sadie. When her arm suddenly gripped his arm, he lifted a hand to cover it, attempting to reassure her.

"Dat?"

His heart clenched at the quaver in Nathaniel's voice.

"Jah, I'm here. We're fine." He kept his voice low, just in case Mason was standing on the other side of the debris that was now blocking their exit.

"What do we do, Ben?"

He was astounded by the trust in her words. And humbled. She was still trusting him, even after he had led them into what might seem like an impossible situation. Sadie wouldn't know it, but he had been inside this cave many times in his life. He had explored every inch of it during his teen years.

Hopefully Mason Green wasn't familiar with the terrain and this particular cave.

"I have an idea," he assured her. "It would help if we had some light."

"Light!" she echoed in a voice of surprise. "That I can help you with."

He heard her fumbling with something in the dark. After a few seconds, there was a click, and a bright beam of white light cut through the darkness, startling him.

"What—"

"I have a flashlight app on my phone."

Ah. He never knew that cell phones came with flashlights.

"What's your plan?" Sadie asked.

"I know this cave. If I remember correctly, there should be another way out."

She sighed. "That's great news. How deep is this cave until we can get to the exit? Do you recall?"

He scratched his head and realized his hat was gone. His hair was coated with debris. "*Nee*, I don't remember. It's been many years since I was here." He hoped that the other exit hadn't become overgrown or caved in. "Shine your light at the ground for a moment, please."

The light shifted lower. Seeing his hat, he bent down and grabbed it. "Walk close together."

He wondered if he should mention the possibility of meeting up with a wild critter or two in the cave. Part of him didn't want to cause them any more worry. On the other hand, it was best to be prepared.

He mentioned the caution to Sadie.

"Yay," she returned sarcastically. "I'll probably have a scared bat get stuck in my hair."

"Do you think we'll see a bear?" Nathaniel couldn't quite contain his excitement at the thought.

"Ah, I don't suppose we'll run into a bear."

"I should hope not," Sadie muttered. He smiled. She was adorable when she grew disgruntled. He had no business noticing that. His smile dropped from his face. Ben was starting to have his suspicions about Sadie's origins. She had some Plain in her background, he was sure of it. Little things about her told him that she wasn't unfamiliar with their ways, at least, not completely. Regardless, she was not Amish.

He needed to remember that. There was no future between them, and he could not allow himself to forget that or become overly friendly and give her the wrong idea.

Deliberately, he turned away and kept walking. They

went deeper and deeper into the cave. The air was still and damp. There was a musty odor.

"Ew. It smells gross in here," Nathaniel commented.

Sadie snickered at the observation. Ben chuckled. Reaching back, he patted his son's shoulder.

"*Jah*, it does smell gross."

"Do you think the bad man is waiting for us?"

With a sigh, Ben pondered how to answer. He didn't want to scare his son, but he would never lie to him, either.

"I hope he has gone away," he said. "If he hasn't, we'll keep hiding from him."

Even to his own ears, the response lacked substance.

"I've been thinking, Ben," Sadie said into the darkness. "I know you believe that God is with us, right?"

He nodded. "*Jah*. With my whole being I believe that."

"So, if He is with us, then it is His job to protect us."

He wasn't sure he agreed with that assessment. It seemed too standoffish.

"*Nee*, not His job. He is our Father. We are His children. Sometimes sin affects the world and bad things do happen. That is true. But *Gott* is always there, loving His children and trying to keep them close to Him."

The light glanced off the walls, throwing long shadows against the floor.

"There's a bend up ahead," Ben announced, the words echoing around them.

He led the way, listening to the reassuring scrape of their boots on the bottom of the cave. He might not be able to see behind him very well, but at least he knew that they were following closely.

"Ben, is that a light ahead of us?" Sadie said at his shoulder.

He frowned. There was a light, but it wasn't as bright as he would have expected it to be. His heart fell at the thought that the second exit might not be viable. Maybe it was just dim due to the weather.

As the small group drew closer to the light, his fears were realized. The second exit was still there. However, the rocks around the exit had caved in. While not completely covered, he could see that they would have to dig themselves out if they wanted to use it. At present, it looked large enough for Nathaniel to squeeze through. Definitely not two full-grown adults.

He set his jaw. *Gott* was with them. He had shown them a way out. They had to work a bit to use the exit, but it was doable. Cautiously, Ben stepped closer to the hole in the pile blocking their way. Peering out, he looked as far as he could in every direction.

No Mason Green.

He bowed his head and sent up a prayer of thanksgiving.

"Are you praying?" Sadie whispered.

"*Jah.* I am thanking *Gott* that we have reached another way out and that no one is waiting for us."

He knew she'd understand.

"Um, we're going to have to dig our way out." She didn't sound too enthusiastic.

"*Jah.* We will dig. But we will get out."

A moment of silence met his declaration.

"You're right," she said finally. "I'm a bit embarrassed by my glass-half-empty attitude. Forgive me."

"*Es ist nichts,*" he responded, telling her it was nothing. He was curious to see what her response would be. Would she understand the German words? He suspected that she would.

"It's nothing?" she replied, confirming his suspicions by correctly translating the phrase. "It's not nothing, Ben. I don't like knowing how cynical I am. We thought we were trapped, and you were right. God has shown us a way out, like you believed. And here I am complaining because I might have to lift a few rocks."

He didn't like the self-recriminations.

"Sadie, you are human. You have also had a very rough few days. It is time to forgive yourself and move on. We need to move these rocks. It will be dark by the time we arrive at my parents' house."

It was too bad it wasn't summer. If it had been, then it wouldn't have been as urgent. They could have rested a bit, knowing that they had a few more hours of daylight. As it was, he knew that the sky would be dark within a few hours.

It took them almost an hour to dig the hole open enough to allow them to exit, one at a time. Ben went first, figuring that if Mason Green was out there, he would shoot him first, giving the other two a warning. He didn't even think about using himself as bait to protect the others. Some things, like family, were worth dying for. He was nonetheless highly relieved when he stood outside the cave in the cold, wet afternoon, unscathed except for a few additional scratches.

Nathaniel came out next, followed by Sadie. The weary trio glanced at the cave for a moment. He saw a shudder rip through Sadie.

"We could have died there," she said when her haunted gaze met his. "We came so close to losing everything."

"We didn't."

She nodded and they continued on with their journey. They kept silent for the most part. Every now and then, he and Sadie would exchange a glance. They had shared a harrowing experience and both were exhausted. They couldn't rest, though.

Mason Green might think he had killed them in the explosion. It would be best if he did.

How long did they have until he realized that they were still alive?

Chapter Nine

They trudged on until Sadie felt as though her legs would fall off if she had to take yet another step. Still they kept going. Nathaniel had reached the limit of what he could bear with patience and was letting them know it. He whined about being tired and said his feet were frozen. Then he complained about how his stomach hurt, he was so hungry.

Sadie completely understood. Her own stomach was hollow. It had gone past the point of rumbling. Now, she was so weary she wasn't sure which was harder, the hunger or the exhaustion filling her limbs with lead.

And the thirst. She was also pretty sure she was slightly dehydrated. Her mouth was so dry, when she tried talking it felt as though the edges of her mouth were coated with cotton.

"*Dat*, my legs hurt." The strength had leeched from Nathaniel's protests and complaints. Now his whining had changed into whimpers.

Ben halted. He crouched down in front of his son. The sunlight had faded and now they were moving in the twilight. His features were blurry, but Sadie could detect the gentle care in the eyes glinting up from his bone-weary face.

"Nathaniel, we are very close to *Grossmamma's* house. I know this journey is difficult. You have been very brave, and I am proud of you. I need you to be strong for just a short while more. *Grossmamma* and *Grossdawdi* will be happy to see you. Can you be strong for a short while longer?" He tapped the boy's chin.

Nathaniel's chin wobbled. He nodded. Probably too tired to speak, she thought, pity for him sneaking up on her. Ben tousled his hair and stood, grabbing the youngster's hand as they continued on. If only Nathaniel were smaller, Ben might have been able to carry him on his shoulders.

Sadie was embarrassed at the tears that swam in her eyes. Yes, his warmth and caring for his child were precious, but certainly she shouldn't be crying over them.

It must be the exhaustion. That and the fact that her feet were just about numb from the frozen ground. At least it had stopped raining. Or snowing. She thrust her ice-cold hands into her pockets.

"Sadie?" Ben's quiet voice broke through her thoughts. Had he been talking to her?

"Sorry? I was thinking. Did you say something?"

"*Jah.* I asked you if you were well. I was serious. My parents live close now. Normally, I could walk there from here in about ten minutes."

"It's probably going to take longer with how tired we are."

Still, ten minutes. Even twenty. She could do it, right? She had to. Even if she wasn't well, they had no choice but to keep moving on. Telling him her woes wouldn't improve their predicament. If anything, it would make him feel bad. And what about poor Nathaniel? If she faltered, what sort of example would that set for him? No, she would keep her aches and her problems to herself.

"Don't worry about me, Ben. I'm sure that we can make it. Especially if we are so close."

He didn't respond for the space of a heartbeat.

"I do worry, though. I know we couldn't wait in the car. It would have definitely been too dangerous for us. And for Braden. However, you were injured recently. This has been a hard journey, even without that."

Warmth tingled in her heart at his words. She tried not to let them get to her, but it wasn't working. This man was breaking through her defenses, and he wasn't even trying. She needed a distraction. She recalled his injured arm. Had that just been this morning?

"How is your arm?" He didn't seem to be favoring it. But then, maybe he was deliberately ignoring the discomfort.

"Ach. It's fine. I barely notice it."

Men. She rolled her eyes. She was pretty sure he was understating the matter.

A few more minutes of silence fell.

"*Dat!* Is that *Grossmamma's haus*?" Nathaniel seemed to regain some of his energy. It was contagious. She straightened her stiff shoulders as hope zinged through her. Could they be nearly at their destination?

The exuberance was clouded briefly by the worry that his family would not want her there. She was an outsider. Not to mention the fact that Nathaniel and Ben had been through horrific things because of her presence in their lives. She should brace herself for their reaction.

She was so tired, though, she'd probably cry and embarrass herself if they didn't want her around. She shook herself free of her misgivings as they walked up the driveway of a large white farmhouse.

An image of another white house filled her mind. It was also two stories, but didn't have the large porch that stretched across the entire front of the house like the one on Ben's parents' house. The one in her mind had a small porch, just big enough for two or three people to stand on. She could see the blueish-gray door on the side. And the smell of apple pie, freshly baked. Her mouth watered.

As the memory, for she was sure that was what it was, faded, she couldn't get rid of the sense of familiarity as they walked up the steps to the door.

She was still in the thrall of these emotions when the door opened and an older Amish woman peered out.

"Ben? Nathaniel!" The woman opened the door, confusion in her eyes, although there was a wide smile on her face as she let her son and his companions into the house. There were no electric lamps inside. Instead, the light in the room was made by natural gas-fueled lights that hung on the walls. She was surprised that Ben's parents used these; she had expected kerosene lanterns. "Ach! You didn't tell me you were coming to visit. Where is your buggy?" She peered around them. "Did you already put your horse away?"

Her brow creased. No wonder.

"*Nee, Mamm.* We walked from the interstate."

Her eyes widened. "Walked?"

"*Grossmamma.*" Nathaniel captured her attention. "I'm hungry."

Her eyes caught her son's. Sadie could see the questions burning there, but the woman smiled at her grandson and bade him to go into the kitchen. She'd get him some food.

"Mamm," Ben said as Nathaniel ran to the kitchen. "I will tell you everything, but first I want to introduce you to—"

Ben's mother turned expectantly to face her. As she took in Sadie's face, her mouth dropped open to form a round O.

"Hannah? Hannah Bontrager?"

Ben felt a shock go through him at the long-forgotten name. Hannah Bontrager had disappeared years ago. And so had her young daughter and his childhood friend, Sadie Ann. Was it possible? Could the woman he'd been assisting really be his friend who had disappeared years before?

Sadie shook her head, eyes wide with confusion. He thought he could also detect a speck of fear in her gaze.

"No, Mrs. Mast. My name's Sadie, not Hannah. Sadie Standings. My mother's name was Hannah, though."

His mother blinked, her eyes still dazed. She couldn't seem to stop looking at the *Englisch* woman standing in her home. Her eyes met his questioning. He shrugged and shook his head, confident that his mother would remember that Hannah had a daughter named Sadie. She nodded at him slightly, then returned her gaze to Sadie.

"Ack. Sorry. Of course, you could not be Hannah. She would be my age, not a young woman such as you. Come in." They followed her into the spacious kitchen.

Ben saw the way her narrow gaze speared him. His mother had questions, and he would be answering them before he was allowed to go to bed.

His father was sitting with Nathaniel when the small group entered the kitchen. The older man's gaze flew to where Sadie was standing. Although he didn't exclaim like his wife had, Ben could see the discomfort on his father's face.

His father, however, was a kind man, and one who took hospitality seriously.

"Benjamin. I'm happy you came home for a visit. Nathaniel here was telling me about your adventure with your friend. Sadie, *jah*?"

Abram Mast stood and made his way across the room to them.

"Yes, sir. I'm Sadie. I'm sorry to intrude on you like this."

"*Nee*, it is never an intrusion to see our son. I am interested in hearing the full story."

There was no mistaking the trepidation in Sadie's lovely eyes. To her credit, though, she smiled and nodded to his parents.

"Come," his mother said, setting a couple of plates on the table. "We have eaten, but there is plenty left."

It had been too long since he had sat and ate his mother's cooking. The talk that ensued while the meal was consumed was general in nature. His parents gave him plenty of significant looks, though.

Ben sighed. He was definitely in for a long talk with his parents. They would wait until Nathaniel and Sadie were in bed for the night. Judging by the way Nathaniel appeared to be nodding off at the table, it wouldn't be long until that happened. He wasn't surprised when Nathaniel went to bed less than fifteen minutes later. He practically had to carry him to his room. He helped him with his clothes and tucked him in under the covers. Nathaniel was growing so fast. When was the last time he'd needed such help? Smoothing his hand over his son's hair, he whispered a quiet goodnight.

Nathaniel didn't respond. He was already asleep.

In the kitchen, Ben found that his parents and a weary-eyed Sadie had waited for him. He wished she could go rest, but he knew her enough to know that she would want to be part of the conversation that had to happen. Knew that in her mind she was somehow at fault for all that had happened. He didn't believe that. She had been a victim, even more than he and Nathaniel had been. It was made worse by the fact that she had no memories to give her some clarity.

Haltingly, they began telling the story.

"I remember the cave," Abram murmured, his face pale after hearing how close he had been to losing his son and grandson. "You must have walked five miles today."

"At least," Ben agreed. "There was nothing else to do. I know that the man we were being chased by would have found us if we had returned to my home."

"Do you think he'll come here?" Esther Mast asked.

Across the table from him, Sadie flinched. He wished he had sat beside her, but knew he was better off where he was. It aroused less suspicion. It didn't stop the longing, though. Longing that he should not be feeling.

He pushed it aside. He could not become distracted. His full attention needed to be on the current situation. Too much was at stake for him to allow this attraction he was beginning to feel to get in his way.

"I cannot promise you he won't. But I think he believes he killed us today." A shudder worked its way through him. "If he had any idea we had survived and escaped, or if he knew about the other exit, I think he would have been waiting for us. Or come after us."

"I will understand if you don't want me here," Sadie

said, facing her hosts. "I'm not part of your community. You don't owe me anything."

Her face was calm, but Ben was sure her hands were clenched together under the table.

"Ach, you are a young woman in trouble." Esther's eyes narrowed in on Sadie's face again. "But you can't stay here dressed in your *Englisch* clothes."

Ben blinked. Even his father looked startled. Dressing an outsider in Amish clothes was something that was not normally done.

"Mamm?"

His mother nodded. "*Jah*, you heard me. Tomorrow morning, I will find you something to wear. If you blend in, it will harder to find you."

Sadie's eyes filled with tears, but she fought them back. He could see the muscle working in her throat as she worked to control her emotions before speaking.

"Thank you. I appreciate it. But I'm serious. If having me here puts your family at risk, I'll leave."

Abram smiled at her, although his gaze was troubled. "Whatever happens, we must remember *Gott* is in control. Always."

Whatever else might have been said was cut off as Sadie yawned. Her hand covered her mouth, but she couldn't hide it. Ben hid a grin as her eyes widened and a blush washed up her face, turning her pale complexion red.

His mother bustled into action. "Ben, you are in the room next to Nathaniel's. Come, Sadie. I will put you in the guest room on the lower level. It should be comfortable, and you should sleep tomorrow morning as late as you need to. You have had a difficult time."

His mother was gone with Sadie in a flash, leaving

him staring at the doorway they'd just swept through. His father chuckled at his expression.

"*Mamm* is a wonder. *Dat*, I appreciate your help. I know that our appearance was sudden."

"I meant what I said, Ben. I am a little concerned about the attachment I sense between you and the young woman." There was no judgment, only caution.

Ben sighed. His father had always been observant.

"We are friends, *jah*? Nothing more. I will not allow it to become more. She is not Amish, although I suspect she might have been once."

Keeping his voice low, he told his father about the small pieces of memory she'd had.

"If she was Plain, she's not now." His father's words were heavy.

"I know, *Dat*."

He left his father a few moments later and made his way up to his room. He stood before the window for a few minutes, staring out into the darkness while he thought about the recent events.

Was Mason Green aware that they had survived? Unless he'd gone back into the cave to check, Ben didn't think he would have any reason to suspect that his explosion hadn't killed them. Even if it hadn't, he was bound to think that they would die buried in the cave. Hopefully he would remain unaware that they had escaped. At least long enough for the police to catch up with him.

If he found them here, there was nowhere else they could hide.

Chapter Ten

The next morning, the sun was out, bursting through the trees and lighting up the house as it streamed in through the windows. It seemed incredible that such a gorgeous day would follow one that had been filled with terror and pain.

Ben had gone out before sunrise to help his father with the morning chores. Then he remained outside for another half hour to walk around. He told his father he was going for a walk to enjoy the uncommonly mild weather. But, in truth, he was really searching for any signs that Mason Green was about.

He relaxed when he found none. Ambling back into the house, he hung his hat up on the rack inside the door and then followed his nose into the kitchen.

His *mamm* had set the breakfast on the table. Coffee, strong and black the way he liked it, percolated on the stove. Helping his *mamm* was a pretty woman dressed in a demure lavender dress that fell to midcalf. An apron was wrapped around her slender waist and plain boots were on her feet. A white prayer *kapp* covered her light brown hair. Hair he had gotten used to seeing pulled back in a ponytail.

Sadie.

His heartbeat was heavy inside his chest. This was not a good idea. How was he supposed to keep the fact that she was *Englisch* straight in his mind when she was attired in Amish clothing? Even worse was the fact that she wore it with a naturalness that stunned him. There was no self-consciousness as she worked. No fidgeting with the *kapp*. She did play with the strings that fell past her shoulders, but that was the extent of it.

The feeling that she had once been a member of a community like this grew firmer.

She wasn't a member now, and once her full memory returned she would go back to the *Englisch* world. He had to keep that in the forefront of his mind. Otherwise, he could find himself in an emotional bind that would cause suffering all around.

"Sadie! You look like us." Nathaniel rushed into the room, skidding to a stop at her side. He grinned up at the woman, and she smiled back.

"I know. Would you like some breakfast?"

Like everything was normal. Shaking his head to clear it, Ben approached the table. He did his best to keep from staring at her throughout the meal. It took some discipline. She looked so right standing in the large, open Amish kitchen working next to his mother. It wasn't hard to imagine her working with Nathaniel on his homework. Or riding in the front of the buggy with him.

Nee. He could not go there. It made the very heart inside his chest ache to know that he must deny himself the pleasure of even considering courting her. It was the way it had to be. He felt guilty, too. The idea that he

was thinking of a woman besides Lydia with longing—
it couldn't continue. He knew that his parents wanted
him to move on, but they would be disappointed if they
knew the direction his thoughts were taking.

He needed to avoid Sadie as much as possible.

He managed to stay out of the house most of the day.
When he returned in the late afternoon, however, he saw
that Sadie was sitting on the porch steps peeling potatoes. He couldn't just walk past her. When she raised
her hand, potato and all, and waved, he gave in. If he
changed direction and went around to go in the back
door, she'd know he was avoiding her.

Holding in a sigh, he strode to the porch and sat on
the top step, being sure to keep the bucket between them.

"How was your day?"

She grinned. "It was a good day. Your mother is great.
She told me some stories about you and your siblings. I
didn't know you have four sisters."

"*Jah*. I am the youngest. My sisters have all married
and have families of their own. One day, my parents
hope that one of us kids will move into this *haus*. Then
they will move into the *dawdi haus*. That's the smaller
haus over there." He pointed to the building situated a
little back from the road. He pulled something out of his
pocket of his trousers and held it out to her. It was her cell
phone. "I had this charged at my *dat's* shop this morning. I thought since you are *Englisch*, you should have
this. Your brother or the police might try to call you."

She frowned. Not a scared or a sad frown. More of a
contemplative expression.

"Thank you. I wouldn't want to offend your family
by having this, but if you think it's okay." She reached
over and took the phone. Their fingers brushed. He kept

himself from jerking his hand away, but only just. Sadie's cheeks became rosy. Without a word, she slipped the cell phone into her apron pocket. Then her gaze flicked over to the house they had been discussing. "*Dawdi haus*. I know that term. That's the house where the grandparents live. Since you were the youngest, and the only son, I would have expected that you would have moved in."

He averted his eyes. "*Jah*. Lydia and I, we had planned to take over the farm. We lived with my parents for a few years. My *dat*, he is still plenty young to run the farm and his workshop. He's a carpenter, like me. My brother-in-law is his assistant."

It should have been him and he knew it. The pain of losing Lydia and their baby girl had been too great to stay here. That and the constant pressure to remarry. He had let the family down; he knew it, but he couldn't change the past.

She tilted her head, her keen eyes making him squirm. He had left instead of taking over. He had done what he thought was necessary for himself and for Nathaniel, but now he was having trouble dealing with the uncomfortable knowledge that he had made such a selfish decision.

"I'm sure they understood," Sadie told him, her compassion for his struggle evident.

He started. Had he said his thoughts out loud?

"How do you know what I'm thinking?" he asked her, not quite able to keep the question from sounding like a challenge. It wasn't that he was angry. He wasn't. What he was, however, was feeling exposed and vulnerable. He had not opened up to anyone about what he had suffered through when Lydia had been lost to him.

"I don't know what you're thinking." She leaned a

little closer. His breath caught. Two inches closer and she'd be near enough to kiss.

Absolutely not. He stood to put some distance between them. She shrugged and began to peel the potatoes again.

"Also, you are constantly looking back at the house. A little line here," she said, touching the tip of her pinkie finger to her forehead. "I just followed the clues."

He was relieved. And, he realized, a little disappointed. If she had already known some of what was on his mind, it would give him a reason to tell her. He suddenly needed to talk about his wife's death. About the agony that had followed them since the day she was diagnosed.

He wasn't sure how to begin such a conversation.

Apparently, he waited too long. Sadie picked up the peeled potatoes and headed back inside the house, leaving him staring after her.

What was she thinking, trying to encourage Ben to talk with her about his personal business? So not smart. He was a good man, a man she wanted to consider a friend, but she was not his confidante. She could not be that person. It was hard enough to keep her emotional distance. She knew that he felt the attraction. Or, at least, she thought he did.

But it was absolutely never going to be more than that. She needed to stop herself before she fell headlong into heartbreak and led a good man there with her.

Her pocket vibrated.

What?

She stopped and placed her hand in her apron pocket. She had already forgotten about the cell phone that Ben had handed her earlier. Nathaniel and Esther were laughing together in the kitchen. She didn't want to disturb them. It didn't feel polite to pull it out in the middle of the house, so she strode quickly to the room Esther had shown her to and closed the door. Heart racing, she pulled the phone out and unlocked the screen.

She froze. Kurt's number was on the screen. She had missed the call from him, but he had left a message.

Or someone using his phone had left a message.

Suddenly, she didn't want to listen to the message alone. Not giving herself time to question her actions, she fled the house and went in search of Ben. If the message was bad, he was the one person she knew could help, the one person she knew she could trust.

Making sure that Nathaniel was still occupied with his grandmother, she stepped quietly out the door. She wasn't quite sure where she should go to find Ben. It struck her that she should try his father's carpentry shop first. That seemed to be a logical assumption. Ben was not a man who liked to be idle. Therefore, it made sense that he would have wanted to go and help his father while they were staying with them.

Having a focus, she walked briskly across the grass and up the path to where Abram Mast had set up his shop. When she got to the door, she paused for a moment. Did she knock? Or was it acceptable to just enter? Biting her lip, she knocked softly on the glass pane of the door. She waited. When no one came to answer the door, she knocked a little louder. Almost immediately, the door opened, and she was relieved to come face-to-face with the man she had been looking for.

A little too happy to find him. She felt the sudden urge to walk across the threshold and hug him. That's when she knew that she was really rattled by the missed phone call. She checked her motion just in time. Rather than moving forward as she wished, she forced herself to take a step back, away from him.

Nonplussed, Ben stopped and stared at her. He had no clue how close he had come to being embraced. She felt the warmth in her cheeks, but decided she had more pressing issues than her near faux pas.

"Can you talk for a moment?" She folded her arms across her middle, striving to keep all her suppressed tension and concern down inside.

"*Jah*. Wait here a moment." He turned back and walked to his father. She could hear the two men holding a low-voiced conversation, but it was too quiet for her to understand what they were saying. Sadie grimaced. They were probably talking in Pennsylvania Dutch, the term used to describe the dialect of German used by the Amish. She was almost glad that she couldn't hear it. It was starting to unnerve her a little bit just how much of the language she seemed to understand. Her brother had given her no indication that she had ever spent any kind of extended time with Amish people before. So where did she learn it?

This was a question she needed an answer to, but maybe right now wasn't the time to explore it. Her brother needed her.

Ben joined her at the door, then gestured that she should lead the way. She had no idea where they could go.

"Maybe we could just walk around for a few minutes. I don't want to go inside because I don't want your folks or Nathaniel to hear."

His brows lowered, letting her know he was a little

disturbed by her words. But he nodded. She waited until
they were far enough from the buildings that she felt
comfortable that no one would be able to tell what they
were saying. Keeping her back facing the buildings, she
drew her phone out of her pocket of her apron.

"I was inside and I felt my phone vibrate." She
watched his expression as she spoke. "I had missed a
call from Kurt. Actually, I should say that I missed a
call from his phone. I have no idea if he was the one
who really called me. The last time I called him, someone else answered it. Whoever it was, they left a voice
mail message."

"Why didn't you listen to the message?" His words
were gruff, at odds with the concerned expression on
his face.

"I'm scared to listen to it." It wasn't easy to admit this
weakness, but she felt he would understand. "At least,
alone. I have no idea what this message will say. I am
imagining all sorts of horrible things."

He stepped closer to her than was absolutely appropriate. A comforting hand settled on her shoulder. "I'm
here with you. I know you're scared, but we will listen
to this message together."

She nodded. She touched her phone to unlock it, but
paused.

"Can we— Do you think—"

"What do you need?"

She pursed her lips and blew out a breath. "Could
we pray?"

She could hardly believe those words were coming
out of her mouth, but they seemed like the right words to
say. Ben's face lit up with surprise, his eyes flared wide
and his brows shot up. Then he smiled.

"*Jah*. We will pray and ask *Gott* for His guidance and help."

Gratitude welled up within her. Then he bowed his head and she copied his pose.

"*Gott*, You alone know what will come today and the day after that. You alone know the future and know what is truly in our hearts. We ask You to be with us, to guide us and to help us bring Kurt home and to help us all be safe."

When he said amen, Sadie echoed it, feeling a little awkward, but at the same time there was a sense of peace.

It was time. Clenching her teeth together, she unlocked her phone and tapped in the four digit passcode. Then she opened up her voice mail and put it on speaker. Hearing her brother's voice come out of the phone nearly brought her to her knees.

"Sadie, it's me. Kurt. Listen, don't call me back. I managed to steal back my phone and get away. But they're after me. I am going to try and sneak into my office. I can't let anyone see me, though. I don't know how, but I believe that my boss might be involved with whoever is after you. And the man who attacked me. I can't go into any details right now. I'm safe for the moment, and if I can I will contact you later. I hope that you are with Ben. He's the one person right now that I trust to keep you safe. I don't know if you've remembered me yet, but I love you and I will do everything I can to finish this up and to get back to you soon. Don't take any chances."

The message ended. Without thinking about it she hit the number to save the message on her phone. Then she looked up at Ben and bit her lip.

"I saved the message, but what should we do with it? It hardly seems feasible for us to travel all the way back to the Waylan Grove Police Department. What do you think?"

For a moment he didn't say anything. She knew from the look on his face he was trying to process all that they had heard and come up with the best solution.

"I agree that I don't think we should go back to Waylan Grove. Even dressed Plain like you are, you could still be recognized. Mason Green has seen me now, so he would recognize me, as well." He tugged on his ear thoughtfully. "Your brother was right. We don't know who we can trust. If his boss was responsible for leading him into a trap, who else might be involved in this? I know your brother fairly well. He has spoken of his boss, Ethan. I know that Ethan is a man that he respects and has always considered a friend. To know that such a man had betrayed him—" Ben shook his head.

Sadie thought about what he had said and her heart broke a little more for her brother. Not only because of the physical danger he was in, but because of the pain he had to be suffering emotionally.

"I'm worried, Ben. Kurt told me not to take any chances, but I think that he will. I'm so scared that he will get hurt, or worse."

He nodded. "*Jah*, I know what you are saying. We will keep praying. And we will do everything we can to help the police find the people responsible for this."

They continued to walk for a few minutes, allowing the silence to settle between them. It was a comfortable silence, one filled with mutual care and concern. Sadie knew that no matter what else happened, she could depend on Ben.

She also knew that as soon as this whole debacle was finished, she would sever ties with him. Not because of anything he'd done. But because if she didn't sever ties with him, she didn't know if she would ever be able to see another man without comparing him to Ben.

The steady *clop, clop, clop* of horse hooves trotting down the road in front of the house caught her attention. Her curiosity grew when the buggy pulled by a chestnut mare with a white blaze on her forehead turned and headed up the driveway. The driver halted the horse, bounded off the seat of the buggy and headed over to where she was standing with Ben.

She turned to her companion. His mouth had fallen open, and joy and astonishment were battling for ownership on his face. This was no average visitor. Whoever this was coming toward them, it was someone who meant a lot to Ben.

"Isaac? Isaac Yoder?" Ben breathed.

Immediately her heart started to beat wildly within her chest. Isaac Yoder. Ben Mast.

She had been wrong. She did know the Amish. Not only that, she knew these Amish.

Chapter Eleven

"Ben Mast!" In seconds, Isaac was standing before them, a wide grin spreading across his bearded face. His blue eyes sparkled with pleasure. "Your father told me you were home. I couldn't believe it. I haven't seen you in years!"

Sadie looked up at Ben. His grin was easily a match for Isaac's. If she wasn't mistaken, his eyes had a sudden sheen to them. He blinked and it was gone.

"You can't believe I'm home?" Ben laughed out loud. "You're the one who left the Amish community altogether to go live with the *Englisch*. I only moved to a new area."

"I did. It's true. I didn't think I would ever come back." Isaac's grin widened. "Nor that I would find a lovely Amish girl who would be willing to marry me. Then I met my Lizzy. And here I am."

"*Jah*, here we both are. You seem happy."

"I am. God is good."

That brought out another grin. This time, she thought that Ben looked like he'd been handed a gift. Had Isaac lost his faith at one point? It was possible, since he'd left.

She couldn't get over the fact that she was again with these two, and they had no clue who she really was. Her throat clogged. She didn't know if she'd be able to talk, emotion was choking her so hard.

The two men seem to realize that they were leaving Sadie out of the conversation. Isaac turned to her with his easy grin.

"I'm sorry. I knew you had a guest, Ben."

"Ack! I am being so rude. My apologies, Sadie. This is my old friend—"

He never finished his sentence. It was too much for Sadie. The emotions that she had been holding back came spilling out of her all at once. The tears streamed down her cheeks and the sob that she had been trying to stifle burst free. Ben's astonished face swam before her eyes briefly before she covered her face with her hands.

"Sadie?" She heard the confusion in Ben's voice. She struggled to answer.

"I remember, Ben," she managed to choke out.

Shocked, Ben stared at her. Isaac's face had gone flat. Not angry or disgusted. Observant. The face of someone used to facing hard situations and making quick decisions.

"Let's get you inside." Before she knew it, Ben was urging her back toward the house.

"Maybe... Should I leave?" Isaac asked.

"Nee!" she said, the Amish word for *no* slipping past her lips instinctively. She ignored it. There was so much going on inside her at the moment, she could not focus on anything other than her recovered memories. "You need to come. You have to hear this."

Distractedly, she was aware of the look that flashed between the two men, but was too distraught to think much of it. Memories were bombarding her from all sides. Memories of being held in a woman's lap while the buggy they were in swayed back and forth. Where had they been going? She had no idea. She had other memories. Memories of baking cookies with an older woman. Her grandmother? She couldn't be sure, but she thought so.

Again and again the images came. They came at her so fast she was having trouble processing them. At one point, she closed her eyes and let Ben lead her. She stumbled once but regained her balance when he caught her around the waist.

"Easy, Sadie. I have you. Just a little farther." Ben continued to support her as the trio walked. Isaac kept his thoughts to himself. She couldn't imagine what was going through his mind right then.

Then they were in the house, and he was leading her to a chair in the living room. His mother came out of the kitchen, wiping her hands on a dish towel. When she saw the tears on Sadie's cheeks, she rushed forward, making clicking noises with her tongue.

"What's this? What has happened?" She edged herself in next to Sadie, squeezing Ben out of the way. Ben caught himself before he could trip, then he moved to stand on Sadie's other side. A giggle burbled up inside her, turning into a sob before she could get it out. Her vision blurred as more tears tumbled down. Sadie brushed them away impatiently. She hated crying. She'd done more in the past week than she had in a long time.

"She said she was remembering," Ben explained to his mother.

Compassion filled her eyes. She placed her warm,

motherly hand on Sadie's cold one. "Dear child. What did you remember? Can you tell us?"

She nodded. With an effort, she calmed herself and drew in a deep breath. "I—I remember sitting on my mother's lap. I'm pretty sure it was my mother. We were going someplace but I don't know where. I could feel the swaying motion as we traveled." She looked up at Ben. He was her focal point. His warm eyes held on to hers, almost like an embrace. She was not alone. Focusing on him helped her to continue. "I think we were in a buggy."

Ben did not look surprised. "I wondered if you had spent some time with the Amish."

That got her attention. "What made you wonder such a thing?"

Ben moved a little apart from her and settled himself on the chair across the way. He leaned forward and rested his arms on his knees. "Several times you have used our language without even thinking about it. Which told me that you had some experience speaking it. Of course, that did not prove anything. It could have meant a number of things. Maybe you had Amish friends. You worked in a school. Oftentimes, we have Amish children with special needs who attend public school with the *Englisch* kids. There were other things, too. You told me yourself how you seemed to remember cooking certain foods with Ruth. Remember that?"

She nodded. She'd forgotten all about that in the panic of the past few days. But he hadn't. She wondered briefly what else he remembered about her.

"Wow. Yes, I do remember that."

"I also noticed that you seem to have knowledge of certain traditions that we have. It made sense to me that you had a deep connection with the Amish at some point in your life but you didn't remember it."

Esther broke in. "Your mother, do you remember her?"

"Yes. I do remember her. And I remember how devastated I was when she and my stepfather were killed in a fire two years ago." She grabbed onto Esther's hands. "I don't remember very much before I was seven years old. I do know that something happened and I was pretty traumatized for a while. I remember not speaking for a long time. Once I started speaking again, my mom and I never talked about what had happened. I do remember that I asked her about my life before, but she would just shake her head and say that some things needed to be forgotten. She always got this look on her face that scared me a bit. I stopped asking. So I'm still missing a chunk of my life. But I have some images."

Esther frowned, but nodded. Sadie could tell that the older woman was disappointed. She didn't need to think very hard about why. She remembered Esther's comments to her on the day that they met. How well had Esther known Hannah Bontrager? Had they been friends?

"My mother," she whispered to the older woman. "Her name was Hannah. Hannah Bontrager. And she was Amish."

Tears brightened Esther's eyes. A smile wobbled on her lips. It was a smile filled with grief. "I knew it."

"Mamm?"

Sadie and Esther both turned to see that Ben had half risen from his seat. No doubt he was concerned that seeing his mother brought tears.

"Shush, Ben. It's all right."

Sadie looked between Isaac and Ben. How could she not have remembered? She was swamped again by bittersweet emotions. Happiness at having her memories back, regret at having missed so much.

"Sadie, why am I here?" Isaac asked her. She could tell it wasn't a rude question. She had specifically told him she needed both him and Ben to be there when she went over what she was remembering.

"My childhood is a blur for the most part. But there are a couple things that I do remember. I told you how I remembered my mother. I also remember playing games and following my two best friends, Ben Mast and Isaac Yoder, around everywhere we went."

Both men's mouths dropped open, shocked, as they listened to the words tumbling from her.

"Sadie Ann Bontrager." The hoarse words dropped from his lips. Ben probably didn't even realize that he had spoken her name aloud.

She nodded in confirmation of her identity. "Yes. I was eight when my mother remarried. I remember that my last name was Bontrager, and my stepfather adopted me and gave me his last name. My mother told me I needed to never again call myself Sadie Bontrager. In fact, she strongly warned me to forget my last name. I had wondered why, but she was so stern, I never questioned it."

"You disappeared. One day you were there and the next day you were gone," Ben mused, his gaze sharp on her face. Isaac's eyes were on the floor.

She nodded, watching them piece together the information.

Isaac suddenly jerked upright, his face intent. "Your father—"

Ben paled. "The flashback you had, the one about seeing the Amish man murdered?"

She already didn't like where this was going. But she had wondered the same thing. Knowing in her heart what the answer was, she asked the question they were all thinking.

"He was my father, wasn't he?" She had no memories of him other than that image, but she knew deep within her soul that she was right. Ben's slow nod confirmed it. New anguish spread through her.

"He was murdered, and a young teenager was sent to jail. Two days later, you were gone."

"You weren't just raised in an Amish community," Ben said. "You were raised in *this* Amish community."

"I don't think you can say that I was raised here. I lived here until I was around seven, then I left. And we never looked back. Until all of this happened, I had forgotten completely about my Amish past."

"Wow." Isaac sank into a chair. "Sadie Bontrager. I don't even know what to say. Just wow."

That surprised a laugh out of her. He sounded so *Englisch* when he said that, his years away from the Amish showing. Ben chuckled, too, although it was a little strained.

Isaac collected himself and looked at Sadie. "I won't get into the whole story, because it's not important right now. But I will tell you that when I left the Amish community, I spent several years working as a cop for the Waylan Grove Police Department."

Hearing that Isaac used to be a cop surprised Ben. Although maybe not so much. He remembered the fight Isaac had had with his father after his brother, Joshua, had been killed. Isaac had been all about finding justice. So maybe joining the police force had been his way to do that.

A thought struck him. "Isaac, did you work with a Sergeant Ryder Howard?"

Isaac laughed lightly. "Ryder? Sure. He's a buddy of mine. He made sergeant just last spring. He has one of my dogs."

Ben didn't quite understand that. "One of your dogs?"

"Yeah. I had gotten into raising service dogs and training them to be K-9 officers. When I rejoined the community, the bishop told me I could keep training the dogs. Well, he gave me permission to train service dogs. I don't train them for K-9 cop work anymore. The one I had trained, I gave to Ryder. It's made him quite the envy of the other officers."

"I'm sure." Ben shook his head, amused in spite of the seriousness of the conversation.

The humor drained out of Isaac's face. "Seriously. He's a good guy. And he's an outstanding cop. I trust him completely."

"Ben, we should tell him about the voice mail."

Ben had almost forgotten about the message. "*Mamm*, could you excuse us for a few minutes?"

Ben rose, and Isaac and Sadie followed suit. This was not something he wanted to discuss while his mother was in the room. He led the others out onto the front porch. After he had shut the door firmly behind him, he looked at Sadie.

Interpreting his look correctly, she pulled her cell phone out of her apron and replayed the message for Isaac. The former police officer listened to the message without speaking. When the message was finished however, he questioned the both of them thoroughly.

"What do you think?" Ben ask him.

"I think we should call Ryder and set up a meeting."

"I'm not sure going back to Waylan Grove would be a wise decision for us."

Ben and Sadie took turns explaining everything that had happened the past few days. Again Isaac listened.

"I understand you not wanting to go back there. Let me contact Ryder and see if he will come here. I'm also curious about this boss of Kurt's. What was his name? Ethan? What do you know about him?"

Sadie tugged at the strings of her *kapp*. "I only met him once, a couple of weeks before the accident. Kurt had invited him and his wife to dinner one night. His wife was nice enough. Didn't talk a lot. Something about him made me uncomfortable, but I didn't know why."

"Last name?"

She shook her head. "I'm sorry. I really don't know. Kurt always referred to him as Ethan."

"I'll contact Ryder," Isaac decided. "Then when he shows up, we can decide where we go from here."

"We?" Ben and Sadie chorused.

Isaac scoffed and cast him a scathing glance. "What? Do you expect me to stay out of this? In a single day I have recovered two of my best childhood friends. Friends that I had thought I would never see again. There's no way I'm walking away from this. The way I figure it, God must have wanted us to meet up again. Who am I to disagree with Him?"

"Denke," Ben said, touched more than he could say. There had been so many times in the past three years when he had felt isolated and alone. He had people in

the community where he lived whom he liked. Caleb and Lovina, for instance. But he really didn't have anyone that he shared a strong bond of friendship with. He hadn't truly felt that bond for a long time. Isaac was right.

"Who are we to disagree, indeed."

Isaac left a few minutes later, promising to bring his wife by to meet them soon. "You'll like my Lizzy. She's from a little town in Pennsylvania. We met when I was a cop."

Intrigued, Ben raised an eyebrow. "She met you while you were Fancy?"

Isaac rolled his eyes. "I was *Englisch*, and yes, that's when she met me. I didn't come back to being Amish because of her, though. I knew that if I came back to being Amish, it was a lifelong choice. Which meant I needed to do it for the right reasons. It would not have been fair to her to join the church and then not be able to truly live this life."

Would Sadie ever— Ben stamped that thought out before it fully formed. She had said she didn't remember very much about her Amish life. For all intents and purposes, she was *Englisch*. And although he could feel the tension and the bond between them growing stronger every day, he knew he didn't have the right to ask her to become anything else. Not for him.

When this was all over, when Mason Green had been caught and Sadie was out of danger, what would she choose? Would she choose to return to her roots, or would she go back to her old job and her old way of life?

He was getting far too invested in her choices. He had a son to think about. He already knew that Nathaniel loved Sadie. Just as he was growing to love... *Nee*.

That was not possible. They had not known each other long enough for him to truly love her.

He decided it was best if he ignored the idea.

But it didn't matter. A hollow spot had opened up inside him and it had Sadie's name on it. Soon she'd be gone.

Whatever was building between the two of them needed to end. Now.

Chapter Twelve

Early the next day, Isaac showed up after breakfast. He chatted with the Masts for a few moments before requesting to see Ben and Sadie privately. The three of them walked out to the barn. Ben had the oddest feeling, being with two friends who had both left his life for so many years. He thanked Gott for the blessing of seeing them again.

"What are we waiting for?" Ben asked.

"Ryder's coming. He has been investigating your brother's boss. Ethan Nettle. The man's record is clean. In fact, it's so clean, he doesn't even have a parking ticket. Nothing."

"And that bothers you?" Sadie asked, her voice slightly amused.

"Yeah, it does. The man drives one of those fancy cars. It's a Corvette or something like that. The ones that go a million miles per hour. Who owns a toy like that and doesn't test it out?"

Ben chuckled. "I managed to drive one during my *rumspringa*. Scared me enough to make me understand the benefit of my nice sedate buggy."

They didn't have long to wait before the sound of a car pulling into the driveway reached their ears. A few seconds later, a door banged shut. Isaac peeked out of the barn. "In here, Ryder."

The officer strode up the driveway, his hard shoes clomping on the gravel as he moved. Within a minute, he entered the barn. With him came a large German shepherd, wearing a bright blue harness with the name Lily on it.

Isaac grinned. "Here's my girl. Ben, Sadie, this is Lily. The pup I trained."

Ryder snorted. "She's not a pup anymore, dude. Now she's a fully trained canine officer, aren't you, Lily?"

The dog sat when commanded to.

"Sergeant Howard," Ben began.

The officer waved his hand. "Ryder. I am really glad to see you two. After you walked out of the police station, we were all a bit anxious about your whereabouts. Isaac's phone call was a welcome one, that's for sure."

Ben felt a momentary pang of guilt over that. He hoped the officer hadn't gotten into trouble because of them. "Fine. Ryder. What have you learned about Ethan Nettle?"

Ryder leaned a shoulder against a post. "Well, that's interesting. It appears that Mr. Nettle has had some success in reporting on social justice issues. For example, he's very well-known for being a force against drug cartels and illegal human trafficking. Particularly when it comes to women and children."

Ben frowned. "I don't see how that is a bad thing. Those are both evils that our world would be better off without."

"Ah, yes, true." Ryder nodded sagely. "Trouble is, it

has long been suspected that Mason Green is deeply connected to both of those markets. It has also come to my notice that quite a few times in the past ten years or so, Mason Green has been spotted in the same place where Ethan Nettle was supposedly working on reporting a story. In fact, in at least three instances, I have witnesses who could place both men in the same hotel. What do you think about that coincidence?"

"I don't believe in coincidence," Ben bit out harshly. He could think of very few things that were as evil as the victimization of children and women. If Kurt's boss was associating with these people, and in fact, profiting from this evil, he needed to be dealt with. Ben remembered Sadie being concerned that Kurt would take chances. She was probably correct. Kurt would put himself at risk to save others. Of that he had no doubt.

"Yeah, me neither." Ryder reached into his back pocket. He pulled out an envelope. When he slipped it open and took out a picture, Ben's stomach clenched. "I actually have a digital copy of this on my computer. However, I didn't know about the service out here so I printed it out so that we could all see it."

He turned to Sadie. "I need you to take a look at this and tell me what you see."

Sadie paled slightly, but she nodded and took a step closer. Her arm brushed against Ben's. He could feel her shivering beside him, and he was fairly certain it was not from the cold. Without giving it a thought, he lightly placed his arm around her shoulders. Isaac raised his eyebrow at him, but he ignored his childhood friend. Right at this moment, Sadie needed his comfort.

"Alles ist gut," he murmured in her ear. "All of us are here with you. No one will hurt you."

"I know," she whispered. "I'm just a little nervous. I can't believe that my brother has been working with this man all these years and has never had a clue. What if Kurt had somehow stumbled onto what he was up to? Who knows what Ethan would've done?"

Ben didn't want to respond to that because he had a fairly good idea of what the man would have done. His arm tightened slightly as Ryder showed Sadie the photograph.

She gasped and swayed slightly.

Instinctively, Ben pulled her closer. She leaned against him for a moment, then she stood straight. He let her go, even though it pained him. She pointed to the red-headed man sitting at the table in a café. "That's my brother's boss, Ethan. And the other man, the one he's sitting with as if they were old friends, that's Mason Green."

She shuddered once, then she looked up at Ben. He saw the anguish in her eyes. "You've remembered something else, haven't you?"

He felt more than saw both Isaac and Ryder straighten. She kept her eyes locked with his. He silently urged her to keep going, knowing that all of this was taking its toll.

"That night my brother had Ethan and his wife over to dinner, they were talking about a story that Kurt was working on. He hadn't told me what it was. I was still pretty torn up because a young girl from the school I work at had been kidnapped and later found in very bad shape. I think it's connected but I'm not sure yet. I didn't mean to eavesdrop, but we have a small house with thin walls. I could hear Kurt trying to convince Ethan to let him write a story. He said he had found some interesting clues and a witness who could prove that someone he was looking into was, in fact, involved in something pretty nasty. I didn't hear what it was, but looking back it was obviously illegal human trafficking. Anyway, Ethan said no. Oh, he was very nice about it. Very complimentary about my brother. My brother did such great work but they just didn't have room for that kind of story at this moment. Maybe later on down the line. I knew for a fact that my brother was anxious to get his hands on a meatier story. He had been researching this angle for so long, just waiting to pitch it to his boss. But Ethan wasn't buying it. I felt bad for my brother but what could I do? I have no knowledge of journalism. I had no idea what would be a good story, or how to even go about finding one."

She turned to look at Ryder and Isaac. "But I had no clue there was anything more going on. Later that evening, I walked into the little office that my brother and I shared. I had a knitting pattern that I wanted to show Ethan's wife. I can't even remember the woman's name at this point. It doesn't matter. Anyway, I knocked some papers off my brother's desk. When I bent down to pick them up, I saw a picture. It was a picture of Mason Green. I believe he was the man that my brother was researching. Anyway, as I looked at the picture, I had a flashback."

Ben could tell she was getting very agitated. Whatever she had remembered, it must've been horrible.

"Can you tell us, Sadie?" Ryder asked, his voice gentle. Ben was a very peaceful man, but he felt a small spurt of anger at the officer for putting even the tiniest bit of pressure on Sadie. He held it in, though, knowing the man was only doing his job. And also knowing that until Mason Green and Ethan Nettle were caught, Sadie would never be safe again.

Sadie drew in a deep breath. "I remember being a

child. I was only six or seven. I was outside, it was a warm summer day. I remember a man grabbing me and trying to throw me into his car. It was Mason Green. He couldn't have been that old. Late teens? Knowing what I know now, I believe he was intending to kidnap me."

Her words sent a chill straight through him. There was only one reason Mason Green would have tried to kidnap a young Amish girl. He had planned to sell her in the human trafficking market.

"What happened?" Ben felt like each word was a chip of ice spewing from his mouth.

Tears welled up in those beautiful caramel-colored eyes and rolled down her cheeks.

"My father stopped him."

She took the handkerchief from Ben's hand and wiped her face. Her story wasn't done. She needed to keep it together for a few more minutes.

"My father heard me screaming. He came out and saw what was happening. He rushed over and grabbed me from Mason's arms. He threw me away from him, and when I looked at him, Mason Green was holding a gun to my father. Before I could do anything, he shot him. Right in front of me. I think between my screaming and the shot, several people on the street came out to see what was happening. Mason threw the gun down and took off. One of our neighbors, a teenager from a non-Amish family, was first on the scene. He was about fifteen or so and had a reputation for getting in trouble."

"He picked up the gun, didn't he?" Ben asked. He remembered very well the day that Sadie's father was killed. He also remembered running out of his house and seeing an older boy holding the gun.

"He did. I was in such shock that I didn't realize what was happening. There were no witnesses other than myself to say that he was innocent. He was literally holding the smoking gun in his hand. I shut down for a while. Mentally. And after that, it was like my mind had closed the memory away. I literally didn't remember what had happened. Until now."

"You can't blame yourself for what happened, Sadie." Isaac's face was so sad as he looked at his friend. "It's horrible. But you were a child."

She nodded to show she understood, but the grief inside her was overwhelming. She had blocked the memory out for so long, she felt that she was only now starting to grieve her father. And that poor kid who went to jail.

"His name was Jeffrey, I think."

"I need you to write your statement out and sign it. There's no statute of limitations on murder. If you give us your statement, it means we can go before the judge, ask for Jeffrey to be released and for the case of the murder of your father to be opened up again."

She thought, *But Amish don't usually give statements or testify*, then rolled her eyes. She hadn't been Amish for a very long time. And there was no one left who could help.

Decision made, she nodded her affirmative. "I'll do whatever I must to help."

Ryder rubbed his hands together in anticipation. "Great! I am so glad that you're going to do this." He hesitated. "Um, today would be good."

"Today? As in, right now?" The idea of leaving and going back to Waylan Grove now, when things were still so up in the air, made her stomach churn. What if Mason Green was still out there searching for them? And now that she knew about Ethan Nettle, there were at least two people trying to kill her. It didn't seem the wisest decision to go back into the middle of the fray alone.

We are never alone.

Suddenly, that peace she had felt once before spread through her. She knew what it meant. Even if it was just her going into battle, God was with her. She needed to rely on him and not on her own strength. Not even on Ben's strength. Because even though Ben was just about the best man she had ever met, he was still a man. Only God was perfect. Only God could truly save her.

"I'll go," she told Ryder.

"Let me tell *Dat* that I won't be here to help this afternoon," Ben announced. "I'm sure my *mamm* would be willing to watch out for Nathaniel while we're gone. She's enjoying having a grandchild in the house."

Surprised, she glanced at him. "You're coming with me?"

He snorted. "*Jah*. Absolutely I'm going with you. Did you think I would leave you to face this danger by yourself?"

"Hey," Ryder protested. "I'm here, too, you know. I'd not let her go by herself."

As he'd predicted, Ben's parents agreed to keep Nathaniel while he accompanied Ryder and Sadie back to Waylan Grove. To her further surprise, as they approached the police cruiser, Isaac hopped into the front seat, leaving the back seat to Sadie and Ben. And Lily. The large dog hopped up beside Sadie and calmly settled on the leather seat.

Sadie felt like she had swallowed rocks for lunch, and now they were sitting heavy in her stomach. She placed her hand over her belly, trying to still the churning going on inside her. The scenery whizzed past. She almost missed the slower pace of the buggy. When you were in a buggy, you could really appreciate the places you were driving past.

The closer they came to Waylan Grove, the tighter her nerves became. She nearly jumped out of her skin when a warm hand landed on top of hers where it was lying on the seat. Startled, she jerked her eyes up. Her gaze collided with Ben's.

"Are you well?" he whispered, concern shining from his face.

Her immediate reaction was to say she was fine. But she wasn't fine. She was far from it. Right at the moment, she didn't want to placate anyone with white lies designed to make them feel better. She wanted to be honest.

"No, I'm really not. I'm learning to trust God, but it's still so hard to understand how anyone could do evil things to another person. And I am so worried about Kurt. All he ever wanted was to make a difference. And now he's stuck in the middle of this mess. It's not fair."

"*Jah*. I know it's not fair. If I could change the situation and make it better for you, I would. But I will not leave you until the situation has been resolved."

And after that? But she knew better than to ask. Ben was an honorable man, but he was still not the man for her.

When they arrived in Waylan Grove, the crowded police cruiser pulled into the station parking lot and Ryder backed into a space. As soon as the doors were unlocked, all four of its human passengers and Lily spilled out into the afternoon light. Sadie sniffed the air. Nearby, someone was burning leaves. She could also smell the faint scent of fresh bread coming from the bakery across the street. Her stomach rumbled. They'd have to get some food after this. She would never make it all the way back to Ben's parents' house without eating again. It would have been nice if they could have waited until after lunch, but they were already here.

Ryder led the small group into the same conference room that she had been in just a few days before. He gave her some paper and a pen and told her to write down her statement. Never having done such a thing, she was unsure how to go about it.

"Just write down everything you can remember," he told her. That was a lot.

Sighing, she bent her head and started. She had no idea how long it took her to get the entire statement written, but her fingers felt cramped by the time she was done. Hopefully, this would be enough to get Jeffrey out of prison. And hopefully her statement would be enough to get the real criminals locked behind bars for the rest of their lives.

She signed her name with a flourish and set down her pen. "Done."

Ryder took her statement. "I have an impromptu appointment with the district attorney. I shouldn't be long."

Her stomach growled again, embarrassing her.

"If it's all right with you, I think I will take Sadie down the street to that restaurant we passed. Neither of us had a chance to eat lunch, and I think we're both in need of some nourishment."

"Perfect. What are you gonna do, Isaac?"

He hesitated.

"You are more than welcome to come with us," she told him sincerely. "I doubt you had a chance to eat, either."

He considered it and finally agreed. "I might as well. I don't have anything to do here. It just feels strange, being in the station and not actually working here."

The three of them headed over to the restaurant. It was one of those places where they could either sit down inside or they could order what they wanted from the take-out menu and have it boxed up to go.

"I don't know that eating in a restaurant would be comfortable right now," she told her companions. "I would be constantly looking around to see if there was any danger."

"*Jah*, that would not be relaxing. Let's grab some food and then we can go back over to the station to eat it," Ben recommended.

Within fifteen minutes they all had their bags of freshly cooked food. The aromas of garlic and butter were too tempting to resist. As they crossed the street, Sadie dipped her hand into her bag and brought out a cheesy breadstick. "I love these things."

She bit into one. The delicious flavors of warm cheese, garlic and butter burst on her tongue. She had forgotten how much she enjoyed Italian cuisine.

The gunshot came out of nowhere, or so it seemed. She had just swallowed another bite of the breadstick when a loud crack split the air, followed immediately by a crash as the window she had just passed by smashed to pieces.

Screams filled the air. The car that was stopped at the red light at the intersection suddenly revved hard. Horns honked in annoyance as the driver cut off those who were coming from the opposite direction. One of the cars slammed on its brakes to avoid a collision. The car behind it tried to stop, but ended up with its hood crunching against the first car's bumper.

It was chaos. The car that had run the red light sped around the corner. As the driver turned, he pointed a gun directly at her. For one frozen second, she stared into the cold, deadly gaze of Mason Green. The memory of his trying to kidnap her as a child sprang fresh into her mind.

"Sadie! Get down!" Ben grabbed onto her and threw her to the ground as the second bullet erupted from the barrel of the pistol. She hit the concrete, hard, but the bullet whizzed past them.

Sirens blared as a police cruiser raced from the station and tore off after the car Mason Green had been driving. Within seconds, both vehicles had vanished from sight. Other officers were at the intersection, helping the two cars that had collided. Fortunately, she could see both drivers milling around as the police took statements, so they must not have been injured.

She sat up, dazed. Frantically, her eyes roamed over to Ben and Isaac, searching for any signs that they had been injured.

Seeing none, her shoulders sagged.

Then they tightened up again. "Ben!"

"What?" He was right beside her again. She had scared him, she could tell by the pallor of his face.

"He recognized me. Even in Amish clothes, he knew it was me. Which means he knows I'm not dead."

Ben's face set. "He must have spotted us on our way into town."

If they didn't catch him now, how long would it be before he discovered her hiding place and came after her there?

Chapter Thirteen

Ben waited for Ryder to finish his discussion with the chief. For once, standing still came as a challenge to him. He paced the confines of the conference room. Isaac was with Ryder, hoping to move things along.

His poor Sadie was exhausted.

He stopped, shaken. She was not his Sadie. He couldn't even begin to think that way. And yet he was. Even after all the warnings he had given himself to keep his distance, he had fallen in love with the lovely young woman sitting so desolately at the table. He had been by her side, but she had informed him that his nervous energy was making her tired.

A total role reversal.

She was so quiet, she was making him worried. What was going on in her mind? With all the things she'd remembered today and then to be shot at. It had to be devastating.

He wanted to go home and see his son.

Nee, more than that. He wanted to take Sadie back to his parents' house and know that she was safe. Being in the police station was making him impatient. Although it was unlikely that Mason Green or Ethan Nettle would be bold enough to come inside to attack.

In his mind he again heard the crack of the bullet and relived the moment when he'd thought Sadie had been shot. He'd been ready to jump in front of the gun for her. When she hit the cement, she'd dropped so hard, he'd thought at first that he'd gotten to her too late, and that she had been hit.

None of them had been shot, though. All three had escaped unscathed, with the exception of some minor bruises from falling to the ground. They were alive. And they were all well.

Ryder came back into the room. Isaac followed him, his expression grim. Ben knew that whatever they were going to say, he was definitely not going to like it. He wasn't going to like it at all. Ryder shut the door to give them some privacy and gestured to the table.

"Let's sit."

Ben waited for Sadie to straighten from her slump. Pulling out the chair next to her, he angled it so that he was close enough to touch her hand if he thought she needed his support. He was somewhat surprised when she reached out under the table and took his hand. Flicking his glance up to her profile, he was amazed. Her fingers trembled in his grasp, but her face was as calm and serene as if she were on her way to a church service, not preparing for news that had both Ryder and Isaac holding their mouths in grim lines.

His patience was thin as it took Ryder a bit to come to the point. Finally, the officer cleared his throat. "Here's the thing. We were not able to catch Mason Green as he fled the scene of the shooting. We have confirmed, both with your statements and with the camera from the stop light, that it was, in fact, Mr. Green driving the car."

"So he's still going to be coming after me."

He hated the dullness that had crept into Sadie's normally animated voice.

"Most likely." Ryder didn't look too happy with that thought. "The positive is that he still may not have an idea of where you are hiding. Yes, he saw you today. Which means he's been hanging around, and possibly has someone else helping him. And he's seen Ben, so he might recognize him. But he has not attacked at the Masts's home, nor have there been any reports of him around there. I have been keeping an eye out for him. So I think he hasn't realized that you're hiding there."

"He does know that I'm alive, though."

It was obvious that Ryder didn't know what they were referring to. It was then that Ben realized Ryder had no idea about what had happened on the trip to his family house. Sadie, apparently, came to the same conclusion. With a halting voice, she started telling about the storm and the accident on the interstate. Ben interjected a time or two when she left a detail out. When he heard about the explosion, Ryder's jaw dropped open.

"That's extreme," he managed to get out.

"*Jah*, it's extreme. It also gave us the benefit of time. He knows that we escaped, now, though I wonder why he was in town."

Again, it was too coincidental, and he didn't believe in coincidences.

"If I had to guess, I would say that he went back to search the wreckage of the cave, just to make you were in there. That would have taken him some time, as he would have needed to dig out the entrance. He might have given you a few days to run out of food or oxygen—"

Sadie's chair slid back and she jumped to her feet.

Ben leaned back, knowing she was going to start pacing the perimeter of the room. Which she did. Now that he knew for a fact who she was, he recalled that Sadie used to do the same thing as a child. It had made her mother crazy.

He shot forward in his seat. Her mother.

"Sadie." She stopped pacing and faced him.

"How did your mother die?"

Her shock showed in her eyes. "How—? She and my stepfather were killed in a fire."

"Was the fire in any way suspicious?"

She nodded. "The police believed it was started by some kids messing around who got careless."

"What if they weren't? What if Mason recognized your mom?"

She looked shaky at his questions. "But it was me—"

He shook his head. "You were a child. And you couldn't speak after the event. She, however, may have seen him around the farm before. He may not have wanted to take that chance."

"He has a point," Ryder mused. "Do you recall if you had seen him before the day he tried to kidnap you?"

Her face tightened, but he could see that she was trying to remember.

"I might have seen him before that, but I was only a child. I can remember nothing about him before the day he killed my father."

Ryder glanced at the clock in the corner of the room. "I think it's about time we got you home. I want to take a different car, in case Green's still out there."

On the ride back to his parents' house, Sadie was very quiet. It wasn't until after dinner, though, that they really had some time to talk.

"I don't know what to do," Sadie admitted. "Should I ask Ryder to hide me someplace else? I hate that I am putting your family at risk."

And he hated hearing her talk like that.

"Sadie, you're here. More than that, you have family here. Tomorrow, I want to take you to meet your grandparents."

"Grandparents," she echoed in a choked whisper. "I can't believe I have grandparents. I have no memory of them."

"They have never forgotten you or your mom."

"Why do you think she took me away?"

He pondered the question. "I think it was either to protect you because you saw your father's murderer, or it was because the pain of your father's death was overwhelming." He swallowed. "When my wife and daughter died, being here was excruciating. My parents wanted me to remarry, to give my son a mother. I couldn't do it."

"Is that why you left instead of moving into the *dawdi haus*?"

He nodded. "I'm a little ashamed now, but *jah*. That's why."

She placed a warm hand on his arm. He could feel the heat from her palm through his shirt. "Don't be ashamed, Ben. Everyone has to deal with pain. I'm sure they understood that you needed a break."

He smiled at her explanation. "I was gone for three years. That's a long break."

A chuckle broke from her. "You know what I mean."

"*Jah*, I know. *Denke* for caring."

For a moment, she didn't respond. He wondered if he had offended her. Then she responded so softly, he had trouble hearing her. "I care, Ben. I will always care."

True to his word, Ben took Sadie to meet her grandparents the next day. The plan was that he would leave her there for a few hours so she could become reunited with her family. She knew that he had plans to help Isaac search the area and see if anyone had sighted Mason Green. Having her at a different location than she had been seemed like a good strategy.

Nathaniel had begged to go with them. The Bontragers, Esther explained, were a large family and had several children Nathaniel's age. Nathaniel was eager to meet them and play. Ben agreed. Until it was time for him to leave and Nathaniel said he wanted to stay and play with his new friends.

At first Ben hesitated. Sadie watched with amusement as a very earnest child managed to wheedle his way through his father's objections until he was allowed to stay with the other children. No doubt he had decided that Nathaniel would be safer in a different environment as well.

Sadie knew that Ben didn't want to leave, but she convinced him that she was well looked after. Besides her grandparents, she had several grown cousins present, as well, with their families. At first she was shy, not sure what they would expect of her or if she would be a disappointment to them, having grown up outside of the Amish life.

Instead, she found her grandparents to be two very warm and caring people. Her cousins seemed to welcome her without hesitation, too. She was amazed at the sheer number of people there. It had always been her and Kurt. Now, it seemed, everywhere she looked there was another relative.

The moment that was really tense for her, however, was when the bishop stopped by to see her. What her mother had done in taking her from the Amish was grounds for being shunned or cast out. Not knowing what kind of reception to expect, Sadie was expecting the worst. When the bishop stood before her, she was sure she was going to get it. In her mind, she had done something selfish by coming to this district when she knew that someone was after her.

The bishop did not scold her, though. Instead, he asked her questions about her life with the *Englisch* and about her mother. He seemed to be genuinely sad to learn of her mother's death. She didn't add in her suspicion that her mother may have been murdered. Mostly because she didn't know yet if it was true.

"I remember your parents," he informed her. "I was not bishop yet when you and your *mamm* left. Your father was a *gut* man. Hardworking and devoted to his family. Your mother was well known for baking the best pies in the district."

She remembered how her mother had loved to bake. A lump formed in her throat. As happy as she was to have her memories back, sometimes they were painful. Knowing that she had almost lost all knowledge of her mother made her ache with longing to see her again. She still didn't remember her father very well.

Lord, please let me get all my memories back.

She bit her lip. Was such a prayer selfish? On impulse, she asked the bishop. She almost regretted asking, though, at the surprised look that covered his face.

"You may pray to *Gott* about anything," he replied, to her relief. "*Gott* likes us to talk with Him."

When the bishop climbed back into his buggy to leave, she watched him go, feeling torn. She had so much to be thankful for. She had family she had lost. Family who truly cared about her. She had friends. Not only Isaac and Ben, but last night, Isaac had brought his wife, Lizzy, by to meet her.

Lizzy was like a ray of sunshine. She laughed and smiled, and joy just seemed to spill out of her. Sadie had been awkward at first, but the feeling had faded quickly in light of the other woman's enthusiasm.

Sadie thought they could become very close. If she were to stay. Part of her yearned to stay so much it was painful. She wanted to remain close to Esther and Abram, too.

But mostly she yearned to be able to stay with Ben, whether he stayed here or returned home. She wanted to have the right to be the woman at his side as he raised his son. She thought that he would move back eventually and take over his father's business. Although he had not said so, she could read his attachment to this place in the way he talked about his family and in the pride he took in helping his father with his business.

Feeling pensive, she remained outside after the bishop left. Without thinking about where she was going, she began to walk along the driveway. Her thoughts returned to Ben.

His parents were right. It was time for Ben to start thinking about marrying again. Not that any woman could replace his Lydia. But she knew that it would be a good thing for him. And for Nathaniel.

She just didn't think she could be that woman. And she wanted to be. So very much.

Could she give up her life and return to the Amish? She grimaced. He had not asked her to. Had not even hinted that he wanted her to.

She had a life in the *Englisch* world. A job she enjoyed. A brother she cared about deeply. One who was still missing.

Had Kurt been able to find the information he needed to put his boss and Mason Green away? She felt that he had been making progress. And she knew that Ryder was looking very hard at the connection between Ethan Nettle and Mason Green.

It seemed too much of a coincidence that Ethan had hired Kurt after what happened with Sadie. And after both of her parents had died in such strange ways. Why had she never been attacked before now? Was it possible that the fact that she never spoke out had convinced them that she wouldn't tell? Or that she didn't know or understand what had happened to her real father?

Could he have hired Kurt to keep an eye on her?

She had been so young when her father had been killed. So young, that she knew she didn't look the same as she had before. And with her not being Amish anymore, could Ethan have questioned whether or not she was the girl who got away, the girl who had seen Mason Green's face?

Maybe it was a test for her brother. Or maybe it was a test for her, to see if she had remembered.

As she mused, she absently walked around to the front of the house and paced on the driveway. Ice slid down her spine. Her entire life seemed like a setup. There were just too many things that led back to that fateful day when Mason Green had attempted to steal her away so many years ago.

"Sadie? Sadie, is that you?"

She turned at the masculine voice. Frowning slightly, she watched as a young man hurried over to her. Through a short beard, a wide smile stretched across his friendly face. He wasn't handsome, but she could see a definite charm about him. He wore a flannel shirt and blue jeans, and a dark brown leather jacket.

Not Amish. As he came closer, she felt no inkling that she had ever seen him before. Had she completely forgotten parts of her adult life, too? She had thought all of those memories had returned, but she must have been mistaken.

The young man, who was about her age, halted a few feet from her. A sense of unease swept over her. She didn't know him. And his smile was wide, but his eyes...

There was something cold in his eyes. And why would she know an *Englischer* out here, when she hadn't been in this area for so many years?

"I'm sorry. I don't have time to talk right now." She tried to excuse herself, backing away from him.

He took a step closer to her, again closing the gap between them. His smile tightened, although it remained on his face. It gained a chilling quality that made her cringe on the inside.

"What's the rush? Certainly you have time to catch up with an old friend?" His voice was pleasant. Teasing, even.

She was now certain that this man was not a friend. She didn't think she had ever seen him before. He was not here to catch up with her, or for any other benign purpose.

Inside, her instincts were telling her to flee. He was so close to her, she could smell the mint of his breath. Normally a pleasing aroma, it made her stomach turn. She was farther away from her grandparents' house than she had thought. If she turned and ran, she might make it. But she doubted it.

As if he sensed her thoughts, his hand shot out and grabbed her. His leather jacket gaped open and she swallowed. He was wearing a gun under his jacket, confirming her suspicions that he was here for reasons that had nothing to do with friendship.

He followed her gaze. His smile morphed into a steely grin. "Ah, yes. You have found out my little secret. It helps to encourage those who are less than willing to hear me out."

She backed up another step. "I don't know you. I need to go back." She tugged at her arm. He held on. His grip tightened painfully.

"I don't think so, Sadie. You have made things very difficult for my father. You and that brother of yours."

Kurt. He was talking about Kurt. Had Kurt been found by the criminals? Her heartbeat was thudding in her ears.

"He has gone into hiding, but maybe if his little sister is in need, he'll come out to help her."

So they didn't have Kurt yet. That was good. How was she going to get away? She glanced around, desperate to find a weapon of some kind. A way to distract him.

"Oh, no. You are not getting away this time. My father has wasted so much time trusting Mason Green to haul you in, but he hasn't. You're too slippery. But you're not smarter than I am. I'm going to be the one to get you.

Then my father will see that he should let me in for a bigger part of the business."

With a sudden twist, she wrenched out of his grip and turned to run. He caught up with her before she'd taken four steps. One hand grabbed her shoulder, the other latched on to her *kapp*. And her hair. Pain had tears stinging her eyes as he pulled her back. Forcing her to face him again, he removed the hand on her *kapp*. The garment fell to the ground.

"That wasn't smart, Sadie. I don't have much patience."

While he was talking, he began to drag her away from her family's house. She opened her mouth, drawing breath to scream.

"You scream and you'll be dead before anyone gets to you. I have people watching the Amish people you're staying with. That little boy is adorable."

His insinuation made her breath stick in her throat, nearly choking her. He'd hurt Nathaniel, or worse. She had no choice. She must protect those she loved at all costs. She stopped struggling. He chuckled and continued to drag her down the block.

"That's right. I knew you were smart."

"Sadie! Let her go!" Nathaniel charged down the street and launched himself at the man. With a growl, the man swatted him away.

"Get in the car, Sadie, and I won't take him with us."

"Stay there, Nathaniel," she told the child, terrified he wouldn't listen. She saw his tear-damp face staring at her, but he didn't move. She was amazed that he was being allowed to go free. He was a potential witness.

They had arrived at a small sedan. Knowing she couldn't let her captor harm Nathaniel, she obediently climbed into the back seat and lay on the floorboards. He threw some blankets over her, covering her up. "You make any dumb move, and the kid will suffer."

She was suffocating under the blankets. Sweat began to pool on her neck. Her forehead grew damp. Something heavy was placed on top of the blankets, holding her in place.

Fear drew her down. She felt more than heard the car start, and the motion as it started moving made her want to vomit.

She was out of time.

Chapter Fourteen

Sadie lost track of how much time had passed or how many turns they had taken. Several times she lost consciousness due to a combination of the heat and the panic that she was swimming in. Would she ever see Ben and Nathaniel again? Her brother?

So many things she regretted not saying, now that it was too late.

Sadie knew she was going to die. But at least her brother and the others were safe. She was very grateful that he had let Nathaniel go. Hopefully Kurt would get the evidence to stop these men before they destroyed too many other lives.

It hurt, the fear and the anxiety that crawled through her. Silent tears slid down her face.

After what could've been half an hour or two hours, the car came to a final stop. She felt the engine turn off. A few seconds later, the front door of the vehicle slammed. When she heard the vibration, she braced herself, knowing that he would open the door and pull her out to meet whatever fate awaited her.

Ethan Nettle had a son. On some level she had been

aware of this. She tried to think if she could remember hearing his name before. She couldn't.

As she had feared, moments later the weights were lifted from her and the blankets came off. Opening her eyes, she once again came face-to-face with her captor. The friendly smile was gone, replaced with terrifying determination. His long arms reached out and he dragged her to her feet. She stumbled slightly as he yanked her out of the car. Her legs were unsteady from being kept in such an uncomfortable position. She fell awkwardly against him. He pushed her away and slapped her face. Her eyes watered in response to the pain on her cheek.

"Come on. Don't make any trouble," he warned her and then proceeded to half drag, half carry her into a building that seemed familiar. He pulled her down a flight of stairs. With some horror, she realized that she was in the basement of the newspaper office where her brother worked.

Forcing her to sit on a chair in the corner, he securely tied her hands and her feet, making her escape impossible. She could barely move, the bonds were so tight. She watched as he reached up and ripped off his beard. She hadn't realized it was a fake.

"That's better. I don't know how anyone can stand those things. I really should have grabbed the kid," he mused, making her blood boil. "It would have been too much trouble, though. It's not like he can identify me." Smirking, he pointed to his now clean-shaven face. Then he pulled out his phone and looked at it. The satisfied smile that crossed his lips was one of the scariest things she had ever seen. "Good. All you have to do now is wait. I have called my father. He's on his way. I'm sure he's bringing that idiot Green with him, but at least he'll know that I managed to do in one attempt what Green couldn't." He snickered. It wasn't an attractive sound. "He couldn't even get you out of the way with explosives."

A sound near the door distracted him. As he peered into the shadows, a figure shot forward and attacked. She watched as the two men wrestled.

Kurt.

Her foolish brother was fighting with the man who had kidnapped her. Fear and hope trembled inside her. And she was helpless to do more than watch. Suddenly, a third person was in the room.

Mason Green. He took one look at the scene before him and laughed before he hefted something in the air and brought it down on Kurt's head. Kurt fell to the ground, and Green let the wrench he was holding drop from his hands.

"So, you can be useful," Ethan's son sneered.

"Can it, Vincent. You almost got taken down. What would your father have said then?"

The amount of antagonism between the two men was frightening. Both of them, it seemed, would do anything for the approval of Ethan Nettle. The man she had thought was her brother's friend was the leader of men such as these. Kurt groaned from the floor. Her shoulders slumped. She hadn't allowed herself to imagine him dead, but the realization that he wasn't sang through her blood.

At least, he wasn't dead yet. They were in a horrible predicament. One she wasn't sure she had a way out of.

Ben would turn it over to God. Keeping her eyes on the two men in front of her, she said a quick prayer in her mind. She asked God to watch over them and help them escape. But if they couldn't escape, she asked Him to watch over Ben, Nathaniel and Isaac. And their families.

"Let's tie him up before he comes completely to his senses," Ethan's son ordered.

"Listen, you, you're not in charge here." Green bristled with anger.

"Really? Because it kind of seems that I am. Now, are we going to tie this dude up, or do you want to explain to my dad why he was roaming free when he arrives?"

She noticed that Vincent stressed the words *my dad*. He was letting the other man know that he was flesh and blood and the other man was merely hired help. Mason Green's complexion changed to a mottled red, his eyes hot with his anger. But he did as Vincent Nettle had ordered.

Within minutes, Kurt was tied up on the floor near her chair. He wasn't completely conscious yet, but she knew it was just a matter of time.

The thump of heavy footsteps coming down the stairs brought everyone's attention to the door. Ethan Nettle appeared and took in the scene. His sharp business suit and carefully trimmed hair was so urbane and the epitome of a charming businessman, Sadie's gut lurched. He used his power, and his job, to enable him to do heinous acts. He needed to be stopped. Only she was in no position to stop him.

His eyes landed on her, and she cringed. How had she not noticed how cruel his gaze could be?

"Vincent, you did well, son. Do you see, Mason? This is how it's done. Both of the Standings, literally at my feet."

Mason Green fumed, his mouth a hard slash across

his face as he glared at his competition. Vincent smirked. Then he rubbed salt in the wound.

"It wasn't hard, Dad. All I needed to do to get her was to make sure she knew that the kid we saw her with would be in danger if she didn't cooperate."

She didn't like the gleam that entered Ethan's eyes as he stared at her. "Maybe he will anyway. As an example."

She struggled with her restraints, knowing it was useless, but fueled with the urgent need to protect Nathaniel from these vicious men.

All three of them laughed.

Ethan stepped closer to her. "You are well and truly caught, my dear." He turned his contemptuous gaze to Kurt, whose eyes were now open and watching. "All you had to do was keep out of my business. I was almost convinced that your sister knew nothing. She would have been safe, because too many accidents draw too much attention. But you had to dig. I knew you had to die," he said, turning back to Sadie, "when it looked like you recognized the picture of Mason that night I ate dinner at your house." He jerked his thumb at the man behind him.

"Did you kill my mother and stepfather?"

The words left her mouth before she even knew she was going to say them. He grinned, a nasty expression that curdled her blood. Kurt's head jerked up. He had never suspected that their parents' deaths was anything but an accident.

"She was a loose end I couldn't afford. She had seen Mason one day, and I knew the risk was too great. Don't worry. They didn't suffer. Much."

She shuddered, and he laughed.

Apparently bored with the conversation, Ethan Nettle turned to his son. "We need to get ready. After these two are taken care of, things will be too hot for us around here. We need to be prepared."

Vincent nodded and started up the stairs. Ethan watched his son leave the room, then he turned back to Mason Green.

Green stood straighter. "You have disappointed me several times now, Mason. I hope this is not a trend that continues."

"No boss. I know what to do."

"Good." Satisfaction settled on Ethan's face. He was a handsome man, but at the moment, he was ugly, marred by the evil that lurked in his heart. "I'll leave you to finish this mess. I don't have to tell you that I am counting on you."

After receiving his employee's nod, Ethan turned on his heel and headed out, following his son up the stairs without a backward glance at the two people he'd just condemned to death.

Sadie braced herself as Mason turned to them. "Well. I see we are to meet one last time, little girl. Too bad only one of us will make it out of here alive."

Ben returned with his buggy to collect Sadie and Nathaniel at the appointed time. He smiled to himself as he recalled her excitement when he'd introduced her to her grandparents. She had been apprehensive, too, but he knew it would be well. The Bontragers had suffered with the death of their son and the disappearance of his widow and child.

They didn't blame Hannah for leaving. The love for a child and the urge to protect her was a powerful force. He wondered what he would have done if something had threatened Nathaniel. He didn't even want to go there.

He stopped his buggy halfway up the driveway and descended. He asked one of the women on the porch to point him to where Sadie was.

"She went for a walk with the bishop. He left to go attend to other duties. She never came back."

"I saw her walking down the driveway. She might have gone for a walk," one of her many cousins reported.

Thanking them brusquely, he hurried in the direction the girl had indicated. He felt a sense of urgency. Something was wrong. Sadie was not one to concern others by wandering off. She had more sense than that. No one here understood the danger as he did. Why had she walked away from the house?

Footsteps ran up behind him. "*Dat!* He has her. The bad man has her!"

His son's words were enough to drop him to his knees. He caught Nathaniel as the child flew into his arms, slamming into his father hard enough to rock him back on his heels. The boy was sobbing so fiercely he was struggling to breathe.

"Settle down, Nathaniel. You have to tell me what happened. Then we can help Sadie. Can you tell me what happened?" he asked when his son seemed to be calmer.

The boy's lips trembled. "A man was dragging her down the street. She was fighting him, *Dat*. She looked scared. I ran after them and tried to stop the bad man from taking her."

His heart was in his throat. His brave little boy had tried to take on a killer to protect Sadie. He'd come so close to having them both taken. He looked down, and paled. Nathaniel had a white prayer *kapp* in his hands. Sadie's *kapp*.

He was afraid to speak again.

"He hit me and I fell. Then he told Sadie he'd let me go if she stopped fighting. She told me to stay. He made her get into his car and made her lie on the floor."

"How long ago was this?"

Nathaniel shrugged, his face miserable. "I don't know. She told me to stay, so I stayed. I sat there until I saw you come, then I wanted to tell you what had happened."

Ben took a deep breath. He needed to find her. *Gott, help me.*

"Nathaniel, I need you to go and stay inside the *haus* with the Bontragers. I need to find Sadie, and it will be easier if I know you are safe."

The little boy threw his arms around his father and squeezed him tight. Ben's eyes closed as emotions swamped him. "Bring her home, *Dat.*"

Home. "I will, son. If it's possible, I will."

He knew better than to promise something like that, but he couldn't stop himself.

Nathaniel nodded, then ran up the drive and into the house. Now that he knew Nathaniel was safe, Ben could work on finding Sadie and bringing her back.

Running to his buggy, he climbed up and turned around in record time. Every second to Isaac's house seemed to be a second lost. Isaac was a former police officer. Ben hoped he would get in touch with Ryder and they would find her.

Please Gott, *let us find her before it's too late.*

He had no doubt that Mason Green had found her. And knowing the history she had with that man, it wasn't hard to imagine what he would do with her. Sweat broke out on Ben's forehead.

He had the fear that they would find her body. He blocked those thoughts from his mind. Sadie would be all right. She had to be. And when he found her, he would forget his pride and all his nonsense about not interfering with her choice and would ask her to rejoin the church and be his bride. Even if she said no, he could no longer pretend that his feelings for her would fade once she left.

Isaac and Lizzy both waved as he pulled into their driveway. One look at his face, though, and Isaac was all business. His friend and his wife were waiting for him the second he pulled on the reins to command the horse to halt.

"He has her," Ben gasped. Lizzy paled. Isaac didn't hesitate.

"There's a phone in the barn," he called out, racing toward it.

Ben was right behind him. Isaac placed the call to Ryder, then he followed Ben back to the buggy. "We need to question the people on the street, see if they have anything to add. Maybe one of them saw something."

It seemed to take forever to get back to where Sadie had disappeared. They questioned the neighbors at each house. The fourth was the home of a young *Englisch* couple. The twenty something husband answered the door, looking startled to have a couple of Amish men on his porch.

"Can I help you?"

"Yes," Isaac responded. "Probably around an hour ago, a young Amish woman was abducted from the Bontrager farm four houses down. A young boy saw her being dragged into a car. Did you happen to see anything suspicious around that time?"

The young man removed his ball cap and scratched his head. "I'm sorry to hear about the woman. A car did come and stop in front of the Bontrager house. I noticed it sitting there when I went out to go to the store. I didn't see who was driving it, but I do recall thinking that it was weird to see a car parked in front of the house."

Ben's heart sped up. Hopefully this man would be able to provide some information that would help them.

Isaac continued to ask him questions. The man hadn't seen the driver, but he definitely got a good look at the car. He was able to provide them with the make and model of the sedan, along with the color and the college sticker in the back window.

"Thanks. This might help us locate her," Isaac told the man.

Ten minutes later, they were joined by Ryder. From where he stood, Ben could see Lily patiently sitting in the front seat.

Succinctly, they told him all they had learned. Within minutes, he had called in the description of the car in what he called a BOLO or *be on the lookout*.

"Once we get a hit, we will head in that direction. I brought Lily along. I know you said Sadie was taken by car. But once she is out of the car, Lily can help. She might be able to track Sadie's scent. If you have anything of Sadie's with you, that is."

Ben started to shake his head, then stopped. Sadie's *kapp*. He handed it over to Ryder, his hands shaking slightly.

Ryder met his eyes. "We'll do our best to find her, Ben. I promise you that I will use whatever I can to find her."

Ben nodded, his throat closed.

Isaac placed his hand on Ben's shoulder briefly in solidarity. The hand slipped off when Ryder's radio started beeping before a feminine voice broke through. Ryder straightened and answered the call. Ben clenched and unclenched his hands, trying to understand the jargon that was passing back and forth between the sergeant and the dispatcher.

"We have a sighting." Ryder turned and strode back to his car. "Let's go. Someone saw the car in the downtown area ten minutes ago."

Ben and Isaac ran after Ryder. Both of them climbed into the back seat.

"I'm not going to use my siren. I don't want to give Green a heads-up that he's been found." He pulled the car out onto the road. When they hit the downtown area, Ben swallowed his disappointment as they hit some minor traffic. Every second wasted was a second longer that Sadie was in the hands of evil men.

"You should hit the lights, even if you're not going to use the siren," Isaac advised tensely. Ben realized that Isaac was affected by the kidnapping of their childhood friend, too.

"Yep." Ryder flicked a switch, and Ben could see the reflection of the flashing lights on the windshields of the cars they passed. The vehicles ahead of them moved to the side, allowing the cruiser to speed up the road uninhibited.

Gib nicht auf, Sadie. Ben whispered the words in his mind, silently pleading with her not to give up. *We're coming.*

He could only pray they'd be in time.

Chapter Fifteen

Ryder turned the corner so sharply that Ben set a hand down on the seat to balance himself. He didn't complain. Anything that Ryder did in pursuit of Sadie was fine with him. When the police officer pulled to a stop behind the car that fit the description of the vehicle the young man had described, he felt his hopes rise.

Three men climbed from the car. Ben didn't recognize the area. Ryder jogged to the other side of the cruiser and let Lily out. He snapped a leash on her harness and then he held Sadie's *kapp* to her nose. Lily sniffed the *kapp*, quivering.

When he told her to search in German, Ben blinked. He hadn't expected that the dog would have been trained in such a familiar language.

"It made sense to teach her in a language I could remember," Isaac murmured, his eyes focused on his former colleague and the canine cop.

Lily put her muzzle to the ground and then shot off to the back door of the building.

Where were they? Frowning, Ben looked around.

Isaac caught his breath beside him. "The newspaper's office is in this building. We need to be careful."

Ryder nodded. "We don't have a warrant, but I think we have a strong case for not waiting for one." He thumbed the radio on his shoulder. When it was answered, he gave their location and the situation. "The situation is grave. I can't wait to enter the building, but I am requesting backup as soon as possible."

"Backup will be there in under ten."

Ten minutes. They couldn't wait. Not for other officers, not for a warrant. Ben didn't care about the *Englisch* laws. He was going in, whether they were allowed to or not. Sadie's life was in the balance, and that mattered more than any law.

"Let's take this slowly," Ryder warned. "I don't want to frighten him. It might go bad for Sadie."

Isaac nodded and Ben understood what he was saying. If they made Mason Green aware of their presence, he might hurt Sadie, or worse, and try to get away again. He was all for going careful if it would protect her.

Lord, please keep her safe. Help us to catch this man and keep him from preying on other women and children.

He thought of how Nathaniel said that the man who took Sadie had threatened to take him along, as well. If that had happened, he might have lost both of those he loved most without any idea of where they should start searching for them. He wasn't sure how he would have gotten through that, although he knew *Gott* would be there to help him.

"Okay, let's go around the side of the building," Ryder whispered, breaking into his bleak thoughts. "There's another entrance there. It might help us sneak up on them."

Ryder went first with Lily. The other two men followed, trying to keep the noise down. Together, they went around to the side. Ryder and Isaac opened the door slowly. A very slight creak sounded from the heavy door, but hopefully it was masked by the other noises around them. As soon as they entered, Lily's nose was on the ground again as she continued to search for her target. The next five minutes felt like an hour as they crept after the canine. At last, they could hear the low rumble of masculine voices. One voice. Two voices. Ben's eyebrow raised. He thought he recognized Kurt's voice. Even though he couldn't understand what his friend was saying, he thought he could detect the fear and strain in his voice.

He glanced at Isaac and Ryder. Both were looking grim.

Suddenly, Kurt shouted out. A second later, Ben heard a scream that made his blood turn to ice in his veins. Sadie. He was done waiting. He took off in the direction of the scream, followed closely by Isaac and Ryder. He twisted around a corner, his blood pounding in his ears.

More shouts by Kurt kept him moving in the direction of the voices. They led him to a staircase. He stomped rapidly down the stairs, not even caring anymore that he was making enough noise to alert everyone in the building to his presence.

Ryder shoved past him, gun out.

"Police! Drop your weapon!" Ryder shouted, pointing his gun at someone still out of Ben's sight. A second later, Ben and Isaac reached the bottom of the steps together and took in the room at a glance.

Kurt was lying on his side, tied up. He must have

fallen over or been pushed. He was awake and had some slight facial bruising.

Directly in front of them, Mason Green was holding on to a struggling Sadie. Ben kept his eyes focused on Mason with difficulty. If he looked at her, he was afraid that the strength of his emotions, one of which was a hot rage that was constricting his chest, would take over his common sense.

She was alive. He needed to focus on that and not let himself be sidetracked by other things. Right now, getting her out of this alive and without further harm was his priority.

Sirens were heard directly outside the building.

"Drop the gun, Green. There's no way you can get away with hurting Miss Standings or Mr. Standings. You're going to be arrested, and any additional violence will only hurt your chances when you go to trial."

Mason Green laughed harshly. Then he sneered. "I'm not the one you should be worried about. The Nettles are long gone. You'll never find them."

Ryder narrowed his eyes. "I wouldn't count on that."

Ben held himself still to keep from drawing attention. He caught Sadie's eye, trying to communicate his love and his promise to free her. She didn't look away. When he looked back at Mason Green for a moment, he saw when the man lost all hope and only wanted his vengeance.

Mason's eyes twitched to where he was holding Sadie. Ben knew he was planning on shooting her.

The moment he brought the gun closer and his finger tightened on the trigger, Sadie yelled out, her voice vibrating with fury, and kicked, hard. Mason screamed in pain as the heel of her boot slammed into his shin.

She jerked from his loosened hold. Ben leaped forward, catching Sadie and dropping to the floor with her in his arms. Kurt yelled. A gunshot went wild, hitting the wall.

Ryder attacked, rushing at Mason and taking him down. Within seconds, the angry man was struggling and shouting, even as Ryder rolled him over and cuffed him while yelling his rights at full voice.

When the man was subdued, Isaac assisted Ryder in pulling him to his feet. He had to dodge out of the way to avoid being kicked. Ben turned away from Mason, his full attention on the young woman who held his heart. Without thinking about it, he kissed her gently on the forehead. Then on the cheek.

He wanted to kiss her lips, desperately. But he held himself back. Instead, he stood and held out his hand. She put hers in his, and he gently tugged her to her feet. Carefully, he scrutinized her, looking for any outward signs of injury. She had a couple of scratches and a bruise on the right side of her face. Other than that, she appeared unharmed. He sighed in relief.

All the fears he'd kept inside for the past hour caught up with him. He could feel himself starting to shake. He slammed his eyes closed and clenched his fists, doing his best to hold himself together. Nothing worked.

"Ben."

He opened his eyes and stared into the eyes of the woman he had risked death to save. She was the most beautiful thing he'd ever seen.

"You came," she choked out. "I can't believe you found me."

"I promised I would protect you. I meant it. With my whole being."

He was unprepared for the suddenness with which

she flung her arms around him and snuggled into his shoulder. He adapted well, though, and his own arms closed around her. He stood there, silently praising *Gott* for protecting her and letting him hold her in his arms.

Sadie wanted nothing more than to stay nestled deep in Ben's strong embrace. But she knew she couldn't. She had to move away from him. Instinctively, her arms tightened in protest. She inhaled his clean, comforting scent.

Enough. This was already hard. She needed to stop torturing them both.

Bracing herself, she backed out of his grasp. He released her, and his arms fell to his sides. She saw his fingers twitch, as if they wanted to reach out and hold her again. They didn't, though.

She was glad, she told herself, even as she wrestled with the regret.

"I thought we were too late," he whispered.

It was then that she noticed Isaac helping Kurt to his feet while Ryder took a handcuffed Mason Green out to his cruiser. The killer impaled her with a deadly glare and sneered as he was paraded past her. "Don't get too complacent, little girl. Ethan will finish the job. Don't you doubt that."

It wasn't over, even though they had caught Mason Green.

Horrified, she swiveled her head and looked at Ben. The Amish man's mouth was a tight line, and his eyes were hard as he watched the criminal being put in the back of the police car.

"Ben?"

She had to call his name a second time before he

stopped glaring after Mason Green and turned his attention back to her. There was no mistaking the concern in those deep eyes. She had grown familiar with his moods.

"They're still going to be after me."

Please say I'm wrong. Please.

He didn't. Instead, his face grew grim as he slowly nodded. "*Jah*. We already knew that Mason Green was working with Ethan Nettle."

"It's not just Ethan. His son Vincent is working with him." She saw the surprise in his eyes. "I so hoped it was over." She couldn't control her glance in the direction that Ryder had taken Mason. She knew that by now, the villain was safe inside the police cruiser. She couldn't see Mason through the walls, but she felt as though his eyes were boring holes in her, even from a distance. "Ethan and his son were here. Vincent was the man that kidnapped me. They were already packed and ready to disappear. After Ethan scolded Mason for failing too many times. In order to make up for past mistakes, Mason's job was to get rid of Kurt and myself."

Ben paled at her words.

Would she never be safe?

"You could come back—"

"No. I'm sorry, Ben. I will not put you or your family in danger again."

He sighed. "They are your people, too, Sadie. You have family there. Family that loves you." He paused, his gaze searching her face. "You could join the church. I'm sure you could find a *mann*. Maybe even one who is a lonely widower, who would open his heart and his home to you."

She couldn't breathe. Ben, the man she had being trying so hard to deny her growing feelings for, was all but telling her he loved her and wished for her to be his wife. The mother of his children.

For the space of three heartbeats, she almost agreed, her heart filling with joy at this gift. Then reality crashed in, shattering the dreams. She couldn't do it. Couldn't put them in danger. The Amish were peaceful people. If killers came for her family, Ben would not pick up a gun to protect himself. He would protect his family, but for himself he would accept death rather than participate in violence. That would destroy her.

She swallowed the pain that started to fill her heart and stepped back from him, deliberately increasing the distance. His face paled, telling her he understood her move.

"I am not going back to the Amish district, Ben. I will not continue to put you and Nathaniel, or my family and friends in danger. It wouldn't be fair."

"You belong with us," he insisted, his voice rough with hurt.

Oh, no. Tears stung her eyes. She wanted to give in and tell him she'd go anywhere he was. But it would never work. And she didn't know if she could live a life under the fear and pressure.

"Nee." The Amish word slipped out. "I do not belong anywhere. I am not *Englisch*, not anymore, nor am I Amish. I won't be responsible for putting anyone in danger. Not again."

Ryder came to where they stood. His serious eyes bounced between them. Had he heard what they had been talking about? His words confirmed that he had.

"If you won't return to the Amish with Ben, you should still go into hiding. Ethan Nettle and his son are both gone. It won't be safe for you to return to your home. I will have to put a security detail on Kurt, too."

Her brother. Maybe she'd be able to be placed with him. Then she wouldn't be alone.

"I can't go into a safe house," Kurt stated in a voice tinged with steel, coming over to their group, dashing her hopes. "Not now that I know Ethan is a part of this."

"Kurt," she started, then paused, unsure what to say.

"My boss is Mason Green's contact," Kurt growled. "I can't believe I never suspected it."

"It's because of me," she whispered. Kurt glanced at her, his face alert. "Oh, Kurt, I had blocked the memories, but Mason Green had murdered my real father, years ago. My mother and I left our home so she could protect me. When Ethan was at our house, I saw a photo of Mason, and my reaction told Ethan that I had recognized it, although I still didn't recall completely who he was."

Kurt shook his head. "He's been playing me the whole time. My guess is in his mind, I was expendable. Maybe he's been using me to figure out what you knew. How much of a threat you were. Once he knew you were remembering, I'm sure he was pretty desperate to get you out of the picture. I can't let them get away with that."

"What do you plan to do?" Ben asked, subdued.

She winced. He was still hurt by her rejection, but she knew she'd made the right choice.

"I'm a reporter," Kurt responded. "I'm going to do my job and expose the truth."

Ryder walked over to Sadie. "I can put you in a safe place. If you are sure this is what you want. I can arrange for a temporary placement for you until we find Nettle and his son. Nettle has a very well-known face. In order to truly hide, he'll have to be in disguise. There's no telling how long this could take."

Sadie bit her lip. She knew that they were all thinking the same thing. What if they never found Nettle or his son? She'd be in hiding for the rest of her life. Never to see Kurt again. Separated from her newly discovered grandparents...and from the man she—

No. That was done. It had to be. There was nothing for her in that relationship.

Turning to Ryder, she tightened her jaw. "That's what I want."

He nodded. Ben's eyes glistened, but he didn't argue. Her heart shattered as she watched him straighten his shoulders and walk away.

Taking her heart with him.

Chapter Sixteen

Sadie opened the door to find Ryder standing on the other side. In the four months since she'd left Ben and gone into hiding, she and the officer had become friends. He was her one connection to Ben and to her brother. The one thing that kept her from going out of her mind as she waited to hear that she could finally go home and begin to live her life again were his visits, where he would tell her how the case was proceeding.

"Ryder. I wasn't expecting you today." She opened the door wider and stepped back, allowing him to enter the apartment she was staying in. She really didn't like the apartment. Oh, there was nothing wrong with it. It was clean, and although it was small, it had everything she needed.

It just wasn't home.

She was distracted momentarily when she realized that when she thought of home, the image that filled her mind wasn't the house she shared with her brother. No, when she thought of home, she thought of Ben and Nathaniel. She had been thinking about them a lot. She couldn't seem to go through an hour without something reminding her of the two of them.

She needed to wrap her mind around the fact that she was not a part of their lives. Not anymore. Ben was an attractive, intelligent man. One who had led her back to God. She would always be grateful to him. But despite the fact that her roots were in the Amish world, she was part of the *Englisch* world now.

Ryder called her name. Shaking herself from the depths of her reverie, she blinked at him, feeling herself flush at being caught daydreaming.

"Sadie, I have some news for you."

She scoured his face with her gaze. News could be a good thing or it could be very, very bad. She had to be ready for anything. That meant fortification. Which meant coffee.

"Come into the kitchen. I just made coffee."

He followed her into the small kitchen area, just large enough to accommodate a small square table butted up against the wall and two wooden chairs. It was sparse, but she found she was comfortable in the simplicity. She would have liked more room so she could bake easily, but she never complained.

Grabbing two mugs from the rack on the counter, she poured out the hot, strong coffee, then put the cream and sugar on the table. She didn't use it, although she had before she knew Ben, but she knew her friend liked to doctor his coffee.

Ben. Why couldn't she get through five minutes without thinking about the man?

"I hope you are bringing me good news." Sitting across from Ryder, she held her mug in both hands, enjoying the warmth. It was bitterly cold outside, with a fresh layer of glittering snow on the ground. There was a lot to be said for staying inside on days like this.

"I think I have good news." Ryder took a sip and set his mug back on the table. He leaned forward. "We found Ethan and Vincent Nettle."

Her breath caught in her throat. Almost afraid to speak, she whispered, "Is it over?"

"Almost. Mason Green is set to go to trial in three weeks. With his partners put away, there is no one out there to go after you."

"What about the man who was sent to prison for killing my father?"

He grimaced. "Unfortunately, we can't give the man those sixteen years back. He was a teenager then. He has spent his entire young adulthood in prison. He's bitter, and of course there will always be people who will refuse to believe that he didn't do anything wrong. But he's a free man. His record has been expunged, so he won't have the limitations an ex-con might face. It's up to him to make a good life for himself."

She'd be bitter, too, if the system had failed her that badly. Would he be able to come to terms with the loss of sixteen years and move on? It would be a shame if he allowed what had happened to ruin the remainder of his years.

She stilled.

"Sadie? Are you okay? You've gone awful pale."

She heard Ryder's voice as if it were coming through a tunnel.

"I want to go back," she said out loud. She felt as though God had given her a sudden clarity. She had hoped Jeffrey wouldn't allow his past to dictate his future, but wasn't she doing the same thing? She had decided that, because of the actions of others, she had to make a life in the *Englisch* world, even if it wasn't a life that she felt she belonged in anymore.

"Back? Yes, that's what I'm trying to tell you. You can come out of hiding and you can go back. I can't promise your job is still there, but I'm sure you can find another—"

"No, no. You don't understand." She stood and moved to the window. "I can go all the way back. Back home. Back to my family."

Back to Ben and Nathaniel.

Fear and trepidation rose up and made it hard to speak. What if Ben didn't want her back? She'd disrupted his life while she was there.

The kiss they'd shared might be the only one she'd ever receive from him, but she needed to know if they could have a future.

There could be nothing between them if she stayed *Englisch*.

"You want to go to Ben." It wasn't a question. Ryder shoved his chair back and stretched his long legs in front of him.

"Is that wrong?" She winced at the defensiveness in her tone.

He shook his head, his face growing thoughtful. "No, not wrong. But I'm just thinking. When Isaac knew he was in love with Lizzy—"

Her face warmed.

"He knew he couldn't go to her without being a part of the Amish community he'd left all those years before."

"Yeah, I can understand that. She was a baptized member of the Amish church. That makes total sense."

"Right. But he couldn't go to her right away."

No. No. No. She'd already waited so long.

"But—"

"Sadie." She folded her arms and listened, not liking where this conversation was going. He continued. "I'm not telling you what to do. I'm just telling you, as a friend, what another friend went through to find his way back to his girl. He said that he had to be sure that the Amish life was what he wanted for all time. And that he couldn't approach her until he was one hundred percent sure."

She sighed. He was right.

And then there was Kurt. She couldn't abandon her brother without warning. He'd be so hurt if she got out of hiding and immediately left. She needed to contact the bishop, privately, and let him know she wished to come home. And then she needed to get the life she was leaving in order. And only then could she go back.

"You're right. I can't go back to being Amish because of Ben. Although he is a major incentive. I have to be willing to live that life even if he and I don't become a couple."

"Exactly."

A new excitement was building inside her. Did she have a future with Ben and Nathaniel? She loved him; she could admit it to herself. And she wanted to be the one he chose to be the mother Nathaniel needed. In her mind, she could envision herself holding an infant, Ben and Nathaniel beside her. She flushed. And smiled to herself at the thought of making a family with the man she'd been ready to give up for good.

"I have so much to do."

"I'll give you a hand."

Ryder assisted her as she packed up her meager belongings. It only took a couple of hours. When they had packed the last box, he pulled out his phone.

"I have a truck coming by to get your things."

She didn't question it until she saw the familiar pickup truck pull into the driveway. With a squeal, she dashed outside without her coat and threw herself at her brother the second he stepped down from the vehicle, never feeling the cold. Kurt's arms closed around her tightly. She could feel them tremble slightly and knew that he was as emotional as she at their reunion.

"Good to see you, sis," he muttered in a rough voice.

"I am so happy you're here." She hugged him again. She mentally thanked God for blessing her with the return of her memories so that she could appreciate what a wonderful man her brother was. She wouldn't lose her connection with him if she returned to the Amish world, she knew that, but it was bittersweet being reunited with him, knowing she'd be leaving again.

But she needed to find the place God had planned for her.

"Hey, buddy, I thought you might want to see this."

Isaac's words cut through the fog that had encompassed Ben's brain since Sadie left him. Or, more precisely, since she'd gone into hiding. It seemed like years ago, yet it had only been five months. Setting his tools aside, he looked up to see Isaac standing in the door to his shop, a newspaper in his hands.

He shrugged and stood back from the table, stretching to work out the ache in his back. It was time for him to take a break, anyhow.

"*Buddy?* That's very *Englisch* of you."

Isaac grinned. "What can I say? I lived in that world for seven years. I picked up some things."

Ben huffed out a chuckle. "What do I need to see?"

"Oh, yeah." Isaac held out the paper. Ben took it, still mystified. "Here."

Following the line of his friend's finger to where he pointed, Ben saw the article and noticed Kurt's name on the byline. "Page one? Kurt's moving up."

"Yeah, yeah. Read the story."

Ben sat down and read. After the third paragraph, he needed to sit as the meaning of what he was reading started to sink in. Mason Green was dead. The man who had murdered Sadie's father and let another man take the fall had been killed in prison awaiting trial. The police had his partners in custody, all profits and assets had been seized and the evidence of their involvement in the drug trade and practice of selling children had been collected and documented. There was enough to put them away for the rest of their lives.

"She can come out of hiding."

The words left his mouth and hung in the air between Ben and Isaac.

"That's what I'm thinking." Isaac leaned against the desk. "If she contacts you and you need my help with anything, just say so. You know that Lizzy and I think the world of Sadie."

Ben was already shaking his head. "It doesn't matter, Isaac. Unless she joins the Amish church, we could never be together. I am grateful that she is free to come home, though. More than anything, I want her to be safe and happy. I have prayed to *Gott* every day for Him to bless her and let her come home."

"He listened."

Sadie.

Ben stood so fast he knocked over the chair that he had been working on. He never even glanced at it. All his focus was on the lovely woman standing inside the door. His heart sped up and his mouth went dry.

She was dressed Plain. He'd never seen anything lovelier than Sadie standing in his workshop wearing a heavy black cape, and under it he could see she had on a rose-colored Amish dress and plain brown boots. On her head, a crisp white prayer *kapp* covered most of her hair. She was holding a black bonnet.

In short, she looked like an Amish woman and not like the *Englisch* woman who had landed in his life so unexpectedly all those months ago. His chest grew tight and his breathing was constricted. Hope flared in his soul, but he struggled to keep it under control. If she wasn't here to stay, or if she wasn't part of the Amish world now, he didn't want the knowledge to crush him.

"Sadie—" he began and stopped, unsure what to start with. So many thoughts were colliding inside him, his mind was having trouble sorting them all out. All he could do was stare at the woman who had stolen his heart, half fearing that she would disappear if he blinked.

"I will see you later, my friend." Isaac placed a hand briefly on his shoulder, wordlessly imparting his support. Ben started. He had forgotten the other man was standing next to him, he'd been so focused on Sadie.

Apologetically, he smiled at Isaac. "Sure. I will see you later."

"Sadie," Isaac murmured as he moved past her. "It's good to see you."

"Same goes, Isaac," she replied, shooting him a tight

smile. Ben could see the apprehension in it. She was as nervous as he was.

Some of his own anxiety dwindled as the urge to reassure her inserted itself.

"I read the article your brother wrote in the paper. Are you out of danger now?" It might have seemed obvious, but he needed to know that she was safe.

"Completely," she whispered. She took a step closer and halted. "The men who were after us are now all out of commission. I was given the news a month ago."

Wait. A month ago? Some of his hope died. If she had waited a month before contacting him... But what about her clothing?

"I'm confused," he admitted. "If you are safe, and have been for a month—"

"Why am I only coming here now?" She completed his sentence. He shrugged. After everything they'd been through together, it seemed to him that he deserved some answers.

"I needed time, Ben. Time to put my stuff in order, time to cut my ties."

"Cut your ties?" He advanced a step toward her. That sounded positive.

"Yes." Her caramel-brown eyes, the eyes that had snared him from the first day, met his. "I needed to cut most of my ties with the *Englisch* world. I have talked with the bishop here. Several times, in fact. He remembered my father and mother. He wanted me to wait until I was sure that I wanted to be Amish before I spoke with you. It was the hardest thing to not run to you the moment I was free, but I knew I had to obey him."

She had been thinking of him. Another step. The distance between them was shrinking. "You have made your decision."

A laugh trickled gently from her lips. "You can look at the way I'm dressed and ask? Yes, I have made my choice."

She took the final step and was suddenly only inches away from him. Her hand lifted and touched his cheek. "Ben, I remember us. As we were as children, and as we are now. There has always been a bond between us, hasn't there? Even when I couldn't remember, I felt that connection."

His hand covered hers where it rested, warm and smooth against his face. "You were my best friend when we were children. I lost so much the day you left. I, too, have sensed this connection."

He lifted her hand from his face but didn't let go. They stood, holding hands, staring into each other's eyes.

"I'm not Amish yet," she said. "The bishop has asked me to continue to meet with him until he feels I'm ready to join the church. I'd do it today if he agreed."

"You know, the moment he agrees, I'm going to ask you to be my wife."

The smile that hovered about her lips burst forth and became a grin. "I hope so. And you know, the moment you ask me to be your wife, I will say yes."

His heart was so full, he found himself needing a second. Her eyes were bright and glistening.

"I love you, Sadie Ann. With all my heart. I want you to be a part of my and Nathaniel's life for the rest of our days." It was as close to a proposal as he could go, but he was at peace, knowing that soon he'd be making a true proposal. Then, during the harvest season, he'd make her his bride.

She sighed, a happy sound that filled all the empty corners in his lonely heart. "I love you, too, Ben. I can't wait until you can ask me to be your wife."

He leaned forward and gently, tenderly, touched her forehead with his lips.

"What about your brother?" He had to ask.

"He knows everything and is happy for me. He'll miss me, of course. But we will stay in touch. Even if I was born here, Kurt is and always will be my brother. The bishop told me that he doesn't have a problem with Kurt visiting now and again. Although I have a feeling that Kurt will be busy with his career for a while. His new boss was very impressed with his work on the illegal human trafficking articles."

He was glad. He would always think of Kurt as a friend. Having him as a brother-in-law would please him, as well.

They left the shop together and headed toward his home. The ground was covered with a fresh layer of snow, and the March air was frigid. He didn't mind. His entire being seemed to be suffused with warmth from the joy of having his love by his side again. He wanted to jump and shout his feelings aloud, he could almost burst with how blessed he was.

He did nothing of the sort, of course. Instead, he and Sadie walked sedately side by side, murmuring softly, making plans for the upcoming months. They might not be officially engaged yet, but he knew that they had already promised themselves to each other.

The front screen door banged open, interrupting their quiet conversation. Sadie laughed as Nathaniel charged out the door and literally threw himself off the porch before running into her arms.

"Sadie! You came back! *Dat*, Sadie *es cumme*!"

A wide grin flashed across Ben's face as Sadie embraced his exuberant son tightly. "*Jah*, I can see that she is home. Are you *gut* with that?"

There was a bit of playfulness in the question. He could see that his son was overjoyed.

"*Jah!* I am happy!" Nathaniel pulled back to look up into Sadie's face. "I prayed and prayed that *Gott* would bring you back. Are you going to be my new *mamm*?"

Both Sadie and Ben flushed at the innocent question. "Easy, son. She just came back to us. She needs to join the church before we can talk about that."

Sadie raised her eyebrows at him. He bit back a smile of understanding. They had talked about nothing but that for the past twenty minutes. But he knew it wouldn't be proper to say anything to Nathaniel yet.

But soon, he promised himself, looking into her beloved face, soon they would marry and become a family.

Later that afternoon, he walked her back to her *grossmamma's haus* where she would live until they were wed. He hesitated to leave her. It seemed cruel that he had her back and had to leave her again. He said as much.

"Only until tomorrow, dear Ben." She reached out and touched his hand.

He leaned forward and kissed her, barely a whisper across her soft lips. "Until tomorrow, my dear one."

And all the days that followed.

Epilogue

"*Mamm*, when will baby Evie be able to play with me?" Nathaniel asked.

Ben grinned at Sadie and waited for her to answer the question. Sadie bit her lip, holding back her returning smile. She was very careful not to give the impression that she was laughing at Nathaniel. At eight and a half, he thought he was quite grown-up. Ben knew that Sadie wasn't laughing at Nathaniel, she just thought he was adorable. Plus, whenever he called her *mamm*, her heart just about melted right out of her chest.

She was so blessed with her men.

And now she had another wee blessing.

Cuddling her sleeping daughter closer in her arms, she smoothed a kiss on the tiny forehead. Sometimes she had to remind herself to breathe, her happiness was so overwhelming.

She thought about the months following the arrests of Ethan Nettle and his son. They had both been convicted, and with the list of crimes against them, they would spend the rest of their lives in prison. Jeffrey was free, and although still bitter, he had told her that he never blamed her. In fact, he said that he would have intervened if he'd seen her getting kidnapped. Ironically, that meant he would have been the one who died that day.

"You're the same age as my baby sister. I couldn't have stood by and done nothing," he'd said.

She prayed for him every day.

She returned her attention to Nathaniel, who was watching her with avid eyes.

"Nathaniel, she won't be able to play with you for a while yet. She's only five days old."

He scrunched up his face and peered at his new sister with disgust. He'd been hoping that she would be able to play immediately, she was certain of it. Evelyn yawned and grunted and stretched in her sleep. Stepping so that he was leaning against his stepmother, Nathaniel placed a very gentle finger in one of the small fists. When Evelyn grabbed his finger and held on tight in her sleep, his scowl softened. Something akin to awe glowed on his features.

"She ain't a boy, and she can't do anything," he announced to his parents. "Still, I guess she's fine, as far as babies go."

Sadie and Ben both chuckled. Her eyes lifted to meet his. The love she saw reflected in his gaze warmed her. Evelyn stretched again, her mouth moving in smacking movements. Someone was hungry. Ben laughed again, bending to kiss his wife.

"Oh, yuck. Kissing." Nathaniel sighed, positively disgusted with the behavior of his parents. Sadie bit back another laugh, not wanting to hurt his feelings.

"Come, Nathaniel," Ben said, standing. "I could use your help in the barn for a bit."

Nathaniel kissed his sister and waved at Sadie before

following his father out to the barn. Alone, Sadie fed the newborn and then put her down in her bassinet to sleep. Hearing voices when she returned to the kitchen area, Sadie peered out the open window, breathing in the sweet-scented spring air. She loved this time of year, with all the blossoms and flowers blooming.

Ah, Isaac had arrived. It was good to see that his friendship with Ben had grown solid and strong, like when they had all been children together. Her memories of her past had returned. Sadie recalled many times when she had followed Ben and Isaac around. Those were happy memories. The dark memories, the ones of her father's death and the period after that, were harder. Between those memories and her near brush with death, she'd suffered from several months of nightmares, and even some anxiety. Thankfully, those had faded since she joined the Amish church and married Ben.

Isaac's wife, Lizzy, was walking toward the house. Sadie threw the door open and moved out onto the porch, not even bothering with shoes.

"Lizzy, it is wonderful to see you. I didn't know that you were coming over to visit."

"Ack, of course I was coming. The minute I knew my husband was coming to see Ben, I knew that I would come and spend time with my dearest friend."

Joy filled Sadie with its warmth. She felt as though she were standing in her own patch of sunlight. She wanted to pinch herself to assure herself that she was truly awake. But she knew she was. God had brought her through the storm and the trials and had blessed her with friends who would stand by her and a man and children who would love her all the days that God had allotted them on His earth.

She was overwhelmed by the blessings she had been given so freely, her heart was near to bursting.

"God is so good," she murmured.

"*Jah, Gott* is very *gut*." Lizzy gave her an understanding smile. Sadie gestured for Lizzy to come inside. As the woman moved past her to enter the house, Sadie's smile widened. Lizzy hadn't said anything, as most Amish women did not speak of such things to anyone beyond their husbands, but even in her Amish attire, it appeared that her friend might be expecting. She hoped so. She knew that Lizzy and Isaac wanted a child. She mentally said a prayer that God would bless them with a large family.

Lizzy caught her glance and laid a hand on her midsection. Although she didn't say anything, her blazing smile and nod confirmed Sadie's suspicions. One more joy to pile on top of all the other sources of happiness in her life. "God is good, indeed," she repeated.

That night, after their guests had left and the children had been put to bed, Ben draped Sadie's cloak around her shoulders and led her out to the front porch. They sat close together on the porch swing he had made her as a wedding gift. She snuggled close to her husband, inhaling the combined scents of the soap she had made and the night air and was content.

"I think Isaac and Lizzy are going to have a child," she said softly.

He kissed the top of her head. With his foot, he gave a small push against the porch floor to make the swing sway gently. "*Jah*, I think so, too. It is *gut*."

"I received a letter from Kurt today."

"*Jah?* What did our brother write?"

She loved hearing him claim kinship with Kurt. "He

said he has a new assignment that will take him out of the area for a bit, he couldn't say what, but I think he was excited. His handwriting was a bit harder to read. Anyway, he wants to come and stay with us for a few days before he leaves."

"He is always welcome." Ben looked up at the stars for a moment. "You know, I will always have a warm spot in my heart for him. It is because of him that we were reunited."

She turned to her husband. "I feel the same. I love you so much, Ben Mast. You and our children have filled all the empty spaces in my heart."

His eyes bright, Ben leaned closer and kissed her. Sadie allowed her eyes to close as she praised her God for His faithful care.

When the kiss ended, she rested her head against her husband, knowing she was where she belonged.

* * * * *

LOVE INSPIRED

INSPIRATIONAL ROMANCE

UPLIFTING STORIES OF FAITH, FORGIVENESS AND HOPE.

Join our social communities to connect with other readers who share your love!

Sign up for the Love Inspired newsletter at **LoveInspired.com** to be the first to find out about upcoming titles, special promotions and exclusive content.

CONNECT WITH US AT:

Facebook.com/LoveInspiredBooks

Twitter.com/LoveInspiredBks

Facebook.com/groups/HarlequinConnection

HARLEQUIN

Heartfelt or thrilling, passionate or uplifting—Harlequin is more than just happily-ever-after.

With twelve different series to choose from and new books available every month, you are sure to find stories that will move you, uplift you, inspire and delight you.

SIGN UP FOR THE HARLEQUIN NEWSLETTER

Be the first to hear about great new reads and exciting offers!

Harlequin.com/newsletters